THE TWO SUNS

To Harriet
Thank you ♡

K.S. Sanral

First Published by Wild Moon Future Press 2025

ISBN-13: 978-1-0687042-6-0

"Without contraries is no progression. Attraction and repulsion, reason and energy, love and hate, are necessary to human existence."

— *William Blake, The Marriage of Heaven and Hell*

CHAPTER ONE

A Gift and A Curse

It's not a question of nurture, as some think. It's a question of nature. You are born either to the Sunrise or to the Sunset (or powerless, but that doesn't matter). It has nothing to do with the time of day or night you are born either. It just is.

She was born to a flash of light that blinded everyone in the room, and the nurse who held her almost let her fall. She was born to the Sunset.

Her birth was a gift and a curse to her parents. Thankfully for them, powers didn't show immediately; it would be ridiculous. Babies need time to be able to sit up, stand, and walk, let alone develop powers.

She had a normal childhood. Her parents were loving people who cared and doted on her, even though they were afraid for her. Afraid of her. The only difference between her and other powerless children was the one rule her parents were strict about. Never reveal your name.

The names of powered people (flairs) have power. In the wrong hands, they could kill you. (The names of powerless people (apos) also can kill them, but they don't matter as much as flairs).

Before she could speak, her parents told others her name was Claire. She hated it even before she understood what hate was. When she started talking, she told a different name to every new person she met, then proceeded to forget which one was which, for she was a child and couldn't grasp the confusion she created. She thought the faces people made were hilarious.

Her powers showed when she was around five years old. It started small, almost untraceable: a gust of wind on a clear day, an object moving a bit towards her extended hand, a bruised knee healing just after getting hurt. It almost passed unnoticed by other people, but she knew what was happening. Her parents had explained, but she also felt it inside.

Once she could connect the feeling in her belly to the events happening around her, she made them happen at her own wish. A kid slipping before he could get on the slide at the park, so she could go first; the veggie soup becoming her favourite ice cream flavour.

Her parents tried to teach her control, not control over her powers, they could never do that, being powerless and all, but control over her actions, when to and not to use her skills.

And like any five-year-old child, she pretended to abide by the rules and kept doing what she wanted behind their backs.

By then she was old enough to understand more of the lessons her parents taught her. Be honest, don't be rude to others, pursue what you love, a kind word can do more than anything else.

Therefore, that night, while her parents were sleeping, she got up, went to their room and woke them with a little shock of static. She told them she loved them. She didn't find anything wrong with letting a little spark ignite the curtains, the bed sheets, then the rest of the room and the entire house. A kind word was worth more than anything else, and she had told them she loved them, after all.

The recruiter found her on the swing in her garden, trying

to swing higher and higher. Unaffected by the blaze that wrapped her house, by the smoke billowing all around her and the entire block. Unaware that she had just killed her parents.

"Where are your parents?" The woman asked. She had salt-and-pepper hair; that's what stood out to the girl. She was dressed in plain black trousers, and a black coat, so were the other two with her. The girl didn't notice if they were men or women; they never looked at her or talked to her.

"Sleeping," the girl shrugged towards what only an hour ago was the parents' window. She didn't stop swinging when the woman spoke. It was funny to see the top of her head getting bigger and smaller, her frame coming into view, then disappearing.

"Don't you think they'll feel hot?"

The girl thought the question was weird, so she shrugged.

"Do you know fire burns?"

"Not me!"She beamed. It was one of the most recent and exciting discoveries. "It doesn't burn me!"

The woman smiled a condescending smile, the same old people usually had for her when she told them something interesting or fascinating she had just found out.

Like the one time she told a grandma friend of her parents that crocodiles cannot stick their tongue out, and proceeded to show she could. The grandma took one glance at her, had that condescending smile, and turned back to continue her conversation with her mum. She made sure the old parrot couldn't stick her tongue out for a week.

"No, it doesn't burn you. But it burns others, doesn't it?"

The girl shrugged again; she didn't really see the point in answering. The woman seemed to pick up her mood.

"Do you mind if we put the fire out now?"

She didn't want them to. She liked the movement of the flames, the creaking of the wood burning, the sparks that danced all around her, but the tone the woman had made her think of the stern neighbour who babysat her on occasions. She always made her orders in the form of questions, so the girl shrugged again.

The woman nodded to the other two figures, a swipe of their hands and a river of water fell on the house all at once. The pretty flames were extinguished, and the girl pulled a face at the damp smell of wet grass. A few seconds later, her swing stopped swinging. She struggled to start it again, but it wouldn't budge.

She glared at the woman, a glare that sometimes made her parents jump and take a small step back, but it didn't work; the old bat wasn't impressed.

"Did your parents tell you about the Sunset Academy?"

They had. They were scared this day would come; someone from the Academy coming to take her away. It was her birthright, but that didn't make it any less painful for them, (they didn't tell her any of that; she heard them talking when they believed she was asleep).

What they told her was that someone from the Academy would one day come and take her with them to teach her. They told her the Academy was a beautiful place, full of children like her, and she would have a wonderful time there. At that point, the girl couldn't remember if that was about the Academy or the book her mother was reading to her about a school of magic.

"Yes," she reluctantly answered.

"We're going there now," the woman extended her hand, fully expecting the girl to take it, like a little toddler.

The girl snorted and jumped off the swing. The woman didn't seem fazed by her rejection and led the way out, the other two following behind her.

CHAPTER TWO

The Sunset Academy

The recruiter took her to their car, parked in front of her burning house. The girl heard sirens in the distance; the firefighters coming to put the fire out. By the time they arrived, there wouldn't be a fire anymore, or anything left of the house other than ashes.

The girl climbed into the sleek, black car and was taken aback by how big it looked inside. It had two seats spanning the width of the car, facing each other. She occupied one, and the recruiters shared the other. It was as big as her bed!

She didn't care to make conversation with them. Her fun-filled night was coming to an end, and sleep was trying to claim her. She let it, not caring much about the road or the people in front of her.

She was roughly shaken awake when they approached the big walls of the Citadel. They were impressive, made more looming by the darkness, but she would've preferred it if they had woken her up when they arrived. The huge, wrought-iron gates opened silently to let the car in, then closed behind it.

The car parked in front of a three-storey building. The door opened by itself, and the recruiters stepped out, not looking at the girl but expecting her to follow. The two silent recruiters left in two different directions, but the woman led the girl into the building and to a room as big as her own, if not more.

There was a bed with a fluffy pillow and soft sheets, a wardrobe, a desk and chair, purple carpet on the floor, which the girl found bizarre, and another door that led to a bathroom.

"Have a good sleep," the woman said before leaving with no further explanation.

The girl shrugged. She knew she probably smelled of smoke, and her pyjamas were dirty with ashes, and she should clean up, but she didn't feel like it, so she climbed into bed and soon after fell asleep again.

The alarm that woke her was the same one her mother had, and for a few moments, she cursed her for letting it sound for so long, but then she remembered she wasn't home anymore.

It stopped only when she got out of bed. The door opened on its own at the same time, so she tried to cross it. An invisible wall stopped her from reaching the corridor. She bounced off it three times before a shimmering sign appeared in front of her, representing a toilet with happy eyes and a smile. She tried to cross again but to no avail, so she got the hint and headed to the little bathroom and found a new rainbow toothbrush, toothpaste, and towels.

Still, the door didn't let her through and showed a picture of a girl dressed in a blue uniform. This time, the girl didn't try to cross it again but reached the wardrobe and found it full of clothes: what looked like school uniforms and some normal clothes.

She took a dark blue polo shirt with two Sunset Academy symbols on each side of the collar and a pair of dark blue trousers, discarded her pyjamas and got dressed. In a shoe cupboard she hadn't noticed the night before, she found black Velcro-strap shoes and put them on. She hoped they didn't want her to fold her clothes or do her bed, because

Mum did that, and she didn't know how. She tentatively tried to cross the threshold again, and to her delight, nothing stopped her from getting into the corridor.

A green, floating arrow appeared mid-air and directed her. The girl thought about ignoring it, but she guessed that whatever other direction she'd try to take, she'd slam into the invisible barrier again. So, with a sigh, she followed the arrow.

Doors just like hers lined the corridor, and the girl assumed they were bedrooms for other students, even though they were all closed. The arrow led her up a flight of stairs to another sober corridor, with big windows letting in the early sunlight. She walked to the end of it, where a set of double doors stood closed. They were the biggest, most ornate doors she had ever seen. She tried to study the intricate design, but they opened, and the arrow advanced through them, so she followed it. The room was equally impressive, with tapestries, a red carpet, and a huge table that felt like the girl had just landed in a fairy tale. The relentless arrow led her to the other side, where a less impressive, less decorated mahogany door was. A golden sign marked it as the Headmistress' office.

The girl reached it and was about to knock when, once again, the door opened on its own.

"Come in," a deep, pleasant voice ordered.

The arrow disappeared as the girl entered the room. It was smaller but as ornate as the antechamber. An ebony desk dominated the room, with two plush chairs in front of it and one behind. The woman who spoke sat on it as if it were a throne. She had the bearing of a warrior queen, and the girl immediately respected her.

Her skin was dark, almost as dark as the desk, and her eyes were a piercing brown that seemed to look at the girl's soul, not at her appearance.

"Welcome to the Sunset Academy." The woman greeted her with a polite smile and gestured for the girl to take a seat. "My name is Magna. I am the headmistress."

The girl nodded but said nothing. She wasn't exactly intimidated, but at the same time, she didn't want to get on the wrong side of that powerful woman.

"Can you tell me what happened last night?" The woman, Magna, enquired.

"I told Mother and Father I loved them," the girl replied.

"What about the fire?"

"I like fire," she shrugged.

"Why?"

"It dances and tickles me; it's warm," the girl stopped for a second, gauging the woman's reaction. She didn't want to see the condescension in her eyes, but she was surprised to see interest. "I like to make fire. It starts here," she patted her belly, "and gets up, fast, hot, and comfy."

"That it does," the headmistress chuckled.

"I don't want to let it out sometimes. I like feeling warm and comfy," she confessed, a light pink colouring her cheeks.

"But you have to," Magna sighed, resigned, like she understood what the girl meant. It was the first time ever someone didn't patronise or dismiss her for what she said, and it was the first time someone understood.

"I like the flames, though," she added. "I like watching them."

"Is that why you started the fire yesterday?"

The girl's eyes lit up as she nodded vehemently. "It was so big!"

"I bet it was," the woman replied. "Do you understand you killed your parents? Do you know what 'killed' means?

"I know what it means."

"So, do you know that's what you did to your parents?"

The girl shrugged; she didn't know what to say.

"Did you want them to die?"

"No."

"Did you watch them burn?"

"No, I wanted to go on the swing and watch the flames dance."

"Why didn't you start the fire when there was no one else

in the house?"

"I wanted to watch the flames dance," she repeated, confused by the question.

"But your mum and dad are dead now."

"Yes," she nodded, still confused.

"But you still wanted to see the flames," the woman said, finally understanding.

"Yes."

The headmistress nodded, and the moment of silence stretched. The girl wondered if she had given the wrong answer, but she had been honest, and the headmistress seemed understanding.

"We rarely accept students as young as you are," Headmistress Magna finally broke the silence. "But your powers have developed ahead of the curve, and we are going to make an exception."

The girl didn't reply. It didn't seem the kind of statement that needed one, so she kept listening.

"You will be joining your cohort tomorrow, but be aware that the students are one or two years older than you. You will not be granted any special treatment and are expected to keep up. Do you understand?

Her tone was still polite, but firm.

"Yes, Headmistress."

"You will attend additional classes to learn to read and write and to catch up with what you missed so far. Those are as compulsory as the rest of your lessons."

The girl nodded. She had never been to school, and she was excited to start it.

"You will always be free to use your powers within the Citadel, but for as long as you will be a student at this academy, you will not kill anyone."

The girl rolled her eyes.

"That is the only rule that, if broken, will result in immediate expulsion."

"I understand," the girl whispered.

"As I mentioned, you will start your training tomorrow.

For today, I suggest you familiarise yourself with the academy and the Citadel. Tardiness will not be tolerated. Do you have any questions?"

The girl thought for a second. "Where is everyone?"

The headmistress chuckled, "Training."

"Do I have to make my bed?"

"No, that is taken care of."

"Is there food?" She hadn't eaten since the previous dinner, so she started to feel hungry.

"Your instructors will take you to the dining hall. For today, you can find something in town, or you can join your peers."

The girl nodded. She thought about other questions, but she couldn't come up with anything.

"You may go now," the headmistress said gently, and the door behind the girl opened on its own again.

"Have a good day," she told the woman as she left her office.

The girl thought about staying in the big room and studying it, but she didn't want to be too close to the headmistress.

She didn't think of which direction to take. She let her feet wander up and down staircases, her hands trying every handle of every door. Most were locked, but one opened onto a dining room with small, round, white tables and red and yellow chairs. The walls between the big windows were painted yellow, the other walls had white bricks and a pattern of zigzag green, white, and yellow patches. The same was true for the middle of the ceiling, but in red and yellow. The centre of the floor was made of dark and light shades of green. She now knew where the dining hall was, if she wanted to join her almost-classmates there later on in the day.

After that, she found the classrooms: boring, bare rooms with wooden desks and chairs, all facing the front desk and a big screen. Some of them were occupied by children in the same uniform as hers, all sitting with their backs straight and their eyes trained on the teacher, who was wearing a more elaborate version of the uniform.

Her next discovery was the gym, a huge, open space with nets and goals, circuit stations, and equipment. It was empty when she reached it, so she went inside to absorb its size. Double metal doors on the other side indicated an exit. She decided to get through them and found herself outside for the first time.

She was at the back of the building, and in front of her lay the training grounds. She could see groups of children of all ages engaged in different sessions. Some were involved in physical combat; some were testing their powers. Instructors circulated among them, correcting the mistakes. That fascinated her, but there was so much more to explore that she couldn't stop.

She was surprised to find a playground, just like the one she used to spend her afternoons. It seemed out of place, but she decided to spend some time there playing. There was a sandbox and a swing, and for the moment, she was content with just that. An enticing little green gate broke the shrubs that enclosed the playground. When the girl was bored with the swing, she decided it was time to move on, she walked towards it and opened it with her powers – just because she could – and emerged back to the front of the building.

It formed a square with two other almost identical buildings and a long long tree-lined avenue leading away. Students were everywhere there, but none as young as she was, and none donning the same uniform. Those kids were older, and the girl noticed they were almost split into two groups: those just a few years older than her on her left, and those even older, in the mid-late teens, on her right. They wore different uniforms, becoming more elaborate as the wearer got older. However, all featured the Sunset symbol on their collars.

At first sight, they seemed intimidating, dangerous even — not that the girl was easily scared — but after she looked at them for a while, she saw they were just chilling. Some were laughing, some were displaying their powers and playing tricks on others. The older students looked more serious, more formal, but they, too, were smiling and playing.

Some of them looked and pointed at her as she crossed the square to get to the avenue. Some had a glint in their eyes she recognised as mischief and shouted at her, mocking her. Some went even further and used their powers on her. Nothing harmful, just a gust of wind ruffling her hair, or the small hole in the ground suddenly appearing to trip her. She started laughing. She didn't care she was the target. They weren't actually hurting her, but seeing powers used so openly, so freely, made her happy. It was the first time she was surrounded by other flairs, the first time she didn't have to suppress the urge to use her powers.

The avenue was long, well-kept, and busy. There were people everywhere: very few students and many adults, most of them in normal clothes. Some were on a bicycle, some on foot. She only counted two cars, which was surprising, she was used to traffic. Smaller roads and streets branched out, but she continued on the avenue until she reached the Citadel. The girl was amazed; it was a town full of flairs. She saw shops, houses, food carts, an amazing ice cream parlour she looked at for a good ten minutes, and trees everywhere. By that time, however, she was tired of walking, and it was close to lunchtime. Her tummy grumbled a bit as she sat down on a bench, right in front of a vendor flipping burgers on a grill; the smell was not helping her stomach settle at all. The headmistress had said she could find food in town, but the girl didn't think of asking for money to pay for it. So, she just looked longingly at the burgers, hoping the vendor would take pity on a lone child.

She stayed there, watching the people coming and going. Men and women dress in all kinds of clothes, some of the older students, even a couple of kids around her age with their parents. There were also soldiers walking around, but they didn't seem to be patrolling, just walking or shopping.

She was looking at one such group when a man in uniform

sat down next to her and offered her a burger with melted cheese and fries.

"I'm not supposed to accept food from strangers," the girl said, while reaching out for the food, not looking at the man at all. At the first bite, she sighed with pleasure, closing her eyes to better enjoy the morsel.

Finally, she looked at the man. He was young, in his mid-twenties, his hair was dark, but cut so short it looked almost blond, his eyes were very dark, but as kind as the smile on his lips. His uniform was the same dark blue as the girl's, but he had a banded collared jacket — with the Sunset symbol on each side — a golden cord around his right shoulder, golden buttons, and a golden insignia on his arm.

"Good?" the man asked.

The girl nodded, her mouth stuffed.

"You know you could've just asked one yourself?"

"I don't have money," the girl replied, annoyed.

"You don't need money. Students can get what they need, and only what they need," he emphasised, "without having to pay."

"That's weird," she pulled a face that made the man laugh.

"It is at first, but you'll get used to it."

She just nodded.

"You haven't asked who I am," the man observed with a smile.

The girl shrugged. "You're a teacher at the Academy."

"Well spotted," the man conceded. "I am Sergeant Major Thomas, and I am the instructor in charge of your class."

She just nodded again.

"I'll leave you to your lunch and your exploration. I will see you tomorrow morning. Be on time."

"I will."

The girl finished her lunch, now lighter than she had been. She could go to any shop and buy stuff without paying, that was a positive note to the day. So, when she finished her food, she sent the rubbish to the bin with her powers. She got an ice cream because it looked delicious and because she could, and she enjoyed it as she strolled through the streets of the town. She found a toy shop and decided to buy some things for her room. She thought about buying pens and other stationery, but she didn't really want to.

She discovered the Citadel wasn't completely enclosed by the big walls she saw the night before, but on one side, it opened up to the ocean. The view took her breath away. She saw a cliff to one side, plummeting down to the water, and she immediately wanted to climb there. There was a long, sandy beach as well, where the waves lapped in a lazy rhythm. She decided that it was her favourite place in the world. She didn't care that she hadn't seen the rest of the world yet, but she knew that was it.

She knew she didn't have the time to go all the way to the cliff, so she stayed on the beach, took her shoes off, and played with the waves until the sun started to set.

When she got back to her room that night, she found the bed made, and her pyjamas folded. She set all the things she got from the shop, and she settled in bed with her new plush animal: a smiling sloth.

Everything smelt different, new, and unfamiliar. She didn't notice the night before, too tired to do anything but sleep, but now she felt tiny and vulnerable. She expected her mum to get in the room and read her a story as she used to, and she kept expecting for a while before she realised it wouldn't happen. She felt a huge weight on her tummy, and tears welled up in her eyes, and she started sobbing so loudly she thought someone would come and scold her, but no one did. She missed her mum and dad, they would come rushing to see if she was okay, but they couldn't, not anymore. So she cried and cried, and cried alone until she fell asleep, her eyes red and puffy, her head aching, but not more than her heart for the loss she felt.

CHAPTER THREE

The Trials

The alarm and the arrow reappeared the next morning. The girl didn't even try to exit her room without first washing and getting dressed. She expected the arrow to lead her to the dining hall, but it surprised her and led her outside. She was tempted to stop following it and go get her breakfast but thought that, for the first day, she should just follow the rules. She was also surprised to see other kids her age in the corridor. Nobody talked to her, or anyone else, but they all walked in the same direction. She wondered if the others could see the arrow, or if it was just for her.

They got out in the front square, and students from the other buildings joined them. They lined up in a precise formation, with the younger students - the girl's class - in front. She looked around to see what was happening and what she needed to do, and she saw the other students were all looking straight ahead, their chins raised, their arms stiff down their sides, their feet together, their backs straight. She wanted to laugh, they all looked like blue broomsticks.

She saw the classmate to her right looking at her without turning his head, a look that meant she needed to get in the same position with urgency. She rolled her eyes but tried to imitate him.

After a few minutes, the instructors arrived. They marched in single file and lined by the avenue side, closing the square. Lastly, Headmistress Magna joined them and took place in front of them.

"Good morning, Cadets," the headmistress's voice boomed through the square. "Today is an important day for our Class 1. They had a taste of our academy, but now it's time to fully join. The Trials will test their mettle; they will show us what these students are made of; and finally earn their name."

The girl was intrigued. The headmistress hadn't mentioned anything about a trial when she met her the day before, nor did Sergeant Thomas. Would she have to take part? Headmistress Magna did say that she wasn't going to get any special treatment, but it still seemed unfair. The girl didn't have a taste of the Academy yet. What if she didn't like it and didn't want to join after all?

"Instructors, proceed to inspection," the headmistress continued. "I will see you all later."

She left the way she came, and the instructors moved towards the three groups of students. The girl wished they hurried up with the inspection - whatever it was - because the stiff position was not comfortable, and she wanted to move.

Two adults stopped at each side of the first row of students, two more did the same from the back.

"First row, step forward," Sergeant Thomas ordered the girl's row. She took a step along with her classmates.

He looked at every student, checking their uniform, their posture, their hair, their socks, and their faces. When they finished with the first row, they moved to the second, then the third, and so on, until the four instructors met in the middle of the group.

The girl didn't get any comments, her uniform was new, clean, and not creased. But one student's hair was messy, as if he hadn't brushed it, so with a stern look he was sent to stand straight and stiff on the side. Another was wearing mismatched socks, one white, one blue. She tried to argue, but was sent to the side as well.

Being in the front row, the girl could see what happened in the other groups more than her own. So she saw when a student of the middle years was found to have not tucked his shirt in, and the instructor made a sharp downward motion with his arm. The student fell to the ground, screaming in pain. He didn't know if he should grab his arm or leg. The other students around him stood still at attention, eyes trained front. The same happened to another student who was less than perfect. Of the oldest students, no one was found to have any flaw in their appearance.

When the instructors were satisfied, they ordered the groups to do an about-turn, which the girl found out meant turning around stiffly, all at the same time and in the same direction. Then, they were ordered to march.

The students in front of her were all taller, so she couldn't see much other than their backs. She just hoped they were going back inside and to breakfast, her tummy was grumbling. She noticed, though, that the students reprimanded during the inspections did not move. The two from her group were still in that stiff, straight position, and the two older ones were still on the ground, writhing in pain. The girl wondered how long they were going to be there. She wished she could go and observe them from closer by.

To her delight, they marched into the dining area. As if a spell were broken, the students' posture relaxed, and the silence broke into chatter as the kids took their seats at the many tables. The girl was the last one entering the room, and Sergeant Thomas stopped her by the door.

"Sit with me," he ordered and led her to one table where three other students were waiting.

As soon as the instructors sat among students, the plates filled with food. There were pancakes, waffles, pastries, eggs, bacon, cereals, and bowls of milk, glasses of juice to choose from — anything she could've wanted.

"You must have questions," Sergeant Thomas addressed

her as he chose his own breakfast.

The girl had a lot of them. Where the food was coming from and how much she could have. What was happening to the students left outside. What the trials were. But she just shrugged, not sure what to ask first.

Sergeant Thomas smiled. “Eat. You’ll need all the energy you can get.”

She nodded and got some waffles.

“Let’s start from the beginning. Every morning, you will assemble in front of this building. You will stand at attention and be inspected.”

“At attention?” the girl asked, confused. How could someone stand at attention?

“It’s just the way it’s called,” Sergeant Thomas explained. “It means face front, stand with your back straight, your arms along your sides, and your feet together.”

The girl nodded.

“I will go through the basic drill commands with you later,” Sergeant Thomas added.

More words she didn’t understand, but she didn’t ask.

“If your uniform, your posture, or your person are not up to our standards, you will be punished. As you grow older, the punishment becomes harsher.”

“How long are they staying outside?” the girl asked, fascinated.

“The Class students, that is, the younger ones, will stay there as long as their instructors see fit. The Recruits will be there until the pain subsides, which means when they feel it less. Then, they’ll spend the rest of the day running the perimeter of the school, and after dinner, they’ll have to catch up on the work they missed today, and tomorrow they will be tested on it. You don’t want to know what happens to Aspirants, trust me,” he winked.

The girl chuckled at the tone.

“Why do we have breakfast after the inspection?”

It was Sergeant Thomas’s turn to chuckle.

“To learn discipline.”

"And we can't learn discipline with a full stomach?"

Sergeant Thomas chuckled again. "I guess not."

The girl made a displeased face that made the sergeant laugh even more.

"On a normal day, after breakfast, you will have physical education."

"What's physical education?"

"It's to keep your body in shape."

"Like the gym?"

"Yes, something like that."

"And it's every day?"

"Yes, every morning after breakfast."

"That's a lot of gym!"

The students at the table laughed and nodded. Sergeant Thomas tried not to.

"After that, you'll be in class learning many subjects. Then, for the rest of the afternoon, you will be back out in the fields, this time for power education."

"That's a gym for powers?" the girl interrupted excitedly.

"Yes, that is a gym for powers," Sergeant Thomas rolled his eyes.

"So, these Trials. They are not every day?"

"No, they happen once a year."

"And I have to do it?"

The other kids took in a sharp breath, as if she said a swear word. Sergeant Thomas didn't seem to take offence.

"Yes, you do."

"It's my first day," the girl reminded him.

"I know," the sergeant was serious now. Any trace of the playful attitude gone.

"Isn't it supposed to be for students who 'had a taste of the Academy'?" she quoted.

"There is no special treatment here."

"There is no equal treatment, either," she replied.

"That is out of line. I'll let it slide this one time. Do not test me again," Sergeant Thomas said in that tone her mum sometimes used when she wanted to make a point. The girl knew what to do. She looked down and nodded, making her lower lip tremble.

"The Trials test your abilities," Sergeant Thomas continued, in a gentler tone. "They test your physical abilities, your powers, and your mental and emotional resilience."

If the girl had to be honest with herself, she didn't care that it was her first day and she hadn't had any training before. She knew she was powerful.

A bell rang. Everything disappeared from the plates, and the students started to get up.

"Speaking of," Sergeant Thomas rose as well. "It is time."

They formed lines; the girl realised late they were in the same order as the assembly, and marched outside.

This time, they didn't exit from the front door, but from a side one, joining the lines of the other classes in the corridors. Once outside, they turned towards the back of the building and reached the fields the girl remembered seeing the day before.

"Welcome," the headmistress' voice boomed. It took the girl a few moments to understand it was coming from the opposite side of the formation, where the aspirants lined up. "Welcome to this year's Trials.

"As most of you know, the Trials are a way to prove yourselves. To prove you belong. They are your chance to showcase what you learnt and what you're made of. It is the only occasion where there are no rules, no limits."

It piqued the girl's interest. No rules? No limits?

"For our youngest cadets, the Trials are even more important," Headmistress Magna continued, suddenly appearing in front of the girl's group, soliciting the ohs and ahs from the younger children. "Pass the Trials, and you will earn your first rank, Junior Cadet. Pass the Trials, and you will earn your token name."

The girl wasn't interested in either. She liked changing names and making people confused. She wasn't sure she wanted to settle on a single name forever. None of them were her real ones anyway, so they didn't matter. The rank? That was even lower on her list of wishes.

"Without any further ado, let's get started!" The headmistress finished excitedly.

Without any other words, the instructors ordered the groups to march to different areas of the fields. They were in a vast clearing where everyone could spread out and have enough space to practice safely.

"When you're called, step to the centre," Sergeant Thomas told his class.

The girl had questions about what she had to do, but everyone was silent, and she understood she couldn't ask any. They were free to relax, and many students sat down, so she did the same. She hoped she wasn't the first to be called, so she could see what the others did. She wasn't worried about her abilities, but she didn't like not knowing.

Thankfully, Sergeant Thomas called another girl. She was small, looked even younger than the girl, and she was definitely terrified. So, the girl wasn't the only one not knowing what the Trials were.

Another student also stood up and walked towards the centre, the girl observed with curiosity. He was older, with the uniform the girl associated with the aspirants, the cord around his shoulder was green, but the girl wasn't sure what that meant. He looked grounded, sure of himself. The little girl looked around, completely lost, trying to understand what was going on and what she had to do, so she didn't see the other cadet charge. It was over before it even started, and the girl understood exactly what the Trials were: in just a few seconds, her classmate was lying on the ground, dead.

Some of the other students gasped in horror, some were shocked into silence. The girl was thinking, though. They couldn't possibly let the older students kill everyone, or there wouldn't be a Junior Cadet class. Maybe that girl was just really weak and never had a chance.

The second cadet from the girl's class faced a recruit. Their fight went on for about five minutes; they exchanged punches, kicks, and powers until the recruit passed out. The girl saw he was still breathing, so killing was not the end goal.

The girl thought the cadet would go back and another one would be called up, but he stayed there, and another aspirant joined him. Just like with the little girl, it was over quickly: her classmate lay on the ground in a pool of blood. It was unclear if he was dead or alive. The instructors took his body away, and the aspirant went to sit down.

Sergeant Thomas called the girl next. Her opponent was a huge recruit girl, tall and lean, who towered over her even at a distance. She didn't waste any time and charged at the girl, who was ready and put up an invisible shield. It wobbled when the recruit slammed into it, but it held.

She looked surprised, and the girl saw an opening. She slashed across the air with her arm - the same movement she saw the instructor do that morning - but the recruit dodged, faster than the girl thought, and punched the girl on her windpipe, leaving her gasping for breath. The recruit moved in for the final blow, but the girl ran backwards avoiding her, but she lost her balance and fell.

The recruit grinned in victory, looming over the girl, even taller now. The girl didn't give up; she didn't want to die such a pathetic death. She looked around and saw a big rock just behind her opponent. She levitated it and slammed it on the recruit's head, who immediately fell unconscious with a big thud. The girl's classmates exulted triumphantly, surprised and excited.

The second opponent was the opposite of the first: a small and thin boy, a bundle of energy always fidgeting in the aspirants' uniform with a green cord. He attacked the girl by running so fast no one knew what had happened until the girl was screaming in pain, holding her arm at an unnatural angle, the boy at the opposite end of the clearing.

Before the girl could turn around, he ran towards her again. This time, the girl ended up with a bloody rivet running down the side of her face. She touched it and looked transfixed at her red hand.

She thought about putting the shield up again, but she wasn't sure the aspirant couldn't get through it. She had to slow him down somehow, but she didn't have time to think that he slammed her on the ground again. Maybe that was the solution, stay on the ground and offer less body to be pushed around and broken. She realised she could feel the vibration of the aspirant's steps as he ran towards her; she could feel the air moving. She acted almost on instincts. The ground around her became muddy and soft, the aspirant halted and the inertia had him fall face first, his shoes making a sloshy, suctioning sound as they left the ground. Now the girl stood, bloody and hurt, and looked down at the aspirant struggling to get up. With a wicked glint in her eyes, she closed her fist. The Cadet started gasping, clawing at his throat, desperate for air. When he was about to pass out, the girl let go. He could breathe again, but didn't have the strength to continue the fight.

This time everyone was cheering for her, even the aspirant's classmates. The only one who wasn't - an aspirant with a gold cord around his shoulder - looked at the girl with an intense glare before he stepped forward to face her. There was something lethal about him. The girl felt a shiver of excitement and fear down her spine. She was tired and in pain, her arm was still hurting, the gash on her face still bleeding. She wasn't sure she could get through another fight.

The aspirant didn't attack. He stood there looking at her. It was unnerving, the others were so quick to charge that the girl expected that to be the norm. They stood still for what seemed forever. The girl's breath was laboured, feeling like a rabbit out of its hole, but was probably just a couple of minutes. The girl was making up her mind and was going to attack first when something heavy hit the back of her head and made her stumble towards the approaching aspirant's punch; the combined hit made her spin and fall, but the aspirant didn't stop. He kicked her in the ribs hard enough that she rolled around, then he kicked her again for good measure. He continued to assault her with powers and physical attacks until the girl was just on the ground protecting her head with her arms, crying in pain from the old and new injuries. She wished he could just kill her, but he didn't; it seemed like he was punishing her for what she did to the others.

Her vision blurred, she felt like she was passing out and coming to in a cycle. The pain was unbearable. She was sure she would die any second. But death wasn't so kind and didn't come. She just wanted for it to be over, to be somewhere else, somewhere safe. Before she could even complete the thought, she disappeared, escaping the aspirant's clutches and reappeared ten metres away.

Before the aspirant could reach her again, she used the last of her strength to somehow stand up to face him. If she was going to die, she would die standing, not cowering on the ground. She knew she couldn't take another blow, but something visceral deep down inside her didn't want to give up either. Her opponent ran towards her, his expression cold and detached. She felt all the pain of the many injuries, the broken bones, the legs shaking and barely keeping her up, the blood flowing out of many cuts. Her vision still so blurred that she could barely see the aspirant. She screamed. A piercing, broken sound that echoed through the clearing and beyond. Something inside her snapped, and something out there answered. The earth rose under the aspirant's feet, launching him in the air, which swirled around him, pushing and pulling him violently. A wave appeared out of nowhere and engulfed him, keeping him under, stealing his breath and starving him of air. Then came fire, enveloping him, cutting through his skin, his eyes, nostrils, mouth, burning him from both inside and out, consuming everything and leaving only a pile of ashes in its wake. As soon as the fire extinguished itself, the girl collapsed on the ground.

The girl woke up in her bed. Her head felt foggy, still sleepy. It took her a few moments to open her eyes fully and sit up. She realised then that there wasn't any alarm, or door opening.

She wondered if she could just go back to sleep then, without having to go to class or assembly. She jumped when there was a knock at the door, thinking one of the instructors had come to drag her out.

"It's Sergeant Thomas," the voice from the other side of the door said.

"Come in," she tried to say, but nothing came out.

She felt like she had a very bad sore throat, and it hurt when she tried to speak. Nevertheless, the door opened, and the sergeant stepped in.

"How are you feeling?" Sergeant Thomas said as he sat down at the foot of the bed.

She shrugged, not wanting to feel more pain.

"Our medics work wonders," he smiled. "You passed the Trials," he said, and the girl looked at him as if to say, "obviously". He guffawed.

"And, you're an elemental!"

The girl looked at him, confused.

"An elemental is someone who can use all the elements equally. And your display was more than impressive."

The girl thought about the third fight. She vaguely remembered the elements answering her plea, but she couldn't take credit for that; she didn't control them; they did everything by themselves.

"Here," Sergeant Thomas continued, unaware of the girl's doubts. "These badges represent your new rank, Junior Cadet."

He handed her two blue sun pins. She studied them, then put them on her bedside table.

"They go on the collar of your shirt," the sergeant explained. "And this is your name tag."

He gave her another pin, a rectangular one. There was nothing on it.

"When you decide on your name, it will etch itself on it."

The girl nodded and put it next to the others.

"It goes on the left side of your shirt," he explained, pointing at his own.

She was about to nod her understanding but was interrupted by the biggest yawn she had ever had. Sergeant Thomas laughed good-naturedly.

"It is late," he conceded. "This one time, you can have some food in your room. I suggest something light but filling. You need to replenish your energy."

She nodded again, this time without yawning.

"I'll see you tomorrow at assembly. With a name etched on that tag."

The girl tried not to roll her eyes. Sergeant Thomas noticed and smiled. He then stood and walked towards the door, which opened when he approached it.

"Well done," he murmured as he left.

When the sergeant was gone, the girl thought of something to eat, and it appeared on a tray right in front of her. She side-looked the name tag, already hating the thing. She didn't want to choose a name. She didn't want to see it written there, even though she couldn't read it yet. Maybe she could just pick something and then change it later. Maybe she could change it at the next Trials, if she survived. Her full tummy made her even sleepier, so she decided to postpone the decision until the next morning.

The blaring alarm woke her up way too early. She stretched and got up. She didn't feel any pain, and when she tried to speak, her voice was back to normal. She washed and dressed, pinning the sun badges on her collar, and picking up the name tag.

She stared at it, willing to do something, to pick its own name, so that she could stop thinking about it. To her surprise, it did. A word etched itself on it. Somehow she knew what it said: Nashel.

CHAPTER FOUR

Nashel

The Trials were only the first hurdle a cadet faced at the academy, even though it was the deadliest. Everything was a competition. A scoreboard was updated every morning and displayed in the dining hall.

"You don't want to know what happens to the bottom five," a child in Nashel's class told her the first morning after the Trials.

Nashel looked at him confused, but he didn't elaborate. She doubted he knew anything, anyway.

By the end of the first lesson, she couldn't read the scoreboard, but she knew she would be last the next morning. She was the only one who couldn't read or write, and, as the headmistress told her, there was no special treatment. She tried her best, but she couldn't understand any of the scribbles the teacher had made on the board.

She learnt a lesson during that class, though. Humiliation.

"Junior Cadet Nashel," the instructor, Sergeant Yaren, called her. "Read the next line."

Nashel stared hard at the squiggles, but to her, they were nothing but black scratches, like little snakes chasing each other.

Her face grew hotter. "I can't see," she replied.

"Then come closer," the teacher ordered her.

She walked to the front with confident steps, but she still couldn't understand the writing she was supposed to read. Her jaw tightened. She knew exactly what he was doing. He wanted to see her fail.

"Read."

The warmth on her face spread, hotter, to her belly. She recognised anger, and she knew it was directed at Sergeant Yaren for tricking her, but also at herself for her inability to pick up the skill quickly.

"No," she answered.

"Excuse me?"

"No."

Sergeant Yaren glared at her, and she glared back. Behind her, the class snickered.

"Go sit down."

She turned and grinned at her classmates as she walked back to her sit. She promised herself she'd learn their stupid symbols, and when she did, Sergeant Yaren would never catch her out like that again.

The second lesson was about numbers. Just like letters, they looked like scratches and were just as difficult to decipher. But numbers weren't new to her.

"Three plus four," Sergeant Harare asked.

Her classmates bent their heads, pens scribbled in their books. Nashel hid her hands under her table, and counted her fingers, muttering under her breath. One, two, three... four, five, six, seven.

She smirked. She got the right answer! She drew the lines of the number on her book, her tongue peeking out of her lips. The boy next to her snorted.

"What's so funny, Cadet?" the sergeant barked.

"Nothing, ma'am."

The teacher walked between the desks, checking the answers. She stopped close to Nashel. "Numbers are a soldier's second weapon," she started. "The first is your head.

If you can't add, you can't fight. If you can't fight—"

"You die," the class recited.

Nashel rolled her eyes. She could count just fine. It was writing she struggled with. But she'd get there. Soon. And she would put a stop to the snorts and snickers. They just had to wait and see.

The following morning she found out what being at the bottom of the scoreboard meant. Every moment she wasn't in class, she had some chore to do. It started with staying behind and clean the tables in the dining hall. She had to run to her first lesson to make it in time, and endure Sergeant Yaren picking on her to read. She refused again, and the teacher informed her he would take points from her, and she'd be at the bottom again. She shrugged it off, but she felt the anger burning inside her. She closed her hands into fists and saw the pencils and pens on her desk shake with the power escaping her.

When the rest of her class had a break, mid morning, she had to return the clean laundry to the cadets' rooms. She complained because she knew it was easily done with powers. Sergeant Thomas heard her and sent her to the assembly square to stand at attention for the rest of the morning. Two other cadets were there from the morning because of issues with their uniforms.

Nashel never had an issue with that. She studied the older cadets, those that were never called out, and copied them. Her chin would be at the perfect angle, her arms so straight and stiff down her side that there would be no gap between them and her body, no light would pass through. She took care of tucking her shirt in, letting the collar on top of the jumper, the two suns shining bright on them. Her hair was tidy, with no wild strands escaping the bun she had learnt to tie.

She still ended up with those sloppy cadets, though, because she didn't know how to read and write, and she struggled to understand what the teacher was saying about terrains and cities, and so many letters and numbers.

That night, after she had to run around the Class building three times, she had to attend extra lessons to catch up on what she missed. Sergeant Yaren was the one delivering, which meant she couldn't learn anything. She hated him.

The morning after, the alarm woke her up, but she soon realised something was wrong. The other students were not up yet, and it was dark outside when she reached the square; only the other bottom cadets milled about. Sergeant Thomas walked up behind her only a handful of minutes later.

"Featherweights, do you know where the armoury is?" he asked them. Nashel had discovered that was the unofficial term used to label them. They carried no strength, no weight.

She nodded, and so did the other four. "Yes, sir."

"Go and polish the weapons. Everything you need is already there."

After the previous day, Nashel had learnt to keep her complaints quiet. It wasn't in her nature, and her emotions struggled to find another outlet. More and more often throughout the day, and especially in Sergeant Yaren's class, her powers escaped her control.

By the middle of her first week, she was so tired she felt like she was sleepwalking. Numbers and letters swam in front of her, making even less sense than before. She dreamt of them every night, but she still couldn't understand them.

She vaguely heard the cadets around her whisper, but she didn't pay too much attention to them until she was in Sergeant Yaren's class the fourth morning since she had joined the academy.

The boy sat next to her poked her arm to get her attention.

"How are you doing that?" he whispered, keeping an eye on the teacher to make sure his back was still turned.

"Doing what?" she drawled.

He pointed at her, not at her face, but at her body. Nashel looked down and realised she was floating a foot above the chair. The surprise knocked her power out and made her drop loudly on the chair. She almost fell off it.

"Junior Cadet Nashel," Sergeant Yaren called her out

without turning. "How is it possible that your stay with the Featherweights has taught you nothing?"

She didn't reply. She couldn't even if she wanted to. Her anger was flaring again, making her stationery smoke. She tried to smother them, to stop them from catching fire completely, but her frantic effort only made it worse. When Sergeant Yaren turned to see what was happening, his nose was smoking too. The entire class burst out laughing, but the teacher was not impressed. He extended his hand to point at the door, an order that didn't need words. Nashel sighed and walked out to the square, standing at attention for the fourth time that week.

"Junior Cadet Nashel," Sergeant Thomas called her after he made her ran around all three buildings three times.

Nashel tried to stand at attention in front of him, but her legs felt like jelly and were shaking so badly they made her sway.

Sergeant Thomas didn't comment on her form, though. "Some of your teachers are very impressed with you. You demonstrated enormous potential at the Trials, and continue to do so in Combat and Power Training, and memory drills."

"Thank you, Sergeant."

"Yet, every single day you are here. Every morning, you are the very last on the scoreboard. Sergeants Yaren and Harare are not happy with your behaviour and performance. Today you set his nose on fire. Care to explain that?"

"I didn't do it on purpose," she pouted.

"You didn't?" he asked, raising an eyebrow.

"No, sir."

"What happened then?"

She didn't want to tell him, so she shrugged.

"Cadet..."

"I lost control," she whispered. She hung her head and bit her lip, her foot scuffing the same spot on the ground, digging a small groove, military form forgotten.

Sergeant Thomas stayed silent for such a long while that Nashel was tempted to look up. She didn't. She didn't want to set his nose on fire too.

"Why?" he asked then.

"I was tired..." her words were so low she barely heard them herself.

"You're trying to do too much. All at once." It wasn't a question but a statement.

"I can fight and I can run," she muttered. "But letters just... don't stay in my head."

The admission cost her. She didn't want to appear weak.

"That's because you're treating them like orders you have to memorise. Letters aren't orders, they're shapes. Patterns. You're good at spotting patterns, aren't you?"

She gave the tiniest nod.

"Then stop thinking of them as words. Think of them as symbols in a code. Each has a sound. Learn the symbols, learn the sounds, and you'll have the whole code cracked."

She looked up, her eyes wide, a grin spreading across her lips. She understood codes. She could break codes.

"Can I write them my own way?"

"You can write them backwards if you want, as long as you know what they mean," Thomas said with a faint smile. "You get the sound right, the rest will follow."

That night, after the extra classes, just before lights out, she sat crossed legged on her bed. Her Slowlyness propped next to her and a book of illustrated letters open in front of her, her notebook on her legs, pencil in hand.

The letter M was a mountain with two peaks. She could remember that.

The letter S was like a snake, curving left and right, ready to strike its prey.

She traced the pattern on the book with her finger. Up, a bit down, then up again, then all the way down. M.

She tried to draw it in her book. It was wobbly and more like a peak and a hill, but she knew what it meant, just like Sergeant Thomas said.

The letter W was just an M upside down, so she turned the notebook that way and drew another M.

For the letter S, she drew a snake, gave it a tongue and dots for eyes.

Her eyes hurt from staring at the pages too long, but at least she knew three letters now. She welcomed the lights turning off and forgot about her woes in favour of sleep.

"Junior Cadet Nashel," Sergeant Yaren was particularly mean the day after the nose accident. "I believe I have overestimated you. Why don't you try to read the first word today, since a sentence is clearly too much?"

The class snickered.

Nashel narrowed her eyes both at the teacher and the board. She wouldn't let her control slip again. She looked at the first word. She immediately recognised the first letter as the snake-y S, followed by the upside down mountain that was a W, next was one letter she didn't practice the night before, but was easy enough to recognise, it was just a line with a dot on top. I. The last one was an M with its two peaks. She pictured it with snow on top.

S. W. I. M. She wasn't sure what the word meant or what it sounded like. She knew the S made the same sound of the snake and the M sounded like 'mountain'. But the other two?

"S... uh... M," she muttered under her breath.

Sergeant Yaren gave her a piercing glare. "Correct," he spat as if the word tasted bad in his mouth, before he moved on to the next cadet.

Nashel couldn't help the little smirk that formed on her lips. She had learnt a new trick. If she knew a few of the sounds and made up the rest (at least until she learnt them well), she could fool Sergeant Yaren. She could already see her name climbing out of the featherweights.

It took her three months to become sixth from the bottom. She progressed more and more each day, but Sergeant Yaren found out her trick and paid more attention to her pronunciation. He was very strict with marking her written work too, and her handwriting was sloppy. Thankfully, she excelled at anything to do with physical education and power training. She could run, she could use her powers (most of the time) and she had perfected her military form to impeccable.

Moving up the board came with new challenges. Free from the extra duties, Nashel gained her breaks back. The Junior Cadets had three breaks during the day. One about mid-morning, one during lunchtime, and one mid-afternoon where they could play outside on the playground Nashel explored on her first day, or in the game room inside, with its comfy chairs and many games.

Nashel had never spent much time with other children before. Her parents would take her to the nearby park for an hour or two, but she had never attended any kind of school or day care. Even at the park, she preferred playing by herself. By the time she had her breaks back, the rest of the cadets in her class were already split in their own little groups. Forming and breaking alliances was encouraged, if not compulsory, to promote camaraderie, teamwork, and to keep the competition up.

Nashel thought she didn't need anybody, but she understood she could climb the scoreboard faster if she gained more points in team activities. She didn't like most of her classmates; they were either sloppy, stupid or had laughed at her one too many times.

She didn't know how to behave around the other children, so she watched them from afar, like a hawk, observing every move they made; the way they spoke, the way their bodies moved. Then, in the privacy of her room, she copied them in front of the mirror.

One of the groups towards the top of the scoreboard like to play a game called tag during the first break in the morning. Nashel had observed them carefully and understood the rules, so one day she asked if she could play too. The classmates had her be "it".

She ran as fast as she could, using her power over earth to boost her steps so she could catch everyone. She reached one of the slower girls and tapped her on the shoulder. The girl crashed down and started to weep like a baby. Nashel stood over her, unimpressed.

"Nashel," Sergeant Thomas admonished her.

She snapped at attention. "She fell, sir."

"No," he contradicted her. "You pushed her."

"I tagged her. That's the game." She wanted so badly to shrug, but she knew better than to move.

"Sit this one out," the sergeant ordered her. He didn't yell at her; Sergeant Thomas seldom did, but she had learnt to recognise his disappointment.

She wasn't really sure why it was such a big deal. She just tagged the girl. It was the purpose of the game. It wasn't her fault if the girl was weak and fell. It definitely wasn't her fault she cried. Criers never lasted long at the academy. To think she was ranking higher than Nashel...

It wasn't the last time Nashel got told to "sit out" during a game. The more she played with them, the more she realised she didn't understand their strange rules. The hidden ones. The rules about when to laugh, when to push, when to stop. Those that weren't written anywhere, weren't even spoken, but decided who reached and stayed at the top.

To win, she needed to learn them.

On one of the rainy days, when they stayed inside the game room, she sat alone with crayons and paper. Not too far from her, a boy was surrounded by a small group of her classmates. He said something, but she didn't pay attention to his words. The ones in the group, though, laughed. One girl threw her head back, one boy slapped the leader on the arm, but he didn't seem to mind, and another girl squealed before covering her mouth. They weren't laughing at him, she realised, but about what he said. Nashel had never experienced that kind of fun; she had never laughed like that.

That night, alone in her room, she sat in front of the mirror. She threw her head back and made a sound, but it came out horribly, not at all like the one the girl made. She practised the boy's arm-slap on the edge of her bed until her palm stung. She squealed like the other girl, but she was tempted to hit herself for how ridiculous she sounded.

Nevertheless, she tried again and again until she could almost sound genuine. Almost.

The next morning, she waited for her moment. It was another rainy day, so they stayed inside for their breaks. She sat closer to the same group, almost in, but not completely. She listened in, waited for the punchline, waited for the others to laugh, then she joined in.

Not too loud, not too soft. Just like she practised. And when the boy next to her smirked, she gave him the light arm-slap she'd rehearsed until her hand ached. A couple of the others glanced at her, then at each other, identical smirks painting on their lips, but they didn't say anything. The group subtly shifted so Nashel was more out than in.

She understood she did something wrong, but she couldn't grasp what. She was sure her laugh was good and the arm-slap looked right too.

Still, it wasn't in her nature to give up so easily. At night, she practised her laugh and the arm-slap. During break times, her eyes didn't leave the group. She sat away from them and just observed them. That's when she saw it. It was in the way their arms or legs would brush against each other when they huddled together. In how they bounced jokes off each other like a ball she wasn't invited to catch.

Her laugh had been good. Her arm-slap had been spot on. The people were wrong. She wasn't part of their circle. They didn't want her part of their circle. If she wanted to achieve higher scores in teamwork, she needed her own.

CHAPTER FIVE

Full Circle

Finding her circle wasn't easy. Nashel had a goal in mind: to be number one and stay there. Because of that, she couldn't choose any lonely cadet. She needed the right people. People who could fill in her gaps, who wouldn't think they could boss her around, who could keep up without being dragged.

She started by learning their names. After she left the featherweights, she regained her privileges, including going to the Citadel. On one of her excursions there, she bought a pack of pocket notebooks to practise her writing. When she decided she needed to learn the names and skills of everyone in her class, she took one and dedicated it to the task.

Following Sergeant Thomas' advice, in the beginning, she wrote the letters however they sprung to her mind, even if they were not the correct shapes. She didn't do it on purpose, not initially. But then, when she got better, she realised no one else could read those early marks, not even Sergeant Yaren. That gave her an idea. Why change them to the right ones if the wrong ones could be her own private alphabet, perfect for recording things she didn't want anyone else to know?

She used one page for each of her classmates. On top, she

wrote the name of the candidate in big, albeit sloppy, 'letters', then she left abundant space for her observations. At first, they were just clumsy words: loud, fast, weak. But as she learnt how to write and observe better, she expanded her records. She noted who was faster during sprints, who was quicker answering the questions in class, or who cried the most. Then even more details: who was punished the most for their uniform. She needed people who could be at her side, not stuck in the assembly square because they couldn't wear two black socks. She dedicated an entire page to their powers. She didn't need rarities, but people powerful enough to work with her and not too much to beat her.

The academy was not a place for the weak. Young flairs with poor control often had accidents, more often than not through their own fault. A few months into her circle project, a promising candidate fell victim of his own stupidity.

It happened during afternoon power gym. Sergeant Thomas instructed them to push themselves to their limit, then further, but to be careful or the powers would overtake them. The boy, Kael, liked showing off, pushing harder when people were watching. It was a point against him, but he was powerful, so Nashel still kept an eye on him.

At first, it was almost impressive: the way he lifted everything around him; weapon racks, rocks, obstacles on the training field. But then he overdid it. Nashel saw the moment it happened. The objects started to move erratically, not controlled. She shifted her attention to Kael. His eyes went wide, but not in fear. They almost looked like they were going to escape their sockets.

He made a sound, then, an ugly thing, like someone trying to breathe underwater. Pink foam frothed at his mouth. Blood trickled down the corners of his eyes, his ears, his nose. Then he collapsed, all the objects with him in a thunderous crash. He twitched once before going still.

The other cadets gasped, shouted even. Sergeant Thomas ran to him, and Nashel move slightly to keep her view unobstructed, her head tilted, entranced.

"Stupid boy," she muttered under her breath, already thinking she had to cross another name off her list.

Still, maybe she could salvage something from that fiasco. As she waited for the training field to be cleared and Sergeant Thomas to return, she focussed her attention on her classmates, studying their reactions, remembering every flinch, blank look, whisper, sob to memory.

When she returned to her notebook that night, she scratched out Kael's name so hard she pierced the page, but she also had a lot of fresh notes on the others. Kael's was the third accident since she started her project, another stark reminder that the Sunset Academy was not for the weak. That night she decided she would wait until at least the end of her first year to make her final decision. She wouldn't waste her energy on candidates who wouldn't survive her entire career.

At the beginning of her second year, she had a list of cadets to test. She set up little experiments for them and tested them one by one. She partnered with them in drills to see who adapted and who failed. She sat close to them in lessons, studying their reaction to the questions, noting who seemed confident and who blanked. She watched how they used their powers, both in drills and free time; how they handled punishment and injuries.

Sometimes she asked them questions. They seemed innocent, about what they were doing or what they did that day, but she drank every word. At night, she noted everything down in her notebook, re-evaluating her list, crossing out unworthy candidates, or highlighting the ones she favoured. Those who passed the first round of tests would move to the next. Not that they knew any of it.

During Combat Practice, Sergeant Thomas paired them off to spar with batons. In their first year, they had padded ones, but now the Academy didn't think they were needed anymore. Each cadet was expected to master a series of weapons, even if they had their powers. Nashel requested Lora, one of the names on her list.

Lora was taller and faster, but Nashel knew speed could be a weakness if not controlled. At the signal, Lora lunged, wide and eager. Nashel let her swing connect with her shoulder, not enough to hurt, just enough to make it look real, and staggered back with a hiss. Lora grinned, triumphant already.

Nashel smirked behind her guard. She'd seen enough. Overconfidence, sloppy footing, no guard on her left side. Nashel waited, let Lora take another swing, opening her side, then slipped in and pushed her baton against her ribs, hard enough that Lora wheezed.

The Sergeant barked, "Point to Cadet Nashel!"

Lora's face flushed red, and she clenched her baton tighter, ready for another try. The more Nashel escaped her attacks, the more erratic and emotional Lora became. That night, Nashel crossed out her name.

Later that month, Power Training gave her another opportunity to further her trials. They were focussing on precision, having to move a stone through five loops, all different sizes and heights. Her test was Kye, a cadet she had been keeping an eye on for a while. Kye had taught her a valuable lesson during their first year, and she kept tabs on him, even though he wasn't at the top of her list.

One lunch as a Junior Cadet, she passed the boy sat next to her the biscuit they were given for dessert. It was a flavour she didn't like, so she just placed it on his plate.

"Thank you," he replied, beaming at her.

The following day she asked him to show her his notes, and he obeyed with a smile.

She started to carry extra food or extra items around her, so she could offer them to others and collect favours. The day after she gave him the biscuit, he sat next to her in all their lessons. She would've minded if she hadn't realised he was quiet and diligent. He was gullible, easy to manipulate, and he would always say yes to her. She wasn't sure if it was because he liked her or feared her. Still, he was smart and was above average in terms of his power skills.

Thanks to him, she noted how being helpful to others brought the praises of the instructors, so during one of the power gym lesson, when one girl fell, twisting her ankle painfully, Nashel was instantly at her side, propping her up and walking her to the infirmary, hoping the instructor would recognise her act of kindness. He didn't, and she almost blasted him with her power. She made sure the girl broke her leg the next time. But that was the previous year, and she had learnt a lot since.

Kye hadn't changed much. He still said yes to her whenever she asked him something, and still displayed prowess with his powers.

When Nashel's turn came, she guided her stone through three hoops with perfect control, then let it wobble on the fourth. It was deliberate. She wanted to see what Kye would do with the opportunity. His reactions had always varied when she was the centre of attention.

His turn followed. His stone passed through all five hoops in one smooth, swift arc, then hovered above his palm before settling back down with barely a sound.

The class clapped. Nashel clapped too, because that's what the others did, but her eyes narrowed.

Kye didn't gloat. He looked embarrassed, but chanced a glance at her. She knew he'd seen her deliberate stumble for what it truly was and gave her a timid smile.

That night, in her notebook, she scratched his name in bold strokes and wrote beneath it: "Sharper than I thought. Useful."

Months and tests went by, Nashel scratched out more names than she highlighted, and her list kept getting shorter, and with it her patience. How was it possible that the cadets were all inept?

When she tested the next person, she devised an especially mean trial to vent her frustration. Siora was an excellent strategist. She could see patterns and provide solutions quicker than Nashel could. And she kept her on her toes. Siora grabbed her attention because she was as observant as

Nashel. While she observed her, Nashel noted Siora would study any room as soon as she entered it. Just like Nashel did. Siora, like Nashel, was quiet, often alone but at ease with her solitude. Even in lessons, she only spoke when asked a direct question, or when nobody else would. Nashel initially thought they were the same, but it turned out they were opposite, in a way. Siora didn't study her peers to imitate them; she studied their behaviour to predict it. She studied them to find their mistakes and avoid them herself.

Nashel approached her. She was almost sure Siora wanted to as well, but she wasn't the proactive type. Nashel had planned to catch the girl alone after studying her routine. Siora liked to stay behind in the study hall when most of the students had left. She enjoyed the quiet. One such evening, Nashel confirmed Siora was there and approached her directly.

To the untrained eye, Siora didn't react, but Nashel had studied her deeply, and she saw her shoulders tensing only a fraction and her eyes darting from the notebook to her surrounding. Nashel smirked, then sat at her table.

"I've been watching you," Nashel admitted.

"I know," Siora confirmed.

Nashel's smirk grew wider. "You've been watching me."

"I know," Siora repeated.

"The next strategy games are in two days," Nashel began. "I want you to pair with me."

Siora looked up at her, then, her expression didn't show any emotion, but she had looked up, and that in itself showed Nashel she had piqued Siora's curiosity.

"Why?"

"Because you're not stupid, and neither am I," Nashel shrugged.

Siora considered it for a moment, and it seemed to Nashel that she understood there were ulterior motives, but she nodded curtly. "Deal."

"Deal," Nashel agreed, stood and left.

The strategy games were held in one of the larger

classrooms, long tables lined with boards carved with grids and markers of different colours.

Nashel and Siora greeted each other with a nod, then sat down together, their pieces spread out before them. The rules were simple: each side controlled a square on the grid. The goal was to capture the enemy's flag without losing your own. Like capture the flag, but on tables.

Nashel leaned forward, her lips close enough to Siora's ear that the girl's shoulders tensed. "Move the infantry to row four. Then the cavalry can sweep around."

On the board, it looked clever. To someone less observant, it even looked like a clean trap. But Nashel knew it was a mistake. If Siora listened to her and moved there, the other team's flank would pin them in three moves, defeating them.

Siora's hand hovered over the piece. Her eyes didn't leave the board, darting back and forth, studying every possible combination. Slowly, deliberately, Siora raised her eyes to Nashel's and set the infantry somewhere else, in a silent challenge.

The other team blinked, surprised. Their careful trap dissolved.

Nashel smirked, but she didn't say a word.

A few moves later, Siora manoeuvred them straight into victory. Precise, like she'd already seen the entire game played out in her head before the others had moved their first piece.

When the instructor announced their win, the other cadets clapped politely. Siora didn't even smile. She only looked at Nashel as if to say, "Did you think I wouldn't notice?"

Nashel's smirk widened. The trap had been bait, and Siora hadn't fallen for it. She'd simply corrected the course and moved on, not calling Nashel out or challenging her loudly.

In her book, she noted: "This one might actually be worth keeping. But keep an eye on her."

She partnered up with Siora for most of the strategy games after that, winning them all.

Break time in the game room was loud with cadets

shrieking, arguing, laughing over card games. Nashel sat with Siora at a table near the wall, silent as usual.

Across the room, a girl let out a high, piercing laugh, throwing her head back as though the joke had been the funniest thing in the world.

Siora's pencil froze mid-stroke. Her jaw tightened. "She always does that," she muttered, low but sharp. "It's not even real. She just wants everyone to look at her."

Nashel's eyes narrowed, following the girl. "It works."

Siora snorted. "Not on me." She went back to her notebook, shutting the matter down.

But Nashel had already tucked the comment deep inside. A new trick. She would practise it later. Another weapon, so simple, and she had missed it. But not anymore. Nashel would not admit it to anyone, but Siora quickly became her social crutch: her observations made Nashel adjust her acts to pass as more natural.

Nashel was aware of the whispers. She didn't care much about them, but they were a nuisance in her climb to the top. Some of the other cadets called her names or made comments. What if she didn't blink the right amount of times when she talked to people? Or if her smile was too toothy for the occasion? Or if she didn't smile enough? She was excellent at what mattered: controlling her powers and winning the games. Something an older cadet told her once struck her, though, and prompted her to rethink her stance.

"You're efficient, Nashel. But you're not invisible. Be careful not to stand out too much. Nobody likes a show-off," the recruit told her after a drill with the older students.

"I'm don't care if they like me," Nashel had countered.

"No, but one day you may need them. Why burn that bridge?"

Nashel hadn't slept that night, replaying the recruit's words in her head again and again. Why burn that bridge? He was right. She had already learnt that some shallow niceties could get her favours, and this wasn't any different. She wouldn't stop excelling. It wasn't her problem if she was better than the rest of her peers, but she could soften the edges by being seen with someone everybody liked. And who better than someone like the laughing girl who irked Siora so much? She could catch two birds with one stone and have a person to keep Siora in check, while also serving as a buffer to Nashel.

Vessa wasn't on her list. She wouldn't have been if Nashel didn't adjust her aim. She wasn't stupid, but she wasn't excellent either. She was frivolous, but that was her purpose, after all. Because she was so different from what Nashel looked for, she was the most difficult to test.

Vessa smiled way too much, but that seemed to make her more likeable. Everyone liked being around her, even though nobody really stuck. Nashel saw an opportunity there, but she needed to make sure she approached her the right way, without scaring her.

After one particularly intense drill, Vessa sat alone on the ground catching her breath.

"Hi," Nashel greeted her.

Vessa flinched. They had never spoken before. "H-hi," she replied tentatively. "Nashel, right?"

Nashel nodded. "Is everything okay?" she put on a mask of slight concern she had practised recently, and Vessa seemed to buy it, as she smiled back.

"Yeah, just catching my breath."

"Do you want some company?" she gave her a half-smile, almost shy. It was her best one; she was very proud of what it looked like when she practised in front of the mirror.

Vessa's smile widened as she nodded. "Thank you."

Nashel sat next to her. She wasn't sure how to continue the conversation, but Vessa did that for her. She started to talk and talk and talk. Nashel realised soon that she didn't have to listen, just nod at the right time, and make non-committal sounds and Vessa would be happy.

Nashel wasn't happy to just approach her though; she needed to make sure Vessa was the right fit. She noticed Vessa could walk into a room and never be alone. She wasn't beloved, and her friends changed from day to day, but her smile, her silly comments, her constant chatter meant she was always tolerated. Always surrounded. Always safe.

That seemed promising, but Nashel needed to make sure it applied to her if she had to tolerate Vessa's presence. It wasn't a simple test for Nashel to devise. In the end, it was chance that made it happen.

It was a few days later during lunch. Nashel carried her tray to one of the long tables. They had just completed a drill with fire, and she had aced it. But nobody liked a show-off, especially not one immune to fire while the others ended up with burns and singes.

In the dining all, someone muttered under their breath. Not loud enough to be caught, but enough for her ears to catch it. She tilted her head just slightly, fixing the boy who had spoken with a look sharp enough to draw blood, challenging him to say more. The beginnings of a smirk formed on his lips.

"Oh no," Vessa gasped, plopping down beside Nashel, unaware of what was happening. "Don't tell me you all got the grey stew again. I swear it's plotting against us!" She prodded the mush on her plate with her spoon, screwing her face into such a ridiculous grimace that a few of the cadets laughed despite themselves.

The boy glanced away, smirk forgotten. The tension dissolved into chuckles and exaggerated groans about the food.

Even Nashel smiled, but she didn't miss the shift. Nobody said anything more about her. She glanced sideways at Vessa, who was already happily chattering about how she was going to bribe the kitchen staff to teach her the trick to the sweet rolls.

Later that night, alone with her notebook, Nashel wrote one word under Vessa's name: Shield.

Siora wasn't happy with Nashel's choice.

The girls and Kye were sitting in the study hall, the usual comfortable silence between them, when Vessa bounced over and dropped herself into the seat opposite with a too-bright grin. She started talking immediately about how hard drills had been, about how the stew at lunch was disgusting, about how someone in a room next to hers had started snoring like a dying boar and she could definitely hear it. Nashel nodded once, lips twitching into her careful half-smile.

Siora didn't bother to hide her scowl. "Why is she here?" she asked flatly when Vessa leaned over to gossip with another cadet across the aisle.

Kye chuckled. He too, had noticed Siora's irritation.

"Because she's useful," Nashel replied without missing a beat.

"Useful?" Siora's tone was almost incredulous. "She's a distraction. She doesn't know when to shut up. She'll drag you down."

Nashel turned her head slowly, fixing Siora with a look that was part warning, part amusement. "No. She'll keep eyes off me. You study rooms; I study people. And they like her."

Siora's mouth tightened. She didn't argue, but her silence was sharper than words. She didn't have to say it; Nashel knew she thought this was a mistake.

"What do I do?" Kye asked in an overly dramatic voice.

He had a sharp eye, as Nashel had noticed when she tested him. He also hated conflicts, even if they didn't concern him, and he would make a light joke or subtly change the subject when he sensed tension.

Nashel smirked. She saw Siora's shoulders relax, her lips tugging up against her will. "You do what you do," she replied cryptically.

Kye shrugged, the timid smile he reserved for Nashel painting his lips.

That quality of his turned out to be very useful when Eira joined the group.

He was the exception. Nashel didn't approach him. He insinuated himself into her life without her permission. He saw right through her, and she didn't like it.

CHAPTER SIX

Eira

"You're trying too hard," he said one day, without looking up from his book.

Nashel blinked. She had never spoken to the boy in front of her, but she knew who he was. His name was Eira, and he was on her list. He was smart, fast, and strong. He was towards the top of the scoreboard, but not part of any group. There was something about him Nashel didn't like. She didn't trust him, and she didn't understand why he was striking a conversation.

"Trying what?"

"That smile you do. It's always half a second too late."

Nashel didn't reply, but tensed. It was true. She hadn't mastered social situations yet, and she was always taking cues from those around her, which led her to be slightly late. She didn't think anyone had noticed.

Eira glanced up, eyes sharp, a playful grin on his lips. "You're not fooling me."

"Okay," she shrugged, finding her composure. "It's not like I care either way."

Eira laughed. It was loud and almost startled her, earning a stern look from the study hall supervisor, which he ignored.

"Why are you talking to me?" Nashel probed.

"Because it's boring being the smartest person in the room all the time," he said.

"You're not smarter than me," she rebuked.

He shrugged. "If you say so."

Nashel wanted to jump across the table and throttle him, but she only blinked slowly.

She tried to ignore him, but from that day, he was everywhere. She didn't seek him out, but he was just there. Two desks over in her classes, a pair away in sparring, just ahead of her during morning runs. He would look at her with an annoying smirk Nashel wanted to wipe off his face with a punch. Somehow, neither Siora, Kye, or Vessa noticed him. Vessa knew him, just like she knew everybody, but she told Nashel he was a loner and a weirdo, qualities that until recently applied to Nashel too but seemed to have been forgotten.

"Are you sure you don't like him?" Vessa teased her one night after she complained again about Eira's omnipresence.

Kye tensed.

"No," Nashel replied coldly, glaring at her.

"If you say so..." Vessa shrugged with a smirk.

"It does seem like you see what you want to see," Siora commented, not raising her eyes from the book she was reading.

Nashel's irritation grew. She wasn't seeing what she wanted to see. He was there. Always. Even then, on the other side of the break room, seemingly distracted by something, but she felt his eyes on her. She would have to take matters into her own hands.

The next morning, during the run, he was a few steps in front of her. She didn't care, but he seemed to make a point of it. Still, she studied him and the surrounding. His uniform was a bit too long, so he could trip on it. Or that root that always stuck out that students learnt to avoid, it could suddenly grow. Or maybe she could pass him a bit too close, an accidental shove.

"Perhaps that branch could poke me in the eye," he startled her, slowing down to her side. "Or maybe a chunk of roofing could drop when we coast past the school building."

"What are you talking about?" Nashel replied, annoyed.

"Accidents. The ones you're planning to get rid of me," he smirked widely, infuriatingly. "I thought I would give you some suggestions."

She rolled her eyes. "I think you're becoming too obsessed with me," she mocked.

"I believe it's the other way around."

"If you say so," she mimicked his shrug and intonation perfectly.

For a fraction of a second, his eyes widened in surprise, then he laughed. "Well played."

"I told you you're not smarter than me."

"Perhaps..." he conceded. "But I'm faster," he sped up, forcing her to chase him.

She beat him to the finish line. "You were saying?" she asked smugly, but when she turned to rub it off, he wasn't there.

If it weren't for Vessa confirming his existence, she would've thought he was an annoying figment of her imagination.

"Did you know the tip of your tongue sticks out when you concentrate hard?" he appeared in front of her in the study hall, slouching on the chair, the following week.

"I thought you said you're not obsessed with me." she didn't look up.

"It's kind of cute."

Nashel's head snapped up, her hands gripped the side of the table, knuckles white. She was sure she would break it... or him. "Excuse me?" she hissed.

He smirked, balancing on the back legs of the chair. "I said," he repeated slowly. "You're kind of cute."

Nashel's powers whipped out without her even thinking about it. The chair moved from under Eira, the legs elongating into the branches they came from, wrapping around his arms and legs, the back rest doing the same around his throat.

"Cadet Nashel," the supervisor immediately shouted. "Stop it now."

She didn't. She was seeing red. Cute meant weak. And if Eira thought she was weak, she would have to teach him a lesson. She cocked her head, having the twine around his neck tighten. His lips were turning blue. He frantically tapped on the floor, as if it was a sparring session and he wanted out. His eyes bulged, his face red. His reduce breath became a rattling wheeze. She smirked. She would show him 'cute'.

She felt more than saw the supervisor move. His arm made a wide arc in a familiar gesture she'd seen multiple times, but never experienced the effects herself. Pain invaded her. One moment she had Eira's life in her hand, the next she was on the ground writhing in pain. It felt as if a current was electrifying her. Even after the current ended, she still felt the pain. It was the worst she's ever experienced. Worse even than breaking her arm the previous year during sparring, or when her partner in Power Training had lost control and slashed her across her shoulder. She still had that scar.

Nashel couldn't keep track of what was happening around her, and she hated being so vulnerable. The pain was everywhere, so much so that she didn't know if the other cadets were still there, or how long it lasted.

When she finally managed to open her eyes and sit up, the study hall was empty and the lights dim. Sergeant Thomas was perched on the nearest desk, with a look of disappointment in his eyes. He didn't say anything to her, just waited until she was able to stand, then turned around, expecting her to follow. Nashel did with wobbly steps, wincing because of the residual pain.

Sergeant Thomas took the long way around. He didn't lead her to her room to pack her things, which she thought it was good, and he didn't take her straight to the gate either. They walked to Headmistress Magna's office. It wasn't that far from the study hall, but the sergeant walked her around the entire building to reach it.

He still hadn't said a word when he knocked on the door.

"Come in," the voice of the headmistress reached them.

He turned the handle and let her inside without following.

Nashel snapped at attention the best she could. She didn't have time to check her uniform, but she imagined it was rumpled and undone. Her stance wasn't as stiff as it should've been, but she still felt the pain and couldn't muster the precise form she had developed.

"Cadet Nashel," Headmistress Magna started, looking at her with piercing eyes. "To say it's a disappointment to see you here is an understatement."

Nashel knew enough of the military protocol by then to know she wasn't supposed to answer.

"I thought I had been clear when I admitted you to this Academy. Killing is forbidden. What do you have to say for yourself?"

"I didn't kill him," she replied, her eyes fixed in front of her. Her legs and arms were shaking. She tried to stiffen them, she didn't want the headmistress think she was afraid.

"Because Sergeant Firwood intervened."

"I wouldn't have killed Eira even if he didn't." Her tone was almost insubordinate, but she couldn't help it.

Headmistress Magna raised an eyebrow. It seemed both curious and warning. Nashel bit her tongue.

"And what, pray tell, did Cadet Eira do to deserve such treatment?"

"He called me cute," Nashel admitted without shame.

Magna chuckled. "Is it a bad thing?"

"Yes," she said coldly. "Cute is weak. I am not weak."

"So you showed him," she concluded. The headmistress had the uncanny ability to understand her.

"Yes, headmistress."

"Be truthful with me," she splayed her hands on the table and looked at Nashel even more intensely. "Would you have stopped?"

"Yes, headmistress," Nashel replied. "I don't want to be expelled."

"I see..."

They stayed quiet for a while, Nashel wishing the headmistress dismissed her soon because her entire body was hurting.

"A week of punishment will suffice this time," the woman decreed.

Nashel almost gasped. A week of punishment, missing classes and remedial tests would drop her to the bottom of the scoreboard. All her progress would be for nothing. She would have to start again.

"Yes, headmistress," she said the only possible answer.

"Consider it a warning. I will not be as lenient if something like this happens again."

"I understand."

"You're dismissed."

Nashel walked the required three steps backwards, then sharply turned and left the office. Sergeant Thomas wasn't there, so she made her way to her room. Stupid Eira. It was all his fault. He riled her up on purpose. He would pay. He had to.

The only upside of the week of punishment was that she didn't see him much. He wasn't fool enough to get punished on purpose to annoy her. Thankfully for Nashel, the punishment was the usual for Class students, not the painful whip of power normally reserved for Recruits. It gave her a lot of time to plot against Eira. She had to be careful, make it look even more like an accident that couldn't be traced back to her. She would have to wait a while, too, just to let the dust settle.

It was the longest week of her life. Every morning she watched her name drop rank after rank, until it plummeted to the very bottom of the featherweights on the third day, so on top of the additional studying she had to do, she also had chores waking her up early in the morning, and study well after lights-out.

When the week was finally over, Nashel had three foul-proof plans to make Eira pay, and at least double the amount of half-formed ones. Vessa and Kye were overjoyed to see her at breakfast. The girl launched into a long rant about how unfair the punishment was, and that Nashel didn't really do anything wrong. Kye nodded vehemently next to her. Siora clicked her tongue.

"Let's not get carried away," she interrupted. "Nashel did almost kill him."

"Yeah, so what?" Vessa replied. "He didn't die, did he?"

Siora rolled her eyes and gritter her teeth. Despite having been months since they started hanging out, she still couldn't stand Vessa. Nashel knew it, but didn't do anything to defuse the tension; she enjoyed it.

"Let's not argue," Kye interjected. "Nashel is back; that's what's important!"

"She's still with the featherweights though," Vessa moaned.

"She'll get out of there soon," Kye asserted.

That was her priority; earning back the positions she dropped. Then she would focus on Eira.

He, however, had other plans. Now that Nashel was back to their normal schedule, he made his presence even more annoyingly. Instead of staying at the periphery, he was next to her at every opportunity. He managed to be her partner for every pair activity, sparring, power practice, strategy games, and class experiments. She had no power over it. It seemed the teachers were oblivious or approved of it.

During the morning runs, she tried to shake him off, but he consistently matched her pace. He even sat next to her group during meals, even though he never spoke to any of them.

If nothing else, it was an excellent lesson in restraint for Nashel.

One afternoon, about two weeks after her punishment had ended, Class 2, Nashel's group, had a practical assessment based on the latest strategy game. The woods surrounding the Academy and Citadel were divided into a grid; each pair of cadets was assigned one. Just like in the games, they needed to conquer the opponents' flag without losing their own.

"Cadet Nashel and Cadet Eira," Sergeant Thomas announced.

Nashel groaned.

The pack they were given was almost bigger than Nashel, and definitely double her weight. She wondered if there was an Expression to make it lighter, but she didn't know it and couldn't ask.

She sent daggers at Eira as they approached the instructor who was to take them to their unit, but he didn't notice, or pretended not to. The instructor grabbed their arms and teleported them to their assigned spot. Nashel had experienced teleportation several times before, but she still wasn't used to it. It was a disturbing sensation, like being disintegrated and reconstituted in another place, with the feeling of having left something behind. It was an advanced technique taught to Aspirants, and it was forbidden outside the Citadel. It was the one thing Nashel wasn't looking forward to learning. She didn't like how it made her feel.

"We're going for the flag," Nashel announced as soon as she steadied herself. She didn't wait for Eira to answer, just started to march.

"We can't leave our flag unguarded."

She rolled her eyes, of course he would argue. "By the time the rest of them gets organised and moves towards us, we'd already captured theirs."

"What makes you think they dropped us off all at the same time?"

She paused. She assumed that.

"As I thought," he smirked.

"It doesn't change anything," Nashel hissed through gritted teeth. "We're going for the flag."

"Stop!"

"I don't take orders from you!" Nashel shouted, the leaves at her feet floating up as her powers showed themselves.

"And I don't take orders from losers!" his powers showed too, pebbles floating around him.

Nashel groaned, stomped her foot and marched away. She wasn't sure she was going in the right direction, but she wouldn't admit it or check her map. For a while Eira didn't say anything, but she heard him walk behind her.

The terrain changed. It was a gradual shift; she almost missed it. The ground became sloshier, her boots sinking into the mud. It wasn't normal, she realised. She raised a fist to stop Eira, a gesture they had learnt in their drills. To his credit, Eira didn't protest this time.

"Ambush," she whispered so low it was almost impossible to hear, but she saw him tense in the corner of her eye.

Two cadets burst from the underbrush, their attacks on her and Eira before they were standing. Pressure slammed into Nashel, as if a boulder was placed on her shoulder and pushing her down to the ground. She shouted, more in frustration than pain, as she saw their flag levitate towards the enemy.

"NO!" hers and Eira's shouts mixed together deafening.

A burst of power surged, Nashel herself wasn't sure whom it originated from, but it worked. The two cadets were blown backwards, the pressure on Nashel's shoulders lifting, their flag flopped back to the ground.

"You're welcome," Eira commented smugly.

"What for?" Nashel turned to look at him as she grabbed the flag. It was dripping with mud, but it was in their possession.

"Saving you?!"

"You didn't save me, if anything, I saved you!"

Eira rolled his eyes and approached the two unconscious cadets. "They don't have a flag," he told her.

She shook her head, still angry she fell into the trap and had her flag almost stolen. All Eira's fault.

"Let's agree we saved each other."

"Let's agree not to get into each other's business."

It was Eira's turn to shake his head and walk away.

They went back into the forest the way they came, then veered deeper into it. Nashel realised then that she had an opportunity. Things could happen in the forest, accidents. She could blame a pair of other cadets, nobody would be the wiser, and Eira would be dealt with.

She studied him as he walked in front of her. He was aware of her eyes; she knew it from the tension on his shoulders, and he was smart enough to know it had been a mistake to have her behind him, but it was too late to change it. He was a fast runner, but not so good on inclined and uneven ground. He stumbled most often than not as they climbed.

Once, he tripped over an exposed root, and she chuckled.

"Ha-ha, funny," he muttered.

That gave her an idea. She commanded the next root to do the same, but this time, it hooked his ankle and held on, making him fall. He stood up, dusted his trousers and looked at his scraped knee with distaste.

"You don't get it, do you!" He didn't shout, but it sounded as if he did. Anger was almost tangibly emanating from him.

"That you're not better than me?" Nashel challenged, enthralled by his loss of control.

"For someone who thinks she's the smarted person in the world, you're really dumb!"

She snorted.

"Headmistress Magna made a mistake, accepting you so young."

"You speak like you're so much older! What are you, six?"

"You're six. I'm seven!" He snapped indignantly.

She raised an eyebrow as if to say, case in point.

He shook his head again. "I don't know why I'm even trying," he muttered.

"Trying what?" she retorted, struggling to keep her own anger in check.

"I'm not here to drag you down. I'm here to push you up."

She froze, stunned by his audacity. "Why would you care?" she spat.

He tilted his head, grin infuriating. "Because you should be higher. Because I need you to be higher. I need you sharp... so I can beat you."

The arrogance in his tone set her teeth on edge, but underneath it was something else. He wasn't taunting; he meant it.

Before she could answer, a whistle cut through the trees. Four cadets charged from the left flank. Two attacked with sharp arrows flying towards them. Nashel raised a shield of power, and they bounced on it. The other two jumped around it with batons in hand, swinging at Nashel. She ducked and swept the legs off one, sending her to the ground. The second came from behind, viciously and cowardly, but Eira intercepted him and stopped him.

Something clicked into place. She wasn't sure what, but she couldn't stop and think what it was. For a moment, they fought like two halves of the same machine. She used branches of the tree around to tie up one of the power attackers, while Eira turned the mud into quicksand and buried the other one up to his torso, trapping his arms in it. They ended up shoulder to shoulder, breathing heavily, studying their surroundings with alertness. When they were sure the only enemies around them were the ones defeated at their feet, they relaxed and took a step away from each other.

"We're better together," Eira stated her, wiping the sweat off his forehead. "Imagine what we could do if we stopped working against each other."

Nashel considered it for a moment. Eira was annoying, but he was also smart. He was too full of himself, but he also pushed her to strive.

"What are you proposing?" Nashel asked cautiously.

"We are the smartest people in a room, any room. Always," he smirked again, a spark of mischief in his eyes. "And you gathered a useful little group."

Nashel's eyes widened in surprise, reading through his

facade. "You won't in."

Eira laughed bitterly. "You're so dumb. I don't care about your group of shields."

Nashel's jaw tightened. It was unnerving how clearly he could read her.

"I could've joined any group. The top of the scoreboard. No problem."

"Why didn't you, then?" she mocked him.

"Because they are stupid and useless!"

She couldn't help but laugh at that; he was right.

"We have the same goal, Nashel," he shrugged. "Be at the top. So why not do it together?"

Nashel thought of the future. Once she mastered social situations, which wouldn't take her too long she was sure, what challenges would she face? Not many. She could grow bored with the academy, the drills, the lessons. But with someone like Eira next to her, pushing her, the challenges would be endless, and she would become even more powerful than she anticipated.

"Deal."

It took a while for Eira to relent and let Nashel lead, but he wasn't interested in being the leader, just in bettering himself. Nashel wasn't that interested either, but she had chosen those people and she wanted to control them. She also wouldn't accept to be their subordinate, as she saw them as less than her.

After they worked through their chinks and oiled their gears, Nashel's group became unmatched. They broke all the records, held their position at the top of the scoreboard without ever faltering. They became the elite squad of the academy. The best, most adored, most hated students, envied even by the upper classes.

CHAPTER SEVEN

The Void Moves Closer

"Void has moved closer."

It wasn't Headmistress Magna opening the assembly that day, but a member of the Sunset Army, a General, from what Nashel recalled from her lesson on military rank.

They all knew about the Void, and had extensive lessons across their entire education on the subject: the wall of power that divided the land in two, separating the Sunset from their enemy, the Sunrise. Everyone also knew that the Void was unstable. It constantly shifted, giving one nation or the other a few more inches of territory before taking them away again. Nashel wasn't sure why then the general was there announcing it to the cadet brigade.

"It is the closer it has ever been," the general continued, without introducing himself.

He was a burly man in his fifties. His face was weathered, as if he spent a lot of time outside, and created a stark contrast with his pristine uniform. He had several medals and award badges pinned to his left side, and the cuff sparkled with the gold insignia of his rank.

It wasn't unusual to have members of the army on campus. They often came to teach strategy and tactics, often using case studies of real ops they took part in. But it was uncommon for a general to be holding the assembly.

"We don't know how long it will last, but as it is, we are in a vulnerable position."

Nashel never understood that. Supposedly the army was there to protect from a Sunrise invasion, and when the Void shifted taking away 'precious' inches of territory, the Sunset faced a higher risk. However, they had been taught that the Void was, indeed, void. There was nothing inside it. No powers worked inside it. People who tried to cross it would die as soon as they got in contact with it. There was no way to go from one nation to the other. So how would they be able to attack each other?

Nashel knew there was something more, something only the top brass knew about. If they were so intent on conquering the other side, or felt so afraid when the Void shifted towards them, there must have been a way for troops to cross.

When Nashel was on one of her residentials, she had been sent to a village very close to the Void, so she had a chance to see it for herself. A way to instil fear in the cadets. When she saw it, though, it struck her as something alive, not empty. Something extremely powerful. Dark, and powerful. She had no doubt that if touched, it would kill, but there was also no doubt in her mind that it definitely wasn't a hollow vacuum.

"We have decided to expedite your training. Aspirants will start their military training from their first year, instead of their third. Recruits will have additional military strategy classes and will have a boot camp lasting between two and six weeks around mid-year. Class will also be introduced to military history and ranks."

The general paused, letting the students take the news in. Nashel wasn't sure what to think. She didn't mind the additional training. She was sure she could endure it, but she was still on the fence about the reasons.

"The Sunset will not perish!" his voice boomed, and the students repeated it as a salutation. The general left, marching towards the Citadel and the main base, and the instructors proceeded to the cadets' inspection as normal.

Nashel had learnt a long time before not to break formation, but she could feel a restless energy spreading through the groups. She wondered if that was the goal: to inspire fear, assuring total obedience and to renew the sense of purpose that was infused into the cadets from their first day. She wondered if any of them would see any action any time soon, but she highly doubted it. Cadets that graduated from the Academy were conscripted into the army for ten years, the first three of which were mostly training and further study to obtain a degree in one of the specialities, and to develop leadership skills. Their fourth year was spent floating throughout the country, learning about the different bases, operations, and customs, just like the residentials were for the academy students. So, even if they expedited their education, Nashel doubted she or any of her classmates would be on active duty as soon as they graduated, let alone that she was still a Warrant Officer and had one more year at the academy before that.

At breakfast, the cadets could finally let their tension go. The dining hall immediately filled with whispered conversations. There was an urgency in the undertones; everyone was wondering what it meant for them, for the Sunset. The older aspirants, those in their final year, seemed the most anxious, and the quietest.

Nashel shook her head.

"Why is everyone so downbeat?" she whispered to her table. "We are not going to war."

Kye shrugged. "It must be important if the general came in person and they decided to do all that."

Vessa nodded. "I read that during the last war, students were drafted. They left the academy before graduation and were sent to the front."

"And when was this war you're talking about?" Nashel asked sceptically.

Vessa scratched her head. "Just before the Void was

created," she admitted in a murmur.

"Exactly," Nashel replied ostentatiously.

"Still a precedent," the other girl tried to defend herself.

Nashel shrugged. It wasn't impossible, but highly improbable. There hadn't been a war since the Void was created, which reinforced the idea that it couldn't be crossed, therefore why should they be worried?

The buzz of the news and the anxiety and restlessness didn't last long. Not because all was forgotten, but because their training did intensify and the cadets, especially the aspirants, didn't have time to worry about anything else.

Their days got longer. They were often woken up hours before dawn to run through drill after drill, before going back to class and being quizzed about all the topics ever covered, then out again for more practice until late in the evening. They were divided into smaller units, teams of four or five cadets, and they would regularly participate in scenarios where they needed to defend themselves and their post and defeat and conquer the other teams.

One night, a siren jump-scared Nashel awake. It wasn't the usual morning alarm, but a piercing, deafening noise that indicated an attack. She quickly changed into her uniform - as it was still compulsory to do so, even in emergencies - and rushed into the corridor. She expected to see the other aspirants briskly moving towards the emergency exit, but most of the doors were still closed. Four other students were looking around just as confused, before recognising each other: it was her squad, the team she was in charge of.

They dropped in a single line behind her, realising it was not an emergency, but rather a drill that involved their squad only.

"Careful now," she whispered, "it's a trap."

There was no doubt in her mind it was. They proceeded with caution along the corridor, checking all the doors, the ceiling, their rear. When they reached the stairs, they stopped.

"Kye, send a feeler," she ordered.

Kye nodded and obeyed. He closed his eyes, concentrating on the task. Everyone could use feelers, but he was the most apt, and it was his squad role. The others waited, keeping as quiet as possible, so as not to disturb him. After a few moments, he opened his eyes and gave the all-clear.

"Nothing in either direction," he said, unhappy.

They all knew that nothing was not good news.

Nashel nodded and moved along. There was no point in sitting ducks. Crossing the corridor was too easy, and as Kye said, there was nothing. No people, no traps. The next corridor was the same, and so was the next. Only when they reached the exit, they faced their first obstacle.

They didn't need Kye's feeler to feel and see the trap on the door.

And if they could see and feel it, then there was another invisible trap somewhere.

"Eira, Siora, keep and eye on the corridor," Nashel ordered.

"Kye, see if you can feel anything else. Vessa, you and I will dismantle this trap. Carefully."

Her squad members nodded curtly and followed her orders earnestly. The first layer of powers was easy to dissolve. It was the flashiest, but also the most innocuous. They worked quickly on that and moved to the next.

"I can't get to the last layer," Kye whispered after a few minutes. "There's too many."

"Is there anything else, not just on the door, but the corridor or outside?"

Kye concentrated again for a few more moments, then shook his head.

"Nothing in the corridor," he reported, "but one of the door's layers is blocking me from feeling the outside.

"Can you move out of its range and go around it?"

He nodded and dashed down the corridor to put some distance between himself and the door.

Nashel and Vessa started working again. The layers were becoming increasingly more difficult to undo, and she wished Kye would return and help.

A scream of pain made them all flinch. It was coming in the direction of the missing member, and it sounded like him. Eira and Siora started, eager to rescue their mate, but Nashel stopped them. They gave her a rebellious glare but fell in line without protest.

"It's the trap we were waiting for," she whispered. "You keep working on the door. I'll go and check it. Protect each other."

"But—" Siora tried to protest.

"Protect each other," she said more firmly, not accepting any argument.

Nashel walked cautiously down the corridor. Other than that first scream, they hadn't heard any more noises. Everything was eerily quiet, and she wondered if powers were at play to keep it that way. She spread her senses, sending feelers in all directions to check for any unwanted disturbance and to see the extent of the door trap, which should give her an idea of how far Kye had to go.

Soon, she turned a corner and saw him on the floor, unconscious or worse. Nothing else appeared to be around, but she knew better than to rush. She sent a feeler to the unconscious figure to assess it. She was surprised to find that it was indeed Kye and not an illusion. He was alive, breathing deeply, but she was too far to feel for any injury that way.

Any other person would've been reassured and approached their squad members, but Nashel wasn't a fool. She knew these drills were mostly meant for the aspirants to fail. They wanted to test how they coped with it, how well they could perform, even if they were doomed. So she knew there was a trap ready for her to step into, and she wasn't eager to do so.

Finding the Trace was not a skill everyone developed. It was so difficult that it wasn't even taught in school. Yet, it came naturally to her. The first time she saw a Trace, her classmates thought she was just joking. It was during her first year at the Academy, so she was young and nobody took her seriously. Sergeant Thomas picked up what she was saying and took her aside.

"What did you tell them?" he had asked.

"The truth," she had murmured begrudgingly.

"Tell me," he had ordered.

She didn't want him to think she was stupid, but she knew she couldn't lie. "I saw something, like a golden thread, around the glass Instructor Kalb was levitating."

"A golden thread?"

"Not a real one," she had explained. "I couldn't touch it or anything..."

Sergeant Thomas had sighed heavily. It had become a habit when dealing with her, as if she aggravated him. "That was a Trace."

"A Trace?"

"Yes, it's the signature of whoever used their powers there. It is extremely difficult to learn how to see them and even more difficult to manipulate them."

"Manipulate?"

"It means to change them."

She had nodded.

"I will have to speak to Magna," he had continued. "For now, do not tell anyone else."

She had cocked her head curiously but hadn't spoken.

A few days later, she had been summoned to the headmistress's office, where she was told never to tell others about her ability to see Traces, and that she was to have extra lessons to learn how to use that skill.

Ten years later, it was still a secret, but one she had mastered. With Kye unconscious and no one else in the corridor, she decided to use it. It had become second nature to her, so it took little energy to see it, and surely, it led her to the trap. It was a clever one. The power was so low that feelers couldn't pick it, but she immediately knew it was going to be very effective. The quiet ones usually were.

Seeing and manipulating a Trace gave her the advantage.

It was much easier to undo the work from the inside than it was from the outside, like they had to do on the door. She dissolved the trap in a matter of seconds, then hurried to her subordinate.

Her first assessment was correct. He was alive and breathing. She couldn't see any physical injuries, but a quick feeler told her he was bleeding internally. She wasn't the best at healing, but she couldn't just leave him be. She rudimentary tried to put a stop to the bleeding, so she could levitate him and take him back to the rest of the squad.

They had made good progress on the door by the time she reached them and they were relieved to see their teammate. Eira, who was more apt at healing, immediately started to work on Kye, while Nashel was briefed on the progress.

"I think this is the last layer," Vessa told her. "But I need help." He said the last sentence so low that it was hard to hear it. Asking for help was not a skill the Academy was too keen on. Nashel knew they were going to be penalised because of that. Vessa should've known better than to phrase it that way. She shook her head and focused on the door. She could look for the Trace and undo it that way, but the squad would have questions she couldn't answer.

It was a hard layer, so faint that at times she couldn't grasp it, but working with Vessa, they managed in the end. They opened the door carefully, expecting a new obstacle ready to stop them.

The air was chill, freezing even, unusual for the season. It made them unnaturally cold within a few moments.

"Keep him warm," she ordered Eira. "We're not done yet."

They were out in the open, with no place to seek shelter, and with hostile weather. It didn't take long before power attacks came from everywhere.

"Shield!" she ordered, and the other two members erected a barrier that deflected the attacks.

"There," Eira pointed towards a crop of trees. "I need to check on Kye. We need shelter."

Nashel nodded and instructed the others to keep the

shield up and run.

They couldn't see their attackers, so they couldn't counter them. Nashel sent feelers, but came up empty-handed. Whoever was attacking them was not here or was invisible.

"Hurry, hurry," Eira muttered, while Kye was convulsing.

They made it to the trees, and Eira directed the others so that they could combine their powers and keep Kye alive, while Nashel kept watch.

"What's our objective?" one of them asked.

"Stay alive," Nashel replied. She didn't know if they had an objective. There had been no directive, no mission briefing. In a situation like theirs, protocol dictated that they find a place to bunker down until the extraction team arrived. She doubted there would be an extraction team.

The cold was settling in their bones. She could feel it making her more and more tired, and she could see the same in her subordinates. Lighting a fire was out of discussion. It would give their position away and make them an even easier target.

"We need to find a better place. We can't stay in this cold any longer, and we can't light a fire here."

She tried to remember the blueprint of the Academy. They were still there, after all. It was clear that they couldn't go back inside, or they wouldn't have been led out.

"The Cell," she whispered, remembering. Not too far from where they were, there was the entrance to the Cell. It wasn't a prison, even though at times it was used for punishment, but a practice room. It could simulate different environments, different opponents. They called it the Cell because it was small and sparse, only containing a narrow coat, a sink and a toilet, just like a prison cell.

"Yes!" Eira exclaimed. "We can run the healing simulation. It should be enough to keep him alive."

"Okay, get ready."

They formed a tight group around Kye. Everyone raised a shield to protect each other from the inevitable attacks. Nashel sent feelers again, trying to catch their attackers off guard, but once more, it didn't bear results.

They moved quickly and efficiently, the drills ingrained into their bodies and minds that they had become second nature. The attacks intensified as they got closer to the Cell entrance, showing that they were on the right path.

"Siora, open the door," she ordered once they reached it. It was a mistake. Vessa was not quick enough to compensate for the shield shift and one attack pierced it. Vessa screamed as a gush opened on her shoulder.

"Damn it!" Nashel muttered, extending her shield to cover everyone. Covering five people with the shield was consuming. She was good enough to have an impenetrable shield, but not for too long. Eira moved to check Vessa writhing on the ground. He shook his head.

"I'm using too much power to keep him alive," he told the teammate. "Toughen up and deal with it yourself."

Nashel nodded at his decision. Vessa was still conscious - not for long, based on her paling face - so she could at least slow the bleeding. Wrenching in pain wouldn't help any of them.

"I'm in!" Siora finally exclaimed as the door hissed open.

Not a moment too soon. The attacks were more and more intense now that they were sitting duck, and Nashel couldn't keep the shield up for longer. Vessa had passed out, her shoulder still bleeding copiously, as she hadn't listened to the order and didn't attempt to stop it. The cold wasn't helping. They were all shivering. Nashel could feel her limbs becoming stiffer and stiffer, her energy depleting quickly.

They retreated inside, Siora dragging Vessa now that she wasn't busy with the door, and locked it behind them. Only then they took a sigh of relief.

The Cell was a self-contained module, untouchable from the outside, unless it was heavily bombarded, so they were safe there for the time being.

Nashel stumbled as she tried to move towards the room's control system. Her head suddenly dizzy, she wondered if the instructors had somehow disabled the ventilation, but the others were alright. Shivering, but okay.

"You good?" Eira asked curtly.

She nodded once, then took another step.

Despite being used as a simulation, the risk of injury was real, and the healing programme was the most used. Once inside the Cell, a cadet couldn't exit until their instructor decided so, therefore they needed all the resources they could get.

With shaky, stiff fingers, she powered the system and accessed the healing programme. A voiceover gave them instructions on how to proceed, and while it worked on the two injured squad members, Nashel turned the heating up so that they could get warm again.

Vessa's arm was easily healed, and she soon regained consciousness, but Kye wasn't so lucky. The system informed them he was in critical condition and would stay sedated until they could be rescued.

"Do you think we are safe?" Vessa whimpered.

"Safe? You know you risk all of our lives?" Nashel's anger surfaced, barely contained.

Vessa looked at her, confused.

"We made it though." At least Vessa had the decency to look away.

"Not thanks to you," Eira commented bitterly.

Vessa protested, but Eira interrupted her. "Why didn't you heal yourself? You could've helped Nashel fend off the attacks again, or even Siora open the door."

"I couldn't, it was too much!"

"Too much?" Eira almost shouted, then turned to Nashel. "It was too much," he mocked the other teammate in an incredulous and cruel tone.

"You're not the squad leader, you don't give me orders!" Vessa protest.

"I—" Eira was about to retort, but Nashel stopped him.

"I am," she stated calmly, "and your pathetic display was beneath this squad, beneath this Academy. He may not be the leader, but he is the healer, and if he tells you to do something, you do it."

"You weren't injured. You don't know what it feels like!"

"I don't care," Nashel snapped. "When the life of your squad or the success of the mission depends on teamwork, you do your part. We were about to fail."

"But we didn't!" she exclaimed, exasperated.

"Again, not thanks to you," Eira muttered.

"Just a few more seconds and we would be dead," Siora said. She had been quiet for most of the exchange, and they all looked at her. "I was about to pass out," she admitted. "I couldn't see, but dark spots in front of my eyes and disabled the final lock only by feeling. I almost triggered a trap."

"My shield was about to fail too," Nashel commented, no shame in her tone, but blame towards Vessa.

She was trying to defend herself again, but a deafening alarm started to sound, red lights flashing.

"Abnormal CO2 levels detected. Use portable canisters until further notice, or vacate the premise."

A cabinet's door opened, revealing the portable oxygen tanks and masks. Nashel distributed them to her squad members. Eira fitted it to Kye's mouth and nose and checked it was working.

They didn't discuss leaving, as they knew that what waited for them outside was worse than what was happening inside. Nashel wondered how long they could be trapped in the Cell when Vessa started convulsing. She clawed at the mask, struggling to take it off as if something else was keeping it stuck to her face. Nashel tried to help, but it wouldn't budge. She saw her teammate paling, her lips becoming blue, her panic receding as energy dwindled, until she stopped altogether, her eyes, devoid of life, staring into the distance.

The alarm stopped, the lights changing from red to green.

"Optimal air levels restored," the voice confirmed.

They removed their masks, Eira checked Vessa's pulse, but there was no need. It was clear she was gone.

The door hissed open. They readied themselves for an attack, but nothing happened.

"Cadets, stand down," the drill sergeant instructed. "This drill is over. You can come out."

They exchanged a glance, silently debating whether this was another test or the truth. They nodded, deciding to keep caution but comply.

The drill sergeant, Sergeant Thomas, and another instructor waited for them outside.

"War room, now," the drill sergeant ordered as soon as they were all out. They filed back inside the Academy and reached the meeting room that was one of the designated "war" rooms. The three adults followed them, Sergeant Thomas closing the door.

"Squad Leader Nashel, debrief us."

The squad stood at attention as Nashel recounted the details of the drill from the moment the alarm woke her up. She only left out the part where she found and manipulated the Trace.

"What do you think you did wrong?" the other instructor asked. It wasn't a question directed at Nashel only, but all the squad members had to answer.

"As Squad Leader, their failures are my failures," Nashel answered last.

"They are," the drill sergeant agreed. "Do you believe you led your squad to the best of your abilities?"

"Yes, sir," she replied firmly.

He raised his eyebrows in disagreement. Nashel wished she could talk freely and shove those eyebrows somewhere she couldn't really say.

"Cadets, you are dismissed," the other instructor ordered. "Cadet Warrant Officer Nashel, you stay."

The others saluted and left, while Nashel stayed at attention. She knew what was coming, and she wasn't surprised they asked her to stay behind.

"Vessa saw you," Sergeant Thomas started, sternly. "She disobeyed your order to stay behind and saw you manipulate the Trace."

Nashel managed to keep a straight face and keep the shock

out of it. She hadn't seen her or sensed her, a massive oversight that was not typical.

Nashel also understood what was said between the lines. Vessa was punished to the extreme not only because of her own mistake of not reacting when injured but also because of her insubordination, but most importantly because of Nashel's inattention.

"I understand," she replied.

"Don't let it happen again."

"Yes, sir."

"You are dismissed," the drill sergeant said.

She pondered on what had just happened as she walked back to her room. She made a mistake, a silly one at that. She should've kept her guard up, split her powers between working with the Trace and sending feelers. She wouldn't make it again.

CHAPTER EIGHT

Field Marshall Stormbreaker

Any thought of the previous night was wiped away soon after breakfast when Nashel's class had another surprise quiz, followed by another surprise drill. Her squad was down one member, but they performed particularly well that afternoon. So, when a message appeared mid-air, floating down, summoning her to the base, she was not worried but thought the brass wanted to inform her who the replacement for Vessa would be.

"Ma'am," she raised her hand to attract the teacher's attention. They were in class for the last lesson of the day.

"Yes, Cadet Warrant Officer Nashel?" the teacher was slightly annoyed about the interruption, but she noticed the floating message and added nothing else.

"I've been summoned," Nashel explained.

"You are excused," her annoyance now directed at the army that kept summoning cadets during her lessons.

Nashel packed her stationery, saluted and exited the classroom. The base was on the opposite side of the Citadel, quite the trek from the Academy, so, even though she hurried, it took her a while to reach it. The walk let her enjoy some time to herself, she thought about what she could say if they asked her if she had anyone in mind as a replacement. She did; it was a cadet a year younger than her, a Cadet Sergeant Major, that she had seen in action in several individual drills, and she thought would fit well with her team. It wasn't forbidden for Cadet Sergeant Majors to join a cadet's squad, but it was uncommon, especially if the other members were older. Nashel had done some research on her candidate and knew they were at the top of their class for both academic and military preparation.

When she arrived at the base, she had a good idea of what to say to sway the brass in her favour. She identified herself to the soldiers at the guard post, who, after a moment, opened the gates to let her through.

"Building B-132 is that way," he directed her. "Second floor. An aide will be waiting."

She nodded, thanked him, and saluted, not letting her curiosity show. The building she was directed to was not the usual one where they had debriefings and meetings. She wondered if this was another test, but doubted it.

It wasn't difficult to find the correct building, even though she hadn't been there before. The base was easy to navigate, and she had seen most of it during her training so far. The door opened as she removed her hat and made her way to the reception.

"Cadet Warrant Officer Nashel," she identified herself again.

"Welcome," the receptionist smiled. "They are waiting for you upstairs," she pointed to the lift.

Nashel followed her directions and landed on the second floor a few moments later. A lieutenant was waiting for her there.

"Follow me," he ordered without preambles. He didn't wait for her to nod, but turned and started to walk down the corridor.

It was a fancy one as well, covered in a red, soft carpet that absorbed their footsteps. The doors were simple, in the sparse manner of the military, but elegant at the same time, with gold handles and name tags.

The lieutenant stopped in front of the fifth door on the left. It wasn't any different from the others, but the golden tag indicated that it was Field Marshall Stormbreaker's office, the highest-ranking officer in the entire Sunset nation.

Everyone knew Stormbreaker. He was an idol, a hero, the best leader the armed forces ever had. Nashel had never met him in person. She had seen him at parades or on the few occasions he made an appearance at the Academy.

"Come in," the voice from inside called before the aide could even knock.

The lieutenant opened the door and gestured for her to step inside before closing the door behind her.

Nashel stood at attention, trying to study the room without moving her head or her eyes and breaking protocol.

"Cadet Warrant Officer Nashel," Strombreaker's voice was deep and rough, apt for his name. "You may sit."

Nashel changed her stance to at ease, then stepped forward to sit on the plush armchair in front of the general's desk.

The office was opulent, with flags, maps, and medals adorning the walls. The desk was of a dark, solid wood, with a lion and an eagle inlaid on the legs. On top, Nashel noticed expensive, thick paper, a pen, and a paperweight that seemed to be made entirely of gold.

Thanks to her training, she also noticed more practical details. There was a hidden door behind Stormbreaker's chair, protected by a power barrier that extended to all the walls, ceiling, and floor. She didn't have time to check properly, but at first glance, it seemed the barrier was there for protection, but also to avoid eavesdropping from the outside.

Stormbreaker kept quiet, looking at her while she looked at him. It was clear by then that this meeting was not going to be about a replacement for Vessa; she doubted Stormbreaker even knew about it.

"I have heard a lot about you," he started, after noticing

the silence didn't faze her.

She didn't have permission to speak, so she didn't.

"Top of your class," he started to list. "Squad leader. Elemental."

She didn't like the general's tone. It felt as if he didn't believe her achievements were genuine.

"You are powerful, disciplined, and determined. With a singular focus."

She wondered if he liked to hear his own voice. Or maybe he was just lonely, up there, at the top of the world.

"Sergeant Thomas couldn't shut up about you, and your other instructors and teachers were an excellent chorus to his praises."

It started to be unnerving. She doubted Stormbreaker called her to his office to compliment her. She wished he'd get to the point, especially because she still wasn't allowed to speak.

"You may wonder why you're here."

She schooled her expression to stay neutral. Of course, she was wondering.

"Let me start by saying this: what you are going to learn here is top-secret. Not a word needs to leave this office. Understood?"

That explained the barrier. "Yes, sir."

"Good, good," he muttered, opening a file he had in front of him. Her picture stared back at her. "Your achievements and awards are impressive, and that is why you've been called here today.

"You are obviously aware of the situation with the Void," he waited for her to confirm.

"Yes, sir," she nodded.

"What you don't know is that we believe an attack is imminent."

So, she was right. There was a way to cross the Void. How could the Sunrise attack otherwise? She painted shock, instead of victory, on her face; the expected reaction after such news.

"We believe the Sunrise wants to take advantage of the Void's movement and strike us."

She nodded, not sure what she was supposed to say or what her role was going to be.

"Our intel is limited," he continued gravely. "But we think their HQ is the Sunrise Academy, their equivalent of our school."

She couldn't keep the surprise off her face this time. Why would they have the HQ for the first offensive in centuries in a school? Surely that was bad intel.

"The Sunrise Academy is slightly different from what you are used to," the general explained. "They don't have a provision for younger children and accept students from the age of sixteen until their university graduation five years later."

"I understand," she murmured, even though she still didn't know why she was called there.

"It is unusual for older students to be accepted, and even more so this late in the academic year. If we were to send one of our young officers, they would draw too much suspicion."

That was when it hit her. "You want to send me," she said, breaking all kinds of protocols.

Stormbreaker didn't seem to mind the insubordination, but smiled patronisingly down at her. "Yes. You are the ideal candidate. As I mentioned, you are powerful, disciplined, and determined."

"Thank you," she replied.

"You are also the right age to start, and it won't seem odd that you started late. I want you to infiltrate the academy, pretending to be a student, while you gather intel on the attack."

"I understand," she said cautiously. She wasn't convinced she was the best candidate, or that the HQ was in a school.

"This is a high-risk mission," the general continued. "You will be on your own. You will have no contact with anyone from this side."

How would she report her findings, then?

"You will not have support or an extraction if things go south. Do you understand what I'm saying?"

"Yes, sir," she said tentatively.

"I see you have questions," he replied, gesturing for her to ask them.

"How will I report back?"

"We will get in contact with you when needed."

"What if I find something urgent?"

"We will know; don't worry."

That was not reassuring, but she didn't press it.

"Will I be able to come back?"

He howled with laughter, "Of course! Of course! At the end of the mission, you will come back."

"What about my studies here?" The thought just crossed her mind. If she were going away for a potentially long time, she would miss the rest of the year, and possibly the next as well.

"What about them?" The general asked, confused.

"I'm supposed to earn the Cadet Under Officer next year, graduate, and be admitted into university."

She had a plan for her future. She would graduate top of her class, which meant she could choose her university path and join the army with an officer rank instead of enlisted. If she couldn't graduate with her class because she was away and had stayed behind, she wouldn't have those options.

"I see," the general muttered. He seemed annoyed at her question. "I'd think that loyalty to your nation and a sense of duty far outweigh personal gains. If you feel that getting a cadet rank is more important, maybe you are not the right candidate for this mission."

"With all due respect, sir, it is not for personal gain. It is making sure I develop at the best of my abilities to serve our nation," she remarked. She knew she was out of line, but she couldn't help it.

"Completing this mission is using you to the best of your abilities, Cadet Warrant Officer," Stormbreaker replied, using her rank to put her back in her place. His eyes sparkled with rage at her insolence. The air crackled with static electricity, the general's power barely contained.

"Yes, sir," she admitted, not wanting Stormbreaker's rage to burst into a display of power she didn't want to see.

"I'm glad we agree," he said through gritted teeth. "You will leave in a week's time."

She cocked her head, curious. If it was so urgent, why leave in a week and not immediately? She didn't say anything, though, not wanting to fuel Stormbreaker's ire.

"You will be excused from your studies effective immediately," he continued. "And spend the week with our Sunrise experts."

"I understand, sir," she replied meekly.

"The Sunrise differs greatly from what you know. You will need to learn everything you can to blend in."

She nodded, understanding now the reason for a delayed departure. However, she now wondered if one week was enough to learn everything, even for a quick study like her.

"You can stay in your room. We don't want people to ask too many questions," the general instructed, "but you'll spend your days here at the base."

"Yes, sir," she replied again.

"I will forget your impudence this one time," he said threateningly.

"Thank you, sir," she answered, looking down.

"You are dismissed. And remember, not a word."

"Yes, sir. Thank you, sir," she concluded, standing and saluting before taking three steps backwards. It was protocol to never turn your back on an officer in charge, and she had already broken too many in such a short time to risk another.

She walked back in a haze, letting her feet lead her home, while her mind replayed the conversation in her head. She was going on a vital mission to prevent an attack on the Sunset. She should've felt honoured, instead, she had more questions than answers. She wasn't sure it wasn't another test, and that she had just failed it.

The next day, after breakfast, she was about to set off for

the base when Headmistress Magna accosted her on the assembly square.

"Let's walk together," she said gently.

Nashel nodded.

"I understand you are worried about your future," the headmistress started, not looking at her. She liked that about Magna; she always went straight to the point.

"I am sorry," Nashel replied, contrite.

"Don't be." There was something in her voice that forced Nashel to look at her and gauge her expression. It seemed as if she wasn't happy about the situation. "Field Marshal Stormbreaker is not used to dealing with children."

Nashel stiffened; she didn't like being called a child.

The headmistress smiled. "I'm sorry I couldn't be there."

It sounded like she had another commitment, but Nashel read between the lines that she wasn't invited.

"It would've been nice," she murmured in reply.

"Alas, it's no use to cry over spilt milk," the headmistress shrugged. "However, I want you to rest assured that your time away will not hinder your academic achievements. You will enrol onto your preferred course upon your return."

Once again, Nashel picked up something in her tone: hostility towards the general and his treatment.

"Thank you, headmistress," she smiled slightly, grateful the powerful woman was in her corner.

"Now, I have to make my way to town. The baker is about to take my favourite pastries out of the oven, and I want to get there before they are sold out!"

They both laughed as the headmistress departed with a wink.

Nashel arrived at the base lighter than she left. She never enjoyed being cornered with no options. It was the one thing about life in the Sunset that she liked the least. So, that the headmistress was not as happy as expected and that she would make sure that she could still progress on her chosen path was a relief.

As soon as the guards let her through, a floating green

arrow directed her to the HR office, where she would be issued a security pass, which would allow her to access rooms and buildings previously out of her reach. Then the arrow led her to another building, and from there to an empty meeting room. She waited there for a few minutes before a captain came in. She hurried to stand at attention, but the captain didn't seem to see her.

"Cadet Warrant Officer Nashel?" he asked her.

"Yes, sir."

"I'm Captain Ashwhisper, and I will be your tutor for the next week."

He seemed aloof, as if his mind were one hundred miles ahead of the rest of him. His appearance was average: average height, average build. His hair was short, in the manner many army soldiers kept it, and his eyes were an unremarkable, watery blue that was made even less remarkable by thick glasses.

"Nice to meet you, sir."

"Call me Ash," he invited her, to her surprise.

"Ash," she said reluctantly, but an order was an order.

Ash laughed. "Let's go; we have a lot to do."

He turned and led her up and down corridors until they reached a door that was barely standing. It was the comical opposite of the Field Marshal's door: as rickety as the other was opulent, as rough as the other was elegant. It almost made Nashel laugh, but she didn't want to offend the captain.

Inside it was a cupboard with a desk, a chair, and more files and folders than it could contain. There was barely any space for Ash to reach his desk and grab a few books and folders, then gesture for Nashel to exit first.

"We're going to the library," he explained. "There's more space there."

Not that it took much.

The library was exactly what Nashel expected: the musty smell of old books, the stuffy, clingy air, shelves on shelves of dusty books.

Ash led her to a smaller room. There were already plenty of books littering the long table, and he dropped what he was carrying on top of the smallest pile. He then gestured for her to take a sit in one of the chairs.

"So, let's start from the beginning," the captain said, already pinching the bridge of his nose as if the mere thought was giving him a headache. "How much do you know about the Sunrise?"

"Just what they told us in class," Nashel answered, shrugging. "That they are our opposite, our nemesis."

"Do you know why?"

"Not really," she admitted. "I only know that we were once one nation, but then the war happened, and the Void was created."

Ash nodded.

"It is a bit more complicated than that, but yes, you are correct. The good news is that we still speak the same language."

Nashel hadn't thought about communication, but it was a valid point. If they spoke the same language, she didn't have to learn a completely new one in one week and pass as a native.

"There are a few differences; I will explain them in the next few days."

She nodded, curious now to find out more.

"You'll have a cover story; we'll go into details, don't worry," he gestured. "But any slip-up could be attributed to that, so communication-wise, you will be okay."

"A cover story?"

"Yes," he nodded, pushing his glasses up, "You don't know it, but you have an accent."

"I do know it," she replied. "I remember from the residentials."

"Fair enough," Ash conceded with a chuckle. "But in the Sunrise, it will be more prominent."

"I understand," she said. "So, I will have a cover story to explain it?"

"Exactly."

"Okay, so the language will be alright," she summarised.

"Yes, we'll go through it tomorrow."

He kept mentioning that, which made her think there was something more important they had to cover for the day, but he seemed reluctant to mention it. So, she waited for that bomb to drop.

"I'm afraid that's where the good news ends," he said after a pause.

"I realised that," she gave him a small smile, wishing he would hurry and tell her.

"It is the power structure," he said, weighing every single word as if to find the right ones. "It is different."

Nashel thought she could detect a bit of disgust in that, and was instantly worried about what she was going to get herself into.

"You see," he said after another pause. "They don't call it power. They call it magic."

"What?" Nashel replied, shocked and incredulous. "What do you mean, magic? Like in the fairy tales?"

She remembered reading some of those stories as a child, with fairies, princesses, and enchantments.

"Yeah, like in the fairy tales," he said. His disappointment and disgust even clearer now.

"But—" Nashel started, but she didn't know how to finish. "What does it mean for me?

"The thing is... It's not just the terminology," Ash continued. "It is the way they feel about it. The way they relate to it. It is appalling," he said fervently. "Appalling."

"That bad, huh?"

"Yes, it is," he firmly replied. "They don't have the same relationship we have with powers. They don't think the powers come within us. That they are a part of us. They believe that magic is an instrument, something that just happens, not something that is. Do you understand what I'm saying?"

"Not really," Nashel admitted.

Ash shook his head. “Of course you don’t. How could you?”

Nashel understood he wasn’t blaming her for her ignorance, but that he felt strongly against whatever they did in the Sunrise.

He took a deep breath, trying to figure out how to make her understand something he didn’t fully understand himself. “They ignore the basic principles of power. The connection between us, them, and the rest of the world.”

That was just ridiculous, but she didn’t say that, Ash was aggravated enough as it was.

“They believe that to manifest their powers, they need to channel them through a wand,” he said the last word as if he was going to throw up.

“A wand?” Nashel asked, confused. All she could think of was a plump woman with too-thin-to-fly wings, a pointed hat, and a stick with a star on top.

“Yes,” Ash sighed heavily. “It’s like a stick of wood. They wave it, and they channel their powers through it. Sorry, their magic,” he said mockingly, making Nashel guffaw. He stood and moved to the far end of the table, where he rummaged through the piles of books until he extracted a long, thin piece of wood.

“This is a wand,” he said to her, and he almost threw it at her, as if he feared that by touching it, he would catch something terrible. “This is your wand.”

“What do I have to do with this?” she asked sceptically.

“Well, you wave it and, um, use your powers normally, but make sure that they go through the wand and not any other part of your body.”

She studied the stick. It was just a simple piece of wood, about thirty centimetres long, polished, but plain, with no decorations or indentations. It was thinner at the point and thicker at the handle.

“This is weird,” she said, while inspecting the wand.

The captain agreed. “Yes, it’s unnatural.”

“Do you know how to use it?” she asked out of curiosity.

She had quite a few questions for Ash but hadn't had the chance to ask them yet.

"I tried, and I failed," he shook his head.

"I'm supposed to learn in one week how to use this?"

He sighed again. "Yes, I know, I'll do my best."

Nashel studied the wand a little longer, as if the longer she stared at it, the more it made sense.

"Does it have any properties?" she tried to ask him.

"No, it's just a stick of wood. We made it ourselves. You can make one all of your own if you prefer. You can have it in any shape or form, doesn't really do anything."

This time, it was Nashel's turn to sigh. "Okay. So, I hold this in my hand and say I want to move that book," she pointed with the other hand towards one of the books. "I'll wave it and point it towards it, then I do what I normally do with telekinesis?"

"Yes," he said tentatively, "but also no. You need to make sure that it goes through the wand as if it held the power, and not you."

"That's ridiculous!" She exclaimed. "It's a piece of wood!"

He sighed again. "Yes, I know."

She realised she did not aggravate him. He was just frustrated with the Sunrise. She wondered if he even liked his job. If he got into that career expecting to solve mysteries that would help the Sunset win, or discover new, fascinating worlds, but what he got in return was just absurdity.

"Come on, try to move the book," he said, as if he already knew that she was going to fail. She wanted to prove him wrong, but she couldn't.

She waved the wand, more obnoxiously than needed - it made him smile, though - and pointed it to the book in question, willing it to move. It did, but she immediately knew she didn't do it through the wand. She didn't know exactly how she knew, but she sensed the power going through her, not through it.

Ash shook his head and shrugged. He wasn't disappointed in her; he just expected that outcome.

"How do I do this?" she asked, almost pleadingly.

"You need to practice. That is your main assignment for the rest of this week. Practice. Spend every free moment you have to practice. This is probably the hardest thing you've ever done in your life, and I've been to the Academy, too."

They didn't start on any of the other topics for the rest of the day. He just wanted her to focus on making herself familiar with the wand, even though she couldn't do anything with it. He wanted her to get used to the weight of it, to the idea that she always had to have it on her.

For the first time in a long time, she was having difficulty learning. Her powers had always come naturally to her, and learning had always been easy because of it. This was frustrating, to say the least. She couldn't figure out how to focus her power through the wand. She didn't understand how those people could not use powers the right way. Why did they need a wand? Power was everywhere around her, in her, in every single thing that existed. All she ever did was commune with it, will it to abide by her commands. Insert herself in the fabric of the world and change it to her pleasure. Now, she realised that to use magic the way the Sunrise did, she had to change her entire knowledge about powers, and she didn't really want to.

By the end of the day, she didn't make any progress. Ash was supportive and often tried his hand at it as well, with disastrous results that made them both end in a fit of laughter. She didn't like not being able to do something right the first time, and she felt he understood that and was making a fool of himself to cheer her up.

When she walked back to her dorm, she was still waving the stick around, and some people gave her the side-eye, not understanding what she was doing and judging her too old to be playing like a little kid. She couldn't blame them; she would've done the same. She hastily put the wand away inside her trousers as she entered the dining hall for dinner. Her squad was waiting for her at their usual table, and they assailed her with questions before she could even take her seat. She realised she didn't have an excuse ready. She hadn't thought about it at all, and Stormbreaker didn't provide one either, just limited himself to threatening her if she told anyone the truth.

"Why were you not there today?"

"Are you still our squad leader?"

"Was it about Vessa?"

"It was just a very long briefing," she attempted, shrugging. "They wanted to discuss Vessa replacement, but they also decided I will not be your squad leader any longer."

"What?!" Eira almost shouted. A few aspirants from nearby tables looked at him, annoyed.

"They had another project in mind for me."

"But!" Siora protested, confused.

Nashel was at the top of her class. If anybody deserved to be squad leader, it was her.

"I tried to tell them I wanted to stay," she said placatingly. "But you know how it is. If they order you to do something, you do that."

They all nodded; she didn't know what else to say to them. It seemed to settle them, though, because after a pause, moved on to describe what they did during the day. About a gruesome drill and how they failed it miserably because they were down to only three members, but it wasn't her fault; that was not what they were saying, of course. About the most boring lesson they had, and how nobody could remember what it was about because they were too focused on not falling asleep.

"Gras actually did, and it wasn't pretty. Hadn't seen that punishment since Recruits," Siora whispered, eyeing the person she was talking about.

When she retired to her room, she stayed up past lights out, waving the wand around, feeling sillier and sillier by the minute. She was trying to figure out how to change her entire nature and fit into a completely different world. She didn't think about anything else, not the language differences, not the way she would have to cross the impenetrable Void, only that little stick, and everything else just disappeared.

She dreamt about it as well. Dreamt of waving it while everything around her exploded, but still not through the wand. Dreamt it was huge, three-story tall, waving itself and pointing at her to turn into a frog, then a book, herself again, then something else she didn't remember, but she knew it wasn't pleasant. The wand started beating her as if it were a cane, and she tried to defend herself, but she couldn't because her powers didn't work without a wand. She woke up in a pool of sweat, hating that thing. She grabbed it from her nightstand and threw it to the other side of the room. It didn't break, of course, but it made her feel a bit better.

CHAPTER NINE
The Wand

The following days were excruciating. Her progress with the wand was too slow; the only thing that grew was her frustration for the piece of wood. She wasn't ashamed to admit that she threw it many times, hitting books, tables, and trees when they moved to a secluded courtyard. She also broke it in half, then repaired it, then broke it again, and the only result was Ash falling prey to a fit of laughter.

"Let's take a break," he wheezed after a particularly intense bout. It was almost the end of the day, and they had already covered everything they needed to for the day.

"You said I need to spend every free moment practising," she said sourly. "I can't take a break!"

"It's an order," he replied, jokingly serious.

"Yes, sir," she mocked him.

Ash wasn't the typical military person. She had understood that from the moment she met him. He didn't like the rigidity of the hierarchy and didn't like to order people around. He was goofy and prone to laughter, which she didn't expect in the beginning. He was smart, probably smarter than the average person his age, and disillusioned. Nashel was usually a good judge of character, but she was right only halfway in her assessment of Ash. He surprised her, and that wasn't common.

They gathered their things and walked together into town. It was a pleasant evening, despite winter being right around the corner. The sun was setting, colouring everything in an orange hue that reminded Nashel of fire. It was her favourite part of the day.

"So, what does one have to do to become a researcher like you? Are you part of a special branch?"

Ash rolled his eyes, laughing. "Nothing special about me. We are part of Intelligence."

That, too, was surprising. Nashel wanted to be part of Intelligence once she finished university, but what she pictured about it, and what they told her during career events, was very different from what Ash did. She imagined a world of risks and dangers, trying to anticipate the moves of a cunning enemy while trying to stay alive. Definitely not sitting behind a desk, bent over books.

He must've seen something in her expression because he added, "Not what you expected, is it?"

She shrugged. "No, I thought you were part of a different branch."

"Like?"

"I don't know, librarians?!"

He laughed again. She liked that sound; it was freeing.

"Fair enough," he replied. "But, no. I'm not a librarian. The actual librarians hate me because I borrow too many books and never return them on time."

"No way! Captain Square doesn't return his books in time?"

"Captain what, now?"

"Square," she smirked.

"I don't get it," he said, genuinely confused.

She had to laugh at his lost-puppy expression. "Square: someone who always follows the rules and never has fun."

It took him a second to realise she was being sarcastic, then he burst out laughing again.

"It's not my fault if I have a lot of work to do and the library due date is too short," he tried to justify himself, feigning being offended.

"You don't seem too sorry about it," she observed, smiling. "Is punishment outside the Academy not as harsh?"

He thought about it for a moment. "Come to think of it, it isn't. I guess if you're in a more active, combat branch, it is probably harsher, but as a librarian," he smiled, "we have more leeway, I guess."

She never thought much about day-to-day life outside the academy. She had a plan to graduate and choose her speciality - Intelligence - but she never thought about what a normal day looked like. And now that she had someone she could ask about it, she was going away for who knew how long. She wasn't sure how she felt about that, so she filed it away for later.

When they reached the town, they stopped at an ice cream parlour - her favourite since the first day in the Citadel - and he insisted they order some.

"It's almost dinner time," she argued. "I can't have ice cream before dinner."

"Who said that?"

"How long ago did you leave the academy to forget all the rules?"

"Did you just call me old?" he asked indignantly.

"I'd never dare, captain, sir," she mocked him.

"I'll have you know I am only three years older than you!"

"Of course, sir," she continued.

"Stop that!" He took a step closer, invading her personal space.

She snapped to attention, staring him in the eyes. "Sir, yes, sir!" She almost shouted it. It was difficult now to keep a straight face, looking at him at the same time.

"I said stop," he whispered, getting even closer.

"Make me," she challenged, her voice barely audible.

He closed his eyes and sighed, as if he were trying to restrain himself. She stayed still, waiting for his decision.

"Scared?" she teased.

When he opened his eyes, she knew she had won. She could see a spark of mischief, guilt, and want before he closed the already small distance and kissed her.

It wasn't her first kiss. There was a sort of rite of passage when cadets became aspirants they would start experimenting with intimacy. It wasn't anything planned or talked about, but it was expected that by the end of the first year, they would have at least kissed someone. Nashel wasn't very interested in any of that, she didn't feel the need to share her life with someone else, and she was indifferent to physical contact. However, she took part.

So that one was not her first kiss, or her second, but it tasted differently. It tasted of victory, of kindred spirits, of forbidden fruit, and rule-breaking. It lasted only a few seconds, just enough for their tongues to meet, before he gently stepped back. He smiled, almost shyly.

"As you were, soldier," she murmured teasingly. He laughed again, the little embarrassment leaving his cheeks. "We should go..." he tried to say.

"Hell no! Now you are going to buy me ice cream!" She pretended to be offended and made him laugh again.

"Yes, ma'am," he mocked her.

They walked placidly back towards her dorm in comfortable silence. She wondered what he was thinking, if he was reliving the kiss, wanting more. She felt a tingle at the idea that he desired her, and she was curious to see his next move. She wished she had more time, even just one more week, to explore what was happening and what could happen. But perhaps the distance would work in her favour, or perhaps he would forget her as soon as she left. She would have to make the most out of the days she had left to make a lasting impression and make sure she had a strong hold on him, in case she'd need him in the future.

At the fork that would take him back to base and her back to her dorm, they stopped.

"Do we need to talk?" he asked tentatively. He looked

younger, slightly embarrassed again.

She shook her head with a small smile.

"Was it okay?"

She couldn't help but laugh. "If it weren't, you wouldn't be standing here all in one piece."

"Fair enough," he didn't reciprocate but did smile.

"Are you worried?" she asked.

"A bit," he admitted in a whisper.

"I'm going away soon, Ash," she murmured. She wasn't sure why she was murmuring, but it seemed fitting for the situation. "There is nothing to be worried about."

He sighed but didn't say anything. She stepped in front of him and gently touched his cheek. "Nobody will find out anything, and if they do, I'll be long gone before they can do anything about it."

He held her hand to his cheek as he replied, "Stop reminding me you're leaving."

She nodded. "Stop worrying, then. Let's just enjoy the time we have."

"I'll see you tomorrow, then..." he reluctantly said.

"Not if you see me in your dreams," she teased, and finally he laughed again.

"You're such a flirt!" He bent down to kiss her again. This time it was just a quick goodbye kiss, but she felt him being more confident, bolder. She smiled on his lips, before stepping back once, then again. Their hands, now intertwined, tried to keep her there, but she kept going.

"See you in my dreams," he shouted, laughing as the distance grew larger.

She laughed in return. "Not if I see you first!"

The following days were a blur of wand-waving, history lessons, language lessons, and some intimacy. Their library room offered all the privacy they needed, if not the comfort.

At the end of the week, she had made passable progress with the wand, and there was nothing else anyone could do about that, anyway. She had absorbed all the knowledge she could about the history. Ash, though, advised her to take it with a pinch of salt, all the differences in vocabulary she could cram into her head, and all the scattered information about the Sunrise Academy.

The only mystery left was how she was going to cross the Void and enter the other nation. She tried to ask Ash, but he didn't know. She believed him, not only because he was enthralled by her but also because he was visibly frustrated by the secret he couldn't crack.

She didn't find out until the very end of the last day. She had packed a few of her possessions, not much because they couldn't be sure if even her clothes were appropriate. She had to take off her uniform, and it felt weird, seeing it hung there, knowing she would not put it on the following day, or for what could be a long time.

She had to say goodbye to Ash too, and she knew she would miss his attentions and his laughter.

"I'll wait for you," he whispered in the late afternoon, their foreheads touching tenderly.

"I don't know how long it'll be," she replied.

"I'll wait for you," he reiterated, stealing a quick kiss.

She didn't reply then, revelling in his desire.

Stormbreaker was waiting for her in front of his office. As soon as the lift doors opened, he stopped her from getting off.

"Stay there, we're going down." With long strides, he joined her.

He took a key out of a bundle, inserted it in the keyhole at the bottom of the panel, and pressed a button without a label.

The ride was slightly longer than the one she had just taken. She reckoned they were going two or three stories underground.

"This is a top-secret section," Stormbreaker told her, as if she could just go out and shout at everyone that there were secret floors under the base.

"I understand," she replied.

They exited on a sterile corridor with rough, not painted

walls and metal doors. She walked a step behind the general, as protocol dictated, and she tried to gauge any information, but there was no tag or sign on any door. There were a few people dressed in camo and lab coats, which struck her as a weird pair. They saluted the general, and one also stopped to whisper something to him and asked him to sign a document held on a clipboard.

He halted in front of a door guarded by a Lieutenant, who snapped to attention as soon as they neared him.

"Is it ready?" the general returned the salute and asked.

"Yes, sir."

Stormbreaker turned to Nashel and looked at her seriously. "What you are about to see has the highest level of security. It is the best-kept secret of the Sunset and the only way to cross the Void."

She tried not to show her curiosity and excitement. She didn't trust her voice, so she just nodded.

"Lieutenant," he implicitly ordered.

The other man nodded and pressed the palm of his hand on the door, and so did the general. The outline of their hands glowed in blue and green for a few seconds, then the door hissed open.

The room inside was completely dark, the only light lasted until the door was shut behind them, and Nashel asked herself what he wanted her to 'see' in such darkness, but he brushed her shoulder, and suddenly she could see. It wasn't as clear as day, it was a more lit shade of darkness, but it was enough. She expected a device - though she couldn't understand the need for the darkness - but she saw something else. She tried to focus on the figure; she wasn't sure if it was a person, a thing, or a monster. It had two arms and two legs and a face, but its features were distorted. Its skin was so pale it almost looked transparent, its limbs were frail and thin, and even its eyes were so white that the irises were indistinguishable from the sclera. She wondered if it looked like that in the light, or if it was just her enhanced night vision.

"This is Nightshade," the general announced. "It's a Drifter."

Nashel couldn't take her eyes off the creature, and she noticed a flicker of anger in its eyes.

"A Drifter, sir?" she asked, absentmindedly.

"They are rare, even rarer than elementals," Stormbreaker was looking at her now. "They are able to drift through the Void and can take a person across with them."

"They cannot live a normal life," the Lieutenant interjected. "As you can see, they are very fragile and cannot tolerate any light. They can eat very little, and it's very difficult for them to control their ability - most get lost inside the Void, actually."

That wasn't reassuring at all.

"When outside the Void, all their energy is spent staying grounded, so they cannot use their powers for anything else."

"Nightshade is very well trained. It will take you to the Sunrise safely," Stormbreaker added, probably feeling her tension. Again, Nashel saw anger in Nightshade's eyes and wondered what they had done to it to make it hate them so much.

"How does it work, sir?" she asked, again not taking her eyes off Nightshade. She wasn't sure she trusted it not to harm them.

"Oh, it's very simple," the lieutenant chuckled. "You just hold on to it, and it'll take you across."

"May I speak freely?"

"Granted," Stormbreaker replied.

"How do you trust it?" she saw that flash of anger now directed at her. "How do you know it'll not go to just drop me in the middle of the Void?"

Stormbreaker laughed heartily. "Don't worry about that! We are our ways."

Nightshade stirred. It was just a fraction of a movement, easily missed, but Nashel was looking and saw it.

"Have you got everything you need?" the lieutenant asked placidly.

"Yes, sir," she answered, shuffling her small bag for emphasis.

"Nothing that would be suspicious?"

"No, sir."

"General, can we proceed?"

"Yes, Lieutenant, I believe so," he replied, then to Helena. "Lieutenant Dustveil will meet you on the other side. The pass phrase is even the sun casts shadows. Ask her to make sure it's her."

Nashel nodded, intrigued. There were other operatives on the other side, yet the general had said she would be alone. She wondered how many there were, how many missions. Would this Lieutenant be on the same mission? Or would she meet and greet Nashel, just to disappear?

"Nightshade, get up. Time to go," the Lieutenant said, kicking the Drifter to make it move.

It stood, tall, probably six feet, but it was so thin and so deformed that it looked bigger and smaller at the same time. It held a hand out for her.

"It can't take you across from here," the lieutenant explained. "It'll take you to this side of the Void, then it'll have to rest for a few hours, then you'll cross. You should be there by dawn."

Nashel nodded, not sure what to say. She still didn't trust Nightshade. It looked, well, shady. And the rage she saw flashing in its eyes was worrying. She was just a Cadet, easy prey if it wanted revenge. Nevertheless, she took a step towards it and grabbed its hand. It was freezing cold, as if no blood was coursing through its veins. It pulled her to its chest and held her in an iron-clad hug. Before she could protest, the room around her disappeared.

Drifting was a weird experience; it felt like moving really fast and, at the same time, not moving at all. She didn't see things rushing around her; it felt like a fog so thick it could've been gelatin that covered everything and blocked her sight. Somehow, though, she felt she was moving. It wasn't easy to describe; it wasn't a physical sensation, but a deeper knowledge she wasn't in the same place anymore.

When they stopped, she felt slightly disoriented. Around her, there wasn't a dark room anymore, but an open space, grass at her feet, the shadows of trees looming from behind her. A garrison cast a circle of light on them, not threatening, but helpful. Her mind registered the five soldiers, one of whom was walking towards her, but the huge, incorporeal black wall that was the Void took most of her attention.

It wasn't the first time she saw it; she had been on a residential close to it once. But it was the first time she had been this close. It was calling to her; she felt the urge to walk into it. She felt its power, immense, almost limitless. She desired it. She took a step forward, but then the soldier stepped in front of her — not on purpose — and broke the spell. Only then did she realise Nightshade had let her go, and fainted right next to her.

"Cadet Warrant Officer Nashel, I presume?" Nashel recognised the soldier; she was one year older than her, and she remembered her from the Academy.

"Yes, ma'am," she replied, snapping to attention.

"At ease, at ease," the soldier replied with a smile. She gestured towards the garrison, and two other soldiers came jogging.

"Take it inside," she ordered them, despite being of the same rank. They hoisted Nightshade and dragged him to the garrison. "Come, get a coffee or something while you wait," she added to Nashel.

The soldiers had dropped Nightshade on a narrow cot, then joined the last one at a table. Nashel and her escort did the same.

It took indeed a few hours for Nightshade to recover, which left Nashel plenty of time to chat with the garrison soldiers, think about how inefficient Drifting was if a Drifter could only carry one person and dropped half-dead after each journey, but also take a nap herself.

When Nightshade was ready, they walked outside and stood next to the Void. Its power called to her again; it made her hair stand on end. Nightshade looked down at her, condescension and superiority in its gaze. Did it know what she was feeling?

It held its hand out, and just like before, as soon as Nashel grabbed it, Nightshade hugged her and everything disappeared. She just had a moment to wave goodbye to the soldiers.

She understood why it was called the Void. Initially, she felt out of breath, as if something had squeezed the air out of her lungs. As if something were squeezing life out of her body. There was nothing around her, yet the nothingness was closing in on her. She panicked. She started thrashing, trying to get free, trying to get out. She couldn't. Something was keeping her there, keeping her drifting. It took her a few moments - or years? Time wasn't the same - to realise it was Nightshade.

Gone was the frail, deformed creature she had seen in that dark room. Holding her was a handsome young man. His skin flushed, his muscles defined. His eyes sparkled with strength, resolution, and resilience. She also realised he was talking to her, making shushing noises to calm her down. Well, not really talking; he was more thinking in her direction, and no word was coming out of his mouth.

She stopped trying to escape, somehow comforted by the strong arms around her. She looked up at him, studying his new, stunning features. She saw pride in the angle of his chin, a challenge, almost.

It struck her then, the reason he looked so irate in the room. They knew he was human, and yet they treated him as if he weren't. They called him "it", they kicked him, they abused him.

"I am sorry," she tried to say, but she couldn't form words. However, she saw the hint of a smile on his lips. "I didn't understand."

"It's alright," his thought-voice reached him, letting her know she did communicate with him.

Her brain was trying to process the experience, but with a

pop, they tumbled out of the Void.

CHAPTER TEN

Crossing the Void

It wasn't dawn; they were ahead of schedule, as it was still dark.

Nightshade collapsed as soon as they crossed the barrier, his deformed, pale form returning. Nashel didn't waste time looking around; she scooped him up and walked towards the crop of trees a few feet away. He was so light she could've held him with one hand, if only he wasn't so tall. She found a spot where they could have cover and gently deposited him back on the grass-covered ground.

Only then she studied her surroundings. The first thing she noticed was the air. It smelt different here. Not the trees or grass around her, but the air itself. The power that permeated the fabric of this side of the world was different too, weaker, its flow broken and scattered. Maybe that was why they called it magic, because it was so sporadic and feeble that they were not used to tapping into it. Maybe that was also why they were using a wand to channel it.

The trees around her were familiar; she picked up a few needles and realised they were the same variety she had just left behind. At least something was the same. She could hear night animals scatter around, but it was faint, as if they were giving the Void a wide berth.

The Void. She had crossed the Void. It wasn't what she expected. It wasn't nothing. Nothing didn't press on you sucking the life out. It wasn't like swimming through molasses. There was something else. It was calling her, even from a distance. And it was hungry. She felt it when she was inside. It wasn't threatening her, not exactly, it just wanted more. More power. More life. More freedom.

Then, there was Nightshade. That was also a surprise. She wondered if, once upon a time, a few years ago, he looked like the handsome boy she saw in the Void.

Saw. She saw. In the complete darkness, she saw. Was whatever Stormbreaker did still working? Or was there light inside the Void? Was Nightshade emitting his own light? She was musing now. She needed to concentrate on her present situation. She was in a foreign land, guarding one of the rarest types of powers, with limited resources and limited ways to use her powers. She checked her watch and saw it was just past three in the morning, which meant she had a few hours before dawn. She wasn't sure she could leave Nightshade to run the perimeter, maybe set some traps, so she stayed put. She took her wand out and killed time by practising.

An hour later, the sky started to light up, to her surprise. It was late autumn, and the sun shouldn't be rising until late. Was it different there? Now that she was thinking about it, it wasn't cold, not the cold the autumn nights were in the Sunset; it was warming, like late spring. Was it possible that the seasons were inverted?

She would've wondered even more, but the rustle of a nearby thicket distracted her. It was closer, and different, not animal, but human. A figure appeared on the strip of dirt that separated the Void and the forest. Nashel couldn't see much, only the silhouette of someone of average height, lean, and a woman. She made a lot of noise that would land her in trouble if they were in the Sunset still. Did this place make you forget your training? She hoped not, but she moved like a trained soldier. Nashel observed her for a few moments, keeping an eye on Nightshade as well, in case he stirred. The woman walked a few steps on the dirt strip, looked around, and then a few more.

"Passphrase?" Nashel used her powers to project the whisper so that the woman wouldn't know where they were hiding. She looked around, surprised, perhaps not expecting them to be there already.

"Even the sun casts shadows," she answered correctly.

Nashel stood and, silently, almost to show her how to do it, approached the woman.

"Lieutenant Dustveil?" Nashel didn't salute or stand at attention.

The woman looked her up and down, then nodded.

"You're early," she snapped, displeased.

Nashel instantly didn't like her. She let the mission go to her head and made her feel like she was more important than her true value.

She was young, in her early twenties, unremarkable, which was probably why they chose her for the missions. She was one of those people that, as soon as they were out of sight, they were forgotten.

"Let's make it quick," Dustveil started.

Nashel shook her head. "Can't go anywhere yet."

"What?" the woman snapped again.

"Nightshade is still recovering," Nashel replied, restraining her contempt.

"The Drifter is still here?"

"What did you expect? That he would throw me out and go back?"

"We may not be home anymore, but I am still your superior," the lieutenant scolded her.

Nashel didn't reply. They weren't home anymore. She was clearly instructed to leave everything, especially anything related to military structures and hierarchy, behind, and she did so.

"Where is it?" the woman sighed.

It took Nashel a few seconds to realise he was referring to Nightshade. "Resting there," she gestured widely towards their hiding place.

"Wake it up. We need to move. It needs to be gone," Dustveil ordered.

Nashel didn't want to, but she also didn't want to fight, so she turned and went back to the Drifter. She gently shook him, and he sprang up.

"It's okay, just me," she reassured him.

His wide eyes locked on hers, and he calmed down.

"We need to go. My contact is here and impatient. Do you think you can travel back?"

She had never heard him speak and wasn't sure he could. Even now, he just nodded. She had so many questions, but no time to ask them. She would have to postpone them and find her answers at a later time.

She helped him up, he stood wobbly, then took a tentative step and almost fell. Nashel held his fragile elbow, hoping she wouldn't break it, and helped him walk back to the Void.

The lieutenant ignored him, she was tapping her foot impatiently, as if Nashel had arrived late instead of early. Nightshade ignored her. She felt him whimper and knew the Void called to him, too. She almost didn't let go of his elbow as he stepped into it, but he turned around and gently removed her hand before giving her a small smile.

Once he was gone, Nashel turned to the woman, who rolled her eyes in an about-time manner. She almost threw Nashel another small bag.

"There's money; you need to use it here," she explained. "There's also a PPad. It's a device, like a tablet, for personal communication. Everyone has one. It is blank. I don't know your cover story, nor do I care about it."

"Understood," Nashel replied.

"You can load up a map on it and find your way to Solned, the capital city."

So, she was going to be completely useless. Good to know.

"You also need to upload your info so that, when they

check, they can find it. I hope you know how to."

"I do," Nashel replied defiantly. The woman was getting on her nerves with her attitude.

"Good. You should be able to arrive in the capital by the end of the day."

"Anything else?" Nashel asked.

"No," the woman retorted. "Go North-East for two klicks: you'll find an old path. It's overgrown and thorny, but will lead you to a dirt road. Follow that West until the village. From there—"

"I get the PPad and follow its directions," Nashel cut her short.

"Yes," the lieutenant glared. "You won't see me again, and if you do, you've never met me."

"I know how undercover works," Nashel rolled her eyes. She emptied the bag into her own and returned it to the woman.

She didn't wait to say goodbye, but started walking in the direction she was instructed. While walking in the forest, she concentrated on her surroundings, trying not to let her thoughts wander too far. As she noted before, the trees were the same as back home. She saw more animals as well. Squirrels, hares, foxes, and they looked the same, too. Still, the absence of power bothered her. About halfway to the old path, she decided to stop. She had to see for herself. Seeing the flow of power was a bit like seeing a Trace, but easier, everyone could do it. It was like switching between the naked eye and sunglasses. She had to concentrate longer than usual. She had to dig deeper. When she finally saw it, like a white thin river that ebbed in and out of everything. Except, as she felt before, this river wasn't flowing steadily. It was disappearing in places, then reappearing, as if an invisible obstacle stopped it.

Nashel had never seen something like it, and she wondered why it was acting like that. She was breaking a sweat to keep the concentration spot on, so she let go. She had seen enough. It was concerning, philosophically, that the power was dwindling in the Sunrise, but was abundant in the Sunset. Was it because of the war? Because of the Void? Somehow, everything brought her back to the Void.

When she reached the dirt road, she was glad she had packed a couple of protein bars and a bottle of water. There was nothing of the sort in the bag Dustveil gave her. She didn't need her new PPad to find West. The sun was out, and as the day progressed, it became hotter.

She was wondering whether she should make a detour and find a stream or a river to get some more water when she heard a vehicle approaching from behind her. It was the first she encountered in the Sunrise, and she half expected it to be some kind of contraption completely different from what she was used to. It was just a normal truck. It passed her, slowing down and coming to a stop just a few feet away from her.

"Hey, you alright there, young lady?" The man leaned on the passenger seat and lowered the window when she reached him.

His accent was very thick, and it reminded her she needed to fake her own.

"Yes, sir, thank you," she replied politely.

"Where are you going?"

"Solned," she replied. She tried to keep her answers short, not too sure of her accent yet.

"Hop in, I'll take you to the train station."

"You're very gentle, but I don't have money to pay you," she shyly replied. She had money, but she wasn't going to let him know that. She also wasn't used to using money. Everything in the Citadel was free as long as one took only the necessities, and she didn't want to be taken advantage of before she could figure it out.

He laughed good-naturedly. "You don't need to pay me; I'm going that way anyway. C'mon!"

He opened the door for her, and after faking another moment of hesitation, she got in.

"Not from around here, are you?" he said once he started

driving. His accent made it sound as if it was only one word.

"No, I'm from a small village quite far from here," she replied. During her walk, she thought about her cover story. They had outlined it, she and Ash, but they left the details for her to decide.

"And you're going to Solned...?" he left the question unfinished.

"My village is dying. My parents wanted me to have an opportunity to do something more," she shrugged.

At that, he gave her a quick, interested look before turning back to the road.

"Have you got any whippers?" he spat the last word with all the vitriol he could muster. It wasn't a word she learnt during her week's preparation, so she wasn't sure what it meant.

"No, we don't," she hoped it was the right answer.

"Good, good," he muttered. "They sweep in with their holier-than-thou attitude, wave their stick, and think they make everything better. Bastards, that's what they are! They steal our jobs, our lives, our products. And if you don't have them or want them, they do something to your land, and it dies. I bet that's what happened to your village!"

She made a non-committal noise in response, as she understood whippers were flairs. Magic, she needed to start calling it that. Was his prejudice a common occurrence? Or was he just an envious bigot? Either way, she was glad her wand was shoved deep inside her bag and not visible.

"Have you walked all the way from your village?"

"Pretty much," she shrugged. "My parents took me as far as they could, then I started walking. Sometimes I got a lift from generous people like you."

He smiled at the compliment. "Well, you're almost there," he said cheerfully. "Once you get on the train, it'll just take a few hours. You'll be in Solned by the end of the day!"

She nodded, then added, almost ashamed, "I don't know if I can take the train. Are the tickets very expensive?"

He laughed again in that pleasant way that she was sure it

would change if he knew what she was capable of. "We'll figure something out."

She didn't like the tone of that. It made her think he wanted to exploit her. She didn't want to kill him, but she wouldn't let him do anything nefarious to her. And if she killed him, she'd earn a car, and probably some money he kept in his pockets.

The forest had left room for fields, some cultivated, some untamed, and as they drove along, houses sprouted like scattered mushrooms. They started to encounter other vehicles too: cars, trucks, tractors, but also carts pulled by horses or donkeys. Slowly, the houses started to multiply and grow together until they formed what was clearly a town. Here, they also saw people walking. It wasn't a big city, but a rural place to cater to the farms they saw driving in. The man slowed down and stopped in front of one of the bigger buildings. It had a sign and, to Nashel's horror, she realised she couldn't read it. It was a different alphabet than what she was used to, and nobody had prepared her for it.

"That's the train station," the man pointed at the building, then turned off the engine and got out of the truck, gesturing for her to follow.

They went inside and reached the ticket office. An old, tired woman sat there, her eyelids half-closed, a knitting kit in her hands.

The man lightly knocked on the glass separating the woman from customers, and she slowly looked up and smiled. The truck driver greeted her and started to speak, just not the language Nashel understood.

"There's a train to Solned in a little over an hour," he turned to tell Nashel, switching languages.

The woman behind the counter seemed surprised for a moment, then smiled. "Yes, at 2.30 pm."

Her accent was even thicker than the man's, and her pronunciation told Nashel that Zakhelion was a second language to her.

The man didn't wait for Nashel to answer, and took out

some notes from his pocket and purchased the ticket for her.

"I can't accept that, sir," she told him, trying - not too hard - to stop him.

"It's alright," he smiled. "Your parents would do the same for my child."

She doubted it since her parents died ten years prior, but she didn't say that.

"I don't know what to say," she mumbled, lowering her gaze.

"You don't have to say anything. Just go to Solned and get your chance."

"Thank you, sir," she replied.

"And see if you can kick some whippers' ass in the meantime," he winked.

She laughed, "I'll try!"

"Here, take this," he handed her some money. "Get yourself something to eat. I could hear your stomach rumble over my loud truck's engine!"

He then leaned over her and planted a kiss on her forehead. Nashel stiffened, but the man did nothing else. He took a step back, looked at her, and wished her luck before leaving. She heard the loud truck start, then the noise slowly faded.

Nashel stood there for a few moments, thinking about what had just happened. Her stomach was indeed rumbling, so she moved towards the station cafe. Calling it a cafe was an exaggeration; it was just a counter that sold handmade sandwiches and freshly squeezed orange juice. She was wondering if the man standing there could speak her language, when the woman behind the counter, now fully awake, shouted across to the man in their weird tongue. He nodded, grabbed a sandwich, filled a glass of juice, and practically shoved it in Nashel's hand with a big smile. She smiled back, gave him the money, took the food, and sat on a bench in front of the outbound track.

She looked into the bag. The money felt weird. She had got so used to not having to worry about that, that the feel of it in her hand seemed out of place. She also powered up the PPad, making sure nobody was watching. While Dustveil told her that everyone had one, she didn't believe a girl from a poor, dying village did. She followed the instructions to make sure her cover story checked out, imbuing the tablet with a bit of power, just to make sure, and then she looked up languages. To her surprise, the Sunrise had a myriad of languages, changing almost in every town, with a common language, Solnedian, spoken as a lingua franca and the main language of the capital. That was a relief; she didn't have the time to learn another language and be fluent in it.

The platform was deserted, and nobody announced the train, but it was the first she had seen, and she doubted the station was very popular. The train screeched to a halt, longer than the platform and more modern too. It felt like a clash of epochs: the rural nature of the town and the sleek modernity of the train made Nashel feel she was about to step on a very long and narrow time machine.

She boarded the train and found that the inside was fancier than she had expected. The red velvet seats were large and comfortable; there was a restaurant carriage, and a sleeping one, as Nashel discovered the train crossed the entire country – We'll take you from Sunrise to Sunrise! was their slogan, which didn't make much sense to her. She found her seat and watched the scenery change as the train sped along. She dozed off at one point, tired after the long journey.

When the train arrived in the capital, the sun had set a couple of hours prior. Fortunately for her, the station was massive and hosted a hotel where she booked a room. Their Solnedian was much closer to her language, with just a slight inflexion, and she decided to spend the night and leave the city exploration for the following morning.

CHAPTER ELEVEN

A New Academy

When she left the station in the morning, Nashel's breath was taken away. Solned was huge. There were people everywhere, different ages, different skin colours, different languages. There were also cars everywhere. Nashel was used to the Citadel, where few people used cars, so it was shocking for her eyes, her ears, her nose to see so many all in the same place. There were streets twice as big as the avenue that connected the Academy to the Citadel proper, but there was no trace of greenery anywhere, not along the walkways, nor on the windows of the four-, five-, ten-storeys tall buildings.

She had to use her PPad to find the direction to the Sunrise Academy, or she would've been lost, despite all her training.

She also realised that if the Sunset forces were to fight in Solned - which would never happen, she was sure - their "urban warfare" scenarios would count for nothing: this was completely different from the simulations and drills they had done. For one, the buildings were sparkling. They were way too clean and mostly made of white marble, which reflected the sun and blinded the people. She looked around and saw that, indeed, most passersby had sunglasses on. She didn't pack any, so she had to just look down and squint, which she hated because it made her stand out from the crowd. After a while, though, she noticed she wasn't the only unprepared one. There were a few other people, some in small groups, some solo, all with their PPads out, a map on the screen, and no sunglasses. She felt relieved Sunrise tourists didn't know their capital was such a shiny trap.

She wasn't sure she was even following the right directions when another blinded and distracted tourist almost bumped into her, her reflexes her only defence against the crash.

"Watch it!" she admonished and squinted to look at the person. She saw a boy about her age with messy black hair and piercing blue eyes. He muttered something in another language, then shook his head and apologised in Solnedian.

"These bloody buildings!" he exclaimed, exasperated. "I'm going to need glasses now!"

Nashel smiled politely and started to walk again, but he stopped her.

"Are you going to the Academy, too?" he asked, surprised. He must've seen her tablet's screen. She took a mental note to either find out if they had any privacy film or use her powers so that nobody could see what she was looking at.

"Do you bump into everyone on the street just to ask that question, or am I the lucky one?" She asked curtly. She didn't like to be singled out when she was already feeling out of her depth.

He laughed, amused. "I said I was sorry!"

"That doesn't answer my question," she wasn't sure why she found herself engaging instead of just walking away.

"Right, right," he laughed again. "No, I don't do it on purpose. And no, you're not the lucky one, just coincidence."

She didn't believe in those, but she let it slide.

"Lucky me," she muttered, but it had little bite.

"Well, I am going to the Academy. And since this city is the most unfriendly place I've ever seen, I wouldn't mind if we put our minds together and defeated its trickery."

She laughed at that, much against her will, because she

agreed wholeheartedly with his assessment of the city. “Alright, but keep up, or I’ll leave you behind.”

He jumped up, his hands in the air, shouting something cheerful in his native language.

“Or that. You do that again, and I’ll leave you behind,” she feigning disgust.

He made an exaggerated, serious face that was comical and made her laugh.

“I’m Alistair, by the way,” he said, as they started to walk again.

“Nashel,” she replied.

When discussing her cover story with Ash, they talked about changing her name but discarded it, considering it wasn’t her real name anyway, and it wasn’t a name that screamed Sunset, anyway. It made her wonder if Alistair was his real name, or if the Sunrise didn’t care to hide powerful names.

“You come from far away?”

“Yeah,” definitely farther than he could imagine, “up North, in the countryside,” she made up. They would have a north and a countryside, and she could use her last residential for details. It was close enough to the truth that she wouldn’t slip, and it could be vague enough that she didn’t need to go into too many details.

“I’m from the countryside, too!” Alistair replied. “My parents have a farm.”

“Why didn’t you join the Academy earlier?” she asked, and she could swear he paled and looked frightened for a moment before he quickly recovered.

“Why didn’t you?” he deflected. She noticed, but decided not to push for the moment.

“My village is very poor, dying. My parents didn’t have the means to send me earlier,” she shrugged, hoping her made-up story made sense.

Alistair nodded and seemed to believe her.

“I didn’t want to leave home,” he finally answered the question. “I’m not used to being around people; we live pretty much in the middle of nowhere. I'm going to miss it," he paused. "Actually, I'm going to miss Peggy more."

"Peggy?"

"She's our mascot. A sheep that didn't grow, but thinks she's as big as the biggest ram. She likes to headbutt you, but can't muster enough strength to be harmful. She's so cute!"

Nashel laughed. "It sounds like she's your girlfriend!"

"Ouch!"

She laughed again. She liked Alistair. He reminded her of her squad members and Ash, not because he seemed attracted to her, but because of his goofiness. He was also powerful, she could tell, and a powerful ally was better than a powerful enemy.

The Sunrise Academy was nothing like the Sunset, so much so that Nashel was about to move on and reroute the PPad, thinking it got them to the wrong place. There were no gates or fences, but a paved avenue where people came and went. Nobody had a uniform on, and everyone was talking to everyone. Nobody was marching or was in formation, and notably, nobody was using powers. The buildings were grand, white and pink marble, and even more blinding than the rest of the city. It was a chaotic and colourful hell; Nashel hated it immediately.

"Now what?" she asked Alistair, irritated. Neither her week of preparation nor Lieutenant Dustveil told her what to do to enrol. She hoped Alistair knew it, and if so, she was glad to have met him.

"We go to Central," he said, shrugging. "That should be the main building where they will point us in the right direction."

She shrugged as well and gestured for him to lead the way. Thankfully, there were maps along the way because the campus was a maze created to distract them, and they had to consult them too many times to Nashel's liking.

They found themselves in front of huge steps and columns so high they made their necks hurt when they looked at the top. In the gloomy hall, marble was replaced by wood everywhere. A single, round information point stood like an island in the middle of it, and an old, grey-haired lady with glasses so thick they made her eyes look like balls, looked up to them.

"We want to join the Academy," Alistair blurted, his voice sounding too high and echoing through the hall.

The lady clicked her tongue, gave them a look over, and turned to look for a stack of paper without saying a word to them. She fished out two clipboards and two pens and passed them over to them.

"Complete these," she pronounced every syllable slowly, as if they were idiots.

If Nashel had a bit less self-control and could use her powers openly, she would make her regret it. Unfortunately, given her situation, she could only ignore her.

The form asked questions about everything from her birth to her weight, height, sleeping patterns, eating habits: everything but her powers. Nashel was once again convinced she was in the wrong place, a different school, not the one she was supposed to be. She looked over at Alistair, focused on his papers, his brows furrowed, but she couldn't guess if it was because of confusion at the absence of power-related questions or just concentration. She didn't want to ask, because she didn't want to expose herself; she still wasn't sure about the Sunrise people's attitude towards powers, and from what she saw, they weren't using them openly. Still, she found it weird that no question asked them what their abilities were.

After a few more moments, Alistair looked up, and she saw the same sentiment in his eyes.

"Isn't this a place to learn... you know..." she whispered so low, she thought he didn't hear her.

"Magic...?" he said even lower.

It baffled her to hear it called that out loud, reinforcing the idea that it was something out of a fairy tale. Something that happened to them, bestowed upon them by some mystical being and not part of their very essence, something they were born with.

Yet, she nodded, and Alistair took a sigh of relief.

"Maybe they introduce it after you get in?" he suggested.

She didn't know the answer to that, so she just shrugged, unconvinced.

They gave the clipboards back to the receptionist, who took them without looking at them and didn't say anything. They shrugged and waited around. People were coming and going, and it was difficult for Nashel to understand if they were students or staff, as nobody was wearing a uniform and they all seemed a lot older than her. She wasn't used to feeling out of place, but here, she felt like a fish out of water, and she hated it. Alistair looked even more distressed.

"Are you okay?" she asked him when she saw him starting to hyperventilate.

"Yeah," he replied doubtfully. "I don't like being at the centre of attention, and I feel like everyone is watching."

"Nobody is watching," she tried to reassure him.

"I know. I just wish we could sit down or something."

She nodded. Standing there, in the middle of the hall, loitering, made her feel uneasy, too.

Time seemed to stretch, but finally, a middle-aged, distinguished man in a suit approached them.

"Follow me," he told them curtly, but not rudely.

They looked at each other, shrugged, and followed. He led them down a corridor, then into a classroom, and gestured for them to take a seat while he leaned against the teacher's desk.

"Welcome to the Sunrise Academy," he said with a smile that didn't reach his eyes. "The selection process is rigorous. You will be tested on your knowledge of Solnedian, the history of the Sunrise, and basic calculations."

No magic? Nashel thought, but didn't say anything. She saw Alistair opening his mouth to say something, but then he closed it without doing so.

"I am Professor Caltren and will administer the exams," he continued. Nashel noted the use of the plural and hoped that at least one of those exams was about her powers. Caltren produced two tests and handed them to them with a pen. "You have one hour to complete this. It will then be evaluated, and you will be notified whether you will progress to the next stage. Understood?"

"Yes," they both replied.

"You may begin."

Nashel was used to acing every test, so it was with dismay that she found herself stuck on the very first question. She didn't know the first thing about the history of the Sunrise. As she skipped to the Solnedian and Maths questions, she tried to think if it were plausible for a girl in a forsaken village to know how to read and write - not even perfectly - and do some basic Maths, but know nothing of history. She hoped so because she didn't know how else to explain her gaps unless she used her powers, which was out of the question at the moment.

"Time's up," the professor said.

If, in the hall, time seemed to stretch to infinity, it snapped back during the test because it seemed like only a few minutes had passed, not an hour. With a sigh, Nashel handed her paper back.

"You can proceed to the next room," he indicated a different door. "You will find refreshments and comfortable seats while you wait for your results."

In the new room, there were two sofas, full and plump, soft velvet covers. which reminded her of the train, big enough that they could lie on them. There was a table with drinks and food, mostly sweet pastries, and some savoury snacks of weird shapes; she wasn't sure what they were. At least the drinks were recognisable as fresh fruit juices, water, and milk.

"Should we address the elephant in the room?" Alistair said once they were both comfortable on the sofa.

"What if they are listening?" Nashel replied in a whisper.

"Paranoid much?"

"Well, it seems weird to me that there is no mention of you know what so far. Maybe this is part of the test, too. Have us marinate here for who knows how long, and observe and listen to what we say, checking if we speak about... the elephant," she ended with a smile.

"Okay, but what if they want us to question it?"

"Good point," she conceded.

"I had this image in my head about a place where everyone was practising magic openly," Alistair said in a daydreaming tone. "And I would come here and just fit in."

"Me too," she whispered back. It wasn't strictly true. She didn't want to fit in, but she did want to use her powers. She had spent the last twenty-four hours without doing so, and it was excruciating.

"Instead, it feels like even the word is unspeakable."

"The word?" she teased, feigning ignorance.

"You know, the elephant," he replied with a smile.

"You mean magic?" she whispered again, looking around suspiciously.

"Shh," Alistair replied jokingly.

"You mean magic?" she repeated at normal volume.

"Shhhh," he laughed.

"MAGIC! MAGIC! MAGIC!" she shouted, laughing as well.

Alistair hid his face behind his hand, pretending she wasn't there, shouting her lungs out.

Caltren decided that was time to enter the room. He looked at the two laughing with an inscrutable expression.

"Mr Corven, if you please," he gestured for Alistair to follow him back to the classroom.

"Good luck," she murmured as he looked at her, panic-stricken.

"You, too," he tried to reply, swallowing visibly.

Not even ten minutes later, he was back there, pale, but not as stressed. He gave her a small smile and filled a glass of water for himself. He didn't say anything, Caltren watching him before beckoning Nashel to follow him out.

"Do you have a wand?" he asked, without preamble.

Nashel nodded and produced it. He took it and studied it. He looked very focused, as if the wand were speaking to him.

Nashel had to restrain herself from laughing. If only he knew it was just a stick of wood they collected from a random tree in an enemy country.

"Simple, but effective," was his opinion as he returned the wand to her. "It seems the right length for you."

They had different lengths?

"It'll do for now."

"Thank you," she replied neutrally.

"You scored extremely well in the basic calculation sections, and very well in the Solnedian section, especially for someone who's not a native speaker."

"Thanks," she replied, trying not to feel offended.

"Do you know you left all the history questions blank?"

She wondered why he had asked her that. He was there while she took the test; he knew her answers were her own.

"Yes, sir," she answered, without looking at him.

"That is a fail."

"I understand, sir," she said. She didn't want to think about the consequences of such a failure if she had to find her way home so soon and with no intel.

"However," he continued, "we believe you have the ability to catch up, and you will progress to the next phase. If you are successful, you will have extra classes to bridge those gaps."

"Thank you!" she tried to be as genuine as she could.

She had a flashback on her first day at the academy, her academy, not this farce. Headmistress Magna had said something similar about extra classes she had to attend to learn to read and write, and starting part-way through the year. The fond memory helped her come across as genuine.

He led her back to the room and told them they would be called once again.

"That was intense, wasn't it?" Alistair asked after Caltren left.

She nodded. She didn't find it tense. He only told her what she already knew and studied that stupid stick.

The wait was another long one. Nashel laid down on one

of the sofas, not sleeping, but relaxing. There was a gnawing inside her, like a barking dog, like a persistent mosquito, like a voice impossible to shut up, that longed for her powers, to burst them out in a fire that would make the one she set on her house pale.

Once again, Professor Caltren called Alistair first. She lost track of time, meditating and telling that voice inside her to leave her alone, and when the door opened again, Alistair was not there.

She got up and followed the professor before he could tell her to do so.

"Take a seat," he ordered her, doing the same on the other side of the desk. "There are a few gaps in your intake form."

"I know," she replied. She had expected that.

"You left your surname blank."

"I don't have one. Nobody does in my village," she shrugged.

"You also wrote 'village' as your place of residence and birth."

"It's a tiny place, sir. It's only six families; we don't have a name."

"I see," he commented, but he didn't seem to believe her. She was tempted to use her powers on him to convince him, but yet again, she stopped herself.

"We have very strict admission criteria here," he started. "And your exam was overall just average."

She tried not to resent that.

"Why do you want to join the academy?" he asked, looking her straight in the eyes.

She saw a movement, barely noticeable, of his right shoulder, then she felt something push against her mind. He was trying to read her thoughts! She pretended not to notice, but didn't let him in. He tried harder, but again she didn't budge, so he gave up.

"My parents and I wanted to give me the opportunity to amount to something. Not be stuck in a dying village."

"I see," he repeated and seemed to be convinced by her

fervour, but she didn't miss the bitterness for failing to read her. "If we decide to give you a spot at the Academy, you will be on probation for your first year. That means we will test you often and observe you closely. You will have progress assessments, and you will need to bridge your gaps before you can move on to more serious study."

"Okay," she shrugged.

"There are strict rules about the use of magic, when and where it's allowed."

She hated that instantly, but nodded.

"Being on probation also means that if you break even the smallest rule, you're out. Do you accept these conditions?"

"Yes."

"Alright, Mr Segast will escort you to your accommodation, where you'll find the rule book, your timetable for tomorrow, the compulsory reading list, and dates of your first assessment."

He didn't say anything else, but it was clear he had dismissed her.

"Thank you for the opportunity," she said humbly.

"Welcome to the Sunrise Academy," he repeated, and again his smile didn't reach his eyes.

Mr Segast was waiting just outside the door. He took her to the hall, where Alistair broke into a huge smile when he saw her.

"Follow me," Segast said when they reached him. The old lady at the desk didn't seem to notice them when they walked in front of her.

He took them out and around the building, on a side alley lined with smaller buildings. Nashel remembered from the map that they were different lecture theatres. The sun was lower now, so the buildings were not blinding her any longer, but she reminded herself to buy sunglasses as soon as she could.

They walked in silence, the two new students exchanging looks and smiles, Alistair mocking the stiff walk of the man in front of them until they arrived at a different section of the campus. The building they stopped in front of was the least opulent and most run-down they've seen so far. It was still made of marble, but it was dirty and unpolished; it was three stories tall, and each story had its own crooked columns, which contributed to the wobbliness of the building.

"This will be your dorm," the man announced, devoid of enthusiasm, and took them inside.

The entrance was stuffed and warm. It smelt like too many people were packed inside and didn't take a shower. There was once-thick worn carpet in shades of red everywhere, a small reception on the right, with pigeonholes behind it, and nobody was standing there to welcome them - a sign said it was only open between 10 and 11 am on alternate days.

The other side of the room had worn-out chairs with springs and stuffing coming out. A big fireplace took most of the middle wall, but big floor-to-ceiling windows at either side of it let in bright daylight and made dust particles dance in it. Opposite the entrance door was a wooden staircase, its steps a shade darker and polished in the middle by the thousands of people who had used them over the years.

Segast took them up to the first floor, where doors lined each side of the corridor, and along to room 17. He gave Alistair a key and turned around, ushering Nashel upstairs before she could even say a word. They stopped in front of room 12, and he opened the door for her. Someone inside screeched.

"Hey! Knock first!" the voice belonged to a girl in her bra who scrambled to find something to cover herself. Segast gave Nashel a key and left.

Nashel was shocked; someone was in her room. Another girl was in the room that was supposed to be hers. She looked around, and all she could see was a mess of clothes and books, and stuff everywhere: on the floor, on the two desks, the two beds, the window sill. In her shock, she also noticed there was no door other than the entrance, which meant no bathroom.

"I'm Lamina," the girl introduced herself, but she didn't

seem happy to have a roommate. “I’ll clean up in a sec.”

And that was it. She turned and flopped back on her bed, a tablet in her hand, completely ignoring the fact that Nashel hadn’t introduced herself yet or had a place to sit.

She spent all her life having her own room, all the time at the Academy having her own bathroom, locking her door at night to avoid people playing tricks on her, and now she had to share?

“I’m Nashel,” she said after a moment, trying to mask her disgust for the whole situation. “Where’s the bathroom?”

The girl clicked her tongue, clearly annoyed, and didn’t look at her at all. “End of corridor.”

As beginnings went, this one left a lot to be desired.

CHAPTER TWELVE
ToM, PoM, and LoM

When she used the communal bathrooms, she was shocked by a parade of naked girls enveloped in towels, coming and going, screaming excitedly at each other. It was an experience she wouldn't get used to. She didn't think she'd miss her dorm or the academy that much, but she did. Everything at the Sunset Academy was regulated. Students' privacy was valued, including personal hygiene. Nashel had changed in front of her squad or classmates, boys and girls alike, but it was a quiet affair: take off dirty clothes, put on clean ones. There was no laughing, no screaming, no squawking like ducks.

Once she entered her room, Lamina hadn't moved even the smallest of her things, so Nashel just grabbed whatever and dump it on top of the rest on her side of the room. She took the satisfaction of sweeping the desk and dropping everything on the floor. Lamina didn't seem to notice or care. She stayed on her bed watching something on her tablet with headphones on.

Cleaning all that rubbish without using her powers was not as effective, not as fast, and not as satisfying. She found the rule book Caltren had mentioned, so she sat at the desk and started reading it. It was a dreadful experience: magic was banned outside of the classroom or unless explicitly allowed by a teacher in writing, and even in that situation, it needed to be under supervision. She would have to find a way, maybe go out of town, maybe just find a place on campus where she could be herself. If she had her own room, she could. Maybe she could make it so that Lamina wasn't there anymore. One way or another.

When night fell, Nashel couldn't sleep. Lamina was snoring lightly – which sounded ten times louder to Nashel, not used to sharing a room – and the bed was as old as the rest of the building, sagging in the middle, with springs digging into her back. The sheets were so stiff that they startled her every time she moved.

She left His Slowlyness - her sloth plushie, the only object she brought with her - in her bag along with everything else she owned and stored it in the bottom of her closet. When Lamina went to the bathroom to prepare for the night, Nashel broke the rules and put a ward on her wardrobe, just to be sure. It was the right move, because Lamina stopped snoring abruptly, and Nashel heard her stand up. She pretended to be asleep then, her eyes closed and her breathing deep and regular. Lamina moved towards her, kicking a few of the things on the floor, and went straight for the closet.

"What do you think you're doing?" Nashel broke the silence before turning on her bedside lamp.

Lamina looked like a deer caught in headlights. "Nothing. I was looking for my sock."

"No, you weren't," Nashel replied. "There is nothing of yours on this side of the room. And unless you're using unauthorised magic, I'm pretty sure you can't see in the dark."

Lamina had the decency to say nothing, turn, and go back to bed.

Nashel turned the light off but didn't sleep, nor did she try. The idea of getting rid of Lamina even stronger after the incident.

At dawn, she got up, used the toilet undisturbed, so she made a note to wake up early every morning, and went out for a run. She didn't see anything in the rule book that forbade that, so she was certain that she wouldn't be in trouble. She thought about stopping by Alistair's room, but it was, admittedly, too early.

She liked the quietness of the deserted hall and campus. Outside, the air smelt of dew and mist, and for the first time it reminded her of home, even though there were no trees. She took a deep breath, closed her eyes, and smiled, pretending for a few moments to be back.

"Couldn't sleep?" a voice from behind interrupted her thoughts.

She turned around to see Alistair and nodded.

"Smells like home," he whispered, and she felt grateful he wasn't like Lamina.

"What are you doing up so early?" she asked.

"I don't know about you, but I'd prefer to sleep on a haystack than in that bed," he grimaced.

Nashel laughed, "Yeah, my bed sucks too."

"And my roommate smells. He refused to shower last night, claiming he didn't like the only shower stall available and couldn't be bothered after."

"That's gross!" Nashel exclaimed, making a face. "My roommate tried to get into my wardrobe in the middle of the night, pretending to look for a sock in the dark!"

"Ridiculous," he commented, while laughing. "You going for a run?"

She nodded again.

"Can I join?"

"Sure," she shrugged. It would remind her of the morning's training. The laps around the campus as a class.

They took their own personal tour of the campus and got back with plenty of time to shower while the other students were about to wake. Nashel wanted to check that Lamina didn't mess with her stuff, and Alistair said he would try to drag his roommate under the shower, but they decided to meet back in the hall to find where they were supposed to eat.

Nashel found Lamina asleep, and she was certain that she wasn't faking. The ward on her closet was also intact, so either Lamina was very skilled, or she actually slept while Nashel was out. She also found her new timetable on her desk, next to the rulebook. It was packed. She didn't have a free period at all.

She took a quick shower and realised she didn't know what to wear, she had worn a uniform every day for over ten years, and she missed it. She got the first shirt and trousers she could find and reminded herself to note what the others were wearing. Once again, she felt like a fish out of water.

She went downstairs and waited for Alistair, who appeared only a couple of minutes later, which was great, because she didn't want to try any of the chairs in the communal area.

"Martin told me that people go for breakfast in the dorm down the street," he shrugged. "I'm not sure if I believe him."

"The rulebook says we aren't allowed to go in the other dorms," Nashel commented, but she wasn't worried about breaking that particular rule.

Alistair nodded. "Martin said that it's fine. But he could have tried to get me in trouble because I basically dragged him in the shower."

Nashel found herself laughing at that. So, Martin was his roommate. She wondered if Alistair wanted to get rid of him just as much as she did Lamina.

They left to find the other dorm and were shocked to see the complete opposite of theirs, the building looked new and shiny, no streaks of dirt, no wobbling columns. When they entered, there was no foul smell, but an amazing smell of bacon and freshly baked pastry. An older student, who didn't seem to mind that they were there, greeted them.

"Follow the smell," he smiled, "and the noise!"

And they did, through the main hall, with its comfy, full

chairs, game stack, pool table, and through another door and into paradise. It reminded Nashel so much of the Sunset that, for a moment, she thought she'd been teleported back.

There was a buffet with mountains of food, and tables, big or small and accommodating all the different group sizes. They all but launched themselves at the food, stacked their plates, and found a small table to sit at. Nobody bothered them, which seemed like a good sign, for now. They took out their timetables and compared them while they finished stuffing their mouths.

She surprised herself when she felt relieved that their schedules were identical. They both needed extra lessons to catch up, and they both failed the history section of the exams. Nashel wondered what kind of life Alistair lived, not to know his own history. He said he lived on a farm in the middle of nowhere, but she felt paranoid that he wasn't who he said he was.

Their first lesson was Solnedian, Nashel tried not to feel offended she had to take additional classes on that. Solnedian was very similar to her Zakhelion, save for some vocabulary and constructions. Yet, apparently, her level was not good enough for those repressed, stuck-up Sunrise whippers.

They asked the friendly student in the reception for directions, as their lesson was on the other side of campus, and they ran through the maze of alleys and arrived as the teacher was about to close the door. They were in a small room with a round table, and half a dozen students already sat, who looked at them curiously.

The teacher closed the door, unimpressed. "You are my new students," he addressed them directly. "I am Mr Cobbler. The only language allowed in this class is Solnedian, so I don't care what dialect you spoke at home; I don't want to hear it."

They nodded.

The two-hour lesson was intense. Mr Cobbler showed no mercy for any of the students struggling, and even less for her and Alistair. Nashel found the pace brutal, but the content wasn't difficult. It helped that she had a good grasp of her language's structure, and Solnedian wasn't too different. Alistair, though, could barely keep up.

At the end of the lesson, Mr Cobbler asked them to stay behind. "Since you joined this class late, catch up on what you missed. Read Chapters 1, 2, and 3 of the first book on your reading list for tomorrow."

He waited for them to nod their understanding. "Now, go to your next lesson, and next time, be punctual."

Nashel knew better than to protest. She doubted that talking back to a teacher led to corporal punishment in the style of the Sunset Academy, yet she didn't test it. They took their bags and rushed to the next class, which, thankfully, was only a couple of buildings over. This time, they were in a big lecture theatre, with plenty of other students chatting in many languages. They found two empty seats and browsed the library catalogue on their PPads to reserve the book they needed to read, while they waited for the teacher to arrive.

She stormed in at the last minute, a flurry of paper and red hair, that stopped by the desk and blinded them with a huge smile.

In Solnedian, she said, "Translations will appear on your PPads now."

Nashel's tablet changed to the random language she picked when she input her details. She now had to remember to look down at it and make a confused face every once in a while.

This lesson was history, which Nashel found refreshingly interesting. The topic was the war, and Nashel couldn't help but compare it to her school lessons, and at times, she wanted to protest when the Sunset was depicted as evil. However, she figured the module was going to be very helpful in giving insight into the Sunrise background, and she could gather important information if she wasn't kicked out for getting angry at the teacher. The more she listened, the more she liked the teacher. She was engaging and made jokes that sometimes were lost in translation, but many students looked at each other and laughed anyway. They had lots of homework for this lesson, too, by the end, and it looked like their life was going to be an endless study session.

They followed the other students to the cafeteria for lunch and found that they had to pay for their food. Nashel was outraged. So it took them a while to figure out they needed a student card to charge with money and use. The lady serving food was generous, though, and let them have a sandwich and water. They ate it on the way to the library, where they were told they could get issued the card and collect the books they needed for homework.

That was their plan, but once there, they found a queue, and they only got their cards done. The photos turned out hideous. It felt like the librarian was waiting for them to blink or turn slightly around or yawn before taking the photo. But they couldn't complain as they had to run to their next lesson to be there on time.

By the end of the day, they have so much to do that they would need to spend the night in the library, if it was permitted. On a positive note, they found the books they needed, mostly because they could reserve them online in between lessons. Some desperate students weren't so lucky and were begging the librarian for a copy that wasn't available anymore.

Nashel and Alistair found a nice table in a secluded corner where they would spread out their books and start studying. It was dark and late, when they called it a night; their eyes got crossed when they tried to read some more.

Nashel found Lamina's stuff all over the place again, and Lamina snoring in her bed.

"Oi," she shouted, startling the other awake, "keep your shit on your side of the room!"

Lamina muttered unintelligible which sounded like an insult, she turned the other side and pretended to be back asleep.

Nashel turned the light on out of spite and made a big deal of noise while she pushed the stuff out of her side. Lamina tried to turn the light off, but Nashel was having none of it and turned it on again, and ignored the insults that followed.

When she was done, she noticed the ward on her closet had been disturbed. She didn't retaliate; however, she put a stronger one on, one that would mark the person who tried to force it, and she also made it so that the floor would creak if anyone but her tried to cross on her side. She wanted to erect an invisible barrier that stopped Lamina's stuff from crossing on her side, but she didn't want to overdo it.

She doubted anyone of the whippers knew anything about Traces, but she masked hers so that it was almost impossible to link it back to her - something Sergeant Thomas had her learn after he discovered she knew how to manipulate Traces. Feeling safer and exhausted from the sleepless night and the late study hours, she fell asleep despite the awful mattress and sheets, with His Slowlyness finally by her side, as it had been for the past ten years.

The morning she was still so tired that, for the first time in her life, she almost fell back to sleep. Her internal clock woke her at the crack of dawn, which was great for using the bathroom, but not for her mood. Still, she got dressed and got out for a run with a zombie-looking Alistair. They ran in silence, both of them too tired to multitask, they also went to breakfast in silence and ate as much as they could, as fast as they could, so they could cram some time in the library before lessons.

Mr Cobbler was not happy with them, even though they arrived on time and had done their homework, he still looked at them as if they were a huge disappointment... but that seemed to be his default.

Pretty soon, they established a routine: they met in the mornings, ran in silence, then had breakfast over homework, went to lessons, Mr Cobbler's was always first in the morning, then at the library till late at night.

Mr Cobbler wasn't the worst, though. He was the strictest

and most unpleasant, but Nashel discovered a profound hatred towards three particular subjects: Theory of Magic, Practice of Magic, and Law of Magic.

As soon as she stepped into her first lesson of ToM - as they called it - she immediately wanted to step out and scream. It was clear that the teacher had no idea what she was talking about. They delved into different schools of thought, each with different ideas of how magic worked or why it existed, and in what form. Each was more unbelievable than the other.

Nashel thought that could just be the subject, or the teacher, but when she went to her first Pom lesson, she realised it was systemic. She probably hated that more, if she were honest with herself, because she still didn't like waving her wand. Half the time, she wanted to laugh, watching her classmates making different movements that were supposed to conjure different spells. It was ridiculous. She got in trouble more often than not, but not as much to warrant an expulsion, just to get her extra homework for punishment.

LoM was one of those unpleasant surprises she started to get once she crossed the Void, along with sharing a room and communal bathrooms. She expected it to be an extension of ToM, that instead of philosophising, it would teach the mechanics of magic. She was completely wrong. LoM was a subject dedicated to learning the myriads of laws the Sunrise had approved to regulate the use of magic and the users of magic, the when and where magic could, but mostly could not, be used. She was going to fail all three subjects, and probably get arrested.

Something apparent from those lessons was that Nashel started to believe the Sunrise magicians - yes, they called themselves that - were incapable of conducting a complex attack on the Sunset. If their magical preparation was as limited and rudimentary as she saw in class, they could barely perform basic tasks, let alone attack and conquer an entire nation. Especially one militarised and trained for war.

Nevertheless, she had a mission, and she intended to

succeed even if the intel she gathered was not what she and her people expected.

CHAPTER THIRTEEN

The Lamina Problem

One night, towards the end of her first week, Nashel came back to Lamina waiting impatiently for her with a very displeased man who greeted her with crossed arms and a muttered "finally". Nashel noticed her roommate's bandaged hands, and she knew exactly what was coming.

"Miss Thalen, here, claims you've been using magic. As you know, the use of magic is strictly regulated and forbidden out of lessons."

"I'm aware," Nashel said curtly. She didn't know who the man was, but she guessed he was a dorm warden.

"Have you been practising?" he clearly wanted to be somewhere else, but she didn't know if he was more annoyed by her or Lamina.

"No, sir," she answered, looking him straight in the eyes, as they taught her at the Academy.

"She's lying!" Lamina almost screamed. "Look at my hands! They're ruined!"

She extended her arms, but with the bandages, nobody could see what was underneath. Nashel knew, of course, but she put on a clueless face.

"There's an easy way to check," the man replied. He

turned to the room and agitated - that's the only way Nashel could describe - his wand in the air. No Trace showed. So, they knew about Traces after all. However, this man wasn't too skilled (maybe none of them were) and couldn't get through Nashel's precautions.

"How do you explain the creaking floorboard?"

"Are you serious? I've been here for a week, and I already noticed that this building is old..." Nashel commented, "...to put it kindly."

"But when you walk, they don't!" Lamina sounded more and more hysterical.

"Would you mind giving us a demonstration, Miss Blaze?" the adult said. Nashel thought he was internally rolling his eyes.

"Sure," Nashel shrugged and walked into the room and towards her bed. All the floorboards she stepped on made a beautiful creaking sound - not as beautiful as the screech Lamina let on, complete with stomping feet.

"It's settled," the warden sighed and left. Nashel was sure he had to leave, or he would just burst into laughter.

Lamina made her best to give her a killer stare that wouldn't frighten a fly and stalked back into the room, floor creaking as she went.

Nashel knew it wasn't the end of it, Lamina was too petty to let it go. She started to find dirt in her bed and her shoes, some of her clothes went missing, only to be found wrenched and used as towels in the showers.

Nashel didn't care about her clothes, but she soon was annoyed. She had to get rid of the Lamina problem.

"Lamina," she called her one night, after a week of tolerating her silly behaviour. "You're from Solned, right?"

Lamina tried to ignore her until Nashel repeated herself.

"Yes," she finally answered in an annoyed tone.

"So, you've never lived anywhere else?"

Lamina sighed exaggeratedly. "That is what 'being from somewhere' means."

It wasn't, but arguing would not help her.

"Have you thought about attending another Academy?" Nashel had learnt that there were other branches of the academy throughout the country.

Lamina paused for a moment, as if the thought had never crossed her mind. "No, my home is here."

"Surely, you're curious about other places?"

Again, another pause. "N-no, I'm not?"

It came out as a question, and Nashel smiled inwardly: it was working.

"Are you scared?"

"No?" another question.

Nashel saw Lamina's eyes becoming cloudier and cloudier.

"Well, I was scared when I left my village," she started to tell, in a particular rhythm she had learnt in one of her last classes at the Sunset Academy. "I've never been anywhere, and everything seemed so big! But as I was on the road, I saw so many new things that I could never have imagined before. I am so glad I left."

"I—" Lamina's words were slurring, and she was slower to form sentences. "I never thought..."

"I know!" Nashel interrupted her. "I would recommend that you travel far and wide. It's eye-opening."

"Far and wide," Lamina mumbled.

"Yes, far and wide. The farther, the better."

"Farther... Better..."

"I would go tomorrow if I were you," she thought about saying 'right now', but she would give the girl the night.

"Tomorrow..."

"Yes, tomorrow. First thing in the morning."

"First thing..."

"Good girl, good girl. Now sleep," she ordered, changing her tone. "Tomorrow morning, you'll wake up, pack your bags, and leave. You'll never set foot in this school again."

Lamina fell into her bed and immediately was asleep.

Nashel had to close her eyes as her head spun. She took a ragged breath, then another, steadier. Influencing someone's will, implanting a brand-new thought, was taxing, and she had just learnt the skill and never put it into practice before. When she opened her eyes again, the dim light blinded her. She turned it off with her powers, not worrying about Lamina, then forced herself to get changed and wash, and finally allowed herself to sleep.

The next morning, she woke to a loud and constant knock on her door. It took her more than a few moments to understand what was going on, get up, and open the door. Alistair was there, looking wildly concerned.

"Thank the Sun!" he exclaimed as he saw her.

"What?" she croaked, eyes still half closed and full of sleep.

"You skipped our morning run. You also skipped breakfast, and you are running late for Mr Cobbler's."

"I what?"

"You need to wake up. I was so worried."

"Why?"

"You haven't heard?"

"Alistair, look at me. I'm sleeping."

He sighed, then gathered his thoughts. "Get ready, quickly. You have ten minutes. I've got you somc toast to eat on the way."

She shrugged, closed the door, and was tempted to go back to sleep, but didn't. She dressed; every morning it took her a beat to remember she didn't have a uniform. Brushed her teeth and hair, splashed her face, then met with Alistair in the hall.

Now that she was mostly awake, she noticed the buzz of whispered conversations, and as she walked to her friend, she caught a few stares and nods from other students.

Alistair passed her the toast, then held her shoulders and basically shoved her out the door. He stopped a few feet away, sitting on a bench.

"Aren't we late for class?" she asked, wondering about the weird behaviour that had descended over the school.

"Yes, but you need to know before we get there."

"Know what?" it seemed like she was the only one out of

the loop.

"Lamina's body was found at dawn, just outside campus."

Nashel looked at him, trying to process what he had just said. She didn't notice that Lamina was not in her room.

"Lamina's body?"

Alistair nodded. He moved to hold her hand, then stopped, his contrite expression telling Nashel he wanted to comfort her.

"What happened to her?"

He shrugged. "Nobody really knows. There are rumours she was brutally attacked, and others that she didn't have a scratch on her."

"That is awful," she replied.

Her mind was racing a mile a minute. Was it a coincidence? Somehow, she didn't think so. There was something that told her it was an unintended consequence of what she had done. Nashel was inexperienced with mind control, so it stood to reason that she possibly did something wrong. Maybe her tone of voice was not the right one. Maybe she didn't carefully plant her words.

She was so focused on her own thoughts, she didn't notice Alistair gently grabbing her by the arm and taking her to class. They arrived late, but for once, Mr Cobbler didn't say anything. He looked at Nashel's shocked face and decided not to reprimand them.

"As you are probably aware," he started, "of the incident that happened this morning."

There was a collective murmur of assent from the students.

"I will address it once, and once only, but I feel it is better than the whirlwind of rumours that had already spread."

He looked at each and every one of them as if they were directly responsible for Lamina's death and the rumours.

"Miss Thalen's death has been a terrible accident, but there was no foul play. She has not been murdered. Despite her young age, she suffered from a brain aneurysm. If you don't know what that is, you can do some research in your own time."

A brain aneurysm. A brain aneurysm Nashel caused.

"Miss Blaze," she shook her head and looked at the teacher. "Follow me outside."

She stood and exited the room.

"Under the circumstances, you are excused from today's lessons."

"I—"

He shook a hand, stopping her from continuing.

"Your other teachers are informed. You will receive a light reading list from each of us, so that you don't fall behind."

"Thank you," she said once it was clear she didn't have a choice.

"The dean has also decided it would be best for you to transfer rooms. You are now assigned to room 21. You will find your belongings already transferred there."

She didn't like the idea of someone touching her stuff, and she hoped they did it with powers and not by hand.

"Thank you, sir," she replied. She hadn't noticed until then, but she was standing at ease, so she shuffled to assume a more relaxed posture.

"Rest. And if you need any psychological support, make it known. Help is available," he finished in a sweeter tone she didn't think he was capable of.

She walked back to the dorm in a haze, still thinking about what had just happened. She wasn't upset that Lamina was dead; she couldn't care less about that, or actually, she was glad it wasn't a problem anymore. However, she didn't like to fail. If she were back home and failed so majestically, she would get punished. It wasn't just that, either. She was too good to make mistakes so big.

She reached room 21 and stopped dead in her tracks. Someone was waiting for her in front of her door. An older man dressed in a pressed grey suit, with a bright red tie that took all the attention. Nashel had to force herself to look up from it and memorise the man's face. She had seen him before, in photos. He had no hair on top, and a little fuzz around his ears and back of the head. He had small, beady eyes almost hidden by thin glasses. His smiled grossed Nashel out, but she couldn't say why. He was the dean of the school.

"Ah, Miss Blaze," he greeted her as if he weren't waiting for her. "I'm glad I got to speak to you."

"It's an honour to meet you, sir." She bowed her head slightly, her eyes darting back to the tie. Was there an Expression on it?

"We would like to offer our condolences for the untimely demise of Miss Thalen."

"I appreciate it, thank you."

"Perhaps we could talk inside." He eyed the door.

She nodded and approached it, finding that her key worked on it. She stopped on the threshold for the briefest moment: the room was a single. Her things were all there in the same place she had left them in her previous room.

"Please take a sit, sir," she gestured towards the desk chair, and sat herself on the bed.

The dean smiled that creepy smile and sat as if the chair were a throne. "We have considered the situation and decided it would be best for your well-being not to be in your previous room. We also considered the impact of assigning you a new roommate, therefore, we have decided to grant you the use of a single, usually reserved for older students."

Nashel didn't understand why he kept using 'we' when it was clear he made the decision, but she didn't ask. She wanted the man out as soon as possible. "Thank you," she muttered, just adding the necessary amount of shy gratitude to her tone.

"Now," he licked his lips, which sent a shiver down Nashel's spine, and she was immediately more on edge. "Mr Cobbler may have mentioned to your class that there was no foul play in Miss Thalen's death."

Nashel confirmed with a tight nod.

"I regret to say it was a necessary lie."

Nashel let her eyes widen in shock.

"We don't want to spread panic, but our healers found the faint trace of a spell that may have caused the aneurysm."

Nashel opened and closed her mouth, pretending to be unable to find the words because of the shock. Her mind raced through scenarios, calculating solutions to the problem if they managed to tie Lamina's death to her.

"Do you know anything about it?"

"About?" she feigned confusion.

"About Miss Thalen's departure. It seemed she was about to leave the academy."

Nashel shook her head. "No, sir, she didn't mention anything to me."

"I see," he commented, not believing her.

"I know she spent all her life in Solned, so maybe she wanted to see the world."

"She didn't inform us of such a decision."

"I'm sorry; I wish I could be more helpful. We weren't on the best of terms," she admitted.

"Yes, I've heard."

"What do you mean?" it came out sharper than she wanted, but the dean didn't seem to react.

"She accused you of performing illegal magic not too long ago, didn't she?"

"Ah," she nodded. "Yes, but it was a misunderstanding. The warden dealt with the situation."

"I am aware. I just find it suspicious that her demise happened so soon after your... how could I say... altercation."

"There was no altercation, sir!" she exclaimed. "The warden checked Lamina's claim and found it false."

"Yes, yes," he replied patronisingly. "Then Miss Thalen took it upon herself to see justice and enacted several pranks on you."

Nashel nodded.

"And then she was found dead."

Nashel knew it didn't look good for her. The more she told him, the more he could see motive in her actions. In her mind, she had two choices. She could try and manipulate the dean's mind, but considering she was still tired from doing the same to Lamina, and the catastrophic result of it, she wasn't too keen on that option.

When she was younger, back at the Sunset Academy, she realised that if a child cried, especially a girl, she could often get away with a more lenient punishment. Nashel wasn't able to cry on command, but she had observed her peers and their behaviour, and after trials and errors, she found a technique that worked for her.

She buried her face in her hands and started to shake her shoulder, hyperventilating. "I—" she faked sobbing and whimpered. "It wasn't me, I swear."

She heard the dean mumble. "No need to cry," he tried to console her. His tone was the awkward one adult men used when they were unsure what to do with a crying girl.

"I don't know what happened," she interrupted the words with hiccups. "I couldn't kill a fly!"

"It's okay, it's okay," he said. Nashel heard him stand. "I believe you," he took a couple of steps and patted her on the shoulder before retreating.

"I'm sorry."

"Listen," he tried in a gentle tone. "It's alright. I had to ask you, you understand. Now rest. Why don't you take a couple of days to process? No need to put in a formal request. Consider it granted."

He started to speak faster, as if that could mask his embarrassment.

"Th-thank you."

"Remember, help is available if you feel the need."

She faked a sob that could pass for another 'thank you' and she heard the dean approach the door.

"Do not panic. We don't think you or any other student is in any danger."

She nodded, her face still covered.

"We will keep an eye on you, don't worry."

She read between the lines, but nodded again.

"Take care," the dean opened the door and left in a hurry.

Nashel clicked her tongue and rolled her eyes, moving her hands away. She would have to be careful for a while, keep a low profile, but she was sure they wouldn't be able to identify the Trace and would leave her alone soon.

In the meantime, she considered her new room. They had transferred her things with magic, as proven by the ward still on the wardrobe. She considered undoing it, as it wasn't needed in a single, but she opted against it. She was too tired to put a ward on the door instead, just like the one she had in her room in the Sunset, so she kept it just in case someone tried any funny business while she slept or was away.

She was glad the dead allowed her a longer absence, she desperately needed to rest and reassess the situation once her mind was cleared. She changed into her pyjamas and laid in bed. The springs dug into her spine in the same spots, and the sheets were still stiff as wood. She wondered if they transported the bed itself or if they were all the same in the building. Still, for the first time since she had arrived, she slept soundlessly.

When she woke up, she planned to make sure her room was her sanctuary, where she was not monitored, where nobody could get in unless invited, and, most importantly, where she could use her powers without restrictions. It wasn't easy, a ward that strong would require all her focus, so she made sure she locked the door. As a last thought before starting, she sent a text to Alistair to say that she was going back to sleep and not to worry.

Unlike mind control, she knew how to do this. It was a sort of homework for cadets to ward their rooms. They started with being able to block access, just like the invisible wall that stopped her from going out if she hadn't brushed her teeth. Then, as the years progressed, their wards became more and more complex and stronger. It took a toll, though, on her energy levels, and since she could, she took the time off. A part of her observed she was getting softer. If she were back home, she wouldn't get a day, let alone two.

She sat on the floor in the middle of the room and closed

her eyes. She pictured what she wanted to achieve and felt for the power around her. It was faint, just like everywhere else in this Sunforsaken country, so she had to dig deeper to reach it. She also found an obstacle: there was already something there. She skirted around it, probing it to see if it was a trap, and when she was sure it wasn't, she opened her eyes. The Trace was also faint, almost difficult to keep in the foreground, and it took her longer than she cared to admit discovering it was an Expression meant for surveillance. That made her pause - and the energy it took, but she wouldn't say that - thinking about her previous room. Was there such an Expression too? If so, did they see her 'practising magic' unauthorised? But then, why did the warden not say so? Was it only in this room to make sure she was okay after the oh-so-tragic death of her roommate? Was it only single rooms, just in case the occupants needed help?

She thought about unravelling it, now that she had a grasp on the Trace, it wouldn't be too difficult, but then they would question why it wasn't there anymore. She hoped she didn't trigger anything yet. She continued with her original plan but made sure the Expression wouldn't perceive any power use.

At the end of her work, she didn't even have the strength to get herself up. The moment she let go of her focus, she fainted on the spot. When she came to, she had no idea how long it had been. Every bone in her body hurt, and she was starving. She managed to reach her bed and vaguely thought of using her powers to make some food appear, but she just couldn't. She looked at her PPad and saw the reading list Mr Cobbler had promised, and a text from Alistair checking in. She was tempted to ask him to bring her food, but a quick glance at the clock told her it was past 1 am, and she didn't want to get out of bed to open the door, either. With a resigned sigh, she tried and sleep some more. She woke up a few hours later to her stomach grumbling.

She still felt exhausted, and her body ached, but she forced herself to get up, get changed, and brave the communal bathroom. Thankfully, it was too early for the screeching girls, so she had time to get under a cold shower and get ready undisturbed. In the spirit of the Sunset Academy, she also forced herself to go for the morning run - at home, she wouldn't have the luxury to choose. It was still dark outside and too early for Alistair to join her, but she preferred it that way. She was too exhausted to have a conversation, and she was sure he would ask her awkward questions. She stopped at the cafeteria on her way back, expecting it to be closed, but one of the catering staff saw her, took pity on her, she must have looked as awful as she felt, and ushered her inside to make her a hot breakfast.

"Thank you," she said when she finished. "I can wash the dishes if you'd like."

The woman smiled warmly at her. "No need, deary. May I say, you look very tired. You shouldn't be up and running this early in the morning."

She prickled at that, trying not to show her annoyance. "I'll go back to sleep in a bit," she explained. "I have the day off."

The woman sighed, relieved, as if she cared about Nashel. "Good. That's good to hear. Off you go, then!"

Nashel nodded and smiled amiably. "Thank you again."

"I hope next time I see you, it's not at such a dreadful time! Have a good rest!"

"And you a good day," she bid farewell and left.

The run, but mostly the food, made her feel better. However, she did as she told the woman; she went back to bed, and as soon as she touched the pillow, she was asleep.

She hated sleeping during the day; it messed with her routine and her usual rhythm, but she knew it was necessary. She woke up again that it was late afternoon, and again because someone was knocking at her door. She thought about ignoring whoever it was but then she got up and opened the door, only teachers and staff members knew about her room change.

"Hey," Alistair greeted her with a whisper and a small smile.

"Hey," she replied sleepily.

"Miss Wynmere told me you were moved here."

Nashel nodded, then went back towards the bed, leaving the door open as an invitation for Alistair to follow her.

"How are you?" he asked her, sitting on her desk chair.

"Tired," she replied, "even though I've been sleeping all day."

He looked at her for a moment, Nashel couldn't identify the thoughts behind his eyes.

"I didn't think you were that close to Lamina," he finally said.

"I wasn't."

"Do I have to kill Martin to get a single, too?" he asked, then laughed.

For a fraction of a second, Nashel thought he knew what had happened to her former roommate, but when he started laughing, she understood he was trying to joke to lighten the mood, and she relaxed.

"You can try," she indulged him.

He looked at her again with the same inscrutable stare, but a grin on his lips.

"I thought you wanted some company," he added awkwardly. "I can go over today's lessons, if you want."

She nodded and offered him a smile.

It took a few minutes for the awkwardness to dissipate, and by then, Alistair had launched into a detailed debrief of everything that had happened in the past two days. Nashel found herself laughing with pleasure at Alistair's impersonations of the various teachers and classmates. He also summarised the lessons, so that she didn't have to do the reading, and she was grateful for that.

"I don't understand how we are supposed to practise PoM if we can't practise magic outside the classroom," he complained at one point.

"Then we get reprimanded if we don't do the homework," she agreed.

"But we can't do the homework if we can't practice!"

That brought another bout of laughter, and she was glad she wasn't the only one to see the nonsense of it.

"I used to use it all the time at home," Alistair whispered, then looked shocked, as if he didn't mean to say it out loud.

She laughed, but filed the information away for the future. It could be useful to know that, outside of Solned, people did break the law, unless he was just an exception.

"Me too," she replied, not wanting him to close up again.

He looked at her in surprise, then relaxed. "Don't you miss it?"

"You have no idea." The words were out of her mouth before she could weigh them properly. Alistair laughed again.

"Sometimes I do something small," he confessed. "Like in my room when Martin is out."

She faked shock and concern. "What if they find out?"

He shrugged. "It's just small things, like making the bed or tidying up the papers on the desk."

"I see," she nodded.

"I know I'm on probation and I should be extra careful," he rushed to say. "But sometimes it just feels like I'm going to explode if I don't do anything."

She understood that all too well.

"I know," she said gently. "I thought that now that I have a single room, I could do some magic if I keep it small."

Not mind control, for example. But she didn't add that.

He nodded vigorously, as to encourage her.

"Do you want to practise for PoM?" she dared to ask.

He thought about it for just a second before agreeing with a loud "YES!"

Nashel's powers were still weak, not that Alistair would notice, and she felt both relieved that she was using them, albeit with a stupid stick, and exhausted again.

"We should do this more often," Alistair whispered to her ear as they walked to the cafeteria for dinner.

She laughed and nodded, still tired but also refreshed.

She wasn't a sharer by nature, but maybe she could make an exception for Alistair and share her safe space with him.

Who knew how useful he could turn out to be.

CHAPTER FOURTEEN

The Glowing Forest

In the weeks that followed, she found it difficult to keep up her Sunset habits. She would go for a run every morning, but that was nothing compared to what she was used to. She had a day full of lessons and a night full of homework, and it was impossible to find some time for herself and her training.

It was also hard to stay focused on the mission. The Solnedian never talked about the Sunset. Even in the history lessons, her home was acknowledged only in passing, and the focus would shift immediately back to the Sunrise. She found it harder and harder to believe there was a group of people - soldiers? Magicians? She didn't know what to call them - planning a big attack right under her nose.

Thankfully, something called a 'half-term' was coming up, and the students were granted a week off meant to revise and prepare for the round of assessments that followed it. She decided it would be a good time to explore the academy and its surroundings more freely and to take at least a small step towards her goal.

She was surprised and relieved when, the last night before the break, she saw many students with small suitcases leave campus. Alistair explained they didn't live in the middle of nowhere like them and that they could go home for the week.

"I wish I could too," he told her, resigned while they watched yet another group leave, laughing.

"Me too," she replied in the same tone.

She wasn't sure if that was true. The Sunset had been her home forever, and she missed the freedom she had there, the routine that regulated her daily life, and the scenery. But she didn't miss anyone of her classmates or teachers.

"I was thinking of taking a trip around the city. I've been here for weeks now, and I haven't seen anything other than this school!"

"Make sure you pack sunglasses," she teased him, and they both laughed.

"Want to come with me?"

The invitation took her aback for the way he said it, awkward, as if he was asking her out.

"I actually wanted to stay on campus," she replied cautiously.

"Oh." To his account, he only sounded slightly dejected.

"I wanted to go on a treasure hunt," she explained, making the excuse up on the spot. "I heard there are secret societies here, and I wanted to see if I could find their lairs."

He laughed at that, seeming relieved. "I've heard of that, too!"

Again, she was surprised. She didn't remember hearing such rumours anywhere, but maybe she had just forgotten or not actively registered it at the time, which showed how out of shape she was, since it could've been important.

"You can join me when you come back, if you don't stay away the whole week," she offered.

"Tell you what, I'll stay and help you!"

"You don't have to!"

"I want to. It's not fun to go around a literally blinding, unknown city on my own."

She looked at him intently. At times, she felt as if he knew she wasn't who she had told him to be and she was suspicious that he was sent there to stop her progress, but then he would do or say something goofy, and she would change her mind.

"Okay," she shrugged. "Let's go find ourselves some secrets!"

The morning after, at breakfast - which, thankfully, was served even during holidays - Alistair showed up with a small stack of books.

"I did some research!" he exclaimed, excitement oozing off of him.

"I can see that," she replied.

"I sent you some articles on your pad as well," he added, dropping the books with a loud thud and sitting down at the table.

"You sure you're not taking this too seriously?" she asked sarcastically and made him laugh.

"I love treasure hunts!"

"I'm starting to understand that, too..."

"According to my research," Alistair started, "There are rumoured to be five different secret societies."

He was half talking so fast it was difficult to follow, especially because his accent became more prominent when he was so excited, and half stuffing his mouth with breakfast, which made it almost impossible.

"It says in this book," he shuffled the tomes on the table. "No, this one... Here... Not all the societies are active at the same time. Some periods there could be five, some just one or two. This book," he took another, "instead says that there had been over one thousand societies in the Academy and that it is impossible to assert with certainty which are real and which are tales."

"Okay," she tried to interject, but he was so engrossed that he ignored her.

"Each society has a different agenda, a different manifesto," he explained. "But they all seem to cater to certain people. And it is said that many of the alumni are now in positions of power in the government."

"What do you mean, certain people?" she asked.

"Well, they only take university students, so we would not be eligible for another year and a half."

"That's not what you mean, though," she guessed.

"It is, but it's not all. Even if we were eligible, they tend to initiate only legacies and the wealthy of the major cities."

Nashel nodded. Not her and her remote, fake village. "No exceptions?"

Alistair shrugged. "There are some mentions of 'charity cases', where some societies let an outsider in, but it never ended well."

"Good thing I just want to find them, not join them!" She laughed.

It took him slightly longer to do the same, and she understood he had entertained the idea of joining one.

"You said they each have their own agenda. What are they?"

"Well, that's the mystery!" His enthusiasm returned. "Some have political orientations, some are said to be sports groups. My favourite though—"

"Wait, how long have you been researching this?"

He looked at her, confused. "Last night."

"And you have a favourite?"

"Yes!" he exclaimed loudly, scaring a couple of students sat a few tables away. "Oops."

Nashel rolled her eyes but smiled.

"It's the most ridiculous thing I've ever heard!"

"Spill it, then!"

"Apparently, the goal of this particular society is to somehow defeat the Sunset," he whispered the last word so low that Nashel had to read his lips to understand it.

Once she did, she stared at him in shock. He laughed at her face, thinking she was too stunned by the nonsense. She forced herself to laugh as well.

"People are weird," she murmured feebly.

Thankfully, Alistair was too excited to see through her poor performance. "I know, right?!"

"What do they think they can do?!" She tried to regain her

composure and focus on what was important, while still pretending she found it funny.

"That's the secret part of the secret society," he commented, "But I don't think they can do much... I mean, I believe they are aware of that slight obstacle that is the Void, right?"

They both laughed, but Nashel knew there was a way to cross it, as she had done it herself. Was it possible that there was indeed a group planning an attack on campus? Or was the intel that prompted her mission just a misunderstanding? Someone who didn't know what secret societies were and what they did thought the threat was real. It was still worth investigating.

"We should focus on that," she proposed.

"I agree," Alistair nodded. "I really want to see what they do."

"Why, you want to join them?"

"It seems so silly, but what if they know of a way to cross the Void?" He whispered, leaning over the table.

"There is no way."

"I know, but what if...?"

She shrugged. "I don't believe it, but it will be fun."

"That's the spirit!" he sat back and smiled widely.

Despite all his research, Alistair had no clue where to look. They didn't know the name of the society, as there was a different name in each book that mentioned it, and they didn't know in which part of campus it could be based.

Nashel thought about checking for Expressions. Surely, if there was such a place, it would be protected from unwanted eyes, but she couldn't practise magic outside of her room and think she would not get caught.

"There must be a sign, like a secret code," Alistair mused when they set off.

"We should start from the university side of campus," she ignored him, her turn to be engrossed in the mission.

"Yes, good suggestion," he nodded, and they started to walk that way.

"But yes," she went back to his statement. "There should be a secret sign. Nobody is allowed to practise magic outside the classroom, not even the university students. There needs to be something non-magical."

"But what if it's something teachers make appear only when the society meets?"

"What do you mean?" she asked, while she scanned her surroundings, hoping to find something out of place.

"Teachers are part of the societies too, and they can practise magic," he explained.

"Not that freely. They still need to follow the law, and I'm sure that making a sign appear to invite members to a meeting is not a 'purposeful use of magic'," she quoted what they learnt in class.

"Fair enough," Alistair laughed.

Their first two days were unsuccessful. There was no sign, no magic arrow that pointed to the society, no tattoo, pin, or badge that exposed its members.

"Maybe we should take a break," Alistair suggested the second night, as they retired to Nashel's room to chill, just like they did most days.

"Do you mean give up?"

"No!" he replied fervently. "But my mum always says that sometimes getting some distance before going back to a problem with fresh eyes helps."

She paused on that. Alistair's approach was new to her. She was not used to letting go; she was used to persevering until the task was done, no matter the cost. However, she had to admit that what they were doing was not working.

She sighed. "What did you have in mind?"

"We could get away from this place for a while."

"You want to explore the city, as you said before I dragged you into this?"

He smiled and shook his head. "No, I did enough exploring for now. I was thinking of going camping. There is a nature reserve not too far, and it'll be a nice change from the city environment."

She considered his words. She missed the nature that surrounded the Citadel, and the Sunrise Academy felt suffocating.

"Okay, let's go camping... If I'm invited, that is," she teased him.

"Of course you are!"

They spent the rest of the evening looking up all the information they needed for their trip: how to reach the reserve, where to purchase the needed equipment, what the weather was like at that time of the year, and what the best trails were.

The following morning, they had a solid plan, and they left the dorm just at the break of dawn. They mutually decided to leave their PPads behind, to be completely disconnected from the academy, even though it was against the rules.

They took a bus that stopped as close to their destination as possible, which was still a few miles away. Next to the stop, there was a small camping shop, which sold them a tent but, unfortunately, had run out of sleeping bags, but the owner assured them the weather was good enough for them to sleep without them. Nashel thought he just wanted them to buy something, as there were no other customers and they were the only two that got off at that stop.

The hike to the actual reserve was easy. They just followed the road for a few miles until they saw a sign indicating it. The terrain was good, and they set a good pace, as they were both quite fit thanks to their morning runs. When they entered the reserve, they slowed down. Not because it was too difficult, but because they were amazed by their surroundings.

Nashel felt it immediately, the difference between inside and out, the difference in the air, in the smells. It was not just nature, it was power. The onslaught was almost overwhelming, completely different from the barren rivulet that trickled everywhere else. It felt like home.

Everything felt better there. The trees were so healthy and green they were almost blinding,a good blinding compared to Solned. The bird's chirping seemed like a wonderful melody. Nashel hadn't noticed until then that birds were few and far between in the city, and they mostly cawed and screeched.

"Have you ever seen anything like this?" Alistair whispered, full of wonder.

"No," Nashel replied. They were both whispering, as if they didn't want to disturb the forest. Her answer wasn't a complete lie; the forest was different, or maybe she had just got used to the dryness of the Sunrise.

Nashel already knew it was going to be difficult to leave the place and go back to the city. It wasn't a conscious decision, or one they talked about, but they just followed their instincts and left the trail to venture into the deepest, untouched part of the forest. They proceeded slowly, stopping to observe everything: every different tree, different shrubs, different insects. They stopped dead in their tracks, holding their breath because an animal was close to them, and they didn't want to spook it, so they waited until it cantered away on its own. While Nashel was used to nature, she had never had the freedom to explore like that, and there was something captivating about the forest and its inhabitants.

They had been walking for a while when Alistair did something that left Nashel horrified and exhilarated at the same time: he made a flower bloom. It was a small thing to do skill-wise, but it was a huge thing to do in the Sunrise. She realised he didn't even do it on purpose; he just brushed his hand against it, and the flower bloomed. He didn't realise what he had done because he didn't turn around, and his body language didn't change.

Of course, Nashel had broken the rules herself, more than once, always being careful not to leave any Trace behind and not doing it in front of anyone, Lamina being an exception. But Alistair, wow, Alistair had just done something in front of her, and he did it so naturally, so freely, that it left her stunned. She was so surprised that it took her a moment to even realise he made the flower bloom without a wand. Suddenly, she felt a cold sweat. It was his idea to go to this forest. Was he trying to get her away from prying eyes to attack her? Was he really who he said he was? Yet, he kept walking, pointing at something that caught his attention, turning around to show her, grinning in awe. If he had nefarious intents, he was excellent at masking it.

"Wow!" he exclaimed in a whisper, snapping Nashel out of her thoughts. She moved to his side to see what was so interesting and saw the canopy open up to a small waterfall and a slow stream. The water was so clear they could see the bottom without any distortion. They saw fish swimming, and on the other side, a deer was drinking. It didn't move when it saw them, just looked at them for a moment, then continued what it was doing and left only when its thirst was quenched.

"Should we stop here for a while?" Alistair asked her.

Nashel nodded and took off her backpack. She didn't need to rest, and neither did Alistair, but they weren't racing, so it was nice to stop and take everything in. She also wanted to find out if he was going to address the flower, or if he finally showed his true colours. They took their shoes off and sat with their feet in the water. It was cold but pleasant. They stayed in comfortable silence for a while, eating a snack. Nashel didn't want to bring anything up, letting him make the first move, but also, she didn't want to break the peace of the forest. It would be in poor taste if she had to fight Alistair in such a beautiful place.

After a while, he started to fidget, wriggling his hands and kicking his feet underwater. She turned to look at him, but still didn't say anything.

"Can I show you something?" he finally said, his tone full of anxiety.

"Sure..."

"It is something weird," he said, still not looking at her.

"That's alright," she tried to reassure him, not sure herself what he had in mind.

"It is also something illegal..." he whispered, as if he didn't want to say it.

"What happens in the forest stays in the forest," she attempted to joke, but he seemed too nervous to smile. "I promise I won't turn you in," she added sincerely.

He took a deep breath and an even bigger sigh. "Look there," he pointed in front of them.

At the bottom of the stream, in the direction he was pointing, there was a red stone. She understood he meant that because it was the only one of that colour.

"Okay," she prompted him.

He nodded, more to himself than her, then he visibly focused on it. A moment later, the stone shot out of the water and stopped, floating in mid-air.

Nashel made herself gasp, the appropriate reaction a Sunrise person would have.

"I know!" Alistair exclaimed excitedly. "It's crazy, right? They always say we need wands, but I've always been able to use magic without it."

He was speaking really fast, rushing through words, his accent becoming more audible. "Not for everything, mind you, but I've always been good with telekinesis."

He finally looked at her, his focus breaking, the stone plopping back in its place. Fear coloured Alistair's face, and Nashel wondered why she thought he could ever be a threat to her.

"Please, say something," he begged.

"You made a flower bloom back on the path." She gestured with her head in the direction they arrived from, but she also smiled.

Alistair's eyes bulged out in surprise that they made her laugh. "I – What?"

"It was quite shocking," she conceded.

"I made a flower bloom?"

"Was it the first time?"

"No, but I didn't notice!"

Nashel shrugged. "It's okay. I'm still not going to turn you in."

"You should've said something!"

"I was shocked!" she remarked.

They both laughed for a few moments before Alistair whispered, "So, I didn't freak you out?"

"No," she reassured him, "you didn't."

He sighed in relief.

Nashel decided to take a risk then. If he could do magic without a wand, he was more powerful than what she gave him credit for. Of course, what he just showed her was a big secret for him, and she could use that information in the future, if she needed it, but she also wanted to reward him, in a way, so that he wouldn't feel awkward or on edge around her.

While he turned to look back at the stream, now more relaxed and not fidgeting, she made a sliver of water flow upward and away from the stream, then made it into a ring, a swirl, a tiny wave.

Alistair gasped, shocked and surprised, his mouth forming a perfect 'O' that made Nashel laugh.

"Wow," he whispered, then change to a normal volume. "You can do it, too?"

"I never had a wand before coming to the academy," she explained, gently guiding the water back into the stream.

"What else can you do?"

A lot more, she thought. How much could she reveal without raising suspicion? How much was Alistair willing to accept without being freaked out and turning her in?

"I'm good with the elements," she replied in a false-modest tone.

"Show me!" he asked excitedly.

Against her better judgement, she decided to indulge him. She snapped her fingers, and first a spark then a flame appeared at the top of her thumb as if it was a lighter. Alistair giggled delighted. She closed her thumb in her fist and extinguished the fire. Then she made the earth rumble under him, and only under him. Again, he laughed after the initial small shock. She made a tiny whirlwind on the palm of her hand, then asked him to open his and transferred it there. He looked at it in amazement, afraid to move.

"Can you mix them up?" he asked her.

"What do you mean?"

"Can you make the water warm, or even boil?"

"I guess. I never thought of it as mixing them, though."

"Can you make fire cold?"

"I don't think so," she was caught by surprise. She had made water warmer, especially when they needed to spend hours in it for training, but she had never thought about making fire cold. Warm water exists in nature, cold fire doesn't.

"Want to try?" he asked with a spark in his eyes.

"It feels unnatural," she answered, shaking her head.

He sighed but nodded. "It'd be cool, though."

"Cold. You asked for cold, not cool," she joked, and he laughed. "What else can you do?" she continued after a few moments.

"Matter manipulation," he told her. "I can, like, reshape things around me, or move them. I am much better at telekinesis than the other stuff."

"Show me?"

He took one of the small pebbles that littered the shore, held it in mid-air, and moved it away towards the other side of the stream. Nashel briefly wondered why before he shattered it into millions of pieces, shards flying everywhere, but fortunately, he held the pebble far enough that it didn't hit them. He then concentrated more and recalled all the pieces together to make the pebble whole again. However, the result didn't look like the original.

"See, I'm just better if I limit myself to moving things."

"The explosion was fine," she joked again.

If he had been born in the Sunset, he would've been a fine soldier. For a moment, she was thankful that the Sunrise had such a rudimentary and limited grasp on powers, so she wouldn't have to face Alistair in combat and kill him.

They got up and walked downstream, using their powers

every now and then, making each other laugh. Her powers came so instinctively to Nashel that she felt almost giddy. There was so much in the forest that it was almost difficult to control her Expressions. After weeks of dryness, of having to use all her energy to focus on each task, it was so refreshing to use powers without even thinking.

When dusk fell, they found a small clearing with low, even grass that looked more at home in a rear garden than the middle of wild woods, but it seemed perfect to set up their tent and settle for the night.

As they were working, an animal, the size of a fox, but as large as three, came out from behind a shrub. It had the fur and tail of a squirrel, but long, bloody fangs and a mouth full of teeth as it hissed cruelly at them. Alistair and Nashel stood frozen, looking at the creature, neither wanted to move, nor back away, or move closer.

The tension broke when Nashel hissed back. It wasn't a conscious decision, and it was a silly thing to do, she could have used her powers instead, or anything else. Surprisingly, it worked: the rodent skittered away, and Alistair burst into laughter, holding his sides as he doubled over. She couldn't help but join him, especially after he mocked her hiss.

"Shame you scared it away," he said after they both had collected themselves. "We could've had it for dinner!"

That prompted another bout of laughs from both of them.

Nashel started a fire. It was ablaze in the blink of an eye, and she giggled, earning a confused look from Alistair. She couldn't blame him. She had never made that sound in front of him.

They looked around to find something edible; they had packed some food ready to eat or to cook, but wanted to try what the forest had to offer. They found a type of berries neither had ever seen before, and they were wary of them, but then saw an actual squirrel and a deer eating them not too far away, so they chanced it. The berries were delicious. They stuffed their mouths with them, eating as quickly as ravenous, starving children, then Alistair got up to pick more because they just weren't enough. At that point, it was more gluttony than hunger, as the berries were extraordinarily filling, but they were also too good to stop.

When they were full, they laid down close to the fire, heads almost brushing, and looked up at the patch of sky over the clearing, now filled with stars.

"I missed the stars," Alistair murmured. "I used to look at them every night."

Nashel never paid much attention to them, except to help find her bearing, but she supposed that a person living on a farm would, with the sky undisturbed by city lights.

"I didn't," she murmured.

"I'll show you," Alistair whispered back, and she nodded, forgetting for a moment that he wasn't looking at her.

They spent sometimes lost in the stars, Alistair pointing at constellations, trying to explain shapes and location, Nashel trying hard not to laugh because she was hopeless at following his directions.

"That's the Guardian," he said at one point, explaining a group of stars that supposedly looked like a person with a spear, at ease but ready to protect its people. "That's how I got my name."

"What do you mean?"

"Alistair means protector of people," he said, and Nashel knew him well enough by now to know, without looking, that he was blushing. "I know it's silly. I'm no guardian, but I liked the idea when I was little."

"I get it," she reassured him.

"I pretended to be a mighty warrior, and our animals were my people, and I would protect them from all evil."

"Did you?" she asked with a smile. "Protected them?"

"Of course!" Alistair puffed his chest in mock pride. "No animal was harmed under my watch! Except mosquitoes. They were the enemy."

They both laughed at that.

"That's the Lovers," Alistair said abruptly after a moment of silence. He pointed at another constellation, representing two people holding hands. "It's us," he said under his breath, but with the silence all around them, Nashel heard him anyway, and she stiffened.

S-Sorry," he exclaimed, his voice suddenly louder as he turned towards her, his eyes wide in shock. "I—I don't mean it like that, let me explain."

She nodded.

"To me, lovers don't only mean people who are in a relationship," he started, after taking a deep breath. "It also means friends who deeply care about each other."

Nashel didn't react, not sure what was the appropriate way. Alistair didn't seem to notice.

"Before I met you, I had no friends, you know that," he continued. "And I was sure I could do without."

She nodded again. "I know what you mean."

"But you showed me I can't, and I don't want to," he said firmly. "I really care about you, and I don't want to scare you off, but I also wanted to tell you for a while."

"I don't scare easily," she smiled and found that she was relieved she didn't have to resort to unpleasant solutions.

"I know," he smiled. "Was that okay to tell you?"

She thought about it for a moment. She thought about her life at the Academy, how she had lots of classmates, but no one she could really call a friend, no one to rely on and share worries with. No one she really missed, or who missed her. Maybe Ash...

She hadn't thought about him in a while. Alistair reminded her of him, but they were also different people. Ash was a means to an end. Funny, flirty, but still, she didn't feel too attached to him, nor did she miss him that much.

Alistair, though, was different. They clicked. Maybe because they found themselves in the same boat, maybe because they were both out of place at the Academy, for different reasons, but she thought about the nights spent in the library together, studying and complaining about teachers and homework, how Mr Cobbler was a pain in the ass and why they had to have him first thing every morning.

She realised what, deep down, she knew all along: that without Alistair, she would've failed on her very first day.

"It was," she finally replied to him. "I think you saved me. I couldn't have done any of this without you."

She wasn't sure what prompted her to say that, she wasn't one to share emotions or admit weaknesses, but it was too late to take the words back, unless she used her powers to erase his memory, and for some reason, she didn't want to.

"Thanks." Alistair's voice was choked by emotion.

"I'm sorry I stiffened," Nashel murmured. "You took me by surprise. I've never had a relationship and, I don't know, you saying we were lovers sort of scared me."

She lied about never having had a relationship, but she felt it was the easiest way to excuse her behaviour.

"I never had a relationship either, and it was pretty scary to tell you that."

Nashel found and squeezed his hand. He squeezed it back with a sigh of relief. She blamed the power overload for her unusual behaviour.

They were quiet for a long time, but they didn't let go of the hands. It was a pleasant night, uncharacteristically warm for the season, so Nashel kept the fire low, more for company and light than for warmth. They dozed off, not bothering to go into their tent, just content with their closeness and the fire. It was probably past midnight, or even one in the morning, when they heard a noise, difficult to describe. It sounded like the deep breath of a huge creature, or like the trees rustled their leaves all at the same time. They both stood up, startled, ready to fight another rodent or something worse. It was like daylight had broken: all the flowers, all the fruit, all the leaves started to glow. It was a rainbow of colours, all the richest greens, the brightest yellows, the deepest reds, and browns. Even the grass of the clearing was glowing. Nocturnal insects swarmed around them, resting on them, enveloping them with their colours. Neither of them swatted them away; they weren't threatening, they weren't biting, or stinging.

The beauty of it all took their breath; if they thought they had seen everything the place could offer during their hike, they were deadly wrong. This was much, much better.

Nashel felt a warmth blooming in her chest that had nothing to do with her. It started to pulsate and grow, pulsate and grow. It was power, she realised. Her power, Alistair's power, the insects', the trees', the forest's power. They were sharing in a symbiotic way she had never experienced before. It was reinvigorating. She felt she could do the impossible with just the vaguest thought.

The warmth grew into light that engulfed everything around them, so blinding that she had to close her eyes. It was a blessing. And in a moment, it was gone. Darkness came back, the forest rested with a noise that seemed almost a sigh.

She looked at Alistair, who looked at her, twin expression on his face. They didn't speak, but cherished the feeling that still lingered.

CHAPTER FIFTEEN

The Treasure Hunt

They woke up when the sun was rising. They found themselves next to the now extinguished fire, hugging each other in their sleep, Alistair behind Nashel, his hands around her waist. She tried not to swat him away, ready for the unpleasant, suffocating feeling, but she didn't experience that.

The forest was not glowing anymore, there was no trace of any of the night's events. They both thought they must've fallen asleep and dreamt all of it.

"Was it a dream?" Alistair murmured.

Nashel shrugged. "A dream we both had?" she asked sceptically.

He shook his head and shrugged too. He didn't have any more answers than she did.

They packed away the unused tent, made sure the fire was truly out, and that they didn't leave anything behind. They stayed in the clearing for a few minutes, just looking around, pondering what they had witnessed and its significance. Already feeling nostalgia invading them.

"I don't want to leave," Nashel voiced their feelings. Her prediction was true; it was going to be difficult. The place was so peaceful and so full of power that the prospect of going back to the dryness of Soloed was unsettling.

"I know, me neither," he hugged her. Nashel froze for an instant, but then relaxed. It didn't feel forced or constricting, so she allowed it.

"We could stay one more day," she mused, already knowing it was just that. She had a mission to complete.

Alistair smiled and nodded, but then they started their hike back, not rushing. They didn't take the same route either but went the opposite way, wanting to explore more of the forest, commit everything to memory. They also talked little, their feelings so in tune that they didn't need words to know when the other wanted to stop, rest, and admire a particular area. They tried not to think about the fact that every step they took took them closer to leaving.

They could almost see the end of the forest when Nashel grabbed Alistair's wrist to stop him, a thought she had to voice crossing her mind.

"So, Alistair is not your true name, right?"

"Why, did you think it was?" he was confused.

"No, I don't think so."

"Why are you asking, then?" he smiled.

"I'm not sure," she mumbled honestly, wondering why she felt the need to ask.

"My mum has magic, too," he revealed. "So, we know about names and their power."

Nashel was surprised to hear that. "It must be nice to share that with your mum!"

"It was nice," he replied sheepishly.

Nashel tried to imagine what it would be like to have a family that understood her powers, that didn't fear her. But then again, Alistair was a Sunrise, albeit a powerful one, but his powers were nothing compared to Nashel's. Maybe having someone like her in a family would create more conflict than anything else. Maybe it was inevitable for her parents to fear her, even if they had powers as well. She had seen it at the Sunset Academy. Powerful cadets going head to head because the tension was too much, clashing and causing injuries or worse. And that was within the rigorous discipline the academy expected.

They stopped at edge of the tree line, as if it were the border of a different realm. Side to side, their hands finding each other's and holding tight for comfort. They looked at each other, took a deep breath, and stepped out. Somehow, it felt like a very hard step to take. It was silly in Nashel's opinion; it was just a forest and just a road. She was getting softer.

They tried not to turn around, but they both failed. They looked longingly at the forest for a few minutes, then they heard it again, the breath of the woods, wishing them farewell. Like two idiots, they waved back, then laughed at their silliness.

Nashel felt exhausted when they arrived back at the academy. She wondered why until she realised that the reduction of power around her was the culprit. Her room felt stiff, suffocating, as if the walls were closing in, and she struggled to fall asleep despite the tiredness. She twisted and turned, the mattress springs digging into her back like never before, the sheets so loud and rough on her skin she couldn't stand them. She gave up and stood, deciding to go for a walk in the fresh air.

It was cold, and she had to stop herself from using her powers to warm herself up. She had also left her wand in her room, and shook her head at her own distraction. It would cost her soon if she didn't get her head straight and back in the game.

"Hey!" Somebody called from behind.

She stopped thinking it was a teacher or security, questioning why she was out of bed, but it was Alistair, jogging to catch up to her.

"Hey yourself," she replied.

"Couldn't sleep?"

She just shrugged. She had an inkling that he felt the same in his room, and there was no need for further explanations.

"Yeah, me neither," he shrugged back with a small smile. "Want to go on the treasure hunt?"

Right. The search for secret societies. She had forgotten about that.

"Why not," she sighed. "I will not get any sleep, anyway."

"You're cold," he observed as they started walking.

"Yeah," she admitted.

"Why don't you warm yourself up?" he whispered.

"I forgot the wand in my room. And we can't use magic anyway," she whispered back in an allusive tone.

He opened his mouth, then closed it. "I forgot about that."

They laughed quietly.

"You can use mine if you want," he offered.

"Al, we can't do magic out of the classroom," she reiterated.

"Okay, I'll wave my wand so that if anyone sees it, I'm the one getting in trouble," he replied conspiratorially. "You warm yourself up."

She looked at him for a moment, the old suspicions stirring back, then she remembered him in the forest and knew he was genuine. She nodded.

They stood by a building in the shadow cone between two streetlights. He waved his wand comically, and she used her fire powers to warm herself up. It made her even more tired than before. She hated that place with all of herself.

They started looking around for clues again without much luck and were about to give up when Nashel thought she saw a flash of gold in the corner of her eye. She stopped Alistair by placing a hand on his forearm, her military training kicking in and telling her not to make a noise. She put a finger on her lips to tell him to do the same, then pointed towards the direction she saw the flash. It flashed again, and this time, Alistair saw it too, because he gasped.

They slowly made their way towards the building, making sure nobody else was around. The flash was coming from the slit window of the basement. They squatted to look inside, but they couldn't see anything, as the windows were blocked out or too dirty. Nashel was pondering the idea of going inside when the door of the building opened and a figure exited. They couldn't recognise it in the darkness, and they waited to see if there were more flashes, or if someone else was coming out.

After twenty minutes of nothingness, Nashel decided it was safe enough to go inside and find out if the flashes were in any way related to a secret society.

The door wasn't locked, so they didn't have trouble getting in, and finding the stairs to the basement wasn't difficult; they weren't hidden or forbidden to students. They stopped in front of a door that Nashel thought corresponded to the windows they had seen from outside. It was a normal door, just like the others on the school campus.

Alistair extended his hand to try the handle, but Nashel stopped him. How could he be so careless? She had to remind herself he wasn't trained like her and to be patient with him.

He looked at her questioning and she told him the door could be enchanted. There was no security camera or Expression, she had noted as they descended into the basement, which was curious in a place where magic was banned most of the time, so she wasn't worried about being caught while she checked the door for wards. There was a very weak one that thankfully didn't take much to undo. Then she opened the door and gestured for a puzzled Alistair to get inside, followed him and created a small sphere of light, just enough to see the outline of everything.

They found themselves in a room that looked like a posh classroom, with rows of comfy chairs all facing a raised stage and behind it, a long banner with a drawing depicting a broken sun and the magical symbols for attack and protection crossed in front of it. The word Alwenach in golden calligraphy on top. Nashel knew, without a doubt, that they not only had found a secret society's lair, but the one they were looking for, the one whose aim was to fight the Sunset.

They both stood just a step from the door, taking in the scene.

"Do you know what it means?" Alistair murmured, gesturing with his chin towards the banner.

Nashel shook her head. If she had to guess, it wasn't in Solnedian, or if it was, it was one of those that didn't exist in her language. "Do you?"

"I think I recognise the language, but I don't know what it means."

"Let's have a look around," she shrugged.

"But—"

"Scared?" she teased him with a grin.

"No, but I don't know. I thought we just wanted to find it."

"And leave without snooping around a bit?"

Obviously, she wanted to find out more about the secret society, find out if there was anything about the attack. But if Alistair didn't want to stay, she would return the next night.

"Okay, but I don't like it. This place gives me the heebie-jeebies." He rubbed his hands up and down his arms.

"The what?"

"The heebie-jeebies," he repeated, turning to look at her confused face.

"I don't know what that means," she shrugged.

"It's the heebie-jeebies!"

"No matter how many times you repeat it, I still don't know what it is," she smiled.

"It's like when something is a bit creepy," he tried to explain.

"OH! The willies!" She exclaimed, understanding colouring her expression.

"The willies?"

"That's what we call it in my village," she said, nodding.

"Well, either way, this place is doing that to me, so let's make it quick."

Nashel went straight to the lectern on one side of the stage. There were a few sheets of paper there, but nothing important. Alistair was looking around the chairs, and they both converged on the bookshelf at the other end of the room. It was sparsely populated, and it didn't seem to be used much based on the dust that covered its shelves. Nashel looked at the titles, but they were just similar to those she had used in class.

"The True History of the Sunrise," Alistair read with a pompous tone that made Nashel smile. "What would that be, I wonder."

They laughed and moved on. That title could be interesting, but it wouldn't say anything about an attack.

"This doesn't have a title," Alistair whispered, pointing, but not touching what looked like a bundle of papers bound in leather.

Nashel took it, not worrying too much about remembering its exact position, as the dust would do that for her. She undid the leather lace that kept it together and opened it to read the first page. She almost slammed it closed; it was written in a different language. If she were back home, she could use a simple Expression to copy the book, then another to translate it, so that she could take it with her in her room. But in that Sunforsaken place, she had to use a wand, and she wasn't allowed to use magic, and the power supply was limited. Even something so simple would require a lot of energy. She would have to find a different way. She put the tome back, and they looked at the last few books.

"This could be interesting. Maybe we should check if there's a copy in the library," Alistair murmured. "The Never-ending War."

She was going to dismiss it. It sounded like a cheap novel, but then she remembered where she was and opened it.

"They don't tell you the truth," she started, reading the first page. "The war is not over. The Void is not real," she harrumphed. "The Sunset bastards are invading our nation, right under our noses, and our government is doing nothing. The Alwenach should rise again. Bear arms, my fellow warriors. Be ready."

"What a load of—"

A noise stopped Alistair from continuing. He froze and paled. Nashel quickly scanned the room, gauging potential hiding spots. The noise happened again, louder, closer. They killed the light - Alistair had his wand tip lit up - and waited. There was nowhere to hide, and Nashel was considering using her powers to make Alistair and herself invisible, even though it would cost her greatly, when they heard the noise again, and she realised it was coming from the outside.

She pointed to the blacked-out windows, and a shadow passed across them. Then she pointed to the door, indicating that they should leave while they still could. Alistair nodded, and she hoped he could be quiet and not bump into anything in the dark.

They managed to get to the door and lock it when Alistair mouthed, “The ward!”

“Shit,” she mouthed back. “Get by the bottom of the stairs and tell me if you hear steps coming closer.”

He wanted to protest; she could see it, but didn’t and followed her orders. Erecting the ward was more difficult than undoing it, especially because she didn’t want to leave her Trace, and she wanted it to be exactly as before.

Alistair came back with urgency, just as she finished and swayed for the effort. He looked at her questioning, but held her to steady herself. She shook her head, and they moved to a classroom two doors down, opposite the Alwenach headquarters, one that didn’t have a ward on it, nor any secret society’s manifestos. They left the door ajar only a fraction and peered outside to the figure moving closer. There was no light, and the crack they left open was just enough for one eye to see, so they couldn’t see who it was, but they waved their wand at the door, the ward Nashel had so carefully crafted opened and let the person in.

“Now,” she whispered and sprinted for the stairs, Alistair two steps behind.

They stopped only when they reached her room. She plopped face first on her bed, exhausted, and he sat on her chair, laughing, exhilarated.

"Wow!" he breathed. "Just wow!"

She made a non-committal sound, muffled by the covers.

"Are you okay?"

"Yes, catching my breath."

Her body might've been tired, but her mind was racing. The last book, The Never-ending War, called for the Alwenach to rise again. Meaning it had risen before, so it was not an invention of a secret society. Or maybe it was, but it was also a secret army made by the elite students of the Sunrise University. Then there was the handwritten bundle she couldn't understand; it was, for sure, containing important information.

"People really believe all that stuff, don't they?" he asked after a minute, his done stunned disbelief.

"I guess," she shrugged and sat up. "It depends on how many people follow them."

"Do you think it's possible?"

"What?" she asked, confused.

"They can cross the Void?"

She wasn't sure who he meant by 'they', but deflected anyway.

"Haven't you heard? The Void doesn't exist!"

He laughed, but she could still see the worry in his eyes.

"I've seen it, you know?" he said. "I know it's there."

"Me, too," she admitted. He looked at her, surprised.

"My village is not too far from it," she lied.

"So, do you think it's possible?" he asked again.

"Are you afraid that, and I quote, 'Sunset bastards' are invading us?"

He shook his head, not humouring her this time. She wondered why it was so important to him.

"I don't know," she answered. "I think it would require a lot of magic to do so, and I don't know how many have that. And even if they do, can they then carry others?"

"Fair enough," he nodded and seemed a bit more relaxed.

"I think this Alwenach society is a bit like the genin: unhappy and bigoted. They are probably also not that good and just talk and never act."

She wasn't sure that was the case, but she still didn't believe some student could plan a large-scale attack. She needed to go back and find out more. She needed to be able to spend time with the books, or take them with her. She needed to join the Alwenach.

The thought came so clearly that she wondered why she had never had it before. She knew they didn't accept students her age, but she would find a way.

"Do you think you can sleep now?" Alistair said with a huge yawn.

She laughed. "I don't know, but I'm willing to try."

"Me too," he said sleepily.

He didn't move, though, just closed his eyes while sitting in her chair.

"Al, my chair is not that comfy; you should go to bed."

"Nuh-no," he drawled, "I'm good here..."

She rolled her eyes, "C'mon, come here. The bed is small, but at least you can stretch out."

He made a noise, but again, didn't move. She got up, grabbed his arm, and dragged him to bed. He followed without protest.

The bed was indeed small, and Nashel wasn't too comfortable being so close to another person, but Alistair fell asleep almost immediately, and after a while, his regular breathing lulled her to sleep, too.

CHAPTER SIXTEEN

Calistelle

Joining the Alwenach proved to be more difficult than initially thought. Mostly, it was because as soon as lessons started, they were drowned with test after test. They were all written exams, even PoM, and they were all packed with abstruse words the teacher may have mentioned once in passing, and that definitely didn't exist in Nashel's language.

For the following three weeks, she and Alistair lived between the classroom and the library, which was open all night for the occasion, seeing their rooms only during the weekend, when they didn't have any assessments. They moved like zombies, half asleep all the time, not even speaking, if not for mumbling some theory or some answers to imaginary questions they hoped came up in the tests. They talked in their sleep. They knew because, more often than not, they were sleeping together in the library, over a stack of books.

When the three weeks of assessments ended, they had the briefest sigh of relief before the teachers started drilling in them the fear for the results. Nashel wasn't one to scare easily. She was trained to handle stress, and school tests were nothing compared to what she was used to at the

Sunset Academy. Yet, she was worried. Mr Cobbler didn't miss any occasion to tell her and Alistair that if they failed the tests, they would be expelled as part of their probation conditions. Nashel wasn't sure she had passed. The tests were not difficult, and at the same time, they were. The vocabulary was a language barrier, but her biggest obstacle was her own knowledge, as often it contradicted what they thought in the Sunrise, irritating and confusing her. She didn't want to fail, not the test, nor the mission just because these people had an alternative version of history.

The day the results came in, a Sunday, Nashel was up at dawn, as usual. She went for her run as usual, but all the while she was refreshing her PPad to see if she received them, despite knowing they wouldn't be sent until the late afternoon.

Alistair was doing the same; he also paced back and forth in Nashel's room so much that she was worried he would wear a hole in the carpet.

Their PPads pinged at the same time, and they took a sharp breath in sync.

The silence that followed was tense as they opened the message and scrolled through the results. Nashel did it slowly, dreading any failure that would mean the end for her, Alistair did it quickly, then again and again.

After a minute, they looked up at each other, both expressions unreadable.

"I passed everything," Nashel told him with relief.

"Same. Solnedian just barely," he plopped down on the bed next to her, all his fidgety energy now gone.

"A pass is a pass," she said wisely, even though she didn't believe that. A part of her was telling her she was a failure for not acing all the tests. She tried to shut it down, but she was too tired to do it properly.

Alistair nodded and told her he was going to call his mum. He always stepped out to do so, she didn't understand why, and her paranoia told her it was because he was hiding something. However, she never questioned him.

Her results gave her an idea of how to get closer to the Alwenach and find out more. She approached Wynmere, who was the nicer one, after the first lesson following the results.

"Ma'am," she stopped at the end of the following lesson. "I was wondering if it were possible for a university student to tutor me. The recent results showed me I have a lot to do still, and I want to be ready."

Wynmere looked at her, pleasantly surprised. "Why, that is very thoughtful of you! Yes, it is possible; we have done so before. Let me get back to you, okay? I'll see what I can do."

"I appreciate it, thank you."

That alone wouldn't be enough. There were many students, and only a few selected ones were part of the Alwenach. Nashel had thought this through, and she had rested and recharged so that she wouldn't make mistakes.

"It'll be better if the student were a member of the secret society called Alwenach," she suggested, her voice becoming the Expression of her powers.

Suggestion and mind control were different. She had slightly more practice with the former, and she was optimistic.

"You will also forget I asked this," she added, which was the hard part.

"Why, sure," the teacher replied slowly, as if in a trance. Then she snapped out of it, smiled, and left.

Nashel hoped she had done everything right and that she wouldn't wake up the following day to the news of the teacher's untimely death. She was glad when it didn't happen, and the teacher was teaching as normal the following day. She didn't update Nashel until later the following week, when she beckoned her at the end of the lesson.

"Good news! I found you a student!"

"Thank you, ma'am," Nashel replied, plastering a grateful smile on her face.

"Her name is Calistelle," the teacher told her. "She is a first year, but one of the most brilliant students we have!

Here are her contact details. She expects your message."

Wynmere sent her said details to her PPad. Nashel looked at it, then nodded and thanked the teacher again. Hopefully, her other request was also granted.

She typed her message on her way back to her room.

"Hey, I'm Nashel. Wynmere said you are willing to help me. Let me know when you're available."

She had to wait until the evening for a reply, and what she got seemed written in a different language.

"Sick! Bet, I got u. HMU when ur sched's chill. XO"

She looked at the text and wondered if this Calistelle person had some learning difficulties, despite the teacher saying she was one of the most brilliant.

"Al, can you have a look at this? I think there is something wrong with my PPad," she asked her friend, passing him the tablet.

Alistair looked at the text and burst out laughing.

"There's nothing wrong," he wheezed. "It's just how some people text!"

"What does it mean, then? And why can't she text like a normal person?"

"It just means to let her know when you are free."

"Why is she sick, then?" Nashel was even more confused.

Alistair laughed again. "She is not sick. It just means 'cool'."

"Then say cool!"

Calistelle was already getting on her nerves.

"What does the rest mean?" she continued.

"'Bet, I got u' means 'alright, she told me'," Alistair explained. "'HMU' means 'hit me up' or 'text me'; 'sched' is your 'schedule' and 'chill' in this case means 'open' or 'free'."

Nashel was shaking her head at every word that came out of her friend's mouth.

"And is too difficult to just write 'okay, let me know when you're free'?!"

Alistair didn't reply, but laughed until his sides hurt.

Nashel met Calistelle two days later, outside of the

Alwenach's HQ building, of all places. She was as tall as Nashel, athletic build that would've fit right in the Sunset Academy, blond hair, blue eyes, and a fake smile on her lips.

"Nice to meet you," Nashel held out her hand.

"Nice to meet you, too," Calistelle replied, and Nashel almost expected her to speak like she texted.

She didn't have an accent, Nashel noticed, and her Solnedian would make Mr Cobbler blush.

"So, Wynmere tells me you'd like tutoring. Which subjects did you have in mind?"

Nashel noticed she had slowed down her speech, pronouncing every word carefully, as if Nashel were a child, or stupid.

"All of them."

Calistelle laughed. It was the opposite of Alistair's and Ash's laughs. If the latter were contagious and genuine, the former was irking and fake. Nashel reminded herself that Calistelle was a means to an end, and she was tougher than the annoyance the girl would create.

"Okay, we can work out a plan!"

And so they did. They met most afternoons after lessons. Calistelle's schedule was freer than Nashel's, so she was always waiting for her outside the building.

The more time she spent with Calistelle, the less she liked her. She was patronising, always looking down on others, always treating Nashel as if she were a lesser being. During their sessions, she always used a voice Nashel associated with idiot people talking to small children. She hated it. Yet, she knew she had to develop a deeper relationship with her, if she wanted to find out more about the Alwenach.

She didn't know how, though. They had nothing in common, and Nashel didn't understand half of Calistelle's hobbies, which seemed to be gossip and fashion. Tactics to ingratiate yourself to someone were taught in the last year of Aspirants, the one Nashel was supposed to start next and would probably never do, so she had to improvise.

Something that worked before was flirting. Ash wanted

her, though, and she wasn't sure Calistelle did the same. She could try, make it happen somehow, and change tactics if she needed to. It seemed her best option.

"Al, how do you flirt with a girl?" she asked him one night while they were in her room studying.

Alistair stopped reading to look at her. She didn't expect him to know; he had said he had never had a relationship before, so he was probably inexperienced.

"I think you need to learn what she likes and show interest in that," he shrugged.

Nashel groaned, "Half the time she is a cipher I can't crack! I don't understand what she says. I don't know anything about fashion, and I don't like gossip!"

"What else is there?"

"Nothing, she is not that deep!"

"Why do you want to flirt with her, then?" he asked, confused.

Nashel stopped for a moment. She was getting carried away and being careless. She decided to take another risk even though she did that too much when Alistair was concerned, and tell him part of the truth.

"I believe she's in the Alwenach."

It came out in a whisper, as if she were afraid of Alistair's judgement, which was ridiculous.

"What?!" he almost shouted.

"You heard me," she sighed.

"You can't join. You're too young!"

"I know that! I want to get access to that book!"

"Why?"

She shrugged, not looking at him.

"Why?" he asked again, more demanding.

"I'm curious," she made up. "I want to understand. They don't teach us much about the Sunset. The Alwenach seem to hate them. Why? Is it true that they are invading us? How are they crossing the Void? I have so many questions, Al, so many!"

Alistair looked at her for a moment, with that piercing

stare that he sometimes had, which made her believe he knew about her.

"Maybe you can find answers somewhere else," Alistair suggested.

"Where? The library will not have any books about any of it, and I wouldn't be allowed to have them even if it did!"

"Okay, okay, but I don't like it."

"You don't have to," she shrugged, coming off snappier than she meant. He gave her a look with raised highbrows and she immediately apologised.

"Are you sure you want to do this?" he asked, concerned now. "You can't stand her."

"Eh, sometimes we need to brave the night."

"What does that mean?"

"It's a saying in my language. Nights can be dark and unpleasant, but sometimes there is no other way than to go through them."

"I see..." he wasn't convinced.

"I'll just try; if it doesn't work, I'll let it go, I promise."

"You promise?"

"Yes," she said seriously.

"I'll hold you to that."

She nodded, and he sighed.

They spent the rest of the evening planning her "courtship," as Alistair started to call it, just to annoy her. The following day, he drilled her on his plan and almost pushed her into Calistelle's arms at the end of the lesson, making a comical face that was supposed to be encouraging.

She ignored everything they had discussed, aiming for a direct approach.

"Would you like to go out sometimes?"

Calistelle looked at her, mystified.

"It's okay if you don't," she added, her eyes flickering down, feigning shyness.

Calistelle preened. Nashel knew her well enough by then that she could play on her vanity and sense of superiority. "No, no," she laughed that high-pitched laugh that made her sound like a duck. "You just took me by surprise. I'm flattered."

That didn't answer Nashel's question, but she knew Calistelle was toying with her, enjoying the position of power she perceived she had. Nashel smiled shyly, waiting patiently.

"Well, you are a bit young," she started, twirling a lock of her hair. "I am single at the moment, so why not?"

Nashel didn't know then the hell she dug herself in. In the following weeks, Calistelle proved not only to be vain and superficial but also mean and controlling.

Nashel put up with it, gritting her teeth, but Alistair would burst into a fit of anger whenever she told him how low Calistelle had stooped that time. She would let him vent, mostly because she couldn't do so herself.

For the same first few weeks, she didn't get far in her mission to find anything about the Alwenach. She only became Calistelle's doormat. She also had to endure everything that came with a relationship, and it wasn't as fun as with Ash. She didn't like how possessive Calistelle was. Even in intimacy, her kisses were aggressive. She was constantly in Nashel's space, pushing for more and more. Nashel knew she was pushing her to isolation. She complained about her relationship with Alistair in jealous bouts that almost became physical, but she stopped just in time - not that Nashel would let her. She also started to look down on Nashel even more, berating her on every occasion, mocking her accent, her opinions, her skills.

One night, finally, she snapped at her to leave her as she had to get ready for an important meeting.

"What meeting?" Nashel asked.

They were in Calistelle's room, a single, much bigger and better than Nashel's. They had finished a tutoring session, which had become more of an insulting opportunity for Calistelle than a learning opportunity for Nashel.

"None of your business," Calistelle barked.

Nashel knew how to make her talk, though. "Alright," she

answered with a shrug of indifference.

"Well," Calistelle purred, sweetening her tone. "It's supposed to be hush-hush, you see. I can't really tell you."

Nashel rolled her eyes. "Don't tell me, then."

"Okay, okay, I'll tell," Calistelle conceded, as if she were doing her a big favour. "I am part of a secret society called the Alwenach."

"Oh! I heard of that," Nashel said with fake admiration and envy.

Calistelle laughed. "Do you want to know what it is?"

"Isn't it a secret?" she replied, making her voice sound hopeful.

"If you promise, I'll tell you."

What a joke this girl was. If she was one of those who were going to attack the Sunset, then Nashel's people had nothing to worry about.

"I promise." She made her voice wobble with excitement and gratefulness.

"It's a secret army to fight those Sunset scumbags."

"What?"

"Are you daft?!" Calistelle clicked her tongue, something she did to an annoying level. "The Sunset, you know who they are, right? Other side of the Void?"

"Yes, I know," Nashel tried to contain her rising anger.

"They are the worst! The word is they throw their children in the Void if they don't have magic."

That was bullshit, but she couldn't say that.

"They also send people here to steal our children and to kill our most powerful. That's why the Alwenach is a secret, so they don't know about it!"

"How can they come here if nobody can cross the Void?" Nashel asked.

"Oh, you are daft, then! They have a way, obviously!"

Obviously.

Nashel sighed. "How do you know all this?"

"That, I can't tell you, sorry," she shrugged, but she was also pleased.

"How do you get in?" she tried to ask.

"They recruit you," she said in a tone that implied that Nashel wouldn't be. "They monitor your school records, see if you have what it takes! But they don't recruit until you are older."

"I see," Nashel commented, then went back to pretending she didn't care.

"Don't you want to know anything else?" Calistelle asked, almost outraged.

"You've already said too much; I don't want you to be in trouble," Nashel said, letting Calistelle believe she was worried about her.

"Look at it this way, if they are stealing our most powerful, then you're more than safe!" Calistelle said cheerfully.

"Yeah, thanks," Nashel deadpanned.

"The Sunset are real bastards. I can't wait to kill them all!"

She wanted to laugh in her face. She was delusional if she thought she could do anything against any of her people. A mere Junior Cadet could defeat her with their eyes closed.

"I wish I could join," she sighed.

"Really?" Calistelle was now serious.

"Yes, really," Nashel replied in the same manner.

"Well, they are very strict about the age limit," Calistelle continued, and for a moment, it seemed like she was genuinely sorry. "But there is a party next week, I can ask if you can come as my plus one. Just to know some people."

"Would you really do that for me?" Again, she used the combination of hope and admiration.

"Yeah, you are my girlfriend, silly!"

Nashel rolled her eyes inwardly. Calistelle had a weird notion of 'girlfriend'. To the other, she initiated one of the kisses she rarely did to show her "appreciation".

"Now, go." Calistelle shooed her, but more gently this time. "I really have to get ready."

Finally, something started to stir. Nashel knew she couldn't take much more of Calistelle's abuse and general personality if she didn't get any results. But now, now not only Calistelle had admitted she was part of the Alwenach and what it was, but she also was going to try to get her to the party with other members. She could bear that.

Somehow, Calistelle did manage to get her into the party. Nashel expected the meeting to take place in the Alwenach's HQ, but they went to a reception room in one of the admin buildings on campus. It was a nice and warm room, made mostly of velvet and luxurious wood, crystal glasses, and expensive drinks, where there was a dress code for even being considered being let in. So Nashel showed up, dressed in an uncomfortably tight dress with too much neckline that made her feel too exposed. Calistelle insisted it was required, and Nashel couldn't make her look bad. She did her hair and put makeup on her, and they spent the last three hours getting ready. It was the most torture she had ever endured. Despite everyone being dressed up, Nashel felt completely out of place.

She and Calistelle lingered here and there, exchanging pleasantries with the many guests. She didn't know any of them, but committed their faces and names to memory. She pretended to taste the drinks, but mostly she waited and studied the guests and tried to learn what she could about them. They were mostly adults, just a handful were university students, most were Solnedian. By their expensive clothes and their easiness around each other and the scene, they were probably from wealthy families, which confirmed what she and Alistair knew about the secret societies. She wasn't surprised at all when Mr Cobbler arrived. She should've guessed he was a member. She tried to avoid him, and thankfully, they were called to order for an old man to make a speech.

He was probably retired, a neat cut parted his white hair, and leaned on an elaborate cane.

"Welcome, welcome!" his voice was powerful, as if that didn't age with the rest of his body. "I see a lot of new faces, and my heart swells! Thank you for joining us today!"

"Hear, hear!" Other members raised their glasses.

"Today, we celebrate our annual induction," he continued with a benevolent smile. "So, I want to take this opportunity to tell you a secret."

He went on to talk about something Nashel didn't understand that mostly comprised of inside jokes only the older members understood. Nashel tuned out, resuming her observations.

"Our glorious Alwenach," he sighed, a hand on his heart. "I am disappointed to see what it has become today, but alas, we do what we can with what we have. Our younger members seem to have lost sight of our goal. Let me tell you, there is nothing more important. You need to imprint it in your mind, and repeat it over and over. Let's see if you know it. What is our motto?"

"Unseen, unforgiving!" the crowd shouted.

"I didn't hear you!" the man shouted.

"UNSEEN, UNFORGIVING!"

"And what does it mean?" the old man asked. "Let the young reply."

"To act in the shadow to defeat the enemy," the younger members replied, Calistelle included, but without the conviction they displayed for the motto.

"Who are the enemies?"

"The Sunset!"

"And what do we do to them?"

"We destroy them!"

The man continued to ask such questions for a while. However, they weren't that useful to Nashel, as they were mostly words and mostly to rouse enthusiasm and adrenaline, a tactic the Sunset instructors used all the time.

When he finally stopped, he paced around the room, quizzing the 'new faces'. When he reached Nashel and Calistelle, he kissed the latter on the cheeks and hugged her, telling her how it was nice to see her, and how he could hear her voice shouting louder than the others, which was a lie, but neither seemed to mind.

He turned to Nashel with a bright smile. "And who is this

beautiful young woman?”

“Nashel, she’s—” Calistelle answered, but the man waved her to stop.

“Nashel, sir,” she replied for herself, holding a hand out for the man to shake.

“It is very nice to meet you, Nashel. I’m Aldenor.”

“Nice to meet you, too, sir.”

“And polite! Your name is not familiar. Tell me, did you just move here?”

“A few months ago, sir,” she answered, and he made a confused face. “I’m only sixteen.”

“Oh, that explains it! I know all the potential candidates, you see.”

Nashel nodded, not sure what to reply.

“Tell me, why would you want to join us?”

“I know I can’t yet, sir,” she said with a regretful tone.

“Nonsense!” he exclaimed. “Tell me.”

“It’s their fault my village is dying,” she made up. “They took our people away, threw them in the Void one night. I don’t know how they came here, but I know it was them. They are evil, sir, evil.”

“That they are,” he nodded solemnly.

“I was little, but they killed my people right in front of me,” she concluded, with a tremble in her voice. She wished she knew how to fake tears, because that would’ve been the perfect moment for something like that.

The man placed a hand on her bare shoulder, squeezing lightly. “Your losses are our losses.”

“Thank you,” she swallowed hard, looking down.

“If you are serious about joining us, I can make an exception,” he told her, much to Nashel’s shock.

“For real?” she asked, her voice filled with hope and excitement. She didn’t have to fake the latter, it’d be a stroke of luck if she could get into the society so easily.

The man laughed. “There are tests to pass to see if you are a good fit, if you have the skills.”

Calistelle clicked her tongue, showing without words what

she thought of that. The man gave her a side look, but didn't comment.

"I'll do whatever it takes!" she ignored her, adding fervour to her tone.

"I will be in touch," he told her, squeezing her hand with both of his and moving on to the next group of people.

For the rest of the evening, Calistelle was colder and meaner than usual, probably because Nashel had outshone her in front of her hero.

"I know you lied," she hissed.

"Excuse me?"

"Don't think he believes for a second your sob story, and neither do I."

"It's the truth," Nashel tried to keep calm, even though the other girl was getting on her nerves.

"No, it isn't. You're a peasant from nowhere," she spat each word. "You mean nothing. You know nothing. You are nothing."

Nashel sighed. "If you say so," she shrugged.

"Don't you dare talk to me like that," Calistelle spewed through gritted teeth. She raised her hand and slapped Nashel hard. Nashel saw it coming; Calistelle was predictable that way, but she let her. The people around them gasped and looked at the other girl as if she were crazy. Nashel saw Mr Cobbler flashing a look in their direction.

"Are you alright, dear?" a woman close by asked.

"No, she is just a little—" Calistelle answered, but the woman put herself between Calistelle and Nashel, giving the former her shoulders.

"I'm okay," Nashel whispered, playing the victim. The slap stung, but it wasn't anything she couldn't endure. She put a hand on her cheek, and for the second time, she wished she could cry at will. "It's my fault."

"Don't be silly," the woman said gently. "I am sure it is not," she looked behind her back and sent daggers to Calistelle, who was too stunned to reply.

"Why don't I take you to the infirmary?"

"No, ma'am, it's okay. I'll just go back to my room," Nashel said with a tremulous voice.

"You need to put some ice on that," the woman insisted.

"I will, I promise. Please," she faked a sob, "I just want to go to my room."

"Of course, dear, of course."

Five minutes later, she was knocking, seething, at Alistair's door. She almost tackled him as she marched in when he opened the door.

"Wow," he murmured under his breath before he realised what her mood was like.

"What happened?" he asked, alarmed.

"That fucking bitch!" Nashel shouted before remembering she wasn't in her room, where the wards allowed her to do whatever she wanted.

"Tell me," Alistair encouraged her, but that wasn't necessary.

She told him everything, even those things about her relationship with Calistelle that she hadn't mentioned before. She didn't even realise that Martin, thankfully, wasn't there. When she finished, she was exhausted and still angry. She wanted to rip the dress off her body, but she resisted the urge.

"I need to get out of this dress," she told Alistair.

"Are you okay with being alone?"

"Yes," she reassured him, mustering a smile. "I'll be okay."

"Okay," he replied, but he wasn't convinced. "I'll walk you."

She didn't argue, but only nodded as Alistair led her upstairs to her room.

"You sure?" he asked as she opened the door.

"Yes," she smiled again. "I'll see you in the morning."

He waved her goodbye, and she locked the door, waiting a few moments to make sure he was gone before she screamed and exploded. An explosion of power that she really wanted to aim at Calistelle, but just aimed it at her room.

CHAPTER SEVENTEEN

Aldenor

A rumble shook Nashel's door, persistently pounding on it. For a moment, she thought it was a residue of her outburst. She usually was very good at controlling her emotions, but Calistelle had driven her last nerve. However, she knew she felt calmer, so her door shouldn't shake, and yet it did. She looked at it questioningly, before realising what was really going on: someone was knocking, and that someone was pissed.

She didn't need to open the door to know who it was, but she did, and a red-faced Calistelle was standing right there. Nashel didn't let her in; she opened the door just enough to square off to the other girl.

"YOU WENT STRAIGHT TO HIM, DIDN'T YOU?"

"I don't know what you're talking about," Nashel replied calmly.

"YES, YOU DO!" Calistelle spat. She pointed a finger at her and poked her chest. "YOU WENT STRAIGHT TO HIM, ADMIT IT."

"I am right here. How can I be there?"

"DO NOT TALK TO ME LIKE THAT, BITCH!"

"Calm down, Calistelle, you're making a fool of yourself,"

Nashel sighed. Some people peered out of their rooms to see what was going on.

"DO NOT TELL ME TO CALM DOWN. YOU HAVE NO IDEA WHAT YOU'VE DONE!"

"I do. I made a huge mistake thinking I could date a self-absorbed brat like you. I should pity you; you will die alone and forgotten, but in truth, I only pity myself."

"YOU'LL PAY FOR THIS, MARK MY WORDS! YOU'RE NOTHING WITHOUT ME!"

Nashel was about to slam the door in her face when the warden rushed down the corridor, his wand drawn.

"What is happening here?" he asked, his tone severe. "Young lady, you are a university student, and you should be in your dorm, not here."

Calistelle pivoted on her heels, ready to fight him, verbally at least, but stopped when she understood he was a warden and he had his wand out.

"I was just telling something to my girlfriend."

"Ex," Nashel pointed. "Ex-girlfriend, thank you very much."

"You are making a ruckus," the warden continued. "And it's past lights-out. Please return to your room, unless you want to face the consequences."

He waved his wand, gesturing towards the exit, but it was clearly a threat of using it as well.

"It's not over," she hissed towards Nashel. "You will pay for this."

"You better not mean with magic," the warden interjected seriously.

Calistelle didn't reply, just turned and left.

"Thank you, sir," Nashel said to the man.

"Go to sleep," he replied, exasperated.

Nashel nodded and closed the door. She was going to kill her. She didn't need her anymore, now that the Aldenor had talked to her, and was willing to let her in despite her age. So, she was going to kill her. She laid in bed, thinking about the method she would use. It soothed her to sleep.

The next morning, it started. It was subtle at first, and it didn't click. People were looking at her, staring, then whispering with their mouths covered by their hands, stealing significant glances. Then the whispered became louder, like they didn't care if she heard them. Then came the texts. Everyone got them except her. They rang in class, in the common room, in the dining halls. They rang every time she was around, and immediately all eyes were on her, and comments were muttered at various volumes with various degrees of disgusted expressions and head shaking. It didn't matter that she was in school and Calistelle a university student; the texts reached everyone.

It took her a while to understand what they were saying. She wasn't familiar with the words in Solnedian, but after ten days, her patient ran even thinner, and she wanted to find out. So, she used her powers to amplify the whisperers to her ears. She didn't expect the results. She was incredulous.

"Did you know this?" she asked Alistair, showing him the text.

He looked shocked. "What's this?"

"You didn't get any texts?"

"Not like this, no. Just my normal texts, mostly from you."

"Have you seen how people look at me? Have you heard what they say?"

He bowed his head. "That I did. I hoped you didn't. That's why I didn't say anything, sorry."

"It's Calistelle," she hissed, furious.

Alistair nodded.

"I'll kill her."

"Try to ignore it," he suggested. "It'll go away soon. She'll find someone else to be obsessed with."

It didn't go away, it increased and became worse. People spat on her, they tripped her up, pushed her, used magic to rip her bag, spill flour, sugar, eggs on her head. No one ever seemed to see anything, hear anything, know anything, so everyone went unpunished.

Nashel reacted; she definitely gave as much as she got,

and she was good enough not to get in trouble, but she was even more resolved than to make her stop. She had planned for this. Calistelle was always surrounded by friends, so singling her out was tricky, but Nashel knew her routine, and, of course, her room. She had already checked if there were wards around Calistelle or her belongings, and there were none; the girl thought she was untouchable, which would be her demise.

There was an old shed on the edge of campus, and she thought it would be perfect. However, it was the opposite way from Calistelle's dorm, or her lessons; she would have to cajole her there, or carry her. Calistelle had an athletic build, despite not practising any sport or running like Nashel did, and Nashel didn't think carrying her would be a problem.

During her next lesson, Nashel sneaked some herbs in her pocket she would need for her plan. She wasn't a big fan of potions, or the way they thought potions there, but she wanted to make sure she did it right, and a little extra help would go a long way. That evening, she mixed up all the ingredients and ground them into a fine powder, and waited until the dead of the night. She used her powers to open Calistelle's door silently, then she woke Calistelle. The other girl took a second to see and recognise her, then she jumped out of bed and had her first insult on the tip of her tongue, but Nashel was faster: she blew the powder on Calistelle's face and whispered the order to follow her quietly. Calistelle did, almost hypnotised, as if sleepwalking.

When they arrived at the shed, she locked and warded the door and broke the compulsion so Calistelle would know exactly what was going to happen.

"What the hell do you think you're doing?" she screamed at Nashel as soon as she could talk again. Nashel wasn't worried. The ward would keep every sound in.

"I told you, you would regret what you did. It's your own fault," Calistelle added smugly.

"Well, it is your turn to regret it."

There was something in her tone that made a shiver ran

down Calistelle's spine.

"And I'm not like you," Nashel continued calmly. "I don't shame people with texts for their sexual preferences, or falsely accuse them of abuse, nor do I plan vile attacks on them."

"No, you're too chicken for that," Calistelle tried her bravado, but her voice quivered and lost its effect.

"No, you're just too stupid to realise who you're dealing with. I'm not chicken, I'm disciplined. If I weren't, you wouldn't have survived for so long."

Calistelle made a confused face.

"You see, you boost about your Alwenach, and how you're going to kill all the Sunset scumbags, and you didn't even realise you were dating one."

Shock was all over Calistelle's face. "W-What?"

"So, now you're going to see what we're really like. Unfortunately for you, it's the last thing you're going to see."

Nashel was aware she was playing right in Calistelle's hand, proving that the Sunset was actually killing Sunrise 'soldiers', but she also knew that Calistelle wouldn't survive to tell the tale.

Calistelle started shivering and shaking her hand, backing away from Nashel, falling and still scrambling away until she didn't have any more space, and her back was against the wall.

"When I said you would die alone, I didn't mean I would leave that up to fate. I knew you would."

Calistelle tried to make herself smaller, as if she could shrink so much that she would become invisible.

"You're going to die today. It will be slow and painful because you wore me down."

"You're crazy," Calistelle said, her voice trembling.

"No, no, I'm not."

Calistelle managed to click her tongue in disbelief.

"Think what you want. You won't think it for long anyway."

"You'll be caught! They'll notice I'm missing!" she was

hysterical now. "I'm popular! I have lots of friends, important ones! They'll catch you!"

"Oh, silly," she mocked the tone Calistelle had used many times with her, like she was a little child and a bit slow. "They won't find you. By the time anyone will come here, there won't be anything that would even resemble you, not the merest speck of dust."

"That's... that's..." but she was at a loss of words.

"Actually, by the time I leave this room, no one will even remember you, not even me. I told you, you'd die alone and forgotten. I wasn't joking, dear."

That was a lie. She wasn't powerful enough to make that many people forget about her, but Calistelle didn't know that.

"Sure, at first there will be questions, but people will know you left for a prestigious private school, and then you'll be off their minds."

Calistelle tried to say something, or her teeth clattered, Nashel wasn't sure.

"And after a couple of weeks, if anyone asks 'where is Calistelle?', the answer will be 'Calistelle who?'"

That was something she learnt from Calistelle, and it was ironic that she would use it against her. The power of rumours and gossip was unknown to her before. She learnt, however, that when something spread, whether true or false, it was impossible to stop it and very difficult to counter.

Soon after she'd leave the shed, she would start spreading the rumour. She wouldn't be able to do it herself. Everyone knew about their relationship and believed she was promiscuous and abusive, so she couldn't put her face to it. She would use Calistelle's own PPad to send a few texts to her closest friends. They would do the rest.

She would need to send something to the Academy's admin, but it wouldn't be a problem; she knew how to forge a document and imbue it with powers so that it wouldn't be questioned. That was how she made all her IDs for the mission, after all.

Calistelle started to cry, sobbing loudly, bawling like a child. She pleaded for her life, she told Nashel she loved her, that she'd been stupid letting her go and spreading all those awful things about her, and that she would be good and do whatever Nashel wanted if she let her live.

Nashel shook her head. "Beg all you want, it will not change anything. I have no use for you anymore. I have my test with Aldenor in two days."

"B-bu-but... we shared..." she grasped for any excuse she could find. Her eyes darting all over the place, trying to find a lucky escape that would not be there.

"What, you thought I was dating you for your personality?! Girl, you're not that special. I'm on a mission. I needed access to the Alwenach, and you were just a tool. A tool I don't need anymore." Nashel smiled sadly, a patronising, pitying, fake smile.

"Any last words?" she added ironically, a laugh barely contained in her voice. She did that on purpose to make Calistelle even more afraid.

Calistelle sobbed even more at that, and she couldn't speak any longer, but she tried to beg again.

Nashel snapped her fingers, and... nothing happened. Of course, it didn't; powers were not tied to gestures unless the user wanted to. Calistelle's eyes grew wider and more horrified when she did it, but then – and that was what Nashel aimed for – when nothing happened, a tiny sliver of treacherous hope flickered in her eyes.

Nashel smirked. She waited a few more moments, letting Calistelle's hope build, then she laughed malignantly. "Goodbye," She whispered and turned towards the door.

Calistelle understood then that there was no hope, that Nashel had orchestrated it all to make her suffer more. Nashel didn't need to wait to see what would happen to her, she knew. Calistelle would start to have trouble moving, her skin would dry, she would have trouble breathing. Her muscles would start to scream in pain, then her intestines would start to digest the flesh. Her arms, legs, and stomach would bloat, causing her excruciating pain. Her tissues would start to liquefy until only bones would be left, which in turn would turn to dust. A fast forward process of decomposition through which she would be conscious for the entire time, thanks to Nashel's power to anchor her soul to the remains until nothing was left. Nashel was going to pay the price; she would be exhausted for days, but the satisfaction outweighed that.

When there was nothing left of Calistelle, the shed door would open by itself, and wind would scatter the dust remaining so that it would never be found.

Nashel left and sent those texts. Replies flooded in almost immediately, full of crying emojis and 'I'll miss you's and undecipherable text slang that she still didn't know how to translate. Then she carefully crafted the email to the university admin and made sure it was imbued correctly before she was too tired to do it properly.

Everything went as she expected. Calistelle's close friends talked about her departure in a subdued way, some were blaming Nashel, but the rest thought she just had an amazing opportunity and took it. She also heard the whispers that the Alwenach had actually sent her on a mission.

Nashel had her own mission to concentrate on: the day of her test had finally arrived. She wasn't sure what to expect. She was used to her people's kind of test, and she doubted they were the same. Part of her also hoped it wasn't. She was still exhausted from the Calistelle business.

It was a nice sunny day. The weather was becoming warmer each new day, which also meant that the sun was blinding her by ricocheting against the buildings. There were no trees for shade around, and she already knew she would hate summer in the city, so she made a mental note to make plans to go away. If everything went according to plan, she might even get back home by then.

Aldenor met her outside the Alwenach's building; not that she was supposed to know that. He smiled benevolently and extended his hand for her to shake it in greeting.

"So, how are you feeling?" he asked her.

"Ready, sir."

"Sad, that business with Calistelle," he said solemnly.

Nashel froze. Had he found out what she did? She was sure she had covered her tracks well.

"I heard she left for another school," she replied, tentative.

Aldenor nodded. "It's for the best. Regretful behaviour at that party. If she didn't leave, she would've not been welcomed back to the Alwenach."

That's what he was talking about! The party, not the murder. Nashel shrugged.

"But let's get down to business and out of this sun!"

"Yes, please," she smiled, and he laughed.

He led her away from the building and into a building that resembled a barn. It turned out to be a sort of gym, with equipment and different sports fields. That day it was empty: no nets, no equipment around, just a wide, open space.

"As you know," the leader started. "The Alwenach was founded to fight against the Sunset. Now, you may think that it's silly, but the Void stops them from crossing, and us as well."

She nodded, despite knowing the truth.

"Well, that is true. The Void stops anyone from crossing to the other side. However, our best minds have been trying to find a solution, and we want to be ready when that happens."

"A solution, sir?"

"Yes, a way to move an army through the Void."

Nashel painted a surprised and shocked expression on her face, internally urging him to give her more details.

"So, we want initiates who can hold their own in battle. You seem to be in good shape. I've been told you run every morning..."

That wasn't surprising; she knew she was being observed, probably everyone was.

"But today, I want to see how you hold your ground with magic."

"Okay," she answered, making her voice tremble as if she

were nervous.

"Don't worry. You don't have to be battle ready. Just show me your potential."

He gestured for her to take centre stage and get ready. She nodded and moved, getting her wand ready.

The first attack came from her left, and she could've dodged it even with her eyes closed. The second came also from her left, after a feint from her right. Both attacks were slow and weak. She hoped the difficulty would increase, but it didn't. It was boring, and she could've aced the test, but she wasn't home. Here, she was a peasant from a small village who barely spoke the language and wasn't very talented. So, after a couple of "lucky" dodges, she let the next few attacks "catch her by surprise". She also made it sound like it was much more painful than in reality. She dodged another one, celebrating exaggeratedly, and let the next hit her. She thought she was doing a good job.

"That's enough," Aldenor declared.

Nashel thought she split the successes and failures evenly.

"Good job," he told her, passing her a towel to wipe the sweat she didn't break.

"Thank you, sir."

"I believe you have potential. You are young, and you have just started your educational journey, but I see it."

"Thank you," she repeated.

"I can't make a decision right now, I need to think about the pros and cons, you understand."

"I understand, sir. I'm grateful for the opportunity," she pretended to be sincere.

"I will be in touch," he dismissed her.

She thanked him again and left the barn. She wondered if she had to use her powers on him to convince him to let her in. For the time being, she would just let him decide by himself, and if that didn't work, she would 'help' him.

It took the man a week to decide, or at least to call her again for a meeting, this time in his office. Why he had an office on campus, she didn't know, but it had a plaque with his name and an assistant ready to welcome her.

"Thank you for coming at such short notice," he greeted her and invited her to sit.

"It's no trouble," she replied politely.

"Always so polite, I like it!"

She smiled.

"Where are you from, Nashel?"

"It's a small village, sir; it doesn't have a name."

"Can you point at it on a map?" he produced a paper map of the Sunrise, the Void marking its borders on one side, the sea surrounding it on the others.

"I think so," she said apologetically. "I don't know the exact — what's the word? — coordinates, but only the general direction."

"That will be enough."

So, she stood to reach the right side of the map and pointed to the empty space where she invented the village's position. "It should be about here," she commented. "The Void is not too far; we weren't allowed to go there as children, but not too close to influence the land."

"And you have your parents there?"

"Yes, sir."

"Are you going back for the summer?"

"I don't think so," she admitted. "I would like to travel around the country for a while."

"That is a good idea," he said distractedly. "When was the last time you talked to your parents?"

"When I left," she answered. She knew they would monitor her PPad, and they would know she didn't send any messages to anyone but Calistelle and Alistair. "They don't have a PPad."

"I see," he sighed.

Nashel understood then that he wanted to tell her something difficult, and he was trying to get the right words out. She didn't know what it was but if he didn't want her to let her join the Alwenach, he could just say so.

"Something happened a few days ago," he started, licking

his lips as if they were dry. “There was an attack.”

“An attack?”

“Yes, a Sunset attack.”

She gasped, hands on her mouth in shock.

“Unfortunately, this time they didn’t just take the stronger magicians. They razed your entire village, and the two next to it, to the ground.”

“W—What?”

“I am sorry. Nobody survived.”

She looked at him in horror, trying to understand if he was testing her, calling her bluff about her village, or if he was serious.

“I know it is difficult to process,” he nodded with understanding. “It is an awful tragedy.”

She just nodded, still not sure what the right reaction was.

“It could’ve been prevented,” he commented almost to himself, his tone full of bitterness.

“What do you mean?” she asked in a trembling, faint voice.

“It could’ve been prevented,” he repeated more loudly, his bitterness even more remarked. “If we had an army, if the government stopped being blind and let the Alwenach grow!”

So, it was not to call her bluff; it was a tactic to foment more hatred in her and elicit allegiance to the Alwenach. She could play that game then.

“Please, sir,” she begged, sobbing, “Let me join. I need to revenge my family, my village!”

“You’re young, I can’t—”

“Please,” she interrupted him, and she saw a glint of victory in his eyes.

“I’ll make you a deal.”

“Anything!” she pleaded.

He smiled good-naturedly. “I will let you join in a limited capacity. You will learn about us, you will participate in our meetings and events, but you will not start training, at least until next year.”

“But—”

This time, he interrupted her. “I can’t let you fight yet.”

“Okay,” she murmured, resigned.

“The Alwenach will take care of you. You won’t have to worry about anything.”

“Thank you?” she mumbled, confused.

“That means that you will have a house, you will have clothes and food. For now, you can stay on campus, of course. If you want to travel this summer, and I think you should, we will give you an allowance to do so.”

“That’s too generous, sir,” she shook her head. “I have some savings.”

“Keep saving them,” he smiled.

“I don’t know what to say,” she replied.

“You don’t have to say anything. You will repay us with your skills and your service.”

She nodded, hopeful. “I can do that!”

“I know I gave you some terrible news today,” he said after a pause. “But do you think you can handle a bit more information?”

“Yes, it’ll keep me distracted,” she said vigorously.

He laughed. “Very well.”

He stood and went out of his office. Nashel heard him exchange a quick word with his assistant, then came back in and took his place behind the desk. He was holding a bundle of papers Nashel recognised immediately.

“This,” he put the manuscript on the desk, “is our history. It was started by the founder of the Alwenach, and every leader after him added their own accounts.”

He opened the leather cover just as Nashel had done a few weeks before, then turned it to show her the first illegible page.

“You see, it wasn’t even written in Solnedian!” he exclaimed with a laugh, and she nodded. “There is a spell I can do to make you understand it. Do I have your permission?”

She hesitated.

“Don’t worry, it is not painful,” he said sweetly.

"Okay," she replied tentatively.

She hoped he was sincere. He took his wand and waved it at her. She didn't feel anything, as he said, and the letters on the page rearranged themselves to form words in her language.

He laughed. "I will lend you this, but you need to be careful; it is very precious."

She nodded vehemently. Excitement now cursing through her, she couldn't wait to put her hands on the manuscript.

"Read it, commit it to memory, and if you have questions, ask me."

"Thank you, sir," she whispered reverently. "It's an honour."

"You have until the holidays. I will need it back then. And the spell won't last any longer anyway!" he laughed at the last sentence.

She nodded again.

He closed the bundle and slid it on the desk so that it was within her reach. She extended her hands and felt it. The power. It wasn't there before when she opened it in the HQ. She couldn't tell what it was exactly, but she assumed it was for protection, to make sure that she didn't tamper with it. Or maybe it was for the translation to work. She would have to analyse the Trace later on.

She didn't hesitate, though. She took the book and held it to her chest. "I will not let you down, sir."

"I know you won't," he replied with conviction.

"May I leave, sir? I think I need to lie down for a while."

"Of course, of course," he stood and opened the door for her. "Take care of yourself. And remember, we are here for you."

She nodded and left.

She had a lot to think about, that was real. And a lot to read. The Aldenor was more cunning than she thought, more ruthless too, making a child believe her parents had died in a Sunset attack, so that she would want to join even more. Maybe they were truly developing a way for armies to cross the Void. Maybe she was wrong in thinking that the Sunrise were pathetic in their use of magic and wouldn't stand a chance against the Sunset. Yet, she had made progress. She was now in possession of the history of the Alwenach, a reading she couldn't wait to start.

CHAPTER EIGHTEEN

The Tale of The Sunrise

Nashel sat in her bed, her pillow behind her back, getting comfortable, then she opened the manuscript. She had a lot to think about: the tactics used by Aldenor, what to tell Alistair, which also raised the question of what to tell him when the summer holiday arrived and she wasn't going home. Yet, her mind couldn't focus on any of it. It had space only for the manuscript. So, she let it win and concentrated on that.

"My name is Iklaurn, and this is the first page of history," pretentious, much. She rolled her eyes.

"The war is finally over. The enemy has been defeated at great cost. Lives were lost, powers were lost." She paused there to read the word again. He had just used 'power', not 'magic'.

"But most of all, our people are now divided. Where there was one, there are now two, two sides of one sun. The war had brought out the worst of people. Now that the enemy is defeated, magicians are becoming greedy. They - I should say 'we' - want more, we want what we couldn't have before and instead of enjoying peace, we are ready for another war, a race to get what the other wants before them. The Void is the only barrier - literally! - separating us, and for now, neither side has found a way to cross it."

Nashel stopped there to take everything in. When they talked about the war, they always talked about the Sunset against the Sunrise, but here, Iklaurn seemed to imply that there had been another, before that, where the two nations were one and had a common enemy. She didn't know what to believe, so for the moment, she continued reading, promising herself she would research it afterwards.

"I saw their greed. I know what they intend to do. They will take the magicians and train them hard. Train them as if the war is not over yet. This side, my side, doesn't want to do that. They are afraid; they want to control us; they want to control our powers. If the Sunset are set in their ways, they will become much, much stronger than us, and I hope they never find a way to cross the Void.

I can't, in good conscience, let this go. We need to be ready. We need to train, too. If the government doesn't want to do it, then I'll do it myself. I hereby declare the founding of the Alwenach, our sacred new army, whose sole goal is to protect our land.

No, scratch that, it will not only protect us. It will make sure that the Sunset is not a threat anymore. We will protect, sure, but we will strive to attack as well. We will research, and we'll find a way to cross that barrier, and we will eliminate every single one of them. And they'll never see us coming. We are not government-sanctioned. We will work in the shadows, keep ourselves secret, and strike as surely and unexpectedly as a snake."

The following few pages were more of the same, with increasing hatred towards the Sunset. Then the leader changed, and the next one spewed more and more hatred and less and less interesting information. Every once in a while, in the chronicles, there was a mention of that elusive research, of forms of magic Nashel hadn't heard of, runic circles, chants, but nothing more than just an update on the progress, which was always the same: some attempts were made unsuccessfully, but they were getting closer. It has continued until the present day, until the page left by Aldenor. Nashel looked confused and turned to the previous page, then to the following, thinking there must be a mistake. The page was blank, only one line written in elegant cursive.

"My name is Aldenor, and I will make history."

There was nothing else, nothing hidden, she tried to reveal it. Somehow, that one line worried her more than what she had just read. She added that to the list of things she had to keep an eye on.

A knock on her door interrupted her musing. She glanced at her PPad. It had two notifications, both from Alistair. and the time told her she spent hours on the manuscript without realising.

She got up, stretching her stiff limbs, and opened the door.

"Hello," Alistair greeted her with a smile. "Rising from the dead?"

She laughed and let him in. "Sorry, I was reading the—" she tried to say the book they saw in the Alwenach's HQ, but her mouth wouldn't form the words. "I was reading," she repeated, but didn't try to say what.

He looked at her, confused, but then shrugged it off.

"Is everything okay?" she asked him.

"Yes, why?"

She shrugged.

"Alright, what's going on?" he asked. "I feel the awkwardness and tension. C'mon, spill it."

She didn't know yet what to say to him. "Aldenor called me in," she started. "He had some news to give me."

"You're in?!" he asked excitedly.

She shook her head. "That wasn't it. He wanted to tell me that there had been a Sunset attack in the area of my village. It has been wiped out, no survivors."

Alistair gasped in horror.

Time seemed to slow down and stretch. Nashel had a choice to make there. She could either tell him she knew it was bullshit and he only did it to incite her, or she could let him believe what Aldenor said.

She nodded to herself to confirm her decision, and to him to agree with his reaction.

"You should've called me!"

"I wanted to be alone," she shrugged.

"Are you sure it's true?"

"I think so. I tried to look for news and found it."

"I am so sorry," he murmured.

She didn't know what to say, so she said nothing. She tried to think about how she felt when her parents died, but she felt nothing. She was enthralled by the flamed, nothing else.

"Can I hug you?" he asked her in another whisper.

She thought maybe she didn't have to cry, maybe she could just pretend to be sad, and he would do the rest for her. She wasn't a hugger, he knew, and that was the reason he asked, but this time, she nodded, looking down.

He got closer, on the bed where she was, and held her tight for a long time. She buried her head in his chest and took that time to think about what to do next.

"Come home with me," he said after some time.

"What?" she asked, confused, putting some distance between them so she could look him in the eye.

"For the summer," he explained. "Come to my place. I don't want you to be alone."

"I don't know," she murmured, taken aback.

"Think about it."

"Okay," she agreed with a small smile.

"What were you reading?" he asked, changing the topic, probably thinking it would distract her.

"A book Aldenor gave me," she managed to say, then she tried again. "The man—" but once again, she couldn't form the word.

Alistair, though, understood what she wanted to say, and the previous excitement came back.

"The manuscript?" he asked in awe.

She could only nod.

"And you can't tell me," he guessed.

She rolled her eyes, as if to say "obviously."

"He enchanted it," Alistair concluded, and she shook her head. "He enchanted you," he corrected, and she nodded.

"Does it mean you're in?"

"Partially," she answered and was glad she could form the words. "He said I'm too young to train, but I can attend meetings and get to know people."

Alistair nodded.

"He used what happened to fuel my hatred. He didn't say that, but it was clear."

"Bastard," he hissed.

Nashel shrugged. "It's an excellent tactic."

Alistair shook his head. "Still a bastard."

She smiled at that and squeezed him a little.

"Are you..." he started hesitantly. "Do you want to join them?"

"Do you mean to kill the Sunset?"

He nodded.

"No, that didn't change. I just wanted to find their secrets."

"Are you sure?"

"I believe something happened to my village. I believe nobody survived. But I don't believe for a second it was some group of soldiers from the other side of an impenetrable barrier."

"You don't?"

"No, I don't think either side has found a way to cross the Void," she admitted. She knew it wasn't strictly true, but she believed neither could send a group of people.

"What do you think happened to your village?"

She shrugged. "There have been threats in the past. The village is small and dying; some rich people want that land."

"Really?"

She nodded, "We had offers before, but none of the families wanted to leave. The offer was for money, not relocation, and our families had been there since the beginning."

"That's awful!"

"It's one reason why I left when I did. My parents were worried something could happen and wanted to send me away a couple of years ago, but I begged them to let me stay, at least until I could join the Academy."

Alistair was left speechless. He only hugged her tight again.

"Let's talk about something else," she whispered. "Okay?"

"Sure, sorry I asked too much."

"It wasn't," she smiled, and he relaxed.

"You have something in mind, right?" he grinned.

"Yes," she admitted. "I was reading, and I found something interesting."

"But you don't know if you're able to tell me."

"Exactly."

"I'm good at charades, so try me!"

She had no idea what charade was, but she trusted him. "The war. What do you know about it?"

"The Sunset wants to invade and conquer the Sunrise, and the Sunrise wants to invade and conquer the Sunset, but the Void divides the two and stops them."

She nodded. That was common knowledge. "What about before?"

"Before the war?"

"Yes, do you know anything?" She was glad she could talk about it so far.

"Not much," he admitted with a shrug. "Why? There is something in there?"

She nodded. "It says there was a—" Again, she couldn't complete her sentence.

"There was a something before it?"

A nod.

He guessed, but didn't get close.

She stopped him and tried another way. "Do you know there was a war?" she emphasised the last word.

"Yes?" he said, confused.

She tried to make a face that told him the clue was in

there. It took him a moment, but then it clicked.

"You're saying the was another war before the war?"

"Yes!" she exclaimed. They were getting there.

"I never heard of it," he said, intrigued and confused. "Another war between the Sunrise and Sunset?"

She shook her head. "They were u—" she grunted in frustration, took a deep breath, and tried again. "Do you remember the constellation you showed me, The Lovers?"

"Yes..." She could almost see his brain's gear turning.

"Lovers are in a relationship, right? They are together."

"Okay," he bit his lower lip, thinking, a gesture she found enticing. "Together..." his eyes widened again. "The Two Suns were together, united!"

"Yes!" she exulted again.

"So, they were united against another enemy!"

She nodded.

"They defeated it, obviously," he concluded, without waiting for her nod. "Then, they started a war between each other."

"Yes, the Void was made then."

"Between the two wars."

"Yes, and I want to find out more."

"Why?"

"I can't say," she replied, not even trying to know what the result was going to be.

"We can have a look, but I doubt there will be anything in the library."

"I agree."

"Maybe that book we saw, The True History of the Sunrise, has something in it. Can you get it?"

"No, he hasn't shown me the HQ yet. He had the book in his office."

"And sneaking in again is a no-no."

"No, but I'd like to avoid that unless there is no other way."

He nodded. "Okay. Well, the Solnedian library may have something."

"The Solnedian library?"

"You never heard of it?"

She shook her head.

"It's only the biggest library in the world!"

"Is it?" she teased.

"Yes!" he laughed. "I can't believe you never heard of it!"

"We don't care about libraries in my village," she rebutted jokingly. "And I never explored the city."

"Fair enough," he made a placating gesture with his hands, then sneaked a tickling attack on her. She let him, letting her guard down, and they soon started to laugh.

"We could go to the library if you want, before we go home," he said, his breath still laboured from the laughter.

"I haven't said I will go home with you," she teased him.

"I know, but you will," he replied with a mock air of superiority.

She rolled her eyes and shook her head.

"We should check the campus library first," she continued. "Maybe we find something, maybe Wynmere knows something. I'll ask her."

"Are you sure?"

"Yeah, it's just an interest in history, nothing suspicious," she shrugged.

He shrugged too and nodded. "Let's go have some food, shall we?"

That evening, when Alistair left to go to sleep in his room, Nashel studied the manuscript's Trace. She found it linked to a Trace with a similar signature that was on her, so she confirmed the Alwenach leader had done both.

The Trace on her, now that she could see it, had the two functions she had already discovered: making her able to read the manuscript, and making her unable to talk about its content. Slowly, she undid the latter, but left the former.

The Trace on the manuscript was more complex. It was linked to her to make it readable, but that was just the tip of the iceberg. It had an Expression that stopped anyone else to pick it up - which wasn't there when they discovered it -

another that was anti-theft, making sure that Nashel had to return it, and another that stopped anyone from copying the content. This could be a problem. She wanted to make a copy and translate it so that she could show it to her people when they called her back. She didn't think Aldenor was good enough to see the signature of a Trace, but she wasn't sure she wanted to risk exposure.

She weighed her options, thinking about all she knew to find a solution, something that let her undo the Expressions and then redo them without altering the signature. She couldn't find any.

With a sigh, she set to work. She had to risk it. The manuscript was too precious to just return it to Aldenor without making sure her people could see it and analyse it. She couldn't claim she lost it, the anti-theft Expression wouldn't allow it, therefore she would expose herself.

She undid the Expressions, which took a considerable amount of energy, then made a copy of the manuscript. By then, she was exhausted. She decided to rest before translating and redoing the Expressions on the original. She needed to make sure it was her best work. She didn't see any sort of alarm alerting someone the Expressions had been tampered with, especially because she undid them from the Trace and not from the outside, so she felt safe enough to rest before getting back to work.

When she woke up, she panicked for a moment as she couldn't find the original manuscript, only to discover it at the bottom of her bed, under the sheets.

She got back to work, now refreshed, and reinstated the Expressions on the book. It wasn't too difficult; having undone them, she knew each detail, but it was time-consuming, especially because she wanted them to be a mirror image of the originals. When she was satisfied with her work, she took out the copy she had made and set to translate it. She soon discovered she made a mistake: the Expression that stopped her from telling Alistair about the content of the manuscript was also stopping her from translating it.

She groaned. "Should've known," she muttered to herself as she undid the work she had just completed. She blamed the tiredness, but she also blamed herself and reminded herself how she had softened in the months she spent on this mission.

The translation itself was not difficult; she already knew the content, and she could check what she didn't remember thanks to the Expression that allowed her to understand the manuscript.

She didn't want to wait any longer, so she also re-did the Expressions on the manuscript for the second time. This time, though, she barely got to the end that she was exhausted. She really hated that place and its weak power!

She passed out and slept until dawn, waking up looking at the manuscript and deciding she would deal with it later. For the time being, it was safe in her room, which nobody could get into, and she would double-check her work at the end of the day.

She changed into her running clothes, washed and jogged downstairs. Alistair was stretching just outside his dorm. He greeted her with a smile.

"I'm glad you're here," he told her.

"Me too," she smiled back.

Alistair sent her worried side looks throughout their run, but didn't say anything; he also slowed his pace for a reason she couldn't understand, but she picked it up to their usual, and he didn't have any other choice than to keep up.

They showered and went to breakfast, then to their lessons. History was the first in the afternoon that day, so Nashel had to wait until then to ask the teacher about the pre-war war. Alistair couldn't believe she was going to do it that day, tried to convince her to take her time, to process her grief first, but she argued it was keeping her distracted from lingering too much on the tragedy.

"Nashel," Wynmere smiled at her at the end of the lesson, when she stayed behind. "I heard your tutor left, but I also heard there was an altercation. I'm sorry to hear that."

Nashel shrugged. "It's okay; it wasn't really working."

Wynmere laughed. "I see. What brings you here today? Would you like me to find you another tutor?"

Nashel shook her head. "No, thank you. The summer holidays are fast approaching, and I wish to focus on the exams."

"Wise decision," the woman nodded.

"However, I found something when I was studying," Nashel continued. "And it caught my attention; I can't get it out of my mind!"

"Why, tell me! Don't keep me so on my toes! Is it a history thing?"

Nashel nodded enthusiastically. "I discovered there was a war before the war between the Sunrise and the Sunset. A war that led to the creation of the Void. I had no idea!"

Wynmere's expression changed from excited to cordially cold. She pursed her lips before replying. "We don't talk about that."

"But—"

The teacher waved her hand and shook her head to stop Nashel's protests.

"It is not part of the curriculum. It was a dark age, and we don't want to relive it."

"So, there is no book, no resource that I can find that will tell me more?"

"Not that you can access," Wynmere said, "Or that I can access."

"Okay," she added, dejected.

"You could try the Solnedian library, but it's a long shot. You're underage, and they are even less likely to show you anything because of that."

She nodded, looking down, making her lip tremble as if she were about to cry. "There was an accident in my village. It has been wiped out. No survivors. My parents just died while I was here, and I couldn't even say goodbye!"

She thought she was doing a good job impersonating a sad

and slightly hysterical teenager stricken by grief.

"They were thrown into the Void; that's why I want to know more about it."

"Oh, dear," Wynmere seemed to be genuinely sad for her. She patted her shoulder and sighed. "I am so sorry to hear that."

"Thank you," she sobbed.

"Alright, listen, there is a book that you can access. It might not have the answers you are looking for, but if you can read between the lines, there is a lot to learn from it."

"There is?" she made her voice querulously high.

"It's a collection of short stories," she laughed awkwardly. "I know, I know, but trust me. It's not for kids, and the library might not lend it to you, but there are copies on campus and in the Solnedian Library."

"Okay..." she wondered how a fiction book could help.

"It's called The Second Sunset," Wynmere continued.

"Thank you," Nashel said with the same querulous voice, now imbued with gratefulness.

"You're welcome, my dear," another shoulder squeeze. "If you need anything, let me know."

Nashel nodded and made her way out of the classroom. Alistair was waiting impatiently outside, tapping his foot and bouncing his leg.

"So?"

"She said it's not in the curriculum and not accessible to me or her," she reported. "She said the Solnedian Library might have books, but they will not lend them out, and definitely not to a minor."

"Bummer," Alistair commented. She had come to understand that expression, even though at first she had no idea what he was saying.

"She gave me the title of a collection of short stories; she said I might find something if I read between the lines."

"Short stories?" he asked, incredulous.

She shrugged. "That's what she said."

"And you can get this book?"

"She didn't know. She said I have more chances with this than any other."

"It's worth a try, then?"

"I guess."

They didn't discuss it further, and for that evening, Nashel left the thought of a fiction book aside to focus on the manuscript that waited for her in her room. She checked her work and found it sloppy, so she redid the Expressions for the third time. Fortunately for her, when she double-checked, she was satisfied and didn't have to do it again. She shook her head, disgusted with herself, imagining what sort of punishment she would've got if she were still in the Sunset. She had to make a plan to re-introduce the rigorous training she was used to and get back in shape. Maybe she could do that during the summer holidays instead of frolicking around with her new little friend.

CHAPTER NINETEEN

The Sun Always Sets

Nashel tried the campus library, but the librarian just looked at her with a vague glance and shrugged. She wondered if the man was bewitched. Either way, she couldn't get it. She didn't know if it wasn't there or if it was on loan. She didn't really care; she was only frustrated that she couldn't get it. She had to try the Solnedian Library, but it turned out she had no time to do so.

The weeks leading to the summer holidays became a hell of exams and study sessions, made even worse by the scorching heat. Walking around campus, and around the city, was a headache-inducing experience due to the bright sun bouncing off the buildings and blinding the pedestrians even more than usual. It didn't help that the sun rose earlier and set later.

Nashel flaunted the rules again and made a small, perennial snow mound in a corner of her room that emanated cold air and made the place habitable. Alistair took refuge there, bringing clothes and toiletries with him, so he didn't have to leave the room. There was enough space for him to sleep on the floor, so he stayed most nights. Not that they slept much, mostly using the slightly cooler nights for their hardest study sessions. Nashel wished they also held the exams at night.

Her plans to resume a strict training regime stayed that: plans. Another reminder that she had grown soft. Part of her also expected her people to contact her; it had been months since they sent her on the mission, and she wondered why, knowing it was the end of the academic year, they weren't interested in any of her progress and updates.

One evening, in the middle of the most packed exam week, she was invited to the Alwenach's meeting. She considered the idea of refusing, but she needed to keep up with her mission.

The meeting itself was interesting only for the first few minutes because she could see who the members were; after that, when the meeting actually started, it became torture. She was finally officially introduced to HQ, and that was the meeting's location. The room didn't have proper ventilation; the small, black-out windows were always closed; someone might think that, being underground, the room would keep cooler. It didn't, and when it was packed with members for the meeting, the heat and the smell of many bodies in a cramped space were a lethal combination.

Nashel didn't scare easily. She was well trained. She knew how to face all kinds of enemies and keep her cool. Yet, that night, she was shaken. Each and every one of the members was a fanatic zealot. They chanted, they bumped fists in the air; they incited each other to hate. They were dangerous, not because they were powerful, but because they were brainwashed. They idolised immolation, and they didn't seem to have any empathy towards possible casualties. They weren't powerful, but if they'd decided to disregard their own lives and kill themselves, they could cause a lot of damage.

It was difficult to pretend to share the same fanaticism, especially when Aldenor called her onto the stage to introduce her to the members, then started chanting an awful slogan, and he expected her to join with passion. Nashel thought she was going to be sick, and the meeting didn't end soon enough. She stumbled back to her room as if she were drunk, her stomach upset.

Alistair was waiting in her room and jumped up to help her take the last steps to her bed, worried because she had refused to talk for almost one hour. He offered her a glass of cold water, courtesy of the snow mound, and waited, trying to hide his impatience.

"El, are you okay? Did they do something to you?" he asked her when he couldn't bear it anymore.

"I'm okay," she said, sitting up and facing him.

"What happened?"

"Nothing. It was just disgusting."

"Disgusting?" he inquired.

"I can't go into details. I'll throw up," she started. "But they would kill their own babies if it meant injuring even just one Sunset person."

"Holy Sun!"

"Yeah," she agreed.

"I'm sorry you had to go through that."

"And I will have to again," she groaned.

"Not until after the summer!"

She nodded, conceding.

"Have you decided if you're coming with me?" he asked, almost shyly.

"Is your place as hot as here?"

He hesitated. "Yes and no."

"Yes or no, which is it?" she said more harshly than she had intended. "Sorry."

He shrugged it off. "The temperature is as high as here, but it's a much more open space full of plants, shade, water, and no blinding buildings. So, it feels different."

"Water?"

"Yeah, there's a lake not too far where kids usually spend most of their summer."

"Sold!" she gave in, smiling.

She had thought about her plans for the holidays. She had hoped for her people to call her, and that was unlikely to happen. She thought about staying on campus, exploring every inch of it to see if she could find any plans of attack, then find a way to communicate them back home. She thought about exploring the country, maybe some of the other major cities to gather information there, in the event there were other Alwenach branches, or other groups or plans. She thought about camping in front of the Solnedian Library until they agreed to let her borrow a copy of The Second Sunset.

However, her people weren't going to contact her; the campus, and the city were scorching hot, and she had no desire to melt, especially because she couldn't use her powers outside her room. The other cities and the country were a stretch. The Sunset intel pinpointed the Sunrise Academy as the focal point of the attack. So, she decided to take some time off, put some distance between herself and the mission, and enjoy Alistair's company.

"For real?" he asked, incredulous.

"What do I pack?"

He laughed, delighted. "Anything light, and swimwear."

"Are you sure it's okay for me to join you? Is your mum okay with it?"

He swatted his hand. "Of course! There's a spare room just waiting for you!"

She noticed that didn't completely answer her questions, but she didn't press.

In the following days, she realised she was looking forward to going, which was a surprising and new emotion for her. Her mind kept shaking its metaphorical head, disappointed - "Softer. Weak," it seemed to be repeating - but she was good at ignoring it. She promised herself that she would use the time off to train, even if she was at Alistair's. She packed gingerly, including the summer clothes and swimwear he told her to, a book to read, and His Slowlyness. The day they left, she made sure all the wards were strong, and added an extra one to seal her room off completely.

They took a train, and Alistair told her the journey would

be long. She spent most of the time looking out the window, fascinated by the change in scenery that had happened in a soothing rhythm. When they were closer, the scenery changed again to yellow fields of crops and grass burnt by the scorching sun. The station they stopped at was barely more than a bench and a sign. It was very different from the farm environment she'd been in during her residential, but it reminded her of the village she first arrived at after crossing the Void. Nobody was there to welcome them, but Alistair told her it was normal: his mum was busy and didn't like to leave the farm anyway.

"We have to walk," he said apologetically. "There's no bus or anything that gets there. It's not too far, though."

He was nervous and worried, but she didn't mind. She was in shape, and it would be the beginning of her promise to train more, so she wasn't bothered at all. They walked between high stalks of corn, passed a thing called a scarecrow, and Nashel stopped for fifteen minutes to study it, because she had never seen one before. Alistair had to explain to her it was to scare crows and deter them from eating the corn, but he was laughing so much that he had to repeat it three times before she understood. She said they didn't have any where she grew up, because it was so far north that there were no crows.

They passed a huge, empty field, with the ground dug up to prepare it for the new seeds, then another field of green, bright grass and huge black and white cows grazing, and another with beautiful horses.

It took them almost an hour to get to Alistair's farm. There was no gate or wall to mark the property, just a post every once in a while, and no house in sight. Nashel was confused, but Alistair explained that their land was huge, not that he was rich. It was mostly uncultivated, but the house would appear in a while. First, they saw the barn, a big, red, wooden building; next to it, a metal, scorching silo that emanated hot waves; pastures where sheep, pigs, and cows grazed; fields of crops; and then, finally, the house. A two-storey building, painted yellow, with a porch all around it and a white fence.

They got to the front of the house, the doors and windows were all open, even though it was so hot and there was no breeze at all.

"Mum!" Alistair called when they entered. "Mum, we're here!"

"Kitchen!" a warm voice replied, clearly excited to hear him.

They left the bags on the floor and went to the back of the house towards the kitchen.

Alistair's mum was a lean but muscular woman, as pale as her son, with the same piercing blue eyes and black hair. Her hands were deep into dough, and the sweet smell of pie was coming from the hot oven.

When she looked up at them, the smile fell off her face, replaced by a look of horror. She took a few steps back, like she was backing away from a ghost or a killer, and spilt a jug of milk that was resting on the edge of the counter, but didn't seem to care about it.

"No," she murmured, shaking her head. "No. No. No!" her voice increasingly went louder and louder until she was screaming, "NO!"

By then, she seemed more angry than scared. Nashel was immediately at ready; something told her what the woman was about to do and made her erect a shield in front of her just as Alistair's mum tried to strike her with powers. She was strong, Nashel noted, very strong.

"Mum!" Alistair shouted back in shock.

She tried to strike her again, but Nashel was too quick. She seemed to give up the attempt, but Nashel knew it could be a trick to make her lower her guard. Yet, she wondered why she had received such a cold welcome.

"Mum! Stop it!"

"Alistair Corven." She was not so happy to see him anymore and was furious. "Do you know what you did?"

Alexis broke into a huge grin. "I knew it!" he exclaimed and made a gesture of victory.

"You knew?" his mum wasn't impressed. "You knew, and you brought her here? You knew, and you've been her friend all this time? What did I tell you? What did I teach you? You stupid, stupid boy."

Nashel didn't know what was going on. The woman who looked so lovely a second before, baking pies for his son and his friend, turned into a formidably powerful flair, then into a fury.

"Well, she's staying, whether you want it or not," Alistair said, jutting his chin.

"Of course you'd say that," she shook her head.

"She's not evil. She's my best friend."

"Only you could dig yourself into such a hole."

"I'm sorry," Nashel interrupted coldly, tired of being left out. "Pray tell, what's going on?"

Alistair turned to her like he had just remembered she was there. He pulled a face and scratched the back of his head.

"My mum, well," he started, embarrassed. "My mum, she has a skill..." he stopped, looked at his mum, who raised an eyebrow but didn't help him. "She can see auras."

"Auras?"

"Yes, auras are a sort of glow around your body. If you have powers, she can see these auras and tell if a person is a Sunrise or Sunset."

Several things happened in the space of a second: Nashel noticed the use of 'powers' not 'magic' and she also recalled all the time Alistair used 'Sunforsaken' of 'Thank the Sun', exclamations typical of her land, that she never heard uttered by Sunrise people. She also understood that she was trapped, alone, against two, and she knew Alistair could be powerful, and his mum seemed as well. She immediately enclosed herself in a protective shield, predicting an imminent attack, all the while studying her surroundings to find the best escape route.

"Wait, wait!" Alistair followed her gaze, and he threw his hands up, palms forward, to show he wasn't a threat. He didn't try to stop her; he actually moved, so the way was even clearer. "It's okay."

"I don't think so," she commented.

"It is," he was talking slowly, as if she was a feral beast he didn't want to scare away or be attacked by.

"You're making things worse, Alistair," his mum sighed, shaking her head again and gently pulling his arms down. She stepped in front of him in a smooth move that could be perceived as just facing her directly, but Nashel knew she was only protecting her son.

"Listen," she addressed her. "That's the door. You are free to leave. We will not stop you or harm you."

Nashel cocked her head, not believing her.

"We are Sunset, too!" Alistair blurted out excitedly.

His mum hung her head, questioning what she had done in her life to deserve a stupid son.

"Let's go sit down for this," she pointed to the living room, still wary of Nashel.

"I'd rather stand," she commented, her voice steely, but let them file out of the kitchen and into the lounge, then followed.

"I'm Ravenspawn, by the way. Raven for short," she told her as she passed sat down before continuing. "My ability is a Sunset speciality. A rare one at that. I've never heard of a Sunrise capable of such a particular feat."

If true, it wouldn't surprise her. The Sunrise had everything but rare skills - or skills in general.

"That's how you knew," Nashel concluded, jerking her chin towards Alistair. She was sure now that he knew since the first moment he had met her, when he had bumped 'accidentally' into her.

"Yes and no," he said, now weary. "I'm not as powerful, so I can perceive the auras, but I can't see them or distinguish them very well."

"So, how did you know?"

"I wasn't sure until now, when Mum confirmed it," he replied. "But your aura stood out to me as different from the Sunrise around."

"How?" she didn't mean how her aura stood out, but how it was possible for them to be Sunset.

Alistair was about to reply, but his mum understood what she meant.

"It happens. Sometimes a baby is born on the wrong side."

"You are both Sunset," Nashel noted.

"Yes, sometimes it is hereditary. I have powers, and I passed them on to Alistair."

"But you weren't born here." It wasn't a question, but a statement.

"No, I wasn't," she confirmed, but didn't add an explanation.

"That's why you don't like to leave the farm," something Alistair said earlier clicked.

She nodded. "Yes, I would be lying if I said I am not afraid of being found out. When Alistair was a child, it was even worse. I was so glad we lived on a farm and not in the city."

"I was a very active child," Alistair commented with a smile.

"He gave me a heart attack every time he used his powers." She had a sad smile and ruffled his son's hair. "You see, a baby born on the wrong side, if found, it would be thrown into the Void."

She visibly swallowed. Nashel looked at her, surprised. She never heard of babies born on the wrong side, nor what would happen to them.

"It would be just easier to kill them," she observed.

"Yes, it would be," Raven agreed. "But you see, throwing them in the Void doesn't kill them. It's much, much worse."

"What do you mean?" Nashel asked, confused.

"That's how Drifters are made."

Nashel stilled. She wasn't blinking; she wasn't breathing or moving at all. She was vaguely aware that Alistair had called her name, but she didn't really hear him. The sentence repeated itself over and over in her head, Alistair's mum's voice slowly becoming Nightshade's. That's how Drifters are made. That's how Drifters are made. That's how Drifters are made.

She blinked, returning to the present, and looked at Alistair. She imagined him deformed, so pale his skin looked translucent, so weak that one Drift would require him to sleep for hours on end; but then she also saw him so strong, so beautiful, inside the Void.

"I see you understand," Raven said, a bitter smile on her lips. "So you see why I was so against Alistair going to the academy, and why I was shocked to see you here."

Nashel nodded.

"I have wanted to go to the Academy since I was little. I couldn't understand why I wasn't allowed, but at the time I hadn't met any other powered person, so I didn't know the difference," Alistair said in a distant tone, as if reminiscing.

"I didn't want him to go," she repeated. "Not even now. I trust him, but it takes only a wrong word. You say 'power' instead of 'magic', or just forget to wave your wand right, and they would know. They would take him and throw him away, and condemn him to a fate way worse than death. You know what Drifters are like. Would you wish that on someone? On your own son?"

"No," Nashel said firmly.

"So, I didn't want him to go. But I couldn't stop him, either. All his life, I clipped his wings. I couldn't bear it any longer."

"I'm fine, mum, I'm still here. Nobody noticed."

Nashel didn't know if it was Alistair's comment or Raven's example, but she recalled again the many times Alistair used the Sunset interjections, he always did it in her presence and she couldn't think of a time he did it in front of others, but still. She opened her mouth to tell Raven, but then stopped. She didn't need to know.

"That's true, ma'am," Nashel lied. "He's been perfect."

Raven sighed, relieved.

Nashel thought about how stupid she had been. About the many times she wondered if Alistair was someone else, why he looked at her in certain ways, some of the things he said to her, and, most of all, how she let them all slide. There she was, in the living room of two flairs claiming to be her people, with no proof of the truth, and no backup.

Yes, Alistair could perform magic without a wand, but she excluded it was impossible for a Sunrise to do the same if they wanted to. Her body reacted before her mind, and she sprinted to the door and outside. She heard Alistair call after her, but she ignored him. He had many occasions to hurt her, or at least try, and never did. He stood by her side and became her friend. Yet, wasn't it also because of him that she became soft? What if that was his plan all along? She knew she needed to face him and his mum, but she retreated to regroup and choose her ground, just like they taught her at the Academy.

CHAPTER TWENTY

Ravenspawn

When she was ready, she let them find her. She didn't attack first; that wasn't part of her plan. She needed to gauge their true strength, and couldn't rush into an attack blindly. They reached her openly, making noise, showing their entire bodies instead of a defensive stance. They approached her as if she were a dangerous beast, and she was glad they recognised that.

She saw Alistair opening his mouth, her name forming on his lips, but his mother silenced him.

"We don't mean you any harm," Raven started. Nashel was still partly hidden, in a tree to get a vantage view, while they were in the field in front of it. They knew she was there, but couldn't see her.

She didn't want to give her exact position, so she made her answer come from behind them, being careful how much power she used in that Sunforsaken weak land.

"Forgive me for not taking your word for it."

She saw Alistair turn, surprised, but his mother's eyes remained trained in her general direction. She was good.

"I can show you my story, if you let me."

"And be blind and deaf to what he does in the meantime?"

She saw him opening his mouth again and saw the murdering glance his mother gave him to make him stop.

"You are right; that would be unfair," Raven admitted. "Alistair, go back home and stay there."

"No!" he protested.

"You either do that, or say goodbye to your friend forever."

Which, in Nashel's mind, translated into "You either go, or we both die at the hands of your friend," and she knew that was exactly what Raven meant.

"I'm not letting either of you hurt the other."

Raven stomped a foot on the ground, frustrated. "Child, listen to your mother for once."

"Yeah, listen to your mother," Nashel echoed.

Alistair shook his head, defeated, turned and walked away. He wasn't very well trained, or he wouldn't have turned his back on an enemy, but she knew that already.

They waited, and when Nashel was sure - she sent a feeler out - that he wasn't in the vicinity anymore, she jumped down the tree and approached the woman.

"It's only me and you now," she said. "We will both be blind and deaf, and you will know if I lie in my memories."

Nashel nodded and offered Raven her hands. She didn't trust her, and she was ready to react, but if she showed her something, they would both be incapacitated.

Raven took her hands; her grip was strong but not violent. In a matter of seconds, Alistair's farm disappeared. With a punch in the gut she didn't expect, she saw the Sunset Academy. She was looking at it from a small height, presumably Raven as a child. The image was accurate to the littlest of details, and it felt as if she were thrown back into her own memories. A younger Headmistress Magna was inspecting a Class. She was wearing a uniform too, the same Nashel was used to seeing Sergeant Thomas in: an instructor.

She saw other cadets, and saw them growing at a fast pace, racing through the memories of the training years, until graduation. She saw her hands - Raven's hands - raise, grab her hat, and throw it in the air in celebration.

She saw her putting on a different uniform, in a different room, and joining the Sunset army. She saw drills, similar to those she had started before leaving, and more training, university lessons, and speciality talks. Raven was shining. She shone through her academy years, and she was shining as a soldier.

She saw her being called to Field Marshall Stormbreaker's office, just like Nashel had been, but she felt the smugness of someone who knew she was going to be praised.

"Second Lieutenant Raven," Stormbreaker greeted her. "Please, you may sit."

He looked and sounded exactly how she remembered him, as if he hadn't aged a day since that meeting and hers. The following conversation was also a déjà vu, as he said almost the same words.

"I have heard a lot about you. Top of your class, squad leader. Auralist."

Now that she was not involved personally, Nashel disliked the general's tone even more. It felt insincere, hypocritical.

"You are powerful, disciplined, and determined."

He did like his own voice, and he didn't like Raven.

"You may wonder why you are here," he smiled slimy.

"I do, sir," Raven replied, unimpressed. She didn't like him, either.

"What you are going to learn here is top-secret. Not a word needs to leave this office. Understood?"

"Yes, sir," Nashel could feel Raven's desire to roll her eyes.

"Your achievements and awards are impressive, and that is why you've been called here today."

He sure liked the preambles.

"We believe the Sunrise wants to attack us."

By then, Nashel knew where the conversation was going, but it still surprised her how close to her conversation with the general this was.

"We want to send you to the other side on a mission. A spy mission, if you will."

"The Void is uncrossable," Raven commented, unimpressed.

"That's where the top-secret part comes into play. There is a way," he smiled, and again, it was almost disgusting to see how false it was.

"This is a high-risk mission," the general continued. "You will be on your own. You will have no contact with anyone from this side."

How would she report her findings, then?

"You will not have support or an extraction if things go south. Do you understand what I'm saying?"

"Yes, sir," Raven replied firmly. Nashel could feel she was conflicted: she didn't like or trust Stormbreaker, but she was also proud to be chosen for such a dangerous mission.

"Wonderful," he laughed. "You will be leaving in a week's time."

"A week, sir?"

"Yes, the Sunrise is very different from what you know. You will need to learn everything you can to blend in. You will spend the week with our Sunrise experts."

"I understand, sir," she replied firmly.

The memory rushed again, a succession of images of an old woman teaching her about wands and languages. Nashel was glad to see she wasn't the only one who struggled with a wand, but Raven was prouder and became more and more excited through the week. She told her squad about it - despite it being a secret - and her boyfriend at the time. She was popular in a way Nashel never was, and she saw how the other soldiers looked at her. Headmistress Magna, or Sergeant Magna as she was at the time, approached her the night before Raven left. They walked together to a secluded area.

"Don't go," Magna said.

"I can't refuse," Raven countered.

"I know, but run away, do something, just don't go."

"What is it?" Raven - and Nashel - understood there was something more Magna wasn't saying.

She shook her head. Either couldn't or didn't want to say.

"Spill it!" Raven ordered her. It occurred to Nashel that Raven was now the higher-ranking officer of the two.

"I can't," Magna replied. "I can only warn you."

Raven was frustrated and angry as Magna left her there to return to the Academy.

Nightshade's room wasn't his yet. Another Drifter, Nashel wasn't sure how she knew it wasn't him, occupied it. He took her to the garrison by the Void, rested for a while, then they crossed the Void.

The feeling wasn't the same as hers. It was way worse for Raven. At one point, Nashel felt her heart - Raven's - stop beating. Rationally, she knew the woman wasn't dead, but it felt like that. When they reached the other side, the Drifter collapsed.

Raven was greeted by a Second Lieutenant, who gave her a bag with a PPad, an ancient model, money, water, and food, then told her the way to the nearest village.

Images again raced each other: Raven finding work on a farm; Raven trying to find anything about an attack with no success; Raven trying to contact her people, again, with no success; Raven falling for a boy, resisting it because she was on a mission. Then, they slowed when a message, a paper message floating just in front of her, appeared one night as she was about to go to bed. Nashel gasped. She knew those kinds of messages; it was from their people.

It said only three words.

"Not a mission."

She felt Raven exhausting herself trying to see the Trace, trying to find who sent it. When she was about to pass out from fatigue, she managed: Headmistress Magna.

Nashel wondered what it meant, but in Raven's mind it was clear. She had doubted it since that night in the woods when the instructor told her not to go.

Raven knew she was powerful. She knew she was strong-headed and not ready to follow orders blindly. She realised the top brass did not like her and that they thought of her as a nuisance. A powerful, unwelcome nuisance that needed to be dealt with. So why not "reward" her with a mission? A dangerous mission her pride couldn't say no to? A risky, bogus mission to the other side of an impenetrable barrier.

Nashel saw and felt her anger; she saw and felt the outburst of powers that almost killed the farm owners who had taken Raven in. She saw the woman coming to accept the truth and finally give in to her feelings towards the boy. She never told him who she was, and he never suspected. When she was with child, she hoped and prayed to the Sun that it was going to be born in the flash of darkness of the Sunrise. But on the day Alistair was born, strictly at home, the farm the owners left her when they passed, the most blinding flash of light greeted the cry of the newborn, horror painted on her now-husband's face.

The final memory she saw was of a fight between the couple. He screamed at her that it was an abomination, that it shouldn't be breathing, and she shouldn't nurse it. He suggested he would take it to the Void and drop it himself.

Raven, of course, didn't agree. To save her child, there was only one thing she could do. She lied to him and agreed to go to the Void. They would do it together, that he shouldn't bear that weight alone. But once they were there, she gently deposited the bundle with the baby on the ground and turned to push her husband, with her powers and her hands, into the barrier. The perfect O of surprise his mouth formed was the last image Nashel saw.

The sun blinded her when they came back to reality. The hot weather took her breath away for a moment until she managed to adjust. Nashel was sure the memories were real; there was a quality to them that was impossible to fake. That was the reason Raven was willing to do it. So, she was truly a Sunset, and Alistair, too. There was a lot to unpack about the memories she just saw: the people in them, the behaviours, the story itself.

"Shall we get out of this scorching sun?" Raven said, shading her eyes with a hand.

"Yes," Nashel conceded.

They were Sunset, but she still didn't know if she could trust them. It was hot, though, so she followed her back towards the house.

"Don't tell him what you saw about his father," she told her halfway through, without looking.

Nashel shrugged.

"He thinks he died in an accident."

"I won't say anything."

They walked the rest of the way in silence. Nashel's mind kept going back to the memories, but she didn't have the time or the mental space to do that right then.

"Don't think for a second I will not keep my eyes on you. He may trust you, but he's not a Sunset like us."

Nashel was surprised by the harshness, not towards her, but towards Alistair.

"I wouldn't dream of it," she smirked.

"Oh, thank the Sun!" Alistair shouted when he saw them coming. He ran from the porch towards them, then hovered to assess any hypothetical injury, as if after they fought, they would both go back walking side by side. This boy might be a Sunset by birth, but he wouldn't last a day in her land.

"So she can stay!" it was supposed to be a question but came out as an exclamation.

"If she wants to," Raven shrugged and went back to the kitchen to resume her cookies baking.

"YES!" he started jumping up and down. He almost jumped to hug Nashel, but stopped before it.

"I'll give you a tour of the house," he said, shouldering both bags. "So, this is the living room, obviously," he smiled. "And you saw the kitchen. There is a guest bathroom there," he indicated a room at the back, then went up the stairs. "Here, there's the master bedroom, my mum's," he indicated to the left. "The bathroom, and my room," he went in and dropped his bag on the floor.

The room was completely different from his at the academy; it was more homey, more lived-in. There were posters of films and music bands, and drawing dating back to various stages of his life, from when he was a toddler to more recent and defined sketches. He mentioned he liked to draw, but he never showed her anything. He said he hadn't drawn since he left home.

It was warm, not just because the day was hot, but the room would have felt warm even if it were chilly. It was the room of a lovely boy who felt at home there and was loved. She could see his mother's touch: the bed made, the sheets looked comfortable and cool, and clothes were folded on his bed, ready for him for the night.

She thought about the contrast with her rooms at both academies. Hers were sparser; there were no posters, no motherly touch, despite the bed being made every day, the clothes being folded neatly, and His Slowlyness ready to welcome her back.

"I'm sorry, but I didn't see another room here," Nashel added, suddenly realising it. "Do I need to sleep in the barn?"

Alistair laughed, "No, no, here, come over."

He moved back to the corridor, and took a little jump to grab a short rope dangling from the ceiling. Nashel hadn't noticed it before, but there was a square-shaped hatch there. As Alistair pulled the rope, a ladder unfolded without a noise. He made a grand, but ironic, gesture to invite her to go up and, when she did, she found a room as big as the house. A nicely made double bed was ready to welcome her; a big wardrobe stood open to show that it was empty and she could use it for her clothes, and towels were on a comfy chair for her bathroom needs. There was actually a smaller room on one end, that turned out to be a bathroom with shower, all for her. Alistair dropped her bag at the foot of the bed and grinned.

"Cool, right?"

"Yep!"

"I always wanted this to be my room, but Mum refused."

"Why?"

He shrugged. "I was very active as a child; Mum thought I

would destroy a place this big with my powers."

That made Nashel laugh.

"I'll let you unpack. Please feel free to explore on your own, as if this were your own home."

"I never had a home home," Nashel said to herself as Alistair was climbing down the ladder.

"What?" he stopped and looked up at her.

"I never had a home home," she repeated louder. There was no sadness in her voice; she didn't feel anything of the sort.

He climbed back up to look at her properly. "So, the village... your parents—" but he stopped himself, realising what the truth must have been.

"Cover story," Nashel confirmed.

"Should've known," he nodded.

Nashel shrugged. She wasn't ready to trust him with her story yet, and she knew she couldn't focus on it while her mind was reliving Raven's memories.

When it was clear she wouldn't say anything else, Alistair sighed and repeated that would leave her to unpack. She put her clothes in the wardrobe, which still looked empty since she didn't pack much. She went to the bathroom and freshened up, then realised that she was with her people: she could use her powers however she wanted. She could use an Expression to keep herself cool. It seemed such a good idea, and it worked for an hour or so, but then she was reminded that the power on this side of the world was weak and required her to use more energy, even for the smaller tasks. She cursed the Sunrise again and resigned herself to let the warmth get her.

She finally went downstairs, making her way back to the kitchen. Raven and Alistair were talking quietly. She couldn't hear what they were saying, but it seemed just small chat.

"She lives!" Alistair laughed and beckoned her to join him at the island. "Have a slice of pie!"

Nashel sat down and did exactly that. "It's delicious! Thank you!"

"Thank you," Raven replied with a smile.

"How do you cope with the lack of power?" Nashel asked the woman.

Raven laughed bitterly. "I guess I just got used to it. It was hard at the beginning, but I've been here a long time now."

Nashel nodded; it made sense. "You still use our language, though," she noted.

"Yes, I also refuse to wave a stick in the air as if it actually did something."

Nashel laughed at that, completely agreeing with the sentiment. "That was the most ridiculous thing I ever heard. When they first told me, I thought they were joking."

"The brass don't joke, though," Raven replied with a grin. An old saying the soldiers and cadets used when they wanted to complain.

"No, they don't," she replied with a knowing smile. It was nice to hear something familiar after all those months.

"What's that?" Alistair commented, gesturing between the two of them, not wanting to feel excluded.

"Inside joke," Nashel replied with a pleased shrug, feeling just a bit more at ease.

CHAPTER TWENTY-ONE

A Taste of Home

"I can show you around, if you feel up to it," Alistair suggested as she finished the pie.

"Alistair, you spent half the day travelling. Leave the girl alone for a while. Let her enjoy some peace and quiet!"

Nashel wanted to protest, but in truth, she was tired. Alistair, too, wanted to protest, but his mum stopped him before he could.

"Why don't you just stay outside, enjoy some shade and a lemonade. You have all summer to show her the fields and everything else."

He nodded, giving up, and she was secretly grateful.

They had yet to move that a ruckus erupted in the kitchen. She didn't have time to register or understand what it was that a furry shape jumped on her legs, and attacked her face. She was about to defend herself, blasting it with powers, when she realised that it was licking her, not attacking.

Alistair's laughter registered in her ears, and she relaxed even further.

When she was able to push the furry thing away enough to see again, she discovered a beautiful, huge, golden dog, its tongue looping on one side, and what could be called a smile, if animals were capable of such a thing. She laughed at herself - how did she get so useless? - and tentatively pet it on the head. It closed its eyes and seemed to ask for more, with a small sound from deep in its throat and the happy thud of its tail.

"That's Neo," Alistair said, smiling. "He's supposed to help us out in the fields, but he's actually a ball of fluffy mess!"

Nashel laughed again, still petting the dog. She never had a pet; they weren't allowed at the academy, and none of the houses she's been on a residential had one either.

"I remember when I first pet a dog," Raven said. "I had the same expression you have right now."

Nashel shrugged, distracted by the dog. It was soothing to pet him; she could see herself do it for long.

"C'mon, let's go outside. I think mum wants the kitchen to herself," Alistair patted his thigh, and Neo followed him, tongue lolling out and tail wagging madly. Nashel followed as well, albeit not with the same enthusiasm.

They went back inside when their stomachs started to grumble, and it was dinner time. Nashel offered to help Raven in the kitchen, but she refused, so she helped Alistair set the table. It was the first time she had sat down to have dinner with a welcoming family since her parents died, and it felt weird. She usually had food in the dining hall at both academies, and she always ended up eating in her room during her residentials.

Alistair was delighted to be home and taste his mother's cooking again. He kept saying that the dish he had in front of him was his favourite and the best he had ever tasted, and he made Nashel smile. The food was good, better than what the Sunrise Academy served, and Nashel enjoyed it as well.

"Is there anything you would like me to cook for you?" Raven asked her.

Nashel shook her head. "Anything is alright."

"You don't have a favourite?"

"Not really," she shrugged.

"Right, I forgot there for a second where you come from,"

Raven laughed without malice.

It felt a bit awkward eating in such a small, cosy setting. There was no cacophony of other tables and dozens of other students chatting all around. It was warmer to just share the meal with two people, share a laugh in comfortable silence, and enjoy a warm plate of something made with love to please and make someone happy, not just for sustenance and quantity. She felt she was intruding, and she didn't know how to behave.

"I'll help do the dishes," Nashel tried to say at the end of the meal but yawned halfway through.

Raven laughed. "You'll help me tomorrow. Now just go to sleep, both of you!"

Alistair was already dozing off during the exchange, and shook himself, startled. They both got up and dragged themselves to their rooms. Nashel wanted to just drop on the bed, but forced herself to the little bathroom to take a quick shower and put on shorts and vest as pyjamas. Then, finally, the comfy bed welcomed her.

Maybe she was too tired, maybe the bed was too comfy, maybe it was too hot, maybe it just wasn't meant to be, because sleep eluded her. She tossed and turned, and tossed and turned. She tried to count sheep, she tried meditating, but still, she couldn't sleep. Somehow, for some reason she couldn't fathom, memories flooded her mind. Memories of when she was little, of warm meals with her feet dangling off the too-big chair; of bedtime stories of magic and dragons and brave princesses with swords; of running around the house and playing games outside. Of warm hugs and gentle smiles, of cinnamon, laundry detergent, and flowery lotion. She hadn't thought about her parents in a long time, and she didn't understand why her brain was playing tricks on her then. Angry, she got out of bed and silently climbed down to the ground floor. Maybe a glass of water, or a walk around the house would help. She didn't expect anyone awake, but the kitchen was lit, and she found Raven there, nursing a glass of something she couldn't guess.

"Couldn't sleep?" she asked.

Nashel shrugged.

"Want something to drink?"

"Just water," she replied and moved to get a glass and some cold water from the fridge. "I was so tired, but sleep just didn't come."

Raven laughed at her moan-y tone. "Do you want to talk about whatever is bothering you?"

"No, not really," Nashel commented, but then started to talk. "I don't know why, but I started to remember my parents."

"Alistair said you came from a small village in the North, but I reckon that was a lie."

Nashel nodded. "Part of my cover. My parents died when I was five, and then there was the Academy."

"At five? That's unusual."

"Yes, they said they were making an exception."

"You must be quite powerful."

Nashel shrugged again. She knew she was, but she learnt throughout the years that people didn't like it when she admitted it.

"You haven't lived in a house for some time; that must be what triggered the memories. I can get you something to help you sleep, if you'd like."

She immediately tensed at that. She still wasn't sure she trusted them, and she wasn't about to let Raven drug her.

"No, thank you. The water will do."

Raven laughed, seeing through her polite decline. "I'm not going to pretend that what you saw in my memories is not shocking, and I will leave it to you and your experience to make your own conclusions. But if you want to talk about them or your mission, I believe I may be the only person on this side of the world to understand."

"Thank you," she replied. "Magna is the Headmistress now," she added, not sure why.

"She is?" Raven laughed and clapped her hands once.

"She's been since I joined," Nashel confirmed.

"Stormbreaker is still Field Marshall."

Raven made a face that made Nashel laugh.

She spent a few minutes with Raven, asking her questions about places and people, and somehow remembering that made Nashel feel better.

"I'm going to try and sleep again," she announced.

"Have a good rest," Raven nodded.

Nashel went back to the room in the attic. It was warmer than downstairs, so Nashel used a bit of her powers to recreate the little mound of snow she had in her dorm room. It helped keep her cooler, but didn't help with sleep.

She was more relaxed now, but her mind went back to the memories. She hadn't heard from her people since she left, now eight months prior. They did say she would be on her own, that she would have no contact unless they initiated it. She had tried her best to find intel regarding an imminent attack. She infiltrated the Alwenach successfully, but even that seemed farfetched. They didn't have a concrete plan, just some research into crossing the Void en masse instead of individually.

The words Stormbreaker had spoken to Raven were so similar to those he spoke to Nashel that they seemed to merge. Nashel still didn't believe that her mission was not real. Raven was a different person, and those were different times.

She knew her worth, and she knew she was more powerful, therefore more valuable, than Raven. Stormbreaker and the Sunset would be fools to send her away and lose her like that. Yet, she wasn't stupid; she saw the similarities in their lives. She saw the achievements Raven obtained and compared them with hers. She knew then that there was a possibility that her mission was bogus, too.

She decided to trust her people and her instincts, and to leave any decision or any further considerations to a later day and finally sleep.

Morning arrived way too soon for her taste. She woke up

at the crack of dawn, as usual, without the need for alarm. True to her promise, she got up and started her day with a run. Alistair didn't join her, sleeping sprawled on his bed, she saw him as she crossed the corridor, snoring lightly.

Raven was awake, already working outside, so Nashel joined her after her run.

"You don't have to help," the woman commented.

"I need to train more; I've become soft," Nashel explained.

"The Sunrise does that to us," Raven replied solemnly.

For the rest of the morning, she assigned her the hardest jobs. The sun was scorching, and the hotness became more and more unbearable, but Raven ordered her not to use her powers to relieve it. She agreed, not because she saw Raven as her superior, although technically she was, but because she agreed it was more formative that way.

Alistair woke up close to lunchtime, his hair all over the place, his cheek marked by the pillow. Nashel laughed when she saw him like that. He looked younger, cuter.

"When did you get up?" he mumbled as he made his way to the dining table.

"Dawn," Nashel shrugged. She had showered, but she was already sweating again. Yet, she felt better than she did in past months, more herself.

"Sun!" he exclaimed. "Don't you know how to sleep in?"

Nashel shrugged. She finished setting the table and joined him.

"What did you do all this time?"

"I worked."

That piqued his interest. "Mum! You put her to work?! She's a guest!"

He sounded offended for her. Nashel laughed. "I asked her."

"You did what?" he said, outraged.

"I need to train more," she explained, but he made a confused face.

After lunch, he took her for the official tour of the property. She had seen part of it in the morning, but now he took her from limit to limit. The fields were huge, so it took them a while to go everywhere. Still, Nashel enjoyed every second. It was good to see open fields, the animals, hear the birds chirping happily again, after the deadness of the city.

She also got to meet the famous Peggy, Alistair's favourite dwarf sheep, the mascot of the farm. She was small and adorable, as he described her. She was all white, except for her face, ears, and the ends of her paws, which were black with a white stripe. She had 'hair' on her head that looked like a floor mop. Nashel wasn't one to feel awe, but she had to admit the sheep was cute.

When they got back, they were dripping wet with sweat, and Raven forbade them to get in unless they showered first. They used one of the hoses outside, which turned more into a game than a shower, a game heavily in favour of Nashel since she used her elemental abilities to douse Alistair completely. They then joined Neo in front of the living room fan to keep cool.

In the next few days, Nashel found it was Neo's pastime: just being lazy and lying in front of the fan. He didn't shy away from pets, but he also didn't ask for them and didn't seem interested in playing fetch.

Nashel kept waking up early in the morning and helped Raven with more serious work, then joined Alistair for the fun tasks: spending a good amount of time each day to try to keep the animals cool. They had sprinkles installed for the cows, horses, and sheep, which they all loved, and shaded areas where the animals could take refuge, with plenty of water to go with. The most fun they had was in creating mud puddles for the pigs. They felt like they were little children again, playing in the mud, getting so dirty it took quite a long time to remove all the mud from every inch of their bodies, but at least they had fun and for a little while forgot how hot it was, and the pigs were happy too.

The nights were her favourite part. The temperature dropped to a bearable degree, and she and Alistair spent them on the reclining chairs on the porch.

Alistair was curious, and it only took him two nights before he bombarded her with questions about the Sunset. Initially, Nashel was reticent to tell him, but he was a Sunset and he never had the chance to experience any of it, so she indulged him as much as she could, without revealing any compromising secrets.

"If not in a village up north, where did you live?"

"My parents died when I was five," she wasn't going to tell him about what happened to them; he wouldn't understand. "So, I moved to the Citadel."

"What's the Citadel?"

"It's our city. It's the capital of the flairs. A fortified heaven. Powerless people cannot get in. We have everything we need there; we don't even have to pay for stuff!" she smiled at the memory of her first time, when Sergeant Thomas told her she could have the hamburger.

"What?"

"Well, that's mostly true for students. As long as we take what we need, there is no need to pay for it."

"That's so cool!"

She nodded, smiling.

"You said you never had a home, though, so where did you actually live?"

"At the academy."

"So, the Academy is not just for kids our age?"

"No!" she laughed at the idea. "Usually, it starts at six years old. I started a bit early because of my parent's death."

"Wow! What is it like, then?" he asked. "Is it like ours?"

She wasn't sure he included her in the 'ours' but she didn't like it.

"No, it is completely different," she answered, outraged.

"Tell me."

"You need to understand that things are different in the Sunset," she stopped for a moment, trying to find the right words to explain. "Do you remember the forest?"

Alistair nodded; she didn't have to specify which forest.

"Do you remember how much power there was there?"

"Yes, how can I forget!"

"Well, the Sunset has almost as much. Definitely more than here."

"Must be awesome..."

"It is," she confirmed. "You don't get tired just doing the smallest thing. And people are way more open to powers, and well, in the Citadel we can use them whenever. There is no limit. The only rule is not to kill anyone."

Alistair looked at her, stunned, as if she were speaking another language.

She smiled, but continued. "So, the academy is a school where you hone your skills from the start, not hide them."

"How?"

"We train. The Sunset Academy is a military academy, because through discipline, we gain control."

"Since you're six?" He sounded confused and incredulous.

"You know how kids are when they start developing. It's better to start early."

"Okay. So, you're a soldier?"

"I'm a cadet. That's what students are called."

"Do you have a rank?"

She nodded. "The academy is divided into three branches. Class, which lasts for five years, Recruits, for another five, then Aspirants, for three years. When I left, I was in my second year as Aspirant and had the rank of Cadet Warrant Officer."

He looked at her with amazement. To her, it felt natural, but to Alistair, it must sound like a story in a book or a far, far away world.

"So you're the second highest rank in the academy?"

She nodded, bitterly. She should be the highest rank by then; a ceremony was supposed to happen at the end of the school year in the assembly square. It was mostly for the graduation of Cadet Under Officers, the last aspirant group, but the other cadets were celebrated, too. Usually, the higher class would pin their rank cord or insignia on the lower class's uniform in a symbolic gesture of passing down the baton. It had always been one of Nashel's favourite moments at the academy, and this time, one of the most important, but she was deprived of it.

Alistair must have noticed, because he lightly touched her and asked what was wrong.

"Nothing." She shook her head. "I regret not being able to attend this year's ceremony."

"Ceremony?"

She realised then that she had zoned out, thinking about the ritual, without saying a word out loud. "The ceremony to receive the next rank."

"Oh!" he exclaimed, his mouth a perfect O that made Nashel smile. "We can do it here if you want!"

She looked at him, confused.

"Yeah, a bit like a birthday party! Actually, when's your birthday?" he asked in quick succession. "Never mind, that's for later. My mum could give you a token to symbolise your new rank, and she could bake a cake to celebrate. What do you say?"

A warm feeling spread inside Nashel. She wasn't sure what it was, but it wasn't unpleasant. "I say you just want an excuse to have cake!"

They both laughed, and Nashel felt a bit of that bitterness flow away.

CHAPTER TWENTY-TWO

Promotions and Lakes

Nashel settled on a routine she found helpful, the morning spent with Raven, doing heavy work, training her body and her powers, the afternoons with Alistair, who tended to wake up late, practising in a more playful way, often showing off or trying to teach him a few tricks he didn't know. The nights were spent relaxing under the stars.

Alistair didn't mention the idea of a mock celebration anymore, and Nashel soon forgot about it. She should've known better.

"Cadet Warrant Officer Nashel!" Raven's voice boomed, amplified by her power, and woke her up with a start. "Assembly outside in five!"

She reacted instinctively, jumped out of bed, put on her working clothes, and rushed downstairs before she realised she wasn't at the academy, but at Alistair's. Nevertheless, she stood at attention in front of the door, waiting. By then, she realised what was happening and felt a smile forming on her lips.

It was the crack of dawn, just a bit earlier than her usual waking time, and Alistair appeared as well a few minutes after her, which surprised her. He tried to imitate her pose, poorly, and she almost laughed, but kept her form. He reminded her of the new Junior Cadets on their first assembly, looking up at the older cadets to get it right and failing.

Raven came out, and Nashel couldn't keep her expression neutral; if she were at the academy, she would be punished. But she couldn't help herself; Raven was donning the full dress uniform of the Second Lieutenant. Nashel didn't know how she had it; she shouldn't, by all accounts, but there it was in all its splendour.

"Is that what we wear for ceremonies, Cadet?" Raven addressed her. Her tone was serious, just like that of Sergeant Thomas during inspections, but Nashel detected amusement as well.

"No, ma'am, we do not," she replied, resuming her composure.

"Well, then, let's make it right." This time, Raven had a small smile.

She waved a hand in front of Nashel, and her work clothes became her beloved aspirant uniform. She looked down at herself without moving her head and took the sight in as much as she could. Alistair guffawed.

"Much better," Raven commented under her breath. "Cadet Warrant Officer Nashel, you have distinguished yourself during your mission, successfully infiltrating the enemy lines, and made progress towards your final goal. There are no Cadet Under Officers here to pass down the baton. However, I am of higher rank and therefore can bestow upon you the rank of Cadet Under Officer."

She produced a cord, a golden one, and affixed it on Nashel's left shoulder where her light blue one used to reside. Raven stepped back, and Nashel snapped to a salute. Alistair did the same in a goofy way, looking lost, but wanting to take part.

"Congratulations," Raven replied, saluting back. "At ease."

Nashel followed her orders with Alistair in tow.

"Dismissed," was the final order Raven gave before

grinning. A grin that was mirrored by both Nashel and Alistair.

Wearing the uniform felt weird. She felt out of place, for one, because she was, but also like she wasn't the same person who had last worn it. She still felt proud even though she knew it was fake, that Raven had no power to promote her, and that the celebration was just so Alistair could have cake. Yet, she liked it. It felt like a small win and a recognition of her efforts.

"Thank you," Nashel told the other two.

"It feels nice, doesn't it?" Raven asked, noticing how Nashel kept eyeing her uniform.

"I don't know; I think so."

"Can I get one, too?" Alistair asked, pouting and making them laugh.

"Sure," Nashel said, and she was in a good mood. She decided using her powers for something silly wouldn't be a waste that day. So she waved her hand just like Raven did and changed Alistair's clothes into the uniform of a Junior Cadet, with a polo shirt, blue trousers, and strap shoes. They fit him, but at the same time, they looked small, just like they would look on a six-year-old. Raven started laughing unstoppably.

"What?! Why?" Alistair asked, at a loss for coherent words.

"That's the Class uniform, what you would wear when you join the academy," Nashel explained, trying to stay serious.

"I'm not six!" Alistair exclaimed.

This time, Nashel laughed.

"Everything at the academy is earned," Raven explained to her son.

"You never talk about that," Alistair whispered back.

"It's not a topic I like to discuss," she replied resolutely.

Nashel saw the flash of anger in her eyes, but Alistair didn't and was going to protest, so she intervened. "I was told there might be cake?"

It did the trick; they both looked at her and then laughed.

"Chocolate," Raven nodded. "Let's get inside."

In the dining room, there was a little feast laid out. There was indeed chocolate cake, but also fruit, juice, pancakes, bacon, eggs, all the options she would find for breakfast at the academy. Raven had gone above and beyond to make that, and Nashel felt grateful.

"The time has come," Alistair tried to say with a solemn tone, but his too-small uniform made him look ridiculous.

"What time?" Nashel asked, muffling a laugh.

"The time for a holiday!" he exclaimed excitedly, a better fit for his look.

She looked confused. She thought they were already on holiday.

"Remember I mentioned the lakes?"

She nodded.

"That's where we're going today."

"But the animals..." she started.

"I managed for months without the both of you. I can manage again," Raven interrupted her.

"Are you sure?" Nashel asked her. The real reason she was opposing the trip was that it broke her training routine, and she didn't like it.

"Yes," Raven confirmed. "You always get a day off for the ceremony."

That was true; she had forgotten it.

"Let's go pack. Travel light," Alistair stood, and it was clear he couldn't wait any longer.

Nashel went to put on her swimming suit; taking off her uniform felt weirder than having it on. She looked at it for a long moment, but it soon turned back into her work clothes, reminding her it was fake. The ceremony, the celebration, all of it was fake. With a sigh, she wasn't sure what it meant. She took a small backpack with a towel, a change of clothes, hat, and sunglasses and went to the kitchen to get a bottle of water and some food. Raven had packed them something already, so she just put it in her bag. Alistair came running down the stairs, rushed to the kitchen too, took the food and water, kissed his mum on the cheek, and ran out, only to come back to beckon Nashel along.

As they walked through the fields, Alistair explained that there weren't usually many people at the lakes, as most families went on holiday during the summer, and only a few farmers stayed, but didn't go there. That year, though, it was extraordinarily hot, and he thought there would be a crowd. Nashel didn't mind; as long as they could find a spot, she would be okay. She was still mulling over the ceremony, the uniform, and the break in her routine. She was also circling back to what Raven had said about her own mission, how it, too, was fake. She felt like her entire life was fake at the moment, so she would embrace the opportunity to dive into the water and forget about everything else.

It took them around an hour to reach their destination. Thankfully, it was still early, and the day wasn't as hot as it would become. The lakes were surrounded by the woods, so there was plenty of shade to relax in, but there were also spots in the sun to sunbathe. There were several lakes; some were as small as a pond, some were bigger, and they all surrounded the biggest one in the middle, which was a decent size for a lake. There weren't many people they could see, but it was still early, so people would probably arrive later on. They didn't stop at the first chance they had; Alistair wanted to show her his favourite spot, which was a bit more secluded and on the side of one of the smaller lakes. It was beautiful. It reminded her of the powerful forest they went to for their trip. Its waters were a beautiful shade of blue, so transparent that they could perfectly see the bottom, which was shoulders deep at its deepest point, and they had plenty of space to unfold a towel and settle down. Nashel almost forgot that Alistair was there, too. She just dropped her backpack, stripped down to her swimsuit, and immediately jumped in the cool water without a second thought.

"I wish I could feel this cool every day, even out of the water," Alistair said after a while, and Nashel realised he was floating next to her.

"Me too," she replied in the same almost-sleepy, relaxed tone.

Then the proverbial bulb lit itself up, and she scrambled to a standing position, with water splashing everywhere. "Al, I'm an idiot!"

"What?"

"I'm an idiot!" she half swam, half walking closer to him because what she was about to tell him was not for prying ears, despite there being no one else there.

"Why?" He stood as well, confused and amused.

"I can!"

"You can what?" more confused.

"I can keep cool all day, away from the water!"

"You can?" he asked, intrigued.

"Yes!" she laughed. "It's going to take some energy, but I think I can do it..." she added, mumbling to herself.

"How?"

"I'm an Elemental," she explained in a whisper. "I should've thought of this from day one! I'm such an idiot!"

"What's an Elemental?" Alistair asked, understanding it was something Sunset-related.

"It's my speciality," she answered. "Elemental Expressions come easily to me. Wait, you know what an Expression is, right?"

He nodded.

"Yeah, so anything to do with water, fire, air, or earth comes naturally."

"I remember you mentioned it in the forest," he whispered, impressed.

"Yeah, that was scary," she admitted.

"What was?"

"Showing you. Now I understand why you showed me you can do it, but I didn't know you were a Sunset too. Then, I took a risk."

He looked at her for a moment, cocking his head. "I haven't thought about it that way, but I guess you're right."

Nashel shrugged. "I took many risks with you; I'm not

sure why," she mused.

Alistair laughed nervously. "Are there many Elementals in the—your place?"

She smiled at how he avoided saying 'Sunset'. "No, it's rare, actually. It is even rarer to be able to control all elements. Some people can do one very well, but not four."

"Thought so..."

"It doesn't mean that others are not good; it just means that it's easy for me."

"Okay, do you think I could do it, too?" he asked, almost shyly.

"I don't see why not," she shrugged.

"Can you teach me?" his cheeks became red, and he averted his gaze.

"You mean here and now?"

He shrugged, still not looking at her.

"It's dangerous. What if someone sees us?"

He sighed and nodded. "You're right. It was a silly idea."

"No, it wasn't," she found herself replying. "I can teach you. Here there's a lot of water, which helps, especially with the little amount of power around, but if we're caught..." she didn't need to complete the sentence.

He nodded reluctantly.

"Tell you what," she said. "Is it dangerous to go back home in the dark?"

He looked confused at the change in topic, but shook his head. "No, not really. We might need some light, but you saw the terrain; it's a nice, beaten path."

She nodded. "So, let's do this: we wait until nobody is around tonight, and I'll see what I can teach you."

"Really?" he lit up.

"Yeah," she smiled back.

"You're the best!" he closed the distance and hugged her. She stiffened for a moment, but then relaxed. He was a hugger. She knew that, and it wasn't the first time, but she still wasn't used to it and wasn't sure she liked it much.

She wasn't sure, either, about the reasons that pushed her

to comfort Alistair and agree to teach him. Normally, she would've just scoffed and moved on, but seeing him dejected made her feel something not pleasant.

They spent the rest of the day playing, sunbathing, and relaxing in the water, and it felt like a weight had left their shoulders, the knowledge that they wouldn't suffer the heat any longer. A few people arrived late in the morning, but not many to consider it crowded. They could hear voices from the other lakes and from the middle one, kids shouting, and water splashing, but their spot remained quieter, only adults and a few teens that wanted to relax just like them.

When the late afternoon approached, most left. A few stragglers stayed until sunset, but then left too, wanting to avoid walking in the dark. They were finally alone. Teaching Alistair to control an element was more difficult than she had thought. He was a Sunset, but he grew up in the Sunrise, surrounded by its culture and restrictions.

She had been right in putting him in a Junior Cadet's uniform: for many aspects, he was as inexperienced as the little children.

"What did your mother teach you?" she asked, trying to keep the irritation at bay.

"Not much," he replied sheepishly. "She thought it was safer to let me learn the Sunrise way."

"That's stupid," she muttered, but he heard and stiffened. "Sorry."

"No, I get it."

"It's just that the Sunrise tells you that magic is some sort of— I don't even know how to explain it. Some sort of out-of-this-world thing that may be used if you wave a stick."

Alistair laughed at the contempt in her voice. "And it isn't?"

He knew it wasn't, but was teasing her.

"NO!" she shouted. "Of course it isn't!"

Alistair laughed again, and Nashel sprayed him with water in retaliation.

"Tell me," he said gently.

"Power is everywhere. It is in everything and around everything. It's in here." She scooped a handful of water. "In here." she dabbed Alistair's chest. "In that tree there, in the owl hooting over there. In the rocks your feet are resting on."

"Okay..." he said, but she knew he was confused. His mother may have told him all this, but he never experienced it for himself.

"Imagine the wind," she tried.

"Okay?"

"You know how you can tell its direction? You feel it on your skin."

He nodded.

"Have you ever stood in a river?"

"Does a stream count?" he was smiling.

"Yes. Did you feel the current around your ankles?"

"Yes."

"Power is like that. It flows." She paused for a moment. "How do you do magic?"

"What do you mean?"

"Say you want to make a glass move from the table to you on the sofa because you're too lazy to get up," she smiled, and he laughed. "What do you do?"

"I concentrate on that," he said, confusedly.

"Do you feel anything when it happens?"

"I think so, like something in the pit of my stomach, and I need to transfer that to the wand."

She groaned at the mention of the stick. "That is it. You're already doing it; you transfer it from deep inside you to the wand. But you know how to use your powers without a stick, too. What do you do then?"

"I'm not sure..." he replied, deep in thinking.

"Try to do something now, and focus on the process," she encouraged him. "Do you think you can make some light?"

It was getting hard to see, after all.

He tried. She could barely see his eyes shut tight, and after a few moments, a small ball of light appeared, floating above their heads.

"Great job!" she smiled. "What did you feel?"

"I felt it deep down," he mused. "And then it was out there."

"This is not going to work," she muttered, frustrated.

"Sorry," Alistair replied, closing in his shoulders to make himself smaller.

"No, it's not your fault," she shook her head. There was another way, something the instructors did with the Junior Cadets when they were struggling, but she knew it would take a lot for her to do it there. Yet, she felt like she had to teach him. He was a Sunset. He had already been deprived of his birthright and had his wings clipped; it wasn't fair.

"Alright," she said resolutely. "Give me your hands."

He did, taken aback by her determination.

"I'll show you."

"Show me?"

"Yeah, I can show you what power looks like, how it moves."

"Oh," he replied in amazement.

"But I don't think I can teach you how to control water after that."

"Why?"

"Because it'll take me too much energy."

"Okay," he nodded. "You don't have to do it, though... we can go home."

"No, I want to."

He nodded again.

"Just close your eyes and relax," she instructed in a whisper.

The light above them flickered and dimmed a bit, as he let go of some of his concentration.

She concentrated, too, knowing it would take a lot not just to see the power flow herself, but to show it to Alistair. When she could see it, it was exactly like the day she first arrived in the Sunrise: spotty, not flowing as it did back home. Her heart ached to see it like that and to have to show it to Alistair. Not its true form, but this diminished, broken version. Alas, there was no other option.

She did what she was trying to teach him: channel the flow that was inside her and around her and in him, and bring it to his eyes.

"Open them now," she whispered.

As he did, she saw his emotion reflected there, thanks to the light ball still floating above them. There were tendrils of power flowing in and out of it, weak, but there. There were some in the water, some in and around the trees. Alistair turned and turned and turned to see them all, Nashel was sure his head was going to spin soon, if it didn't already.

"It's—" he was at a loss for words. "It's—"

"I know," she smiled. She really wished he could see it in the Sunset.

He turned once again to face her, and when he looked down to meet her eyes, his widened even more.

"You're beautiful," he whispered, entranced.

His hand rose to cup her cheek, moving a strand of her wet hair behind her ear. For once, she didn't move.

"You're glowing," he continued. "You're like a sun."

Nashel didn't have time to reply that he leaned down and kissed her.

CHAPTER TWENTY-THREE

First Love

It was a gentle kiss, leaving her all the time she needed to decide whether to allow him or not. It was pleasant. She liked the warmth his lips carried, and his hand on her cheek felt right.

She thought back, fleetingly, about Ash and Calistelle. She couldn't help the comparison, but they were all different. She didn't have time to dwell too much on it at that moment, but she knew she would go back to it as soon as she was alone.

"Alright?" his whisper was so low that if they were even just a hair more distant, she wouldn't have heard it.

"Alright," she answered in the same tone, smiling a little.

He took half a step back, and she stumbled, her head suddenly spinning. He was quick to step closer again, and hold her, alarm painted on his face.

"Are you okay?"

She leaned on him to stay upright and nodded. "Just tired."

"You did say it," he recalled. "We should go home."

She wasn't sure she could make the trek back, she wasn't even sure she could get to shore. It took her a lot more than she anticipated, and she felt completely drained. How much she hated the Sunrise!

He held her and gently dragged her back to where they left their belongings. The little light ball followed them, illuminating the way. When she sat down, she sighed with relief, but she felt the urge to lie down.

"Give me a minute," she muttered, closing her eyes and using her backpack as a pillow.

"All the minutes you need," he replied gently.

"I didn't think it would drain me so much," she commented.

"Shh, it's alright, rest now."

She felt herself drifting out of consciousness; she didn't want to be that vulnerable, not even with Alistair. She hated being the weak one even more than she hated the Sunrise. She couldn't help it, though. She blacked out.

When she came to, she realised something was wrong. The earth was shaking. She opened her eyes, ready to fight whatever was causing the earthquake, because she knew it wasn't normal. But when she did, disorientation took her. She wasn't lying down, she was standing against something warm, and when her eyes focused, she saw Alistair's face way too close. She frantically turned around and realised there was no earthquake, but Alistair was carrying her.

"Calm down, calm down," he said, shifting her weight not to drop her as she moved around.

She stopped, taking a deep breath to calm her heartbeat.

"It's okay," Alistair added. "I can put you down, if you feel you can walk."

"Yes," she murmured.

She wasn't sure she could stand. Everything was still fuzzy, but she didn't want to depend on him.

She tested her balance, and it seemed to hold. She let go of her hold on him to see if she could walk on her one and her steps, wobbly at first, grew stronger.

"What...?"

"You passed out," he explained. "It was getting late. My mum is probably worried. So, I thought I could carry you for a while, until you recovered."

"You should've called me."

"No, I don't think so," he smiled, but she understood there was no point arguing.

Their progress was slow, thanks to the darkness and her tiredness, so it took them well over an hour to get back. They barely saw the house lights when they heard Raven's voice booming, as if she was next to them, startling them.

"WHERE HAVE YOU BEEN?"

They didn't reply until they arrived on the porch.

"At the lakes," Alistair murmured awkwardly, scratching the back of his head.

"And what time do you call this?"

"It's my fault," Nashel said.

"That's not the question I asked," Raven snapped, reminding her of the instructors at the academy.

"We know it's late," she started to explain, her voice losing the apologetic tone and becoming firmer. She unconsciously stood straighter, her shoulders square, almost at attention. "I exhausted myself. It was a silly mistake. But Alistair was kind enough to wait for me to recuperate a bit before coming back."

Raven studied her for a while, then nodded curtly.

"Go to bed," she ordered.

They didn't argue. They filed upstairs and stopped in front of Al's room.

"Are you okay going up by yourself?"

"Yeah, thanks," she nodded.

Somehow, though, she didn't move. She felt a little awkward, not sure if she needed to do something or if she just had to go. It was weird, the embarrassment. She had relationships before, she knew how to behave in those situations.

Was it because she perceived Alistair's awkwardness, too? He stood by his door, no intention of moving, slightly rocking on the balls of his feet.

This was silly!

She closed the distance and kissed him, just a quick peck, but enough to break the embarrassment. He made a surprised sound that made her smile, but he leaned in after just a moment.

"Goodnight," she whispered, and she was pleased to hear her tone was back to normal, with just a hint of flirtatiousness.

"I—," he was speechless. She liked it. "G—Goodnight?"

She laughed and walked away.

The climb up to the loft wasn't as easy and she was so glad when finally she could lie in bed. She sprawled on it, like a starfish, which was not her usual composure, but there was nobody to see her.

She looked at the ceiling without actually seeing it. She was exhausted, but she knew she would not be able to sleep, at least not until her mind was clear.

It brought her back to the Sunset, to that last week she spent there learning about the Sunrise and practising waving a stick. It brought her the image of Ash: his smile, his laugh, the easiness of their relationship, how she was in control of the situation, how she knew exactly what to do and when, and how easily she read Ash and his desire.

It brought her back to Calistelle, too. To her superiority complex and the way she constantly looked down on Nashel. How she hated being intimate with her and how Calistelle would try to force herself on her. She remembered how possessive her kisses and hugs were, how kissing her felt like her lips, then her face, were sucked away by Calistelle's lips. She remembered how uncomfortable she felt at having to do it.

She had compared it in the past with her experience with Ash, but she found herself doing it again then. His kisses were charged with tension, with want - mostly on his part -, with playfulness; her kisses were possessive, aggressive, like she was marking Nashel as property, like she was trying to teach her her place, to annihilate her.

The kiss with Alistair was not like either of them. It was

awkward, clumsy even, timid. She wasn't sure why, she wasn't inexperienced, he was, but it shouldn't influence how she felt. So, what was different?

She mulled over that question, interrupted by the memory of the kisses, and how they made her feel something in the pit of her stomach, something she couldn't identify. It wasn't unpleasant, but it was distracting. Sleep was also distracting, wanting to claim her for the rest of the night. She was about to lose that battle when it hit her, the difference. She accepted Ash's advances, and she initiated Calistelle's relationship because they were both means to an end. And while she liked Ash in the end, she still got into it because she thought he could be useful. Calistelle was more obvious. Nashel's intent was never to have a romantic affair with her. It was to gain access to the Alwenach. But Alistair. She didn't have a use for Alistair. And yet, she felt something for him, something that people might describe as love.

She didn't have much experience with love, she never thought she would feel it, and she wasn't sure that was what she was feeling for Alistair, but she was feeling something. Before she could dwell more on that, sleep finally claimed her.

She woke up at her usual time, surprising herself. She stretched, got dressed and went downstairs, feeling well-rested, full of energy, and ready to work.

"You're awake," Raven looked at her, surprised.

"Yeah, I feel great!"

"I bet," she commented.

"What do you mean?" Nashel asked, confused.

"Oh, honey, you didn't realise, did you?"

"Realise?"

"You slept all of yesterday," Raven explained, offering her a mug of coffee.

"I what?"

The woman laughed.

"You were completely out of it."

"I—" she didn't know what to say.

"It's okay, Alistair explained what happened."

"It shouldn't happen though," she commented, frustrated. "I shouldn't pass out for over 24 hours just because I showed him something."

"You know that seeing the power flow is not normal, right?"

She looked at Raven, confused.

"Only a few can do it, and even less can do it as naturally as you do."

She nodded, she knew that. "But I do, so I shouldn't be that weak."

"You're not weak," Raven shook her head for emphasis. "The power here is weak."

She groaned at the reminder.

"I wish I could go back," she admitted in a rare moment of vulnerability.

"I know, me too sometimes."

That surprised her. Raven had been in the Sunrise for a long time, and it wasn't an amicable separation, so Nashel didn't think she would miss her homeland.

"Of course I do," the other woman laughed, reading her expression. "I don't miss the people, but the place? You bet I do."

That made more sense.

"Let's go to work and forget about our woes," Raven gently put a hand on her shoulder and directed her to the door.

"Alistair told me something else," she said, about halfway through their usual chores.

"What?" she said, feeling that feeling in the pit of her stomach at the mention of the boy. Somehow, she also knew what he told his mum.

"He told me you kissed."

"We did," she admitted, trying to be as nonchalant as possible.

"He really likes you," Raven continued.

Nashel had seen enough films to know what was coming next, and she wanted to laugh, but restrained herself.

"And he is my baby boy," Raven added.

"I understand," Nashel replied.

"You are powerful, that was clear since the first moment I saw you."

"Thank you?" it came out with a slightly increasing intonation, as if it was a question.

"But I am powerful too, and I am more used to the flow of the Sunrise. So, do not even think about harming him in any way, or you'll pay harshly."

"Understood," she nodded once.

With that out of the way, they worked the rest of the morning, mostly in silence, then went back inside for lunch. The sun was out and scorching, just as usual, so it was a relief to be out of it and in a cooler environment. She knew she told Alistair she could command the elements and make herself feel better, but she was wary of how much energy it would take.

Alistair had just woken up, as usual, and he was making his way downstairs, his hair ruffled, the mark of his pillow red on his cheek. The sight made Nashel's stomach twist. His smile broadened when he saw her awake.

"Hey," he uttered, his voice husky with sleep.

"Hey," she said back and saw Raven roll her eyes.

"Listen, lovebirds," she said once she soon took his place at the table. "I'm not going to tell you what you can or cannot do, but I'm going to set some ground rules."

They both groaned.

"Use protections—"

"Muuum!" Alistair exclaimed, shocked and embarrassed, but she glared at him.

"Use protections," she repeated. "Be kind to each other. And, for the love of the Sun, don't make me hear you."

Nashel felt her cheeks grow warmer, and she knew they had pinked. It was a weird feeling and a weird situation. She never had to deal with parents. Even when she started exploring physical intimacy at the academy, the parents of the other students weren't that involved.

Alistair was as red as a tomato, he couldn't meet either her mother's or Nashel's eyes and only looked down at his still-empty plate, while he fidgeted with the fork.

Raven rolled her eyes again. "There's nothing to be embarrassed about."

"Mum, just stop talking, please," he muttered with the voice of someone who would love nothing more than to disappear.

She was right, though. There was nothing to be embarrassed about. Maybe it was different for Alistair, since it was his mother, but she wouldn't know.

Raven put them out of their misery after lunch, letting them do what they wanted, while she would take care of the farm. Nashel wished she was back at the lakes, chilling with Alistair, without thinking about intimacy or relationships.

"Are we boyfriend and girlfriend now?" she asked him while they were sunbathing on the porch.

"If you'd like," he replied, shrugging.

She didn't have to see him to know he wanted to say yes, probably shout it as well.

"Okay," she said.

"Okay?" he asked, hopeful.

"Yeah," she smiled.

"I've never had a girlfriend," he murmured.

"Wait," she realised something that made her sit up, lower her sunglasses and look at him. "Was that your first kiss?"

"No," he replied in a small voice.

"Oh, okay." She didn't know if she was relieved or sad.

"But I've never been in a relationship," he repeated.

She wasn't sure what to say, so she laid back down, sunglasses back in their place. "We'll learn together," she muttered.

"Have you ever had a boyfriend?" he asked her when she wasn't looking at him any longer.

She realised she had never told him about Ash. She could lie, make him feel better, but she didn't want to.

"Yes, back home."

"Is he waiting for you there?" there was something in his tone that made her prickle.

"Are you jealous?"

"Maybe?" he replied defensively.

She laughed. "No, he's not waiting for me. Or if he is, it's his loss."

He sighed.

"You don't have to be jealous," she reassured him. She hoped he wouldn't because Calistelle had been jealous to the point of obsession, and she didn't want to repeat the experience or be reminded of it.

"Sorry," he said in that same small voice he used before.

She shrugged, "It's alright."

"I like you, you know?" he said suddenly fast. "I liked you since the moment I saw you."

"So bumping into me was your first move?"

He laughed. "No, I was distracted. I didn't do it on purpose."

"Distracted, but you saw me and liked me?"

"I was distracted by you, El."

"Oh," she realised.

"And by your aura," he added truthfully.

Of course he was. The only Sunset he ever encountered other than his mother. It would distract anyone.

"I wasn't sure you liked me," he continued. "I wasn't sure you liked boys, actually."

"I do," she replied, suddenly shy.

"Thank the Sun for that," he breathed, and they both laughed.

"I like you too," she said after a pause. She felt the need to reassure him of that, even if she couldn't explain it.

He didn't reply, but she didn't mind, she knew he heard her.

"About what my mum said..." he spoke after a longer pause. "We don't have to... I mean, you don't have to worry about it."

"Worry about it?" she asked, confused.

"What she said about using protection, and making noise," he replied awkwardly. "It doesn't mean we have to, you know, do it."

"Oh," she felt her eyes grow wider and was thankful she had the sunglasses to hide them when she realised he was talking about sex.

She wasn't stupid. She knew couples had sex, but somehow she never connected the dots and engaged in the possibility of 'doing it' with Alistair, at least not until he mentioned it.

"I just wanted to let you know there's no pressure, okay?"

"Okay," she said, swallowing, her mouth suddenly dry. "It goes for you too," she added after a moment. "No pressure."

"Okay."

She could hear the smile in his voice.

"We just take it one step at a time and see what happens," she declared.

"Agreed," he replied with a laugh at her serious tone.

That's what they did. They spent time finding out what they liked. Their kisses became more intense, deeper. They explored their bodies, and Nashel found she liked it when Alistair kissed her neck, she pleasantly shivered, and she found he liked it when she kissed his earlobes. She enjoyed kissing his body, and when he kissed hers. She felt like he was worshipping her, like a saint, like a god, so she returned the favour. They mostly kept their underwear on, but Nashel often took her bra off, or let him do it, and let Alistair touch her breasts. Most of all, she found that she really liked cuddling in bed, half-naked, spooning. She liked the warmth of Alistair's skin against her. It wasn't the warmth of the weather outside, the heat that clung to your skin disgustingly. It was a warmth that told her she was safe, that told her for the first time in her life she was not alone, that she was loved.

It shocked her to realise that. It turned her world upside down and made her feel everything differently, as if she had never experienced it before. Again, she thought she might be in love with him, even though it was a foreign concept to her.

"Your scars," Alistair murmured one time, tracing the shape of one on her shoulder. "How did you get them?"

"Accidents," she replied lazily.

"Abuse?" he insisted, tensing up. She could feel he was afraid he had crossed a line.

"No, no," she replied calmly. "Accidents, for real."

"There are so many..." Alexis whispered almost reverently.

Nashel chuckled. "That's life at the Academy."

She never thought about how many scars she had and what they'd look like to someone who didn't grow up at the Academy, but now she felt self-conscious.

"What do you mean?"

"We are encouraged to experiment. We use our powers freely, and we train in different types of combat. It definitely leads to accidents."

"It sounds brutal."

"It's not. It's just that when people, especially children, are inexperienced, it's easy to make mistakes."

"Some of them look really painful."

"You should see the other guy," she joked.

"Do people die?" he gulped.

Nashel thought about lying for his benefit, but she didn't want to be dishonest. "Sometimes, yes," she braced herself for the inevitable next question.

"Have you...?"

"Died? No, definitely no, never," she tried to joke, but Alistair didn't let her distract him from the topic.

"I mean, has somebody died because of something you did?"

She didn't know what to say. Should she lie? Would telling the truth make him look at her differently?

"Yes," she let slip before she could think about it too much.

Alexis hugged her harder. "I'm so sorry," he said, his tone full of compassionate concern.

She didn't understand why. Except for the Trials and

Calistelle, she didn't go on a rampage and killed hundreds. If someone died, it was truly an accident, and it was probably their own fault, because she was really good, and she shouldn't feel guilty about it. Like Vessa, for example. She died under Nashel's command, but it wasn't Nashel's fault. She didn't know what to say, so she didn't say anything, she just enjoyed Alistair's hug.

"Do you want to talk about it?" he asked her.

"No, if that's okay." There was nothing to talk about in her opinion.

"Of course it is," he said gently. "But can you tell me what life was like there? From what you just said, it sounds like hell!" he laughed.

"No, it wasn't. It was tough at times," she answered, "but not hell."

"I wish I could see it," he murmured, his face buried in her hair.

"Me too," she replied and was honest. She really wished he could see it, not only because it was his birthright, but because she wanted to show him her favourite places, the places where she grew up, even the places where she got her scars. Once again, what she was feeling was foreign to her. Sharing had never been her strong suit, and she generally found couples sharing everything cringey, but there she was, wishing nothing more than to share her home with Alistair.

CHAPTER TWENTY-FOUR

Farmers' Fair

"What's your mission?" Alistair whispered one night while cuddling in her bed.

Nashel tensed. They had shared a lot in the previous days, but that was a very direct question, and her instinct screamed at her to run. She didn't listen, but she tensed.

"It's okay," he continued. "You don't have to tell me."

Then why did he ask?

"What I really meant is, do you think it's real?"

If it were possible to tense even more, she did. She turned around to face him, confused by his questioning.

"What?"

"My mum told me about her past, how she was sent on a mission that was just an excuse to get rid of her."

"Mine's not," she tried to stay calm and not snap at him.

"Okay," he said, but he didn't believe her.

"It isn't. I know about your mum, she showed me. But we are not the same people. If we were, this," she gestured between them, "would be very awkward."

She laughed softly at his disgusted expression.

"I'm not sure if I can look at you ever again," he said dramatically, closing his eyes tight.

She laughed again.

"Can I help you?" he said in a small voice after a while.

"Help me do what?"

"With your mission. Can I help you?"

"I—" she thought about it. She thought about the progress she had made in her months at the Sunrise Academy, admittedly not much.

Could enlisting his help make a difference? He already knew who she was. Would it really hurt to tell him about the mission? It wasn't a complicated one, he probably already figured it out. She managed to get into the Alwenach, but it wasn't enough, she needed to find more. If it were enough, they would've called her back by then.

"Okay," she said tentatively.

"Okay?" he replied, surprised.

She chuckled. "I don't know how much you can help, but you are welcome to try."

"Okay," he nodded, trying to psych himself up. "What do I do?"

She laughed at that. "You don't even know what the mission is!"

"I don't need to! It's a top-secret mission, need-to-know only. I don't need to know. You tell me what to do, I do it."

She got into a fit of giggles, and when she stopped, she caressed his cheek and quickly kissed him.

"The mission is to gather intel on an imminent attack on the Sunset," she whispered.

"What?" he said it in a normal tone, but it was a stark contrast to her whisper. He also put some distance between them, as if looking at her better could change what she said.

She just nodded.

"That's why you wanted to join the Alwenach!"

She nodded again.

"Are they the ones attacking?"

"I don't know," she shrugged. "I haven't found any proof of it yet."

"Is it possible it's going to be a different group?"

"Could be. My briefing told me their headquarters is at the academy, but the only hint I have is the Alwenach. I haven't heard of any other group even remotely that extreme."

"Sometimes, it's the least suspicious that causes the most damage," Alistair whispered.

That hit her hard. It was the simplest truth. Sometimes the best hiding place is in plain sight. The least noisy, most inconspicuous group is the one plotting an attack. Why didn't she think about it? It was Strategy for beginners, and she was supposed to be a Cadet Under Officer, for Sun's sake!

She nodded slowly, cursing her own stupidity.

"We'll look more when we get back, deal?" he whispered gently.

She nodded again, sighing. "But for now, let's enjoy the summer," she added. "I'm not too keen on going back to that stifling place."

They laughed, and it turned into a fight of tickling and blowing raspberries.

"Listen," Alistair whispered later when they were both about to fall asleep, or at least Nashel. "There's this fair in town later this week."

"A fair?" she asked sleepily.

"Yeah, it's like for farmers to sell their products, and for the kids to have fun at the carnival."

"Okay?"

"Would you like to go? With me?"

His tone was so hopeful it sounded weird. As if he were too invested in this and hoped she would accept.

"Okay," she said, because she didn't want to deal with the other option. She didn't want to hear the hurt in Alistair's voice or see it in his eyes. She was too tired to argue.

"Thank you!" he hugged her happily and pressed a kiss to her forehead. She still found the enthusiasm weird, over the top and out of character for him, but she didn't question it.

The next morning, she discovered the fair was a big deal for Raven, too. She was snappier than usual and swapped their chores for preparations for the fair. Everything became even more hectic when Alistair joined them.

It wasn't until the day itself that she understood their reasons. When she woke up that morning, Raven was busy in the kitchen, baking a batch of cookies, several pies, and a huge chocolate cake.

"Oh!" she exclaimed when she saw Nashel. "Don't tell me I forgot to tell you!"

"Tell me what?"

"There's no work this morning," she explained.

"How come?"

Raven answered, opening her arms and indicating the whole kitchen.

"I see," she replied, and she meant it in the literal sense, not the metaphorical, because she didn't understand why Raven was so busy so early.

"Should I go feed the animals, anyway?"

"No," Raven shook her head. "They'll get a week's worth of food at the fair."

"Okay," she said doubtfully.

"You can go back to sleep if you want," Raven added gently.

Nashel shrugged. She was used to waking up early; she liked it, and she wasn't really into sleeping in, anyway.

"I'll go for a run and practice for a while, if that's okay?" she had a feeling something she didn't know was going on, and she wanted to make sure she wasn't making a mistake.

Raven just nodded.

"Raven," Nashel asked as she turned to leave. "What is going on? Why all of this?" she made the same gesture encompassing the kitchen the woman had done a few minutes earlier. "Why is this fair so important?"

Raven looked at her, shocked, so shocked that she dropped the whisk in the bowl and splattered chocolate all around her.

"You don't know?" she asked, incredulous.

"Know what?"

"It's not the fair that is important," she explained. "It's Al's birthday."

"It's what now?"

"Today's Al's birthday. I can't believe he didn't tell you!"

"And the fair?" she asked in confusion.

"When Alistair was very young, he wasn't too good at controlling his powers, so I wouldn't let him go to town often. The fair was the exception. I had to go, and he couldn't stay home alone. I made up a story, that the fair was for him, for his birthday."

Nashel smiled.

"I was very strict with him," Raven continued, picking up the whisk and resuming baking. "I was terrified. So I kept him here, away from anyone and everyone. I regretted that decision every single day, but I stuck by it. I know he didn't have friends and he was lonely..."

She trailed off, shaking her head.

"You did what you had to do," Nashel replied firmly. Raven was startled, as if she had forgotten Nashel was there. "And he turned out alright, I'd say."

Raven smiled.

"I don't have a present for him," she said after a moment.

"You didn't know," Raven shrugged. "I think he wanted it that way."

"But why?"

"I don't know, but I can tell you I've never seen him happier. Perhaps you are the only gift he needs."

Nashel thought about that for a moment. She recalled a conversation they had a while ago; he asked her when her birthday was, but then they changed the topic to her ceremony and she never got to answer or to ask it back.

As she went for her run, she couldn't stop thinking about it. She never cared for birthdays; at one point she'd even forgotten when hers was. Some cadets were really into celebrations. They would get special permission to go back to their families, or to organise a party with their classmates. But to her, it was just like any other day. Maybe that was why she never asked Al when his birthday was.

Still, she felt she needed to give him something. She didn't know what exactly, she didn't have any experience with those sorts of things, and time was not on her side.

Perhaps you're the only gift he needs, Raven had said. Nashel was sure she didn't mean it in a sexual way, but maybe, if she couldn't get anything else, giving herself to him could be her Plan B.

She was so wrapped up in her own mind that she couldn't focus on practice. She went back inside to shower and get ready for the fair in a haze. She didn't realise the bathroom door was closed until after she opened it and stepped inside. She was startled hearing the water running, but mostly by the shriek that rose from behind the curtain.

"Mum!" Alistair squeaked indignantly.

"Shit," Nashel muttered. "Sorry!" she added a bit louder, taking a step backwards.

She stopped. Was this her cue to give him his present? It would be so easy to slip out of her clothes and in the shower with him, and she wouldn't have to think about something else.

"Oh," he replied, his head taking a peek from behind the curtain. His cheeks were flushed.

"Sorry, I was distracted."

"It's okay," he replied awkwardly. He hid back behind the curtain.

He didn't tell her to get out. He didn't seem that bothered about her being there. Was it a sign? The silence stretched uncomfortably.

She turned, locked the door, and took her clothes off. With a deep breath, she stepped quietly into the shower.

Alistair's back was turned towards her, so he didn't seem to have heard her. She kissed the spot between his shoulder blades, and he yelped, tensed, then slowly turned around.

"What?" he mouthed, or whispered, but with the water running, she only read his lips.

"Happy birthday," she whispered back, getting on her tiptoes to kiss him.

"I—" he was speechless.

It was the first time they were completely naked in front of each other, and he hadn't looked anywhere but her eyes. Nor did she.

"Is this alright?"

"I—" but he still couldn't utter a full sentence. She smiled and kissed him again, her hands on his bare shoulders, the water running down both of them.

Suddenly, she didn't want to continue. She wasn't uncomfortable, but she had just realised that she was his first girlfriend, that he had never done anything like this with anyone else. She looked into his eyes and she saw more fear than desire.

"I'll shower later," she whispered with a smile and took a step to get out of the shower.

He gently grabbed her wrist and made her turn around to face him again. "It's okay, I was surprised."

"No, you're terrified," she said, caressing his cheek.

He swallowed visibly and pulled her closer. "I've never—"

"I know. It's okay," she tried to back out again, but he was holding her tight.

"This is okay too," he nodded and kissed her.

The power-amplified voice of Raven reached them before anything else could happen and made them jump. "Kids, it's time! Are you ready?"

They briefly laughed before drying themselves and being very careful to leave the bathroom one at a time, ten minutes apart.

She put on a summer floral dress, braided her hair, and put on a wide-brim straw hat. She also concentrated and made the air around her felt cool instead of stifling hot. It would take energy to keep it up all day, but it shouldn't drain her. It also gave her an idea. She had yet to teach Alistair how to do it as well, so maybe that could be her birthday present for him.

They squeezed into the truck and left as soon as she

landed downstairs.

“You look lovely,” Alistair whispered in her ear as Raven started the truck and rolled her eyes.

The fair was not what she expected. It wasn’t in town, but just outside it on a massive field. It was a patchwork of animals, animal products, crops, crop derivatives, tractors and machinery, a carnival with more rides than she could see, and a hay maze.

Nashel and Alistair helped Raven unload the truck and set her stand before she told them to make themselves scarce because all “the lovey-dovey, teenage-y love was making her sick”.

Alistair took her for a tour of the huge grounds. It was interesting to see all the farmer’s friendly banter about who had the best cows or the best honey. She enjoyed the fact that it wasn’t a market, but that even the farmers could have fun in not-too-friendly competitions of pie baking, mostly tasting, tractor races, and beauty pageants for pigs. By the time they got to the carnival area, it was lunchtime, and their stomachs were full already because they had stopped at all the stands and took tasters from each.

The carnival was a completely different world from the rest of the fair. It seemed like all the teenagers of the country converged there. It was packed with people, loud noises and colours. Alistair also transformed. He was beaming, and every single teen was waving at him, smiling, stopping to ask him how he was or wish him a happy birthday. Nashel lost count of the girls that stopped to kiss him on the cheek, just as she lost track of how annoyed she was.

“Oh Al, every time I see you, you become more and more handsome,” a tall, blond girl stopped them as they strode down the main aisle.

“Thanks, C,” he replied slightly awkwardly.

She took him by the arm, completely ignoring Nashel and she proceeded to shamelessly flirt with him for half an hour, as they just walked up and down. After the second lap, Nashel decided she had had enough and stopped following them like a loyal dog and stopped at one of the stands, a shooting game.

She dealt with guns before, not often, as she didn't need them, but she was good enough that she could win the biggest prize. She decided not to, to miss some of the shots so as not to attract too much attention, but most of all, she imagined C's (what kind of name was that?!) face was the target.

She won a huge teddy bear she had to carry piggyback or she wouldn't see where she stepped. She thought about going back to Raven's and leaving it there, as it was bulky and she couldn't humiliate herself by going on a rollercoaster with a stuffed animal "sitting" next to her, but it would take her too much time, and frankly, she wanted to keep an eye on C as they strolled along. So, she hid behind one of the stands, making sure nobody would see her, and used her powers to reduce the size of the bear to a more portable, pocket version. It wasn't a big effort, but she was already keeping up the cool air around her, so she was dizzy for a handful of seconds.

She re-joined the crowd and queued for the rollercoaster, then for the drop tower. From up top, just before she was dropped, she saw Alistair - it was impressive that she could recognise him from such a distance in the middle of a packed place - with C still holding him by the arm.

More than an hour passed before he was alone again and started looking for her. She avoided him and went on to the skydiver before he finally saw her and waited for the ride to end.

"There you are!" he exclaimed, as if he had looked for her the entire time.

"Yeah," she replied with an implied "obviously".

"Have you been to the Ferris wheel yet?"

She looked at him blankly for a moment while she took a deep breath. She didn't want to snap at him; it was his birthday after all. "No," she replied curtly.

"Let's go, then," he nodded towards it, grabbed her hand

and dragged her to the ride.

They queued in awkward silence, and didn't speak until the wheel started to spin.

"I'm sorry," Alistair said, not looking at her. "C is a handful."

She shrugged, not trusting her voice yet.

"She's been hitting on me since the day I met her."

Her brows furrowed.

"I don't like her. I'm not attracted to her, and I told her too many times to count, but she never gives up."

He was rumbling, but she was enjoying the grovelling, so she didn't say anything yet again.

"I'm really sorry. I should've tried harder."

"Why didn't you?" she finally said. "Is she that strong that you can't get her arm off you? Have you told her you have a girlfriend?"

"I—" he opened his mouth, but closed it again, gathering his thoughts, but failing.

"Exactly," she snarled.

"I did tell her I have a girlfriend," he added shyly. "But she didn't care."

"And you just couldn't twist her arm."

"I didn't want to hurt her," he explained.

"But it's okay to hurt me?" she rebutted.

His eyes widened, and she thought she saw tears welling up. He hadn't realised how offended she was. She felt something tagging in her stomach at his distress.

"I won a giant teddy bear," she offered as an olive branch.

He swallowed heavily, trying to push back the tears. "Did you?" he tried for an incredulous and sarcastic tone; after all, the plushie was nowhere to be seen, but it came out querulous.

"Yep." She took it out of her pocket and showed it to him.

"I thought you said giant," he said, confused.

"It was," she nodded. "Too bulky though," she smirked.

It clicked, and he smiled a small smile.

"I am sorry, El," he said when they started their descent. "I really am. I'm not sure how to deal with C. She is so aggressive that I don't know how to react. But I should've done more. You're right, I should've just shoved her arm away."

"I accept your apology," she replied with a sigh. "Next time, try harder?"

"Absolutely. And if she dares mouth you off again, I won't be as nice as I was," he promised.

"Mouthing me off?"

"Shit, sorry, I didn't mean to say that."

"What did she say?"

He pretended not to hear her.

"Al, what did she say?" Nashel insisted.

He sighed. "She said you're bland and probably dumb," he said, then rushed to add, "But I immediately told her she was completely wrong!"

"Is that all?"

"Yes, she recommended I forget you and choose someone more 'my type'."

"Meaning her," she finished.

"Yeah," hc tried for a smile.

The ride ended, and she stood to get off, but he held her hand and guided her back to the seat. He also gestured with his other hand to the ride controller they would go again.

"Please?" he whispered to her.

She nodded once and sat back down.

"Are we staying here for the rest of the day?" she asked sarcastically.

"No, just until you forgive me."

"Oh, Sun," she muttered.

"So the sooner you forgive me, the sooner we can enjoy the carnival together," he joked.

"I already accepted your apology, didn't I?" she reminded him.

"Yes, but am I forgiven?"

Nashel sighed again. "Yes, Alistair, you are forgiven."

"Hooray!" he exclaimed with a little victory dance.

He was bumping fists in the air, then with a smooth move, he wrapped an arm around her shoulder and kissed her on the cheek.

"You are not bland," he whispered in her ear, making her shiver. "Nor dumb."

"Thank you," she replied cheekily.

"Sorry I didn't tell you about my birthday," he added. "I didn't want you to fret about presents. I don't need one."

"What was this morning, then?" she asked, faking being offended.

He flushed at the memory. "This morning was—" he mumbled, embarrassed. "It was amazing."

His voice was so low that she struggled to hear him.

"Good," she said smugly, which made him flush even more.

They stayed in silence for a while, this time it was companionable, and watched as the world below got smaller and smaller.

"Quick, kiss me like your life depended on it!" Alistair exclaimed, grabbing her by the waist and holding her flush against him.

He didn't wait for her to process what he had just said that he kissed her. When her brain finally caught up, she did what he asked. The kiss felt different, not genuine as they usually did, maybe because her life didn't depend on it and she was pretending, but she wondered why Alistair told her that.

After a few moments, when they had to breathe, and she looked up at him, she saw him grinning.

"Turn around," he whispered in reply to her questioning look.

She did, and saw C standing a few meters away, her face a mix of shock, lividity and heartbreak. As soon as Nashel spotted her, she spun around and hastily lost herself in the crowd.

"That was mean," Nashel told him, feigning reproach.

He looked sheepish and shrugged.

"I loved it," she added with a grin.

"And I love you," he whispered.

CHAPTER TWENTY-FIVE

Interlude

Shock cursed through Nashel. For the first time in her life, she didn't know how to react. She had always been quick on her feet, making firm decisions in a split second, most of the time, right decisions. Her instructors praised her, and it was one of the main reasons they chose her as squad leader.

Years and years of training had prepared her for almost any and every situation, except that one. There were no classes on emotional responses, or how to deal with a boyfriend, especially one she cared about.

She was completely frozen.

"I'm sorry," Alistair murmured, caressing her cheek. "I didn't mean to blurt it out."

She looked at him but couldn't react.

"It's alright," his voice stayed calm. He wasn't disappointed, nor hurt by her silence. "It's okay. You don't have to say anything."

He kissed her forehead, and she flinched. That made his smile falter just a little.

"I'm sorry," she muttered under her breath.

He shook his head almost imperceptibly.

She took a deep breath, then looked him straight in the

eye. “I’m sorry. I shouldn’t have flinched, and I shouldn’t have frozen.”

“It’s alright,” he repeated.

She never found herself in a more difficult situation or having to have a more difficult conversation. “Nobody has ever said that to me,” she admitted. “So I don’t know how to react or what to feel.”

She saw his eyes widen at her confession, then soften, and then he nodded with a small smile.

“Is it okay if I think about it?” she added, almost shyly, and for once she wasn’t faking it.

The entirety of the last few minutes had been surreal. She had never felt those emotions before. She didn’t even know how to identify them, or if she could.

“Can I kiss you in the meantime?”

She laughed a shaky laugh. “Of course you can!”

He laughed too and kissed her. It was another different kiss. It wasn’t insincere as the previous one, but it was also different from the previous, genuine kisses they shared. It was deeper, he was trying to communicate what he felt and that it was okay she didn’t know what she felt. She, on the other end, wasn’t sure what she was communicating. She knew she cared for Alistair, she liked him and enjoyed being around him, so maybe that was what she was telling him.

They spent the rest of the day going on every ride, laughing, kissing, eating all kinds of sweets. They went back towards the farmers’ stands and had another round of tasters. Nashel fleetingly thought she would explode, but then the thought was replaced by more food.

They challenged each other on the mechanical bull, betting on who would last longer. Alistair turned out to be quite good on it, even better than Nashel, though she came close.

They went back to Raven to help her pack everything, but were surprised to see a small crowd gathered around. The stand was sorted already, and in the middle of the table, there was the huge chocolate cake Nashel saw that morning and completely forgot about it. It had seventeen candles lit up waiting to be blown by the birthday boy. There was also a little mound of parcel to its side.

Alistair grinned as he blew the candles. Everyone around him sang a traditional song Nashel couldn't understand, but she clapped along and watched him open his presents, trying not to think about the absence of one from her.

When darkness fell, they gathered in one of the bigger fields to watch the fireworks display. Nashel was used to a spectacle of Expressions, fireworks powered by powers, making the most intricate, the most impossibly beautiful figures and patterns. The show she watched with Alistair and Raven was, like everything else in the Sunrise, not. It was underwhelming. The fireworks were pretty, colourful, but nothing special. Apo fireworks. Not for the first time, she wished she could show Alistair what her world looked and felt like.

That gave her an idea.

They went back home straight after the fireworks to catch a couple of hours of sleep before doing it all again the following day. Or Raven would, but she told Nashel she and Alistair didn't need to go with her unless they wanted to go to the carnival again, and even if that was the case, they didn't need to do it so early.

"Get ready and come upstairs?" Nashel asked as Alistair stopped by his bedroom.

"What?" he asked, confused.

"Come upstairs?"

"Now?"

"If you want," she shrugged. "I'd like to shower first, though."

He nodded, dumbfounded, but didn't move. She chuckled.

"I just want to give you your birthday present."

His eyes widened in surprise, and she chuckled again.

"Now?"

"If you want," she shrugged.

"O-okay," he stuttered.

"Meet you upstairs, then?"

He nodded.

When she got out of her little bathroom, her towel around her, Alistair was awkwardly standing by the feet of the bed. Only her bedside lamp was on, but even with that, she could see his cheeks become red when he saw her. She ignored him and put her pyjamas on. It wasn't the first time they shared a bed, they did so every single night since they first kissed, so she wasn't sure why he was so awkward.

"Are you alright?" she asked him as she patted the space next to her, inviting him to join her.

"Yes," he replied, swallowing visibly and taking some tentative steps towards her.

He looked at the bed, at his clothes, at her, then at the bed again.

"C'mon, sit down!" she said impatiently.

"Should I—" he paused, uncertain. "Should I take my clothes off?"

She looked at him blankly for a moment before she realised what he was thinking. She should've thought about that. On the Ferris wheel, she told him what had almost happened in the shower was his present, so it was reasonable for him to think that the invitation to join her in her room would lead to a continuation of it.

"That's not what I meant," she murmured, suddenly not wanting to look at him, not wanting to see disappointment in his eyes.

He didn't reply.

"Sorry," she added.

The sheets ruffled, and she felt him sit next to her. His hand gently lifted her by the chin, he smiled, then kissed her.

"Thank you," he whispered after.

"What for?" she asked, confused.

"I don't think I'm ready for that."

No need to ask what that was. He put enough emphasis on it that it couldn't be clearer, even if he said the actual word.

"Why did you come then?" she asked with a nervous little

laugh.

"Because it's you. I want to spend time with you, no matter what."

"No," she said, shaking her head. "That's not fair."

It was his turn to be confused. "What?"

"I don't want to force you to do anything you don't want. Neither I want you to force yourself."

"I—"

She stopped him. "Promise me you will always tell me if we are going too far or too fast. Promise me you will stop me and yourself."

He studied her for a moment, then nodded. "I promise."

She sighed in relief and relaxed.

"So," he said after a moment of silence. "What is this present you wanted to give me?"

He tried to be nonchalant about it, but she saw right through it and knew he was curious and excited.

"Well," she started with a knowing smile. She briefly thought about teasing him a bit longer, but decided not to. "For a while now, I've been wishing for you to be able to see the Sunset."

He nodded.

"Tonight, while we were watching the fireworks, I got an idea," she explained. "I can't take you there, but I can show you."

"Show me?"

"Yes, kind of like what I did at the lakes and kind of like what your mum showed me when we arrived here."

"Wouldn't that take a lot of power?" he asked, concerned.

"Yes, but we got the day off tomorrow, right?" she smiled.

"Okay," he offered her his hands, just like the night at the lakes.

"You'll feel a bit disoriented at first," she explained as she started to concentrate.

"Okay," he whispered, shivering with anticipation.

She had thought it over on the way back from the fair. What to show him and how to do it efficiently.

It wasn't a memory that she was going to show him like Raven had done, it was a reconstruction. She started on her favourite place because she knew every detail of it. She took him to the beach at sunset.

It wasn't the main beach she saw on her first day, but a smaller, secluded one between two cliffs. She had found it soon after when she explored the area and it immediately outclassed the bigger beach. That one was exactly the same, but hers. She had never met people there, no matter how many times she visited it, the time of the day or the season. So she loved it. Now, she was sharing it, albeit virtually, with Alistair. She thought about that on the ride back home, she could've chosen the bigger beach, she could've shown him anything else, but she decided to share that part of herself with him.

His reaction didn't disappoint her. She heard him take a sharp breath as the initial disorientation wore off.

The setting sun shone on the sand, colouring each grain a different shade of gold. The small waves lulled gently just a few feet away, and the seagull called each other from up high. But most of all, power was flowing freely everywhere.

Nashel knew it was a product of her mind, but it still felt like something was squeezing her heart tight.

"It's beautiful," Alistair murmured.

"This is my sanctuary," she explained, heading towards the rock she always used as a seat. "It's the place I go to whenever I need to put some distance."

"Put some distance?"

"Yeah, some distance between me and other people and between me and my thoughts."

He nodded, sitting next to her.

"Can you feel it?" she asked him.

He nodded. "Is it always like this?"

"More," she smiled. "Even I have limits."

"I forgot we are not really here," he laughed at himself.

"C'mon, I'll show you the town," she said, standing and holding her hand out to him. "Close your eyes."

To get to town, they would have to climb the cliff, then descend it to the other side and walk the rest of the way. If they were really there. She asked him to close his eyes because she would just change the environment around them and didn't want to break the charm for him.

"Open them," she whispered.

He looked around and took a full turn to see everything. There were people around, faces she knew and faces she just saw around and remembered.

"All these people," he said. "Are they all flairs?"

"Everyone in the Citadel is," she confirmed.

"It's amazing."

"I know," she smiled.

They walked around the town centre for a while, Nashel pointing out the shops she liked, the food stands, the bench where she first met Sergeant Thomas. She pointed towards the avenue that would take them to the Academy and the one to the base.

"Can you show me?"

She nodded and didn't even have to tell him to close his eyes that time.

With a pang of nostalgia, she manifested the academy square.

"So, that's the Class building," she pointed towards the middle one, directly opposite the road she had just shown him from the other end. "That," she pointed to the left one, "is the Recruit's. And that," she pointed to the last one, "is the Aspirant's. My room is in there."

She explained they would assemble in the square every morning for inspection. She didn't say what would happen if a cadet was found in breach of regulations, she didn't think Alistair would understand. She showed him the fields, behind the buildings, cadets were there training. Faceless cadets, because she was feeling too tired to conjure up accurate people.

Alistair was too amazed to notice, he was trying to take everything in, and she knew that, at the same time, he was trying to imagine himself there, what his life would look like if he was born on the right side of the Void.

She swayed, the academy flickering to black. She wasn't sure if she was just blacking out or if the Expression was failing.

She felt Alistair's hands steadying her, but then she felt herself falling and falling. She gasped a moment before she hit the ground, only to realise that she wasn't falling anywhere. She was lying in her bed in the loft of Alistair's home. His face was looming over her, all shadows eclipsing the nightstand lamp.

"Are you okay?" he asked her gently when he saw she had regained consciousness.

"Yes," she replied croakily.

"Thank you," he murmured, kissing her cheek. "Best present ever."

"I should faint more often, then," she replied weakly, making him laugh.

"Rest now," he said sweetly, and moved to get up.

"Stay," she whispered. "Stay with me?"

He didn't reply with words, but laid back down and hugged her. She felt exhaustion claiming her again and didn't fight it, but just before she fell asleep, she thought she heard him mutter something.

"I love you." She thought she heard, but didn't have the time to process or think about it.

When she woke up, she knew that once more it wasn't dawn. The light from her window told her it was around midday, but she wasn't sure if it was the day after Alistair's birthday or if she slept for another entire day. Alistair wasn't there, which made understanding time even more difficult.

She stretched and made her way downstairs. She stopped by his room, but he wasn't there either, so she kept going. She found it in the living room, plastered in front of the fan with Neo.

"Hey," she announced herself.

"Hey," he tried to say, but he was so close to the fan that it came out distorted and made her laugh.

"What time is it? How long did I sleep?" she asked.

"Lunch time!" he exclaimed. "And you slept about ten or eleven hours?"

"So not an entire day."

"No," he laughed, and the sound that came out of the fan was almost scary. "I think it helped that you were already in bed when you passed out."

She nodded.

"Lunch?" he asked, standing up. Neo looked at him, wagging his tail, but lost interest when Alistair took a step away from the cool air.

"Yep, I'm famished."

Raven wasn't there, but they had carried home enough food from the fair to feed an entire army, so they didn't miss her too much.

"Did I say thank you for your birthday present?" Alistair asked her, stuffing his mouth with a bit of everything.

"Yes."

"Thank you," he ignored her. "I really appreciate it."

"You're welcome," she smiled.

She wondered why his tone was so serious, she hadn't done anything special other than exhausting herself, and that seemed to occur more often than not those days, she had just showed him where she lived, where he belonged. She didn't even do a good job towards the end, the faceless cadets would haunt her dreams for a while. Yet, for some reason, she also felt proud and pleased that he was happy.

As they sunbathed in silence, her mind kept going back to the moment, just after they shocked C with their passionate kiss. To when Alistair said he loved her.

"What kind of name is even C?" she said abruptly, trying to think about something else.

Alistair chuckled. "It's short for Shierzha," he explained.

"Why not Shie then?"

Alistair laughed again. "She's weird that way."

Nashel could feel the shrug in his voice even without

turning to look at him.

"She's apo, right?" Nashel asked, and she hated the note of desperation she felt in her own tone.

"Yeah, and she doesn't know I'm not," Alistair replied. "Not many people in town know."

That made sense.

"How did you meet?"

She heard him shuffle on the sun lounge as if was sitting up. "Why are you asking so many questions?"

It wasn't a defensive tone, but a curious and slightly ironic one.

"I was just thinking about it," she shrugged.

"Are you jealous? I told you I don't care about her."

"No, I'm not jealous. I was just chatting," she scoffed. "I'll go back to just sunbathe, don't worry."

He laughed again. "You're cute when you're all worked up," he whispered.

"Cute?" she said, offended. Nobody ever called her cute. To her ears, it sounded too similar to weak.

"Yeah, cute," he repeated defiantly.

"I'll have you know I am a fierce warrior!"

"Yes, and a cute one."

"Stop saying that!" she snapped, but it didn't have any bite.

"Cute."

"Alistair!"

"Cute."

"You're going to pay for that!"

"Still cute," he kept teasing her.

She mentally scanned her surroundings for something to throw at him, maybe some water or, even better, mud, but there was nothing. She huffed in frustration and resignation. Alistair laughed, enjoying the win.

With that conversation over, she had no choice but to go back to her thoughts. Alistair said he loved her. And she froze.

Love was something she didn't know. She wasn't sure her

mother and father ever loved her. They cared for her, they were affectionate at times, but they were also fearful. The academy was no place for love, only discipline and training. Her relationships were always of convenience or fun. She knew what she felt for Alistair was different. But was it love?

If it wasn't about him, she would ask Alistair, but she couldn't, not yet, at least.

For what she knew, love was caring for a person more than oneself. She didn't feel that. She cared for Alistair, but she would put herself first, always. She tried to think about what else she knew about love. It wasn't a topic that ever interested her, so she never paid too much attention to romance in books or films. She thought one of the common tropes was wanting the other person to be happy. On more than one occasion she felt that. She didn't like when Alistair was sad or disappointed, and she felt the urge to change that. She thought about how upset with something deeper than anger she was when C, or Shie, took him away from her. She'd never been jealous before, but she was when it concerned Alistair. She wanted him close, she wanted him for herself.

She had never been interested in physical affection, either, but it felt good with Alistair. She liked when he hugged her, when he caressed her cheeks, when he kissed her. She wanted more. More of everything. More of him. She wanted him by her side.

So maybe, just maybe, that was love. Or the version of love she experienced.

Was she going to tell him that? There was a lot of herself she didn't want to share with him yet, a lot that he wouldn't understand. Would he understand that? Or if she said "I love you", would he think she felt the same way he was feeling? Did it matter?

She groaned. She didn't mean to, but all those thoughts kept going in circles and were frustrating her.

"El?" Alistair called sleepily.

"All good," she replied.

"Why did you groan then?" he asked, amused.

"I have a song stuck in my head," she lied. "One of the jingles from the carnival."

He laughed, and she took a moment to enjoy it. He didn't laugh like that with Shie. She had heard him "laugh" with her. It was a nervous sound, awkward. The sound of someone who wanted to escape and didn't know how. In fact, even at the academy, she only ever heard him laugh like that freely with her. Something not unpleasant knotted her insides, affection. Love?

She smiled to herself.

"I love you," she mouthed without sound, just to see what the words felt like on her lips.

Weird. They felt weird, out of character. But she also felt something else. A desire to get used to those words, to tell them to him. She was a very disciplined person, so she knew better than to blurt out words without thinking. Yet, once again, in the span of just over a day, her training failed her.

"I love you," she said out loud.

Alistair drew a sharp breath.

The silence that followed was tense. Maybe it wasn't the right moment. Maybe she should've said it while looking at him, maybe when they were lying in bed with their faces so close together their breaths mingled.

She wasn't afraid to move, but she also didn't want to see whatever emotions were crossing Alistair's eyes, so she stayed perfectly still. He, on the other hand, slowly sat up. She felt him staring for a moment before she heard him stand up.

He took the few steps that separated their sun lounges and looked down at her. She had her eyes closed, but she knew he was doing precisely that.

He knelt beside her, placing a gentle hand on her cheek. "Look at me," he whispered.

She pretended not to hear him.

"Please."

With a deep breath, she opened her eyes and turned

towards him. His hand on her cheek was warm, but she leaned into it. He had a resolute look in his eyes, and before she could utter a word, he bent closer and kissed her. It felt as if he was kissing her like his life depended on it. He was very good at communicating with gestures, and that kiss told her he was overjoyed by what she had just said and filled with love for her.

She wasn't sure she had made the right decision in telling him that. She wasn't sure she had made the right decision starting that relationship with him and letting it get so deep. Those were all considerations she made after, because, in that moment, the power of that kiss took her breath away.

CHAPTER TWENTY-SIX

The Solnedian Library

The summer holidays passed in a breeze, and soon it was time to go back to Solned and the Sunrise Academy. Nashel hated to admit she wasn't ready, or better yet, she didn't want to. The weeks she spent at Alistair's were the best of an awful situation. She was freer there, she could use her powers she wasn't constrained by absurd rules and she could train and keep up a semblance of normality. And it didn't last long enough.

The weather was still unrelentingly hot when they left, and it was even more suffocating in Solned, surrounded by the blinding buildings, the dry city air, the scorching cement. She groaned loudly as they got off the train, making Alistair laugh.

Alistair. He was the only positive aspect of all of it. She knew she was neglecting her mission in favour of her newly formed romantic relationship. She knew that if she were back home, she would get disciplined for that, but she wasn't home and there was nobody there to order her around.

The journey was long and it didn't do anything to improve her mood. She couldn't wait to reach her room and sleep. If she could, she would sleep until the next holiday.

"Hey, it's okay," Alistair whispered as they paused to look at the looming campus, giving her hand a squeeze. "We'll be okay."

She groaned again in response.

Their PPads pinged as soon as they crossed the gate: they had been assigned new rooms in a different dorm. It was the building they went to breakfast every day, the better building, the one that wasn't falling to pieces.

"At least there's that," she conceded as they moved towards it.

"A single!" Alistair yelped as they opened his new room door. He got in and twirled around, laughing. "And it doesn't smell!"

Nashel laughed too, then let him enjoy his newfound freedom, and went to her room. She was surprised by it. It was a single too, but it was much nicer than what she had. The mattress was newer, springs were not going to dig into her back or creak so loudly they would wake her. The wardrobe and desk were much nicer too, more spacious, less damaged.

She immediately went to work to erect the wards she had before, for her own peace of mind. When she finished, she finally got to try the new bed. Before falling asleep, she managed to send a short text to Alistair, letting him know she was going to rest.

"We should try to get that book," Alistair whispered the following morning at breakfast.

Nashel took a few seconds to understand what he was talking about. She was about to ask him, when she remembered: the collection of stories Wynmere promised would give her answers if she could read between the lines.

"We will have to try the Solnedian library."

"We have the day off," Alistair shrugged.

She nodded, agreeing.

The Solnedian Library was a huge building, the biggest they had seen other than the academy campus. It was all white marble, like the majority of the city. A sign on the side of the main entrance recited: "The Antique Solnedian Library is the biggest historical repository of the Sunset."

When they got inside, they discovered that only a small fraction of the books were available to the public. It was still a big number, but Nashel knew it would make finding the information she was looking for even harder.

"Hello dearies, how can I help you?" the librarian asked as they approached the information desk.

She was an older woman, kind, used to smile judging by the wrinkles at the corner of her eyes.

"We're looking for The Second Sunset," Nashel told her.

"The Second Sunset?" the librarian asked. Her tone was not suspicious; hers seemed like a genuine question to check she understood correctly.

"Yes, please," Alistair replied.

"Let me see," she said gently, tapping on her screen for a few moments. "Ah," her expression changed, and Nashel knew what was coming before she could add another word. "Unfortunately, you are not on the authorised list to borrow this book."

"Can we consult it without borrowing it?" Nashel asked.

"I'm afraid not," the librarian shook her head.

"Can we get authorisation in any way?"

She shook her head again. "Unless you become a scholar overnight, it is not possible."

"Thank you, anyway," Alistair told her with a smile.

He put a hand on Nashel's shoulder, squeezing it, and guiding her away from the desk. He knew she wanted to argue, but it would be a lost cause. She knew it too.

"How important is it for you to get that book?" Alistair asked on their way back.

"Important," she replied.

She didn't know how to describe it. It was a gut feeling; the book contained the answers she needed, whatever the questions were.

Alistair stayed quiet for a while.

"We have two choices," she broke the silence. "We either

break into the library on campus or the Solnedian."

Alistair looked at her incredulously. "We what?"

"You're right," she muttered, her mind already lost in thoughts of planning. "I can break in. You are invited to come, though."

"El, I don't think it's a good idea."

"I need that book, and neither library wants to lend it. So I'll have to take it for myself."

"The campus library is smaller," he mused.

"Yes, but the librarian might remember I asked for it and lead them straight to me."

"True," he conceded. "But the Solnedian is protected by magic. Don't tell me you didn't feel it."

She grimaced at the word 'magic', she hated it when Alistair used it. But he was right, the library was heavily protected. "I know it is," she nodded. "But I won't let that stop me."

"You're powerful, El," he said, squeezing her hand gently. "But even you have limits. What if you pass out, like at the lakes?"

"I'll be careful."

Alistair was right. While they walked back, she kept thinking, trying to run over the viable plans in her head. It had been impossible not to notice the power that surrounded the library. It was the highest concentration of power she felt other than that mystical forest they went to for their getaway.

Alistair was right: she was powerful, but in all the scenarios, she thought, she didn't have enough to break the barriers or go undetected. She didn't even know what Expression protected it. She would have to reveal them first, just that would take energy, then she would have to use her remaining power to camouflage herself, as she knew already that undoing the Expressions would be a lost cause. Then she would have to find the book, which she reckoned was protected, and get out before she couldn't sustain her disguise and trigger the alarms.

It didn't take much thought to know that she would never

succeed, not in the Sunrise. Not alone.

"Is there a way to share magic?" Alistair asked in a whisper as they arrived back on campus.

She stopped on her track, looking at him.

"What?" he asked, confused.

"What are you asking?"

He blushed. "I was just thinking," he said awkwardly, scratching the back of his head. "If we can share power, we can probably get past the security."

"It is possible," she replied. "But it's going to be risky. Do you really want to come?"

"No," he said. "But I don't want to leave you alone either, so I will."

He smiled, a bit shyly.

She smiled back. "Thank you."

They spent the rest of the day planning. They had seen too little of the library to draw a complete blueprint, and they couldn't go back to check without drawing suspicion. They knew the layout of the entrance, the reception area and the first section in front of it, but that was it. They didn't know how the library was organised or where the book might be.

"Let me recap," Alistair said, slouching on her bed. "We are going in blind. We don't know what protection the library has. We don't know where the book is or how it is secured."

She nodded at each fact. "Once there, I can check the Expressions to see how to fool them. Then we just need to find the book and either see if we can take it or make a copy."

"How long?" he asked.

"Probably an hour, maybe longer."

"That is, if there is no other security feature other than magic."

"Yes, if there are guards, we would have to deal with them, too."

"Cameras!" he shouted. "We forgot the cameras!"

"I didn't," she grinned. "Cameras are easy to fool, don't worry."

"But it's more magic—"

"Stop saying that!" she snapped.

He laughed. "But it's more power we need to use, and we need to be careful not to get spotted before we disable them."

"Relax, cameras don't take much."

"Okay, so we share powers, which take power. We disable the cameras, again power. We take out the guards? We camouflage somehow, and guess what, it takes power. Somehow we find the book even though we have no idea where it is, then we take it or copy it. And finally, we get out."

"Yes, but sharing powers will sustain all of that."

"Will it? It seems like a lot."

"It is a lot, but not too much. Trust me."

He nodded, but she could see he wasn't confident. She wasn't either. Alistair was powerful enough, but there was a lot to overcome. She hoped there was no guard. Humans would make everything messier, and she couldn't kill them, not if she wanted to keep Alistair by her side - and not get caught.

They waited until the dead of the night and reached the library. There weren't many people out, but the city was still active. It was a different look than in daylight. Nashel took some time to enjoy it now that it wasn't blinding. The architecture was majestic, over the top, but majestic. The library, when they got closer, took her breath away. Lights were illuminating the building, creating a stunning play of lights and shadows. They stopped around the corner, out of the eye of the cameras.

"We didn't account for people," Alistair whispered.

He was right, again. They didn't think there would be passersby, they thought that like on campus, people would be sleeping. But in a city as big as Solned, there was always something to do, day or night.

"There should be a side entrance, right? For workers, deliveries and everything else."

Alistair nodded. "Let's try it."

They strolled down the road, Alistair's arm around her shoulders and hers around his waist, like a couple enjoying a night out, taking a wide berth of the building, not to get spotted by the cameras. They took a side road that circled back to the side of the library and stopped when they saw it but were still out of range. This side wasn't illuminated, and thankfully there weren't people around. There were cameras on the metal door and at the corners of the building.

She quickly got to work on those, and as she predicted, it didn't take long or much energy.

"Clear," she whispered to Alistair once she finished.

"Should we share now?" he asked back.

"Yes," she held out her hand. He squeezed it nervously. "Now, just like we practised."

They concentrated on their locked hands, on getting the power flows through them until they met. Nashel immediately felt the boost, she closed her eyes to appreciate it, reminiscing of home.

"Wow," Alistair breathed.

She quickly snapped out of the stupor and got to work on the door. She expected it to be protected by an Expression, similar to the one she put on her door in the dorm. But when she tried to reveal it, she found nothing. It was surprising and unexpected. She didn't trust it, but trying to reveal the Trace would take more power she didn't want to use. However, she didn't want to waste time outside at the mercy of the first passerby, either.

"Damn," she muttered under her breath. "Keep watch."

"What's happening?"

She didn't reply, she just concentrated on the task ahead. Revealing the Trace was easier while sharing powers with Alistair. It didn't take her long to find there was one indeed. Pleased that she was right, she worked on undoing it, bit by bit, thread by thread. She had a moment to appreciate the masterful work they'd done on it. It was the first time she saw an Expression done properly in the Sunrise. It was almost a shame she had to ruin the work. Almost.

The door opened with a satisfying click and she smiled. "Let's go," she told Alistair.

The room they entered was dark. It smelt of dust, old books and metal shelves. She didn't need a light to know that's what surrounded her. Still, some light filtered from the edges of the door opposite them, the one that would lead deeper into the library. She grabbed Alistair's hand and walked towards it. She quickly checked if there was any protection, but she found none again, so she turned the handle and opened it slowly. A smaller room with a soft light greeted them, and they could see boxes, shelves, and books. More light was coming from yet another door. She checked that as well, and was about to open it when she heard a noise.

She held up a fist, an instinctive gesture stemming from her training. Alistair made a noise, half a laugh, half a squeal of surprise.

"What?" he whispered.

"I heard a noise," she replied in the same small voice.

She pressed her ear to the door, trying to discern if she heard something or if she just imagined it. She heard nothing for a long while, and she felt Alistair becoming impatient next to her, shuffling his feet and making it harder for her to hear anything. She shot him a stare, but he didn't understand. He wasn't trained, after all.

"Can you please stay still?" she snapped with gritted teeth.

"Sorry," he whispered back, contrite.

She closed her eyes to concentrate on hearing. There it was again, a soft thump in the distance, followed by another and another in a rhythmic pattern.

"Steps," she murmured.

She listened as they grew louder, closer, then slowly got fainter again. She counted the seconds until she couldn't hear them anymore, then waited to see how long it would take for them to return.

"What's happening?"

"Please, just wait quietly," she replied again, losing her patience.

The steps returned, then moved again in the opposite

direction.

"We only have three minutes before the guard returns to this area," she explained, her hand already on the handle. "C'mon."

They walked into the library itself. The entrance and reception were to their right, the desk now empty. In front of them was the large expanse of shelves and reading tables. The lights were dimmed but still enough for them to see without problems.

She nodded towards the first row of shelves and moved towards them.

"What's next?"

"We need to take out the guard. There may be more, so we need to keep watch."

"Take out?" he asked with a scared look in his eyes. She really wished he had just did what she said without questions. Or that he grew up in the Sunset and knew what an op looked like.

"Incapacitate," she answered.

He nodded, relieved. "Magic or brute force?"

"Force," she replied.

They waited for the guard to return. She thought about what would be the best way to accomplish that without using too much energy and she came to the conclusion that sometimes it was better not to use powers.

The guard was a burly, middle-aged man who was strolling more than patrolling, which meant he had no idea what was coming for him. Nashel waited for him to pass in front of their hiding spot before jumping out and putting an arm around his neck, using her other arm to tighten the grip. The guard took a moment to realise what was happening before he started to fight her. By then it was too late, his oxygen level was decreasing rapidly, and the more he struggled, the more he used, the quicker he passed out.

Nashel dragged him towards Alistair and the aisle between the two shelves. Alistair was a mess of emotions: disbelief, stupor, fear, pride. He jumped a little back when she dropped the guard unceremoniously, but thankfully, he didn't make any noise.

"There could be more in other sectors, but let's start looking," she instructed. "Don't touch anything. We don't know what protects them."

"I think this is the public section," Alistair replied. "It should be fine."

"Don't touch anything," she repeated more sternly. "We don't know what they do, even to the public section after closing time."

He nodded. They looked at the books, trying to figure out what system they used to organise them. There were no signs that told them which section they were in, and she wondered why that was the case, but she didn't linger on it too much. By reading some of the titles, it seemed they were in the science section, so she hurried on.

"I think the Scholars' Archive is that way," Alistair pointed.

"The Scholars' Archive?"

"I read that's what it's called while you were talking to the receptionist."

She gave a small nod, her eyebrows slightly raised in acknowledgement, a silent "fair enough" in her eyes.

There wasn't a barrier or even a cordon to separate the public section from the Scholars' Archive, but Nashel held out a hand in front of Alistair to stop him, anyway. He grunted, and she realised he would've stopped on his own, because he, too, felt it. There might not have been a physical barrier, but power was. And if one looked closely, they could see a shimmering gold, almost translucent shine separating the two sections.

"There must be a door," Alistair murmured. "An opening to let authorised people in."

She nodded. "You go that way," she pointed to her left. "I go right. Keep an eye out for guards."

He opened his mouth, then closed it again. She shrugged and walked away. She sent out feelers to see if she could perceive any difference in the barrier. She checked a direct line from the reception desk, the entrance to the library and the Scholars' Archive barrier, to see if the path was in direct line with those, but she found nothing.

CHAPTER TWENTY-SEVEN
The Heist

She continued on her path until one feeler caught something. To her surprise, it wasn't coming from the barrier, but from the public section shelves. A guard? She sent another feeler, but it didn't return any feedback. She took a couple of steps and tried again, and there it was, and after a moment, it was gone. She concentrated and tried to distinguish a pattern. It seemed like a regular, rhythmic ping, like a radar. A feeler! It was a feeler, just like the ones she was sending. Was it Alistair? It was impossible. He went the opposite way, and the library was way too big for him to have circled it, even if it were possible to do so. Also, this feeler was different, it didn't react to hers, as if it was someone programmed to recognise powers and not do anything about them, unless it triggered a silent alarm, but enough time passed for a response team to converge on her position.

So, it was a programmed feeler, probably to catch intruders, or recognise authorised personnel, maybe it was near the entrance they were trying to find to screen scholars. It was static, so it wasn't a guard on patrol, but it would probably trigger the alarm if she moved forward. She could try and go around it, sending more feelers to pinpoint the

Expression's exact location before undoing it.

She took a wide berth back into the public section, afraid to get too close and trigger a response. She managed to find the location of the Expression, and she stopped to think about how to proceed. Once again, she was reminded why she hated the Sunrise so much. If she were back home, she wouldn't need to stop and evaluate her options; she would have enough energy to just act. She decided that screening the Expression would be the best cost-effective option. It wouldn't touch it directly, so it was safe, and not having to undo it and redo it reduced the risk of being noticed.

Once she'd done it and could get closer, she realised that the Expression was not there to identify authorised people. There was no entrance to the Scholars' Archive in its proximity. She found it curious. What was its purpose, then? Just a security feature? Were there more? Was Alistair going to trigger one because he didn't notice it? She couldn't answer those questions unless she kept moving, so she resumed her inspection, sending her feelers, ears and senses open to anything out of place.

She felt another of those feelers after a while, and at the same time, she heard the steps of a guard coming her way. She hid and observed. The guard seemed to be on the path to cross the Expression, and she was curious to see if there was any change or recognition. The guard passed through, but nothing happened. There was no change in the Expression and nothing happened to the guard, who continued his patrol. She waited until he was out of the Expression's range then quickly took him out the same way she did the other. She screened the expression and continued, finding another at regular intervals, but still no entrance to the Archive.

When she finally reached the end of the library, she was frustrated and angry. There was no entrance, no gap, no indication of how people were able to get into the restricted section. She had screened all the feelers and knocked out another guard, and she still had nothing. The barrier between the public and restricted areas was too powerful for her to undo, even while power-sharing with Alistair. Even if she managed, then she would have to find the book, copy it and get out without passing out and without getting caught.

She was about to go back, meet Alistair in the middle, and hopefully get some good news from him, when she noticed a small gap between the barrier and the wall. It was tiny, just a sliver, but it was there and it gave her an idea. Maybe the entrance was not detectable, maybe it was only activated manually when someone had to gain access, but usually there was an emergency exit, so that people would not be trapped inside. She concentrated and sent a small amount of power through the gap, just enough to create an Expression, once on the other side, to search for the emergency exit from the inside. She couldn't send it across the Scholars' Archive to find the book, as it needed to stay close to her to work, but it should be enough to find the exit.

She walked back slowly, now her focus split even more, checking that the guards were still out, the Expression still screened and her exit finder still working, as well as being alert for anything new. She had to go all the way back to where she started for her Expression to alert her of the emergency exit and she could finally see it. It was so subtle, no wonder she missed it the first time.

Alistair came back a few minutes later, his expression grim.

"What happened?" She asked immediately.

"Guards," he grimaced. "It was hard to knock them out."

She fought the urge to roll her eyes.

"What about the feelers?"

"The what?" he asked, confused.

Before she could answer, she heard a noise: the rhythmic click of boots on marble. Fast approaching.

"What have you done?" she hissed through gritted teeth.

"Nothing!" Alistair exclaimed on the defensive.

Nashel shook her head. She didn't have time to recriminate now. The noise was coming closer and closer. Her Expression on the other side of the Scholars' Archive was faltering slightly, as Nashel focussed on the approaching unknown. She wasn't sure she could make it open the door in time for them to escape.

"There's an exit there," she whispered, pointing towards it, not that he could see it.

"An exit?"

She nodded. "I have an Expression on the inside."

He looked at her as if she spoke a different language and, for a moment, she wondered if she did.

The noise was too close now; they would not make it.

"Hide," she ordered Alistair and gestured towards the shelves.

They both rushed to put some distance between them and whatever was coming. Nashel felt a tug as her Expression was getting too far for her to keep it up. She stopped, grabbing her stomach. She wasn't really feeling physical pain, but it was an instinctive reaction.

"W—" Alistair was about to ask, but her hand shot out and pressed hard on his mouth. His eyes wide in warning.

The noise kept its rhythm as it reached the spot they had been moments prior, then it abruptly stopped. Nashel peeked from behind the shelves, a risky move, but she needed to see. The tallest man stood looking around attentively. He had a hand-held device that emanated a red light, and he pointed it in front of him, slowly turning.

"Damn whippers," he muttered.

Nashel hid back.

"We got intru—" Nashel heard static and chanced another look. The guard was shaking his hand, and by his side, swans a smoking radio.

Nashel hid again, confused, only to see Alistair grinning. He must've done something to the radio.

Nashel thought about her options. If she used her powers to knock the guard down, she would jeopardise the rest of the mission. But the man was over six feet tall and as wide as Nashel and Alistair shoulder to shoulder, making it almost impossible to do it by force.

One of the first lessons cadets was taught was to study and use one's surroundings. The shelves were too tall to move them, even with Alistair's help, but the books were heavy tomes and she had a good arm. She looked at Alistair and tried to communicate to him to follow her example.

She took a random volume and threw it at the guard, aiming for his head. She caught him by surprise and hit him. A gash opened on his forehead, but he didn't falter. She threw another, then another. Alistair did the same until the guard was under heavy "fire" and couldn't do anything but protect himself.

Nashel ordered her Expression to open the door to the Scholars' Archive, hoping that in the mayhem she still had enough of a hold on it. It did, and she gestured for Alistair to run, while she threw more books at the guard as she went around him.

She threw the last book, the guard swayed, blood covering his face, obscuring his vision, but he managed to point the device at her. Nashel expected the red light to do something to her, but what hit her were two small prongs that released a high voltage current. Nashel fell through the Archive's door, just as her concentration faltered and the Expression dissolved. She convulsed on the ground, vaguely aware of Alistair calling her name in panic.

It took several minutes for her muscles to stop trembling and her mind to clear enough to start processing everything again.

"El?" Alistair murmured, from close by.

Nashel turned her heavy head and saw him crouching down next to her. "Help me up," she told him creakily.

She looked around and notice the barrier separating the sections up again. She took a moment to assess herself, but found no injury, just muscle soreness and probably a bruise forming because of the fall. Alistair helped her from sitting to standing, and she nodded a thanks.

The building must have been expanded with an Expression because the Scholars' Archive was immense, at least three times as big as the public section and definitely bigger than the building they saw from the outside.

"It's bigger than I expected," Alistair whispered in wonder. She didn't reply; he was stating the obvious.

"Let's get searching. The guards won't stay knocked out forever and there's only one exit. They'll be waiting."

It was almost a literal needle in a stack of needles. There was no rhyme or reason as to how the books were displayed. If the public section was chaotic, there were no words to describe the Archive. It was as if the library was messing with their mind, if it was enchanted... It was. Expressions were keeping her from finding the right book.

"Stop," she ordered.

Alistair stopped mid-step, and she smiled at the comical effect.

"We'll never find it," she explained. "The library doesn't want us to."

"The library doesn't want us to?" he repeated, confused.

"Yes, Expressions are stopping us from finding the book because they recognise we are not authorised."

"So, how do we find it?"

"Do you think you can carry me out?" She asked with a sigh.

"Carry you out?"

"Yes, can you? Can you get past the guards unnoticed and get us out?"

"What are you thinking of doing?"

"We need to find the book. I need to bypass this Expression and locate it."

"No," he said firmly.

"Excuse me?"

"No, you are not going to do that."

"I don't think you can give me orders," she rebutted.

"Okay, I'll leave then," he shrugged.

"Good luck opening the barrier," she shrugged back.

"You think you're the only capable person?" he snorted, turned his back to her and started walking towards the exit.

She didn't call him back, she didn't say anything, she just focused on the powers around her. They made her head spin. There were so many Expressions overlapping that it was impossible to distinguish them all. Each book had at least one, keeping the books from leaving the library. Most had one to prevent copies, and some had others she didn't have time to distinguish. On top of them all, there were multiple Expressions meant to confuse the patrons, and she still felt the effect of the taser.

She wouldn't admit it out loud, but she would never be able to find the book. There was too much chaos, too many Expressions to get through; she wouldn't be able to disentangle them from each other or undo them.

She felt frustration and anger rise. She didn't get to that point only to give up, even if she had to check every single book manually or fend off an army of pathetic Sunrise, while navigating the maze that was the Scholars' Archive.

Navigate. A memory flashed in front of her eyes. When she was very young, a Junior Cadet or a Cadet maybe, her Class took a trip to the Hreystisafn, the Citadel's repository of Sunset's history. It was a library, a museum, a sentient entity. Open to all Sunset, all day, every day. The opposite of the Sunforsaken place she was in at the moment. When her Class went there, she remembered, they were all excited to see the wonders of the place. But the Hreystisafn is huge and kids could get easily lost, so each and every one of them was given a guide. It wasn't a human guide, but a wisp: a little ball of power with a tiny antenna that bobbled every time it moved, its shape changing to mimic human facial expressions. Nashel became so obsessed with it she recreated it and kept it as a pet in her room for over two months. But the wisp guide knew the Hreystisafn and could take its patrons around wherever they wanted to go, finding whatever book or artefact or piece of knowledge they needed.

She smiled as she realised she had found the solution. She concentrated, feeling her power flow through her body, connecting with the rest of it around her, with Alistair's not that far yet, still within the barrier. She willed the wisp into existence, carving a space for it within the flow, until the blue ball of power squeaked, floating at her eye level, its features turned into a smile.

"I'm looking for *The Second Sunset*," Nashel told it.

It turned and looked around, left and right, then turned back to Nashel, nodding, its antenna bumping up and down. It made another small noise that wasn't a word, but at the same time it sounded like "this way".

"Let's go," Nashel instructed.

"What's that?" Alistair's voice behind her made her jump.

She cursed herself for lowering her guard.

"A guide," she replied. "Hopefully."

"How?"

"Something I saw when I was a child. Something we have back home."

"It's kind of cute," Alistair commented, and she could hear the peace offering in his tone.

"It is," she replied, accepting it. "I kept one as a pet."

He chuckled. "Of course you did."

She rolled her eyes but didn't comment.

Despite the wisp seeming to know where to go, the Expressions were still messing with their head, as Nashel tried to keep track of the turns, to understand how the books were catalogued, but she couldn't.

"Are you sure it knows where to take us?"

"Yes," she replied, sounding surer than she was.

She lost track of time, her head spinning with each turn, another effect of the Expressions. At one point Alistair had to steady her, which she hated.

The wisp finally stopped and turned to her with its satisfied and open smile, squeaking an excited noise, like a puppy happy to have brought the ball back after fetching it. Nashel turned to the shelf it was pointing out, but she still couldn't see the book. The titles on the spines were swimming in front of her eyes, turning and changing, blurring her vision.

"You need to point exactly at it," she told the wisp.

It nodded with a squeak and gently bumped itself against one of the books.

"Thanks," she grinned in victory.

Now that she knew where the book was, looking at it didn't confuse her. She could see the title shimmering in gold in the library's light, slightly raised from the purplish spine. She promptly swatted away Alistair's extended hand, stopping him from touching the book.

"Expressions," she murmured without further explanation.

She let the wisp dissolve, needing all her focus for the next step of the plan. She directed all her attention to the book, trying to isolate the Expressions linked to it.

"What can I do?" Alistair asked in a whisper.

"Nothing," she replied.

"C'mon, El, I didn't come here just to be your power supply," he snapped.

She sighed.

"What do you want to do? You're not trained to do anything I need help with!"

She didn't usually lose her patience, but Alistair was getting on her last nerve.

"Stop thinking I'm incompetent!"

"You are!"

She knew she had to stop arguing and start working on the Expressions. The guards wouldn't stay knocked out forever, and they would raise the alarm once they regained consciousness. They had spent too much time in the library already. She shook her head.

She tried to focus again, the many Expressions dizzying her. She swayed, Alistair's hands immediately stabilising her.

"Let. Me. Help. You," he hissed through gritted teeth.

"I don't have time to teach you," she replied.

"You don't have to teach me anything. Just let me help."

"Can you distinguish Expressions and their uses?" she asked accusatory.

"I—" he started, but stopped. "Not that well."

"Exactly, so let's stop arguing and let me get to work," she said, shaking her head.

She knew Alistair wanted to protest, but he stopped, and with a nod, she closed her eyes to focus.

With a lot of effort and energy, she managed to stay focused on the book she needed. She realised that the confusion-inducing Expressions were the ones giving her a hard time, but she wanted to identify the rest before undoing anything.

"There are five Expressions on this book," she whispered, hoping that saying it out loud would help her stay focused. "Two to confuse unauthorised patrons; one to prevent the book from being taken from the shelf without permission; one to prevent it from being taken outside the library; and the last one is the anti-copy one."

Alistair let out a low whistle. "That's a lot."

"Yeah," she replied with a sigh, rubbing her forehead where a headache was starting to form.

She let go of the focus for a moment, taking a breath and relaxing her muscles. She didn't realise Alistair was still holding her upright.

"I think I can make a buffer between you and the Expressions we don't need to deal with," he said after a pause. "I think if you focus on the anti-copy and the shelf one, we should be okay without touching the rest."

His tone was soft, uncertain, and she knew he felt like he was walking on egg's shells because of her outburst. But he was also right. They didn't need to undo all the Expressions, just the ones that would stop them from copying the book.

"Can you?" she asked, her tone less blunt.

He nodded.

"Okay," she whispered and stood up straighter, away from his support.

They both concentrated on their task, and after a few minutes, Nashel felt the difference Alistair's help made. It was like a weight was lifted from crushing her. Her mind felt cleared, and she didn't need to focus on the book so intensely just to keep it at the centre of her mind. She could perceive the remaining Expressions better as well, which allowed her to work on them quickly and efficiently.

She extended a hand to grab the book, careful not to touch the ones next to it, and held her breath for a moment, waiting for an alarm to be triggered. Nothing happened, and she grinned, victorious.

She nodded at Alistair to let go and relax. Now that the book was in her hand, she wouldn't be confused by the Expressions. He did and stumbled before righting himself .

"You're okay?" she asked, extending a hand to help him.

He nodded, but looked pale, about to pass out or throw up. She waited a minute, making sure he was recovering and not getting worse.

"I'm okay," he confirmed.

"Can you hand me the blank?" she asked him then.

He rummaged through his bag and produced a blank notebook. They had decided it was easier to copy the book onto an existing blank instead of making one out of thin air to save energy and time.

"Hold it steady," she instructed, then placed the original next to it. She opened it to the first page, and Alistair did the same, while she focussed on transferring the words. It was an easy Expression, cadets used it all the time on tests to copy from one another or to mess with another cadet's test, but it took some time to go through the entire book page by page, waiting for Alistair to make sure the words stayed on the blank before moving on.

She didn't like how much time it took them to get to the book and copy it, and then they had to redo the Expression to avoid detection. Alistair created the buffer again as she worked on the anti-copy and shelf Expressions, making sure they looked like the others around her, linked to the other books. She noticed different Expressions had different 'signatures' even when the books were next to one another, and she relaxed, thinking it wouldn't be too out of place if her remaking was not identical.

When they finished, they were both exhausted. They still needed to get out, and Nashel was almost sure there were guards expecting them.

"If I spend my powers covering us," she told Alistair. "Will you be able to carry me back to campus without arousing suspicion?"

He looked like he wanted to protest again, but he must've seen the steel in her gaze. "I believe so."

Nashel didn't trust easily, and if she did what she had in mind, she would be completely at Alistair's mercy. This time they weren't on a dirt road in the middle of nowhere, and she wasn't sure he could pull it off. Yet, it was the only option she could think of.

"Alright," she nodded and led the way to the only door they had found.

Thankfully, the barrier separating the Scholars' Archive let them through, its emergency exit override making an opening for them. Nashel called on all her power to camouflage herself and Alistair so that they could move along the shelves undetected. The tall guard was there, his scanner back in hand, but Alistair had the promptitude to make it short-circuit like he had the radio. They moved quickly away from the door as the guard shouted for them to stop. Some of the other guards regained consciousness and were in the vicinity, but didn't hold scanners.

Nashel and Alistair had to progress slowly. Her camouflage worked by bending the light around them just enough to make them blend in with the background. Moving too fast would cause the layers to overlap, revealing their position to the observing eyes.

She hoped that none of them had seen their faces because she didn't have the energy to erase their memories. The cameras weren't a problem, as she had disabled them when they arrived.

Many elements were down to hope and luck; if she were home, she would be punished for her ineptitude. She hated herself for being so sub-optimal, but she didn't have the time to dwell.

The back door they used to enter seemed to have moved farther away, and for a moment Nashel wondered if there was an Expression preventing them from reaching it, but then realised it was just tiredness. She started to see black spots in her vision and had the peculiar sensation of being taken away from her body. Alistair held her up and took the lead, as she tried not to pass out before they were outside.

As soon as she took a breath of crisp night air, she collapsed, leaving it to Alistair to complete the last leg of the mission. She regained consciousness sometime later and found herself in her bed. She had a fleeting thought about the fight with Alistair; she knew they would have to talk about it, and she couldn't wait to read the book and find the promised answers, but she couldn't even finish the thought that sleep claimed her.

CHAPTER TWENTY-EIGHT

The Triggennan

The book was a collection of three stories. Or three versions of the same story. Nashel was rapt from the very first word, and she couldn't put the tome down. It told a story spanning millennia, culminating in the creation of the Void and the Two Suns.

It answered her questions of the war before the war, even though, she realised reading it, neither was an actual war.

Before the Void, there was the Triggennan: three supernatural beings who united the land and prompted a Golden Age - at least for flairs, according to one version.

Nashel was fascinated by them, by how otherworldly powerful they were in all versions, how good or evil they were depicted depending on whose account the story was based on. She found herself invested in the story, loving and hating the Triggennan according to each version. It felt like the author was speaking directly to her, and their funny commentary made her smile; it was clear which version they believed was true.

Nashel understood what Wynmere meant when she said it wasn't a kid's fairy tale, it was violent and explicit, but it didn't bother her, and it felt real, not fiction.

Each version ended the same way: a group of flairs wanted more, they didn't want to be ruled, so they rebelled. Not an all-out war, just a group of people overthrowing their overlords. They somehow found a way, called Draining. She never heard of it. It stripped the Triggennan of their power and contained it in the Void. Nashel had to agree with the author that it was suspicious how the all-powerful Triggennan were so easily defeated.

As a consequence, the once united land was split into the two nations Nashel knew, each side led by half the rebel group, deciding how to manage powers, how to prevent anyone from becoming too powerful. The Sunset opted for training and discipline, the Sunrise for repression and wands.

There was never an actual war between the two factions, never a battle, a fight, or a skirmish. If she were to believe the book, everything she ever knew was a lie, a way for the leaders to keep people in check, to keep the leaders in power unthreatened.

While she enjoyed the book and believed the author thought of it as the truth, she was aware it was a volume found in the Sunrise, a place that for whatever reason didn't like flairs.

Her conversation with Raven replayed in her mind over and over, and she realised she needed to find the truth for herself. She had to go home. If she found the book or any record of the same story in the Sunset, she would know it was the truth; she would know she was sent on a bogus mission to get rid of her.

The problem was how. Her people had not been in contact with her at all. There was no way to cross the Void without a Drifter, and while she knew she could "make" one out of Alistair, she didn't want to lose him, not even after their fight.

As if on cue, a rap on the door told her he was there. He let himself in after a moment and saw she was reading the book, nodded towards it and asked, "Good read?"

"Very," she nodded and passed him the volume.

He shook his head. "I think we need to talk," he said, scratching the back of his neck without making eye contact.

She sighed and patted the bed next to her, and he sat down. It was the first time the silence between them felt awkward. She knew he wanted to talk about the fight, but she didn't see the point. She may have been blunt, but she only told the truth. He wasn't trained, he didn't know what to do, and his constant questions and interruptions disrupted the mission. He expected an apology, and she considered whether she should just say it to make him happy.

"I am competent," he started in a small voice. "I may not be as trained as you are, but I am capable."

She waited a moment to see if he would say more. She considered her words carefully, she didn't want to argue again, and she had more important things to think about.

"You are," she said placatingly. "But not for what we needed yesterday."

He started to protest, but she stopped him. "I don't want to dismiss you. I do think you are powerful."

"But not enough to help you."

"Not when we are on a time-constrained mission and you don't know how to do what we need to do."

"Couldn't you show me before we went?"

She thought for a moment. "We didn't have much time to practise other than sharing power."

"We could've waited another day."

"We have lessons to attend," she countered.

"We could've done it next weekend and practised in the meantime!"

"Need I remind you it was your idea to look for it?"

He opened and closed his mouth.

"I'm sorry if you thought I don't value you," she said finally. "That was not it. We were on a mission, I can get really focused when I'm on one."

She wasn't totally honest. She thought he was not up to it, and she hated incompetence, but she also knew it was not his fault, and she wanted him by her side.

He nodded. "What's the book about?" he asked after a brief pause.

She offered it to him again. "It's the legend of the Triggennan. Very interesting."

He took it and scanned through the pages, not really reading them. "Did it answer your questions?"

"It raised some more," she smiled bitterly.

"What's next?"

She sighed. "I need to go home."

"Home?" he said, his eyes widening in surprise.

She nodded. "What the book says is interesting and concerning. I need to go home, find records on that side too."

"How does that help with your mission?"

"It doesn't, but if the book is right, then your mother is right and there is no mission."

This time, his jaw dropped. "How will you go back?"

"I don't know yet," she said in frustration.

"Can I come with you?"

She looked at him in shock. "No!" she almost shouted.

"I thought we were done fighting!" he exclaimed.

"We are, but you can't come. You're a Sunset born on the wrong side, you can't cross the Void!"

Realisation hit him. "Oh, that."

"Yes, that!" She couldn't believe he forgot. "I wish you could. I wish I could show you everything in person, not just from my memories. But it's not worth it."

She extended a hand and squeezed his, leaning in to place a soft kiss on his cheek.

"But that's it!" he exclaimed, lighting up. "I can take you!"

She looked at him, appalled. "Do you understand what the Void would do to you? What you'd become if you touch it?"

"Yes, I do," he replied firmly. "But you need a way to go home, and I can finally help you with something."

"I thought you loved me," she retorted.

"I do...?" his tone rose, confused.

"Then why are you so eager to leave me?"

"I am not!"

"That's what would happen if you became a Drifter," she said sternly. "It's a non-life. An existence of pain, torture, not being able to withstand anything more than breathing without passing out. There would be no future for you. For us. Is that what you want?"

"No," he admitted, horrified. "I—"

"I know you want to help," she said gently. "But this is not the way."

"I feel useless," he admitted in a murmur.

"Don't. You're not useless. You are my love, isn't that enough?"

He smiled sheepishly and nodded. "Say that again," he asked, a teasing glint in his eye.

"You are my love," she repeated.

He closed his eyes and sighed, as if he were tasting particularly delicious food. He leaned in and kissed her then, deep and charged, all the tension from the night before and the fight forgotten.

"How do you plan on going home?" Alistair asked her, the morning after as they walked towards their first class.

"I don't know yet," she replied with a sigh. "There must be a way to send a message."

"But you don't know what it is."

She shook her head. "I may need to go to the drop-off point, where I first arrived."

"Wasn't that random?"

"I think so, but maybe not. Maybe the Void is thinner there or something."

He nodded.

"I need you to cover for me, can you?"

A look of surprise and hurt crossed his eyes for a split second, but enough for her to see. "I know you wanted to come with me," she added before he could reply. "And I do too, but I also need someone here to tell the Academy I am sick or something."

"But what if you can send the message, and they whisk you

away there and then?" he pouted.

"I think they might not come if someone else is there. And if they find out you are a Sunset, they might force you to cross the Void."

"And we don't want that," he sighed.

"No, we don't," she placed a hand on his cheek. "But I promise, if they take me home, I will come back for you."

He held her hand there with his and nodded.

The following weekend, before dawn, she gathered a backpack of supplies and left. The journey back was long but uneventful. The train stopped at the first village she ever saw, which brought a smile to her face at the memory, but this time there was no surly old farmer with his loud truck to give her a lift, so she had to walk. She didn't mind, she was in shape, having kept up with her training, and the journey gave her the chance to think about how to contact her people, what to say, and how to convince them she needed to go back home. A plan started to form and she was confident she would be successful.

It took her a while to find the right spot, the vegetation around it had grown, and she noticed the Void had moved, not by a lot, but enough for her to see the difference.

If she believed The Second Sunset, the Void in front of her was what remained of the Triggennan, raw power yearning to be let out. She remembered her first and only trip through the Void, how she felt as if it tried to squeeze the life out of her. At the time, she thought it was nothingness, but now, thinking back to the feeling of it pressing on her, how could that be nothingness? Nothingness wouldn't make one feel out of breath.

As usual, its power was calling to her, inviting her to touch it, to step into it and join it, feed it with her life, her soul. It also felt amazing, finally being surrounded by power, a large quantity of it, not the trickle the rest of the Sunrise provided. She closed her eyes and embraced, being careful not to let the Void suck her in.

After a moment of pure joy, she concentrated on her task.

Seeing the flow wasn't difficult, but unfortunately, it didn't show her anything. There was no difference to the Void there, there was no difference to everything around it. She walked for a while in one direction, but nothing changed; she rounded back and walked the same distance in the opposite direction with the same fruitless results.

On her journey there, she thought about that possibility. It was the most likely outcome. Too much time had passed for any residual trace of hers, Lt. Dustveil's, or Nightshade's presence.

Nightshade, a Drifter.

A being linked inexorably to the Void. If they were connected, maybe it was possible to send a message inside it, and he might somehow get it. It was worth a try; she didn't have any other choice anyway.

The boost the Void was giving her made it easy to concentrate. An Expression message was common at home, more common than electronic messages, so it wasn't hard to conjure it. The hard part was sending it into the Void without it absorbing it and destroying it. Perhaps, if she gave it something stronger to feed on, she could sneak the message in intact. She approached the Void cautiously. She wasn't completely sure she wanted to do what she planned, but it wouldn't be the first time she had to do something unpleasant.

With a sigh, she extended her hand, stopping just a few centimetres from the Void, its power intoxicating so up close, it took all her willpower to just not take another step. Her Expression floated next to her, straining to jump in itself. Nashel took a deep breath, gathering her strength, then plunged her right hand into it. She gritted her teeth, expecting searing pain, but nothing came. She thought, perhaps, the adrenaline was keeping her from feeling the pain until the job was done, so she focused on that. She let her message travel down her arm in a shiver, letting it slip through the gap her hand had created, hoping the Void would prey on the bigger prize, her, and not it, then retreated her hand. She looked down at it with a sort of detached dread and was surprised to see it whole and uninjured. She looked closely, bringing it up to her face and turning it front and back. It was just her hand. The same calluses, the same small scars dotted here and there, the same olive skin colour. It puzzled her. The Void was supposed to suck all life out of anyone and everyone except Drifters, but there she was, willingly thrusting her hand in and getting it out unscathed.

Was everything she's been told a lie? Was the Void harmless? A scarecrow to keep the two sides separated and under control? Or was there another reason? Maybe one hand wasn't of interest to it, maybe it was too powerful to even notice such an inconsequential ripple.

She would love to have some way to experiment and find an answer, but unfortunately, she was there alone, and she wasn't irrational enough to risk her own life.

She retreated inside the forest, hidden by vegetation, but was able to keep an eye on the Void. She waited, and waited. And waited. She lost track of time, but realised the sun had set when the barrier assumed a more silvery tone, typical of night. She tried again, emboldened by her first success, and stuck her hand in again. She dared to go a bit further, halfway up her forearm. No pain, no injury when she retreated it. With a sigh, she went back to her hiding spot, resuming her waiting.

She was getting ready to call it a night and get some sleep, when something from the corner of her eye caught her attention. She didn't see it happen, despite having an eye on the Void, but right in front of it, laid in a heap the deformed shape of Nightshade. He had got her message.

She hurried towards him, checking that he was alone first, and knelt at his side. He was out cold. She sighed and lifted him, ravelling once again at how light he was. She kept watch and waited for him to recover.

"Hi," she whispered when she saw his eyes open.

He blinked a few times, focusing on her, and gave her a nod. It was hard for him to speak - or do anything other than breathe outside the Void.

She offered him something to eat, but he shook his head. She wondered what he ate, if anything, and where.

After a while longer, he managed to stand with her help and shuffled to the edge of the Void. He looked at her with a warning in his eyes, and she held him tight. A second later, they had left the Sunrise and were in the nothingness of the Void.

Like the first time, she felt the pressure of it trying to squeeze her soul out of her, but unlike the first time, she didn't panic. Nightshade's arms were strong around her, and when she looked up to see his handsome face, for the briefest moment, she saw Alistair.

"Thank you for answering my call," she thought in his direction, knowing spoken words didn't work in there.

"It was impossible not to," his voice was deep but gentle in her head. She could see the hint of a smile on his lips. "But you must be warned, they'll be waiting for us."

"I expected that," she nodded, a gesture that seemed at odd with telepathy. "How long can we stay?" she asked him after a moment.

"As long as you like," he replied, and she could feel the confusion and surprise in his tone. "As long as you don't let go."

"To send you the message," she explained, "I had to create a gap. I shoved my hand in the Void."

Nightshade gasped, his eyes widening and his jaw dropping almost comically.

"But nothing happened to my hand," she continued. "Is that normal?"

He looked intently at her hand, then shook his head. "No, people die when in contact with the Void."

"Even just a hand?"

"Even less. Even just the tip of a hair."

"That's an exaggeration," she commented.

"No, I've seen it happen," he replied seriously.

She sensed more to the story, but she didn't press it and

he didn't elaborate.

"Only Drifters can survive the Void," he said instead. "And you are not one."

She knew that, but found his certainty curious. "How do you know?"

"I'd have felt it the first time I took you here," he said. "And if that failed, I would've seen it once on the other side."

"Drifter transformation is instant?" she asked, and once again she saw surprise in his features.

"You know..." he whispered. "It is immediate, but not extreme. You don't become like me on the first Drift. But the changes start nonetheless."

"So you would've noticed," she concluded, understanding. "What are the first changes?"

"No energy, pale skin," he replied, "and the dead dull look in your eyes that'll never go away and only worsen."

She nodded, filing away her newly acquired knowledge. "Thanks for telling me."

"Don't tell anyone you touched the Void," he warned her. "If they knew, no matter which side, your life would be over."

"I won't," she replied firmly. "One more question."

He smiled.

"If you could choose, would you live in the Void permanently?"

He thought for the briefest moment. "Yes, I would," he replied, his words steel.

"I may need to leave the Sunset and cross again," she started, looking at him straight in the eyes. "Would you help me if I could set you free?"

"I would help even if you couldn't," he replied.

She gave him a smile and a nod that were both understanding and a go-ahead to end their crossing.

Her ears popped when the pressure was lifted. She felt Nightshade's hand go weak and limp and him starting to drop to the ground, but she never heard the soft thud or got to focus on her surroundings that she was assaulted by several Expressions in such a rapid succession that she couldn't count them, let alone counter them.

She lost consciousness before she hit the ground.

CHAPTER TWENTY-NINE

A Dangerous Path

Even before opening her eyes, she knew she was home. She felt it in the air around her, the power flowing like a strong river, not the trickle of a leaking tap she had to deal with in the Sunrise. If she were a weaker person, she would've broken into tears of delight. As it was, she only revelled in it, relaxing and feeling herself be one with the flow.

Even before opening her eyes, she knew she was in her room. She felt her bed hugging her form, the softness of her blanket, her pillow embracing her. She smelt the familiar smell of her favourite detergent, and for a moment, it was as if she had never left.

When she finally opened her eyes, she took in the sight with a small smile. Everything was exactly as she left it. She stretched lazily, her body was sore, but when she examined it, she found no wound. They must have healed her, but the soreness and headache remained. She got up and took a shower, changing clothes after the long day of travel felt great. When she finished, she glanced at the door. She didn't try to open it, she didn't even need to see the Trace to know there was at least an Expression on it preventing her from getting out. She knew her people too well to even think they would let her go free without questioning her after the stunt she pulled.

Food appeared on her desk at the usual lunchtime. She ate eagerly and wondered only briefly how long they would keep her locked up before they marched her to interrogation. She found she longed to see the Academy, the Citadel, and even the base. She missed home more than she had thought. And yet, they kept her from it for three days. She tried to create a routine, waking up when breakfast appeared on her desk, training in the confines of the room, then lunch, then studying, the books on her bookshelf were all the textbooks she would need if she were still a cadet. She didn't care about it, not after everything she had found out recently, but she knew they were observing her and she wanted to give a good impression.

On the third day, when she woke up, she found her uniform hanging on the wardrobe door. It was perfectly pressed, the collar starched, the shoes resting on the carpet below it, shiny, the gold cord around the shoulder almost took her breath away. Gold was the colour of the Cadet Under Officer, the rank she would've earned if her education had not been suspended.

She looked at it while she had breakfast, wondering if the promotion was a trick to make her complacent. It seemed weird that they would promote her after what she did and before hearing her out. She donned the uniform, and she didn't recognise the person looking back in the mirror. The door opened, with two soldiers waiting for her outside. They didn't say a word, but she didn't need them to. She put her hat under her left arm and let them lead her out. She realised she was slouching. She lost that martial posture students at the Sunset had learnt to keep at all times. She wasn't marching, just walking, less stiff, less straight. It was impressive how just a few months could erase years and years of formal training. She tried to regain it, mimicking the soldier in front of her, but it was a lot of effort, always reminding herself to keep her shoulders straight and square, her chin up, her steps in rhythm. The walk to the base wasn't too long, but it tired her and felt unnatural to put all that effort into just walking, but once again, she had an impression to make.

And because of all that, she couldn't take in and enjoy the walk as she would've wanted. She hoped she would have time later, that they wouldn't throw her in a forgotten jail. The soldiers at the base entrance let them through without checking any identification. The guards marched Nashel through the buildings and up to General Stormbreaker's office. The lieutenant aide knocked on the door and opened it for her to get in, the guards waited outside.

Nashel stiffened to attention to salute and waited for him to order her to be at ease. He didn't. He didn't even look at her for several minutes, reading or pretending to read a document on his desk and letting her stew. She kept her breathing steady, her expression schooled and waited.

"Cadet Under Officer Nashel," he finally sighed, looking up at Nashel. "At ease."

She did it as crisply as she could.

"Explain your exploits. What prompted you to cross the Void unauthorised?"

"An attack, sir, is imminent." She used the three days she was trapped in her room to come up with a plausible excuse that would get her out of trouble. She needed to be free, not in jail, to find out what she wanted.

"Elaborate," the general sounded sceptical, still not giving her his full attention.

"The Sunrise is planning an attack. They are gathering troops in the north. They say the Void is thinner there."

"Bah," he blurted, then added dismissively. "They don't have enough Drifters for that."

"No, they don't," she improvised, hoping he wouldn't see her bluffing, "but they found another way; that's why they do it where the Void is thinner."

The General couldn't know how many Drifters the Sunrise had. She didn't think there was anyone infiltrated deep on the other side or they wouldn't have sent her. If her suspicions were right, and there was no mission, then the general wouldn't have that kind of information either.

"What other way?"

Nashel could swear the general started to sweat then. She had to keep a grin from her schooled expression.

"I don't know, sir," she said apologetically. "I've infiltrated a militia group, but only the higher-ups know. I couldn't get the info."

"Report from the beginning," the general ordered.

Nashel nodded once, sternly, then recounted her experience, glossing over Alistair and embellishing her time in the Alwenach, making up plausible details the general could not disprove.

General Stormbreaker finally stopped pretending not to listen and gave her his full attention. His eyes were piercing and cold, processing the information and calculating possible next moves. He was an intelligent man; he probably could've figured out she was lying if the Void didn't prevent communication between the two sides. Or maybe he could communicate with them and knew exactly that she was lying and was just waiting for her to finish and arrest her or kill her. It was a risk she had thought about and was willing to take.

He didn't interrupt her, but when she finished, he asked her some follow-up questions, clarifying some of the points she made.

"I reckon that was a deserved promotion, after all," he concluded, but his tone sounded more disappointed than satisfied.

"Thank you, sir," Nashel replied nonetheless.

"You will go back as soon as I convened with my advisers and decided on a plan, but you earned some R&R."

"Sir," she let her tone rise in a question, and Stormbreaker cocked his head, surprised and not too happy by her lingering.

"What?"

"I would like to help if there's an attack," she told him. It wasn't true. She needed the time and space to pursue her goal, but it would be out of character for her not to want in on the action.

"You're still a cadet," the general replied curtly. "Cadets cannot be on active duty on the front line."

"I understand, sir, but—" she started to insist, but Stormbreaker glared at her. "I understand, sir."

"You are dismissed."

She saluted, took three steps backward before stiffly turning her back to him and exiting the room. The guards were not there anymore, and the aide gave her a nod as she passed his desk.

The general wasn't clear on how long she could stay, but she was sure it would be at least a couple of days, and she needed to make the most of them. She needed to find out if the story of the Triggennan was true, if her mission was just a ploy to send her away.

She was about to leave the base, when she remembered Ash. His job was dedicated to studying the Sunrise, he may have encountered something about the Triggennan or anything about the time before the war. She changed course and headed for his office, even though she thought she would find him in the base's library. She almost missed his nondescript door and halted abruptly.

Her knuckles rasped on the door, and she heard the shuffling of paper and feet inside for a couple of seconds before he opened it. She smirked at his shocked expression.

"Have you seen a ghost?" she teased him.

She realised she had missed him. Alistair was amazing, but there was something about Ash. Maybe the fact that he was older, or that whatever it was between them was forbidden, that added a thrill she enjoyed experiencing.

Ash didn't let her in, the room way too small for both of them, but took a step towards her and closed the door behind him. He was still speechless. His eyes didn't leave her, as if she would disappear if he did. His mouth opened and closed several times before he found his voice.

"Hi," he breathed.

"Hi," she smiled back at him.

His hand tentatively tucked a strand of hair behind her ear, lingering there a moment too long. He took a deep breath, undoubtedly trying to steady his racing heart. Then, without warning, he hugged her tightly. She huffed as her breath was taken away, but reciprocated with a small laugh.

"Missed you too," she murmured in the crook of his neck.

"Can we go somewhere more private?" he whispered in her ear, and she nodded, taking a step back.

He led her out of the building and into another one. It was deserted, and she soon found out it was a dorm, which explained why there was nobody there: everyone was at work.

He strode down the corridors and up two sets of stairs before stopping at one of the many doors. It opened for him without the need for a key, and she found herself in his room. It wasn't too different from hers, just bigger, with space for a living room corner and a kitchenette. It had a big window, but the view was just of another base building.

He led her to the small couch and started the coffee machine before joining her.

"How are you?" he asked, his tone still tinted with surprise.

"I'm okay," she replied. "You?"

"I didn't know when to expect you back," he admitted.

"It wasn't planned," she told him with a shrug.

His eyes widened, and a question painted itself on his features.

"It's classified," she replied apologetically.

He nodded. "Can you tell me anything about the place?"

She did. She told him everything about Solned, how it was so blinding all the time, how people despised powers and how gullible they were because of it. She told him about the Academy, and the difficulties she had adapting to the wand, and never truly managing. He gasped whenever she said something particularly outrageous, and shook his head almost constantly.

It was nice to tell somebody who could understand what she had to go through just to pass as one of them. Liberating. Alistair had grown up in that environment, so he couldn't truly get her. Raven was too bitter about the Sunset to have such a conversation. Also, she needed to impress Ash, needed him to push her to break the rules and tell him more, so she could ask forbidden questions. She tangled hints and prompts here and there in her tale, hoping he would take the bait.

"I wish I was there," he commented wistfully at one point.

"No," she laughed, "you really don't! Powers are so weak there, I don't know how they—" she stopped herself.

"How they what?" he pressed her.

"Classified."

"Tell me," he whispered. "Nobody can hear us in here. I won't tell anyone."

"I can't," she shook her head. "I shouldn't."

"Please!" He was not trying to trick her. He was genuinely curious.

She feigned reluctance, and he tried to convince her again, but then she gave in.

"I guess you're going to find out soon enough," she whispered, resigned. "They are planning an attack."

"They what?!" he shouted. Shock making him recoil.

She gushed out the information she gave the general, pretending to be relieved to tell someone, and she knew she had him wrapped around her fingers.

After he recovered from the shock and the anger at the general for sending her back ("Haven't you done enough already?!"), she tried to ask him what she was really after.

"I found something while I was there," she said tentatively. "Something curious."

"What is it?"

"An account of the war."

"Oh," his eyes sparkled with curiosity again. "I might help,

I know more than most about it."

"I thought so," she smiled at him. "Well, the thing is... That account claims there was never a war." She paused, gauging his reaction. He looked surprised, but she wasn't sure if it was because she had found something like that or because it was the first time he had heard such a theory. "There were these powerful beings, the Triggennan, and they were controlling everything, until a group of flairs staged a coup. The Triggennan were so powerful they couldn't be killed, but they were Drained of their power, and it was contained in what we now call the Void."

"Wow," he sighed, sagging against the couch's backrest.

She waited, letting him process what she said and decide what to tell her in return. She got up and refilled their coffee cups to give him time.

When she offered him the steaming mug and sat back down, she also gave him a smile. "Hey," she said softly. "You don't have to say anything."

"It's only fair," he muttered, looking at the coffee.

"It's alright." She scooted closer to him, placing a hand on his forearm.

"I've seen something like that before," he finally told her. "There were a few books telling a similar tale. When I inquired about them, I was strongly encouraged to drop it."

"So, do you think it's true?" she asked eagerly, scooting even closer to him, as if the proximity made it safer to tell secrets.

He looked up at her with a pained glance. "I've seen a lot of different takes, some more plausible than others, but they've all been classed as fakes."

"Classed as fake doesn't make them fake."

"It's dangerous territory, you're trying to wade in," Ash warned her. "Traitorous."

Nashel raised her hands in surrender. "You're right. Sorry."

"That's not what I meant," he rushed to reply. "Just be careful."

"If any of it is true, I've got nothing to lose." It was meant as dismissive, but it came out steely, almost challenging.

"What do you mean?"

She decided to tell him the truth. She was confident of her hold on him. "I think my mission never existed. That I was banished."

An array of emotions flashed through his eyes: shock, surprise, rage, incredulity. "What?"

"I've met someone over there... A Sunset like us. When she was about my age, she was chosen for a top-secret, very dangerous, very honourable mission: to spy on the Sunrise."

Ash gasped.

"Except when she was about to leave, someone told her it was all bogus. There was no mission. She was undesirable, and they just wanted to get rid of her."

"That's im—"

"I've seen her memory." Nashel shook her head. "She wasn't lying."

"But the attack? What did you find?"

"I made it up," she admitted. "I needed an excuse to come back, to find out for myself if what I found about the Triggennan, about my mission, is true."

Hurt crossed his features for a brief moment.

"I'm sorry I lied to you," she hurried to say. "I wasn't sure I could trust you."

She looked away, pretending to be ashamed. He reached out, a finger under her chin to make her look back at him. "Of course you can trust me."

He kissed her, tentatively, barely restraining the desire that had lit him up since he saw her.

"Will you help me?" she whispered against his lips.

"Yes."

She kissed him, then, pouring gratitude instead of victory into it to further her hold. They made out for a while, telling each other how much they missed each other, how scary it was for Nashel to feel abandoned by her people, and other soothing, meaningless words. She thought of Alistair, of how different it felt to kiss him. How freer it was without an agenda. At the same time, she liked Ash's attention and desire. She liked being above him, owning him. But, if she were honest to herself, she liked he understood her in a way Alistair never could. She wasn't in love with Ash, but there were benefits of being with him.

They parted ways later that evening; she was in R&R, but as a student, she was sure she still needed to obey the curfew. He promised her he would look into the books he had mentioned before. It was safer if he did it, and she would just peruse the Hreystisafn, the Sunset repository of knowledge, for lower stakes, under the radar information, and they would reconvene. She had no intention of just casually perusing the library, but Ash didn't have to know that. She would find as much as she could, no matter what she had to do.

On her way back to the Academy, she took the time to enjoy her home. The sun was setting, painting everything orange and red, giving the impression that the Citadel was on fire. It was such a stark difference from Solned. The buildings there reflected the light harshly, blindingly; in the Citadel, the buildings were interspersed with green plants and not made of the same reflective marble. They embraced the light instead of repelling it.

The Academy buildings peeked out from the end of the avenue, a welcoming sight for Nashel. She smiled as she approached them, taking in their stocky shape and reliving the memories of ten years of stepping in and out of them. It was bittersweet, being back. It was still her home, but something had shifted. All the blood, sweat, and tears she poured into her training seemed to be in vain. If there had never been a war, if there had never been a mission, what was it all for? She was enraged by her people, who made her waste so much of her life for a cause that didn't exist. She would make them pay, even if it meant razing the Sunset to the ground.

CHAPTER THIRTY

VN-EX

The morning after was awkward. Nashel had had a very restful night's sleep, but going to breakfast in the dining hall, joining her classmates again, felt out of place. They bombarded her with excited questions she couldn't answer, and she felt miles away from them, as if they were in two different worlds. At the end of the meal, she asked Sergeant Thomas if she could have her meals in her room. He conceded it fairly easily after she told him the general ordered R&R before she would have to leave again.

With newly acquired freedom, she set off for the Hreystisafn. The Hreystisafn was more than just a library. It was the biggest repository of knowledge of the Sunset, and it was open to everyone. There was no forbidden knowledge, no Scholars' Archive hidden under heavy Expressions. Because of that, it was one of her favourite places. Whenever she had questions the teachers didn't want or didn't know how to answer, she would head there and find whatever she needed.

On the outside, the building was nothing as grand as the Solnedian Library. It was bigger than the buildings surrounding it, but not any different in style. There was a square in front of it, with benches and a fountain in the middle, that was always busy with people enjoying the good weather while reading a book they just borrowed, and for once, Nashel paused, took the scene in and appreciated the freedom her people had. There was no censorship, no ban on powers. The Sunset were always displaying their powers, even for the smallest thing. It was a beautiful sight.

Once inside, she paused to take that all in as well. The Hreystisafn was always busy, but not chaotic. Books were floating around, summoned by patrons who didn't need wisps to direct them. Little blue blobs of light were helping those in need. The inside of the Hreystisafn was bigger than the outside, teaming with power, a maze of shelves and rooms, stained glass windows providing brightness and airiness. There was an information desk, but nobody needed to stop there unless they needed information. Nashel skipped the desk, she didn't need anyone knowing her business. She called a wisp, who appeared squeaking in front of her, and asked it to direct her to the pre-war tales' section. The wisp expression changed to confusion for a moment, then it changed again to smiley eyes, its antenna bobbing up and down, before turning and floating away at a pace she could follow. They turned around a few aisles, until the wisp stopped with a squeak that sounded like "we're here".

Nashel looked around in disappointment. The section the wisp took her to was a subsection of fiction. She rolled her eyes and was tempted to tell the wisp to take her somewhere else, but then she stopped. The Second Sunset was classed as a fairy tale after all. Maybe she could find something interesting. She dismissed the wisp and started to look around the books. She took a book and skimmed through it, but it was a tale of a long time before the war, more legend than history. She put it back and took the next one, then the next. She found nothing. She moved to a quiet area and called the wisp again.

"I want to know about the Triggennan," she muttered, keeping her voice low despite nobody being around.

This time the wisp didn't hesitate and led her away, its antenna bobbing in an excitement that didn't encourage Nashel. It suggested to her the wisp misunderstood her. Her confusion and distrust increased when the wisp took her not to another aisle of bookshelves, but to one of the rooms. It made that "we're here" sound, and bumped itself on the door. Nashel dismissed it doubtfully and opened the door.

The room inside wasn't a room at all, but a meadow. It wasn't a surprise. Each room was unique, could be a meadow, a cosy beanbag in front of a fireplace, a pier on a rough sea, or a rocking chair on a wooden porch. Each room had its own function; some made the user relive their past, often forgotten, memories; others made a book into a full immersive reality.

A meadow, then, wasn't a surprise. Nashel took a few steps towards its centre, looking around to see what the room would bring her. She sat down, the shift of reality could make people dizzy, so it was better to sit down and enjoy the scene. It shifted into a gloomy room with no windows, a big wooden table in the middle, wooden panes on the walls, and high-back wooden chairs occupied by a group of dishevelled people. They seemed to be aggravated and were arguing.

"That's not going to work," one of them shouted, pounding his fist on the table.

"What will, then?" hissed another one. They spoke with the heavy accent that was neither Sunset nor Sunrise.

"I don't know!" the first man shouted, throwing his hands up in frustration.

"Let's all take a breath," the one at the head of the table told everyone. His voice was deep and calming, and Nashel guessed he was the leader. "What are our options?"

"We could kill them," a woman shrugged. She looked bored, as if she wanted to be anywhere but there.

"They cannot be killed, and you know that," the first man rolled his eyes.

The woman huffed, annoyed. "If you're not contributing with any idea, just shut up."

"We can Drain them," another man, very young and shy-looking, spoke so softly it was almost inaudible.

One of the other women gasped. "Drain? No, that's forbidden."

"Is it?" The annoyed woman raised an eyebrow. "They're not people. Can't be that bad."

Everyone around them was about to protest, but the leader stopped them. "We can consider it, but let's think of something else first."

Nashel understood what they were talking about then, and how it tied to her request. This was the group of people who had defeated the Triggennan, and Draining was how they did it, even though they dismissed it at first.

They continued to bounce ideas off each other while arguing and shouting, not getting anywhere, until they circled back to Draining.

"It's our only option," the leader commented, resigned.

"We need a container," the annoying woman said.

The leader nodded. "Yes, and a space where to place it."

"The wasteland," the shy man said. The others paused, then nodded.

"It will split the land in two," said the quieter woman. "And take a big chunk of it as well."

"It's an acceptable loss," the angry man said, and the other muttered their reluctant agreement.

The scene shifted to an open place, it was dry and barren, sun-scorched. Nashel reckoned it was the wasteland. The group of rebels was there, directing about twenty other people to different spots. When they were ready, they united their powers and summoned the Triggennan.

They looked human, but also not human. There were two men and a woman, though the distinction was not as clear. Nashel couldn't tell what was human and what wasn't. She just knew something was different, and she could feel their immense power even through a fake reality. They looked around, taking in the people who had summoned them. They didn't seem scared or concerned, just mildly annoyed.

Nashel understood what the author of The Second Sunset meant when they said the Triggennan gave in easily, and seeing the scene unfold, she wondered why.

At a signal from the leader, the Draining process started. The Triggennan screamed and doubled down in pain. The people around them intensified their efforts, elated by their initial success.

It was difficult to watch, even for someone accustomed to pain. And it looked unbearable, the vilest form of torture. Nashel understood what Draining was: forcibly taking powers out of people, which was like taking away a piece of one's soul. And yet, she couldn't look away.

The Triggennan slowly collapsed on the ground, their breathing laboured, but impossibly slow. A group of the captors changed stance, moving away from the circle and lining up, facing each other a little away. As soon as the Triggennan stopped breathing, the rest of the circle moved, keeping formation between the two lines. Nashel couldn't see it, but she could feel the power held between them. She could see their effort, the sweat on their foreheads, their bodies shaking. They couldn't hold on much longer, and she wished they wouldn't.

The lines started to create a wall, then another, and another, until the circle was contained, and slowly the people inside walked backwards, crossing the invisible barrier, but leaving the power inside it. As soon as they left, they scattered, running away as if an explosion was imminent, and so did the line. And indeed, there was a sort of explosion. There was a collective sigh as the container expanded with the power, but kept it inside itself.

And so that's how the Void was created. Nashel watched it expand in the straight line of black she knew, creating the barrier between the Sunrise and the Sunset. Half the people who performed the Draining were left on one side, half on the other. She could somehow see both sides, as if from above, setting the foundation for the societies she knew. Their goal was the same: preventing another Triggennan from being born. The Sunset decided to train its people, keeping them under a military state, while the Sunrise limited the use of powers to one speciality. They started rumours of war to keep the truth hidden. By the third generation, they had forgotten what it was like before, brainwashed by either side's new philosophy, any mention of the Triggennan erased from records, just as they erased people who spoke against them.

The scene shifted again into a cosy cabin surrounded by the woods. Nashel gasped as she recognised the place. Not the cabin, but the surrounding forest. She didn't know why she was sure, maybe something in the air, but she knew she was in the same place she and Alistair visited. The one where they experienced that rush of power that seemed much like a dream.

When she made the connection, the scene moved her inside the cabin, letting her phase through the closed door. There was a woman sitting by the windowsill holding a journal of sorts, with a quill and ink bottle next to her, and in the rocking cot on the other side, a newborn baby sleeping soundly.

"It's not a question of nurture, as some may think," the woman said out loud while she wrote. "It's a question of nature."

Nashel felt surprise course through her. She knew those words! They were the incipit of The Second Sunset. The woman must have been the author. She looked curiously as the woman continued to write and narrate the story of the Triggennan.

"It was a Golden Age," the woman turned, smiling towards the baby. "Everything was flourishing; power permeated everywhere. You would have liked it."

Nashel realised what it meant. The creation of the Void or, better yet, the stripping of the Triggennan's powers left the world drained of power too, the Sunrise being the worst off.

The woman continued the story, adding little comments she had left out of the book. "But you see, my darling baby, they didn't know the Triggennan was never made of just three people," she bopped the baby's nose, who continued to sleep. "They were a triplet, linked together not just by blood, but by power. When they were lured into 'the trap', the fourth remained behind as a failsafe. She lost her powers when they were defeated. But she survived. And you, my sweet miracle, you are their heir, our heir."

Nashel looked at the woman again, paying more attention to her. She was older, more human, but she could now see the resemblance; she still had an otherworldly aura about her.

"And you are destined to avenge us," her tone lost all the sweetness, and when Nashel looked back up, the woman was looking not at the baby but straight at her.

Before Nashel could process it, the scene change again, speeding up, following the life of the child as he grew up as the fourth Triggennan died of old age, as her son had a child of his own, then became a grandfather, and so on down the generations until it abruptly stopped, stilling on a backyard with a swing set she instantly recognised. A little girl was on the swing, using her power to go higher and higher, laughing almost manically, while her mother told her to stop, but powerless to make her.

Nashel hadn't seen her mother since the night she killed her, and except for a few weak moments, she hadn't spared her a single thought.

Now she looked at her with detached eyes. She was an apo, so it couldn't be, could it? Nashel looked more intently, trying to understand if she was influencing herself or if she was actually seeing the resemblance, vague and almost undetectable.

Considering the scenes she saw and how they ended with her as a child on the swing, she knew she was the last Triggennan's heir. As soon as the realisation hit her, the scene dissolved, and she was back in the meadow.

She was the heir of the Triggennan, the beings that provided a Golden Age of power brought to a despicable, evil end by the greed of men. She had to avenge them. She had to reclaim what was hers.

A message appeared, floating in front of her, snapping her out of her thoughts. She grabbed the piece of paper and scanned the words. It was Ash, asking her to meet him in his room. The message burst into flame when she finished reading it, as she got up and left the Hreystisafn.

The guards at the base gate let her in after checking her identity, and she made her way to the dorm building. Ash intercepted her along the way and redirected her away from it.

"Too many people," he explained as they walked back the way she had just come from.

They exited the base and walked away from it, and the Citadel, towards the wall that separated them from the apos. They found a quiet, deserted spot, but Ash made an Expression to grant them additional privacy. Only then did he spoke. "I found something," he was jittery, eyes darting everywhere.

"What?" After the revelations she had that day, she had no patience to coddle him.

"I couldn't find anything about the war," he told her, whispering despite nobody around. "But then I thought about what you said, about your mission, and looked a little deeper."

She cocked her head, curious.

"You were right," he said apologetically. "There were others before you, and there was never an actual mission."

"What?" she replied. "How do you know?"

"I've found your file. Highly redacted, but I have high clearance." He gave her a bittersweet smile.

"If it's highly redacted..." she started doubtfully.

"There was a code," he answered. "I didn't know what it was. I'd never seen it before, so I searched for others sharing the same code."

"And you found we were all sent to the Sunrise," Nashel concluded.

He nodded vigorously. “Not only that, but you all had other things in common.”

“Such as?”

“Top of your class, very powerful, strong will...”

“Not easily bent,” she muttered to herself, but he nodded. “Not easily brainwashed.”

“That in itself doesn’t mean the mission was fake,” he continued. His voice growing volume as his excitement seeped through.

“Just based on that, it seems we were the perfect candidates for such missions,” she agreed.

“But then I found the actual meaning of that code. An oversight on their part,” he grinned, but didn’t explain further.

“What’s the code, then? What does it mean?” she asked impatiently.

“VN-EX,” he returned to whispering. “Volatile Nature, Expendable Assignment.”

Volatile nature? That didn’t sound like Nashel at all. But at least it meant they recognised she was powerful to the point of being dangerous, to the point where their best option was to send her away for good. It also meant Raven was right, the mission was fake.

“I’m sorry,” Ash told her, misunderstanding her silence.

“Don’t be,” she shook her head, already thinking through everything she had found, calculating what the next move would be.

“I am still at an advantage. They don’t know I know,” she said.

“And they believed you about the attack,” Ash placed his hands on her shoulder, squeezing gently. “Stormbreaker already mobilised the troops.”

Nashel’s eyes widened. Ash grinned and nodded. “Nothing big, just some shuffling things and people around. He spent the day with his advisers.”

“How do you know all that she chuckled?” she imagined Ash as a busybody.

"I have ways," he winked.

"That gives me more time, I guess," she muttered.

"What do you need?"

She looked at him, confused.

"What can I do to help you?" he clarified, reading her expression.

"You did enough," she replied.

"Seriously, tell me. I'll do it."

She thought about it. Maybe she could use him, as he was so eager to help. "I'll let you know," she replied. "I need to make a plan."

He nodded with a smile. "Can I tempt you with some ice cream? For old time's sake..."

She rolled her eyes and laughed. "Sure," she conceded.

He undid the Expression and held her hand, leading her to the Citadel.

They were halfway through when a message appeared in front of Nashel.

"What is it?" Ash enquired.

"It's from the base," she told him distractedly. "What's the EC?"

"Ethical Committee. Is that where you need to go?"

Nashel nodded, still looking at the message, so she missed Ash's worried expression.

He stopped her, making her look up at him. "The Ethical Committee is the one that told me to 'drop' my searching into the pre-war."

Nashel raised an eyebrow questioning.

"You went to the Hreystisafn today, right?"

Nashel nodded.

"What did you look for? I told you I would check the tricky stuff."

She felt her instinct to react, but realised he wasn't angry. He was worried.

"I had to look some stuff up," she replied.

Ash shook his head. "You triggered something. That's why they want you. You need to go. They are known for being inflexible. They didn't do me anything because I have high clearance, but I heard stories... and you're just a cadet."

"There's no forbidden knowledge in the Sunset!" Nashel protested.

Ash left out a bitter laugh. "Yeah, that's what they say, but there are some things they don't want public. They suggested I don't look into anything per-war, and I had to drop it."

She nodded. "So what do I do? Should I go anyway, see what they have to say?"

"Well, I wouldn't. But at the same time, if you don't go, you'll get in bigger trouble. I don't know, it's a mess," he concluded. "If you go, I'm not sure that you're going to be free to come out."

"That bad, uh?"

"I've never seen a cadet being summoned by the Ethical Committee, and you're not a normal cadet, you're already 'volatile nature'," he used air quotes.

Nashel laughed bitterly.

"I don't want you to go and then disappear on me again before we have a chance to, you know, sort everything out," he smirked.

"I'm not here to sort things out, I'm here to find the truth," she snapped, but apologised immediately.

"I know, I know, I was trying to lighten the mood," he raised his hands in surrender, smiling. "I don't know if you can have an exit strategy if you go there," he sobered up quickly. "They'll take it to a room where your powers will not work, they did that with me. So if you go there, you won't be able to escape."

"Well, until they get me out of that to get mean to a cell or take me back to the Sunrise," she shrugged.

"Possible. But do you want to risk it?"

That was the question, wasn't it? Did she want to risk being captured? Just now that she found the truth, not just about her mission, but about the Triggennan. Now that she found she had to take back what was hers, and she didn't have a plan for that yet.

"But if I don't go, they're going to hunt me down. So I'd either go in hiding or they'd send me to the Sunrise anyway. And I don't think I can go there now. Not yet. Still have to find some information. And it's not that easy to do that over there. It's easy to do it over here, even with the Ethical Committee summoning me."

"What if you tell them you just wanted to check on something you found in the Sunrise?"

She thought about it for a second. "That could work."

"It's worth a try," he shrugged. "If you can keep your freedom, then you can make a plan and leave on your own accord."

She looked at him at the choice of words. "How did you know?"

"I know you're going to leave, anyway. I know you're going back to the Sunrise or wherever you need to be, because it's obvious that you're not going to stay here."

"This is my home, Ash," Nashel remarked, steel in her voice.

"Yes, but it's a home that will haunt you down because you're too good for them to keep alive. And if you don't go back to the Sunrise or go somewhat else, somewhere safe, they're going to kill you. And honestly, I don't want them to kill you even if I can't be with you. I want you to be alive and well."

The heartfelt confessional surprised her. Was he in love with her? Or was he just caring? She wasn't sure what to make of that, so she didn't say anything, just nodded. "So I'll go. Can you take me there? I don't know where they are."

"Yeah, sure, let's go back to the base then," he sighed. "Ice cream will have to wait."

CHAPTER THIRTY-ONE

The Ethical Committee

Nashel imagined the EC room they were taking her in to be an interrogation room, sterile, with neon lights blinding her to make her uncomfortable, but it was the opposite. Comfy chairs, no steel table, warm lights, which definitely made her uncomfortable.

"Cadet Under Officer Nashel," an older woman in civilian clothes smiled at her, making her shiver. "Thank you for coming. I'm Commander Iklaurn and he is Major Vorrick."

She was creepy, too nice, too Sunrise-y. The man with her, lean and thin as a nail, was just as creepy. She wondered if it was part of the job description, or if they became so after starting to work for the Ethical Committee.

Nashel sat, back straight, taking in the room. Ash said Expressions were there to prevent her from using her powers, so she studied the two people and what it would take to take them down, and studied the layout to find ways out.

"We just have a few questions about your recent visit to the Hreystisafn," Vorrick told her, taking a seat on the chair in front of her.

She nodded but didn't speak.

"You visited the Hreystisafn this morning at

approximately 10:00 hours. Is that correct?"

"Yes, sir," she replied.

"What did you do there?" Iklaurn asked.

"With all due respect, ma'am, I need to know your clearance."

The woman stiffened, her expression souring. "That is out of line."

"No, ma'am. If you want me to be completely honest, I need to know what your clearance level is."

The two exchanged a look. "We know of your mission, if that concerns you."

"Thank you," she replied with a nod. "I can answer your questions now."

"What did you do at the Hreystisafn?"

"I was looking for something I read while I was over there," Nashel had discussed the excuse with Ash, so she had something more detailed to say. "I read something concerning about the war. Well, just before it."

"Which is?" they urged her.

"In the Sunrise, power is weak. It is barely perceptible, and very tiring to use."

"What does that have to do with anything?" Vorrick snapped.

"I found this paper at their Academy that claimed we stole their power. I know that's not true," she urged to add when she saw the man ready to protest. "And I thought I could find what really happened, because I trust our sources."

"And what did you find?" Iklaurn asked. She was the calmer of the two.

"Nothing," she shrugged. "I asked a wisp to take me to the pre-war section, but all I found was fairy tales."

The best lie had a seed of truth, she had known it for a long while, and she was an excellent liar.

"What about the second ask? We know the wisp took you to a Vision Room."

She let out a laugh, feigning nervousness. "I wanted to relive something." She said, looking away.

"What?" Vorrick asked.

Nashel couldn't blush on purpose, but she could act like it. "My first kiss," she whispered shyly. "I know it wasn't part of the mission, but I had a boyfriend. My first."

Vorrick groaned, rubbing a hand across his face.

"Did you include this in your report?"

"My boyfriends?" she asked, feigning shock and embarrassment.

"No," Vorrick snapped. "About the per-war rumours."

She sighed with exaggerated relief. "No, I remembered it last night and thought it was irrelevant, given what else I reported. I thought I could check if there was anything I could find before I said anything."

"Stupid girl," he muttered under his breath.

Nashel pretended to flinch; if being seen as a silly, love-struck teenager helped get away scot-free, she'd let them.

"You should've included it in your report."

"I apologise."

Iklaurn sighed. "If you have questions about the pre-war, there are channels to ask them."

"I understand," she nodded eagerly.

"Do not go to the Hreystisafn for it," she insisted.

"Yes, ma'am."

The woman shook her head. "You may go."

When she crossed the threshold, she felt something, a tingle raising the hairs on the back of her neck. She thought it was her power being reachable again, but it persisted as she walked out of the base.

Ice cream? She sent the message to Ash, hoping he would understand the implied meaning that she was free.

She reached the Citadel and stopped in front of the ice cream parlour where they first kissed. He would know it. She waited for him or a message, looking at people coming and going, trying to figure out what the Expression she felt was, but she couldn't without trying some of her own and there was something about the feeling and the secrecy that stopped her.

"Hey!" Ash whispered to her ear as he hugged her from behind, taking her by surprise.

"Hey," she whispered back, cursing herself for letting her guard down.

He kissed her lobe before letting her go, but holding her hand. "Let's get that ice cream."

"It's late," she protested. "I can't have ice cream before dinner."

She tried to keep the grin from her lips as she recreated the scene from their first time.

He laughed, not taking the bait but ordering her favourite.

"So?" he asked wearily as they strolled down the promenade, looking into the sea.

"It was alright," she shrugged, wishing he hadn't asked. "They asked me a couple of questions, then told me not to go look for that stuff."

He nodded. "I'm glad."

The exchange was somewhat strained, both tip-toeing around it not to say too much.

"I better go," Nashel told him when the sun set. "Curfew and all that..."

"I'll walk you."

They stopped a while away from the Academy, just to avoid any unwanted eyes. While she was not exactly a student at the moment, she also was still a ward of the Academy and still underage. Also, the secret added to the thrill.

They kissed goodnight and went their separate ways, Ash making her promise she would let him know when she had a plan and how he could help.

Food appeared on her desk as soon as she stepped into her room, and she eyed it without an appetite thanks to the ice cream, but she sat down and ate anyway.

When she went to take a shower, she felt a weight being lifted. She almost let it slide, when she reconsidered. She focussed on seeing the Trace, going off a hunch. She almost flinched when the Trace showed her a human silhouette on the other side of the door. She was ready to blast it when she realised it wasn't an actual person (it couldn't be, she had wards up that prevented uninvited people from entering) but an Expression. It was standing there in front of the door as if waiting.

Nashel studied it more, stepping closer but keeping the door closed. She itched to take it apart, but restrained herself, working around it instead, trying to understand its extent, but it didn't seem to be any. She kept the focus on seeing the Trace and stepped out of the door. The Expression latched itself to her, like a shadow or a cape. She moved around the room, sorting through her possessions just to do something while observing what the Expression did. It was difficult as it was behind her, but when she levitated her books back to their shelves, she saw something in the corner of her eye, a fraction of the Expression detaching from it and leaving in the base's direction: a message. She went back to the bathroom, and it stopped by the door. So they were spying on her, but let her have privacy in the bathroom. Good to know.

She sent a message to Ash. Got eyes on me, just to let him know to be careful about what he said in front of her. She thought about their last conversation when he made her promise about the plan, but she reckoned they didn't say anything too compromising. They may have talked about her plan for the next day for all they knew.

She would have to be careful about what she said or did and how much time she spent in the bathroom, too.

She was pretty certain the Expression could not read her thoughts, she didn't see or feel a link to her mind, so she assumed it was safe to think about her plan. She knew what her goal was, how she could avenge the Triggennan and reclaim what was hers. She didn't yet know how to reach that goal.

Nashel thought about what she saw in the meadow, recalling the formation the rebels took to cast the Draining spell, but more specifically how they Contained the power and created the Void. She would need information, but she couldn't use the Hreystisafn, and if the Expression monitored everything she said, she couldn't ask around either. She could go to the Sunrise and try to find the information there, but as they were so guarded with their knowledge, she doubted she could find anything useful. That left asking Ash for help or finding a way to cheat the Expression.

The former would be easier but she would be completely dependent on him, and, she didn't like it, let alone that she would have to tell him everything, including what her plan was, and she was sure that while he wasn't happy about the sunset's treatment of her, he wouldn't be thrilled by what she wanted to do. Which left her with finding a way to cheat the Expression.

She spent the night wide awake, planning. She could use Ash's help, get some of the info or some of the materials she may need later, but her first steps needed to be her own. She wouldn't give up control.

She reckoned that between the report and the spying Expression, she would still have two days, three at most. Maybe she could be reckless and go to the Hreystisafn to find anything she needed, then run away before they could catch her. She didn't know how many Drifters her people had, but she could take a risk, use Nightshade and disappear once on the other side. She was more used to the Sunrise, and she was sure she'd be able to lose whatever pursuers would come after her.

The only problem was that power in the Sunrise was so weak it would make what she had to do much more difficult. If she had to do it, though, she would. Maybe she could learn to Drain and use that to accumulate the power she needed.

She went through all the options, not realising the sun had gone up until breakfast appeared on her desk. She got up to eat it, then headed to take a nap. She didn't have anywhere to be, anyway. She dreamt of the Triggennan looking down on her, telling her to hurry up, that they had waited long enough.

When she woke up, she had a lingering feeling that she had to act. Maybe it was the dream, or maybe she sensed she was running out of time. She donned her uniform and went to the bathroom, leaving the door open so she could pack a bag without them knowing exactly what she packed.

She made her way to the base, waited for Ash outside, then they silently strolled down the road, his eyes asking her the thousand questions he was thinking and she couldn't answer.

She wanted to test a theory, so she led him to a popular spot where couples used to make out. He raised an eyebrow suggestively, and Nashel smirked with a nod.

"I like where this is going," he told her, enveloping her in his arms and teasing her with a quick kiss to her neck. She gently cupped his cheek, guiding him to meet her lips. She felt a shiver running down her spine, but she wasn't sure if it was arousal or the Expression, so she kept going. When she took a breath, she felt the lightness telling her the Expression had left her to give them privacy. She laughed, making Ash look at her curiously, but she shook her head and whispered into his ear.

"Privacy when I use the facilities. Privacy when I'm making out."

"Oh, is this why we're doing this?" he replied with a hint of amusement.

"Well, yes, why else?" she feigned naïveté.

"Of course," he chuckled, biting her lobe gently, making her flinch and chortle.

"At least we can talk," she gasped, as his next bite was more aggressive, but not painful.

"Okay," he breathed on her lips. "If we're not too distracted."

She teased him, getting closer to his lips, so they brushed against hers. "The Expression monitors everything I do or say."

"I see," he quickly kissed, just a peck.

"I need to find information about containers," she told him, closing her eyes to stop her arousal from getting the better of her.

"Containers?" he asked, surprised.

"Yeah, they can store powers."

He moved to look at her, but she stopped with a warning look. He rolled her eyes and stopped. "I'll see what I can do," he replied. "Can we stop talking now?"

She chuckled and let herself feel. "Yeah, let's..."

Later on, when Ash remembered he had a job and couldn't just do whatever he wanted and Nashel felt the weight of the Expression back as her shoulders, she made her way to the Hreystisafn. She decided to take the risk and look up Draining, thinking she should have enough time to find something helpful before they tried to stop her.

She summoned a wisp and asked it to direct her to knowledge about Draining, and quickly. She wasn't sure it helped, but she thought the wisp was going faster. When they arrived at the right session, it bumped its head towards a particular tome in that adorable way that never failed to make her lips twitch in a smile. She took the time, making the pages turn to the right one with a spark of her power, and started copying it, so she could read it later, when she was safe to do so. Nashel left the Hreystisafn in a hurry, knowing that if they wanted to get her, they would already be on the way. She was almost sure they were. She had a "Volatile Nature", after all. She was dangerous – they didn't yet know how much she could be – and she was stirring up a lot of dust.

She teleported to the spot near the wall where she and Ash talked the previous day, where she asked him to meet her if he had any news about containers. She gave him a time frame and set out to wait, on high alert, ready to run if needed. She hated running, she preferred fighting and facing her enemies head on, but her plan had other stages and she couldn't take the risk. She was about to leave, the time almost up, when a rustle of leaves, then Ash's figure, appeared.

"It's me," he whispered. "Sorry it took me so long?"

"I was about to go," Nashel replied.

"I thought I had a tail," he explained. "I had to shake them off."

She nodded. "Any news?"

"Yeah, here," he passed her a book. It looked old, its leather cover crumbling, the pages yellow, but still legible. She delicately put it in the backpack with the copy she made in the Hreystisafn. When she put the pack back on her shoulders, Ash grabbed her by the shoulders and hugged her tightly.

Nashel let out a gasp as the air was knocked out of her and tentatively returned it.

"You're going, aren't you?" he whispered in her ear.

"I am," she confirmed. "Have to. I had to go to the Hreystisafn to look for something, and I have a feeling they're closing in on me."

"I haven't heard anything," he told her, releasing her from his hold.

"If it's not today, it'll be tomorrow," she told him. "If not for what I searched, then because my R&R is up."

He nodded dejectedly.

"So, I need to be going," she concluded.

"What else can I do?" he asked. "Where will you be going?"

"Nothing else," she told him, forcing a smile. "I think it's better if you don't know that. For your own safety."

"Oh... Yeah... Sure."

Nashel resisted the urge to roll her eyes. That was the reason why she was on the fence about Ash: the attachment.

She plastered a sweet smile on her face and caressed his cheek.

"I don't want them to hurt you," she whispered. "I don't want them to send you away."

That was the truth. She didn't want them to send him to the Sunrise. She might need him more in the future, and for that, he needed to be exactly where he was.

"Be careful," he told her, rubbing his hands on her arms.

"I will," she nodded.

He took a deep breath and a step back, a sadness in his eyes. "I hate having to let you go again."

Nashel managed a smile, wondering about the best way to end the conversation and get going. She couldn't wait to have the time to sit somewhere and read the books. She also missed Alistair. Ash was fun in the beginning. He was at first; he was funny, and bolder than Alistair, but then he also was falling for her and that made the excitement dim.

She was almost grateful when she heard voices in the distance. They exchanged a look, then turned towards the source. Two guards were lazily approaching along the wall.

"That's my cue," Nashel said in a whisper.

"They're just patrolling; they're not looking for us," Ash dismissed her. There was desperation in his voice, and for a moment Nashel wondered if he was stalling, keeping her there to let them catch her.

She shook her head. "I need to go."

Before he could protest, she kissed him one last time, then she teleported to her next checkpoint.

Teleportation was not too common. It required a lot of energy, and it was forbidden to teleport outside the Citadel without explicit permission from the brass. But Nashel was past the point of asking for permission. She knew that, thanks to the spying Expression still on her, they would find out where she teleported to soon enough, but she should have enough time to get herself out of the Sunset.

CHAPTER THIRTY-TWO

The Last Resort

Nashel contemplated the Void while she waited impatiently for Nightshade to arrive. She paced back and forth, her mind running faster than her body could ever catch up. She hoped Nightshade would be in shape to travel immediately, because she didn't have time to wait.

It was still daylight, maybe it was why her Drifter took so long, but he finally appeared, crumbling to the ground. Nashel crouched down, ready to hoist him up, when he reached to grab her.

"Incoming," he whispered before passing out. She cursed, standing to move in front of him, ready to defend him, her back to the Void.

They appeared all together, surrounding her on the three free sides.

"Cadet Under Officer," the one right in front of her, a captain, started to speak. "We need you to come with us."

"I don't think so." It was the first time in her life she had disobeyed a direct order. "Sir, respectfully." There was some sarcasm in the last word.

"It wasn't a request," the captain told her.

"Well, still not going to happen."

"Don't be foolish, girl," he growled.

Nashel rolled her eyes. She was tired of talks, and the best defence was a well-timed attack. She targeted the captain first with a jet of white-hot flames that engulfed him before anyone even realised what happened. They were Sunset soldiers, though, which made them highly trained. They spread out, the typical tactic when dealing with elementals, and attacked her in rapid succession. It was only basic blasts meant to disorient her until she would lower her guard somehow and they could attack with something stronger. She was grateful that they had started to teach the cadets army tactics before she was sent away, she could read them better now. She sent a barrage of power projectiles towards the two on her right, while also raising a shield of shimmering light to protect Nightshade. Elements were her biggest strength, but they were far from her only one.

They dodged most of her projectiles, but some grazed them, which was something.

"Dammit, Nightshade," she muttered as she attacked one of the soldiers that was getting too close. She made a sturdy branch of the closest tree extend and grabbed another one of the soldiers and dragged him away, a smaller branch wrapping around his throat.

Unfortunately, doing that exposed her right flank, and the soldiers on that side took advantage of that. She felt the stab of a power projectile lodging itself in her ride. She grimaced and attacked him back, mirroring her wound.

She thought she had a good chance of overcoming them when a new squadron appeared. Nashel wondered how they called for reinforcements, but she couldn't linger on the thought. She used the sand on the ground to raise a wall between her and them. She could handle a leaderless squadron, but two, while protecting an unconscious body, were a stretch.

The sand wall helped, but it wouldn't do much for long. Their leader was smart, she made them team up and coordinate attacks, as opposed to single multi-directional attacks.

They plummeted with an incessant stream of powerful blasts. The only thing she could do was defend herself. They had her step back, the Void looming at her back, she could feel its crackling energy tingle the back of her neck. Nightshade was still out cold, and they were closing in on her. She released an energy blast with a shout. It only made them stumble back, just enough that she could crouch, grab Nightshade's arm so tight she probably broke a bone, and drag him back.

Nashel took a gamble then. She hoped the Void wouldn't swallow her and kill her. She hoped her experiment with her hand extended to her entire body. She also hoped that, if that didn't work, holding Nightshade, even if unconscious, would spare her an awful death.

She felt a lot in the span of a second: a weight lifted; she imagined it was the spying Expression; then she felt the arm in her hand twitch, telling her Nightshade was finally stirring, then she felt the Void closing in on her as it always did. She also felt something else. Something that was always there, but she never identified. A call. A call that vibrated in her blood, at the core of her power. That immense energy was hers by birthright, and it was calling her. It was screaming for her to free it.

"Soon," she whispered to it. "Very soon."

Nightshade stirred again, this time more firmly. He slowly stood, even though there wasn't a floor to stand up from.

He looked around, shock painting his handsome features as he realised where they were. "How?" he told her, turning towards her and hugging her.

"Hey, it's okay," she replied with a smile. "I told you it doesn't hurt me."

"It's impossible," he muttered.

"It's not. I'm here. For once it was me taking you into the Void for once," she laughed. She didn't feel the need to tell him she hadn't been here until she stepped in and didn't die.

"Never thought I'd see the day..." he chuckled.

“The power know it’s master,” she said cryptically. “Can I ask you a question?” she added before he could ask more.

He nodded.

“If I had a way to destroy the Void, would you like me to do it?”

He looked at her so intently she could almost hear the gears in his brain turning.

“Only if I’m in it,” he finally replied.

That surprised her.

“I can’t live outside the Void, and certainly don’t want to even if I could,” he answered her unspoken question.

“I will do it,” she said.

“I can’t go back, so if you don’t mind, I’ll wait here until you do.”

Nashel nodded.

“Thank you,” he said as he started to withdraw from her as he pushed her towards the Sunrise.

“You’re welcome,” she replied, helping him out by taking a step for herself.

She gasped as she stepped out, an arm instinctively rising to cover her eyes from the blinding sunlight. Why did that stupid place have so much sun and so little power? Nashel felt it immediately, the lack of power, like a gut punch taking her breath away. She groaned, disgusted by the place. She wished she could’ve stayed in the Sunset. It would’ve been much easier to do what she planned from there, let alone that now she had to face Alistair and probably tell him she wanted to destroy the Void. She wasn’t sure how he would take it, but he probably wouldn’t jump for joy.

First things first, she needed a place to bunker down and read the books, then practice, and Sun knew she needed a good place for that. She started to walk away from the Void, just in case her people found a way of following her, even though she doubted it. She was out of their way now, not a threat anymore and, if they still believed an attack was imminent, they would dismiss her in favour of the bigger issues. She had only spent a couple of days back home, but they were enough to make her used to the power, and the absence of it was almost unbearable. But she was a soldier, and she'd get through. She had a mission to complete, not a bogus one this time.

After she walked a few miles, it was clear she had arrived at a different spot than the one she had used before. There was no town in sight with its tiny train station; there was absolutely nothing but woods. She was about to give up and just make camp in the next spot large enough, when the path opened into a village. It was small, just a handful of huts around a clearing. Smoke was coming off a couple of chimneys, and some women were milling around.

Nashel stopped before they could spot her. She didn't plan for this, and she wanted to take a moment to do so. She walked away, giving the village a wide berth, and settled, weighing her options. She could make her presence known, say there had been an attack on her village and she ran away and had been walking ever since, trying to find shelter and food. But then she would have to keep up appearances and pretend not to be a flair (she was almost sure those village people were apos and didn't like flairs), which was even more difficult since she was wearing her uniform.

She needed the space to read in peace and practice, and she preferred to do that unobstructed. Still, she wouldn't say no to a real bed and a warm meal.

Nashel waited with night fell and the last of the smoke dissipated from the chimneys, then she ventured into the village. She used an Expression (that cost her way too much than it should've) to make herself quieter and searched the huts for food leftovers that wouldn't be missed and a tattered blanket on it seemed in that part of the wood's temperatures plummeted at night.

She made her way back to her camp when she stumbled upon an abandoned hut. It wasn't in perfect condition, half the roof had crumbled, taking two walls with it, but the other half would do. She could light a fire without being seen, maybe set a trap or two and procure herself some food instead of stealing it from the village. It seemed a good plan, so she got to work. She was about to light a fire with her power but she realised she would use too much for such a mundane task she was able to perform without, so muttering curses under her breath, she collected wood, while also set wires all around her base, then she rubbed two sticks together until a spark started then another, then she had the smallest flame ever, but she cupped her hands around it and nurtured it to a full blaze, smiling softly to it as if it was her baby.

She ate the leftovers as she opened the first book and read it by the firelight, only stopping when her eyes were too tired to work properly.

Nashel woke up sweating, and it was barely dawn, but the sun was already scorching. She set out to check her traps. Most were empty, but she had caught a mangy rabbit. She had to think for a long moment to remember how to skin it without power. She also charred it to a crisp because she wasn't used to cooking without power, but it was enough for breakfast.

She went back to reading about Draining. It was such a brutal Expression, so violent that almost made her squirm. But it was also fascinating, titillating. So dark, so tempting. And she knew she soon would itch to try it. She set a trap close to her camp to catch the next game alive, and when she did, she tried Draining it. The book was vague about how to actually do it, but she thought she had figured it out. She watched as the rabbit writhed in pain, squealing and twisting, unable to run away.

She felt a tiny amount of power entering her as the rabbit stopped moving. It felt unnatural, almost wrong, but then it settled inside her and the feeling went away.

Over the course of the following few days, she practised with a series of different animals, trying bigger ones.

Once she thought she had perfected the technique, she moved to the next phase of her plan: human experimentation. Power was still weak, but what she absorbed from the animals was probably enough to lure one human away from the village. She had studied the routines of the people. The men would leave at the crack of dawn to work as lumberjacks. They would accumulate wood, then someone from a bigger town or city would come after three days and collect it. The women stayed around the village, gathering the spare edible plants the woods offered, trying to grow a few vegetables and fruit. It was a miserable life in Nashel's eye, she was doing them a favour.

She positioned herself by the tree line, just in sight of one of their vegetable gardens a young woman tended every morning at the same time, like clockwork. When the girl was bent over to check on the plants, Nashel cast her Expression to control her. She didn't have much experience with mind manipulation. The last time she did it, her roommate was found dead. She hoped she could keep the girl alive long enough to do what she had set out to do.

The girl was so compliant that Nashel had to check multiple times that she was still following and still under her influence. She led her not to her camp, but farther away, just to make sure her screams wouldn't attract unwanted attention from the other villagers.

The girl sat down meekly when they reached her chosen spot, and Nashel set to work. Her screams didn't take long to follow. Humans were more difficult, she learnt. They put up a fight, their survival instincts kicked in hard. And the girl was just an apo. Nashel wondered what a flair would be like to Drain and understood why the rebels needed so many people to Drain the three Triggennan.

When the girl let out her final breath, the meagre amount of power she had transferred to Nashel. She was amazed that an apo had power at all, but she knew everything and everyone was connected. Still, it wouldn't be enough to boost hers for longer than one simple Expression. She needed to find some flairs. Before leaving, though, she tried three more times, just to make sure she was doing it right and in the most effective way. She felt slightly more like herself after, and she cherished the feeling for as long as it lasted.

She wondered if there were flair villages and towns; if the apos hated and shunned them so much, it made sense that they would form communities of their own. She wished they had taught that at the Academy instead of stupid propaganda. But maybe she could go back and find out, or she could ask someone to find out for her. With a resigned sigh, she set off for the nearest town she could find and sent a message to Alistair to meet her there.

The town she found was medium-sized and more on the industrial side rather than agricultural. Nashel found a place to stay, one of those places where they didn't look you in the eye as long as you put sufficient money on the outer. She waited there and started reading on Containers. She needed to understand how they were created and if it was possible to dismantle them, but also how she could absorb the content without wasting any or causing unnecessary damage. It was a frustrating read, as she could barely scratch the surface of what she needed, so when Alistair arrived, she welcomed the distraction. She met him at the train station, and he smiled at her like she was the sun itself, and she realised she had missed him. She hugged him tight, smiling back.

"How? Why? What?" he pummelled her with questions, all in one breath, and she let out a laugh.

"Long story," she replied, taking his hand and leading him to her dodgy room. "Tell me about you first," she added knowing he would gladly catch her up on all she missed, while giving her time to think about what to say to him, because despite the wait, she wasn't any closer to figuring that out.

"You seem preoccupied," he noticed as he looked around the room, his mouth agape and slightly disgusted.

"A lot happened," she replied. "I don't even know where to start."

"But why coming here instead of the Academy?" he asked, reluctant to sit down anywhere.

"Because I need to do something, and I don't want the

many eyes of the Academy on me while I do it."

"Okay..." It wasn't a question, but it sounded like it.

"It's not that I don't want to say," she explained, keeping the irritation out of her voice. "I want to have the full picture first."

He nodded sheepishly.

"But I can tell you something..." She recounted her journey to the Void, then how she called on Nightshade and wasn't sure it would work but then it did, and how they kept her locked in her room for three days before interrogating her.

Alistair was appalled until she told him they gave her food and water, of course, and she didn't mind because she had missed her room and the feel of it. She didn't go into the details of what she told Stormbreaker or her reunion with Ash, but she told him how she was able to visit her favourite places.

"Did you find what you were looking for?" he asked when she finished. "The truth about the mission?"

"Yes," she told him with a sigh. "It appears your mum was right."

His eyes widened in shock.

"There's been several people sent here on a false mission to get rid of us."

"That must be awful for you," he whispered, hugging her.

She shrugged, not sure what to say. It had been infuriating to find out that most of her life had been a lie, that there was never a war, or that this so-called mission was just an excuse to get rid of her, but she wouldn't say 'awful'. Despite the premise being false, the Sunset was the place that shaped her, trained her to hone her skills and power, and she was relieved she had grown up there instead of the Sunrise.

"What now?" Alistair asked after a while.

"I need to find a place with flairs," she told him.

"A place with flairs?" the word was tentative on his tips, reminding Nashel that over there they didn't use it.

"Yes, like a village, a community, but away from big

cities."

"Oh," he exclaimed in realisation. "I think I know a place!"

"You do?" She didn't expect that. She thought they would have to research it to find it. "Well," Alistair replied awkwardly scratching the back of his neck. "I don't know it *know it*... I heard of it."

"What did you hear?"

"There's this town apparently made for magicians," she clicked her tongue at the term. "By magicians."

"And do you know where this place is supposed to be?"

"Nobody knows for sure. They say it's warded and can only be found by the most skilled. But the rumours say it's in the south, on the other side of the desert?"

Nashel hadn't paid too much attention to the geography of the Sunrise, but she recalled a big desert to the scorching truth.

"Well then," she nodded, satisfied. "That's the destination!"

"But it's warded! How would we find it?"

She tsk-ed, swatting a hand dismissively. "Please, what passed as 'most skilled' in this part of the world is like a ten-year-old's level on my side."

Alistair seemed slightly offended, but didn't reply, only nodded.

"You should go back to the Academy, though," she told him, trying to convey concern.

"What?! No, I'm not letting you go alone!"

She thought he would say that, and she didn't mind him journeying along with her, but she knew he wouldn't be okay with her Draining an entire community (or even just one person). If he did go along with her, she would have to find a way to leave him behind or to convince him she was at doing anything "wrong". She could play into his need to prove himself capable and send him on a wild goose chase in the wrong direction once she knew where the town was, or she could try to tell him the truth and control his mind if he didn't agree. She didn't really want to do either, but desperate times call for desperate measures, and she would do it if she had to.

CHAPTER THIRTY-THREE

A Monstrous Act

The journey south took them longer than expected. They spent three days in the nameless town figuring out how to travel. Nashel was wary of public transport, as to get tickets they would need to provide IDs and they were supposed to be at the Academy. She didn't want them to give them grief and send them back.

Alistair suggested taking a car. He knew the rudiment of driving, but he wasn't thrilled with the idea of stealing it (renting would require ID and an address).

"We could hop on a train without tickets," Alistair suggested.

"We can hitch-hike," Nashel countered for the umpteenth time. It was her preferred way, but Alistair was being fussy about it.

"Can we not forge IDs?"

"We could..." she pondered. It wouldn't be too taxing to do it. It was one of the first Expressions she did when she arrived in the Sunrise and wasn't even used to the weakened power.

"We can take the train then, to Amasyr, then find some form of transport through the desert."

Nashel thought about it for a moment, then conceded.

Nashel thought she knew hot, but she wasn't prepared for the scorching sensation that hit her as soon as she stepped off the air-conditioned comfort of the train. She was immune to fire, but this felt as if her skin was burning and peeling off her body. Alistair was gasping and panting, trying to take in air that felt like liquid flames. They stumbled away from the train and into the station, but there was no relief. The inside felt stuffy, which made it even worse.

They asked at the information desk about directions to reach the desert, and the woman behind the counter looked at them as if they were fools wishing to die, but she told them how to get there and which tours were available at that time of the year. She also pointed them to a shop selling useful supplies like sun cream, appropriate clothing and gear. Despite her attitude, Nashel appreciated the info and made their first stop at the shop mentioned. There they found items of clothing that would keep their temperature constant (she wondered if Expressions were applied to them, but didn't dare ask), which would come in handy in the shadowless desert where temperatures were sky high during the day only to plummet to freezing at night. They would still feel hot or cold, but it would reduce the risk of heatstroke or frostbite.

They bought head and face covering, canteens, bedrolls and dried food advertised for "the ultimate extreme adventure" but would come in handy in their search.

They decided to join one of the tours the following day, now that they had suitable transport that could take them at least part of the way through.

Nashel had to restrain herself from killing everyone on the tour, they were all a bunch of overly excited middle-aged apos who started complaining as soon as the temperature rose just a fraction and became even more insufferable when they drank all their water before noon. The organisers had more (once again Nashel thought there were powers involved) but they were giving them out slowly, which prompted the apos to complain even more. Alistair made everything worse by laughing at her the entire time.

The tour was supposed to last two days and a night, but by late afternoon, the rest of the party decided they had had enough and wanted to go back. The organisers tried to convince them to continue, but they were overruled.

“Can you leave us here and collect us tomorrow?” Nashel asked them.

“No, it’s a liability, and you’re too young.”

She rolled her eyes.

“We can sign any documents needed,” Nashel insisted.

“No, sorry.”

Nashel smiled but wanted to rip his head off. She concentrated, checking that nobody was looking at them.

“You think it’s dangerous,” she whispered in the particular intonation she was taught.

“Yes”, the organiser replied. Nashel noticed his eyes becoming glassier immediately.

“We take full responsibility.”

“You take full responsibility.”

If she weren’t busy controlling his mind, she would be impressed by how easily she was doing it, the power she Drained boosted hers nicely.

“You will forget about us,” she added, because she didn’t want anyone looking for them.

“We will forget about you.”

“You’ll leave now and won’t look back.”

“Leave... Look...”

She let go of her hold on his mind, and he immediately turned towards the rest of the group, ordering them to get back in the truck. Neither he nor his colleague looked back at Nashel and Alistair.

“You convinced them!” Alistair exclaimed, surprised.

Nashel grinned. “Yeah, it wasn’t too difficult.”

“Where to now?”

She shrugged. “Pick a direction.”

They started to walk in the opposite direction they came

from, the scorching heat now on full blast in the noon sun and the absence of a climate-controlled truck. The clothes were helpful, though. Nashel felt the effect on her body.

"Would you tell me why we are in the middle of literal nowhere?" Alistair was losing his temper. They had been walking for a few hours, and there was no trace (or Trace) of the flairs.

"I told you, I need to do something away from prying eyes," she was losing her temper too.

"What do you need to do?" he asked again. "You know I don't like it when you leave me in the dark."

"Not everything I do concerns you," she replied coldly.

"It is my concern when you drag me to literal hell!"

"Nobody said you had to follow," she seethed.

"Nashel," he growled.

"Let's camp here for the night," she took a deep breath. Arguing was not going to lead them anywhere. They were both tired, hot, and dehydrated.

"Not until you tell me!" Alistair continued.

"Suit yourself," she shrugged with a laugh as she started to set up camp.

He growled, throwing his hands up and sat down on this bed roll.

Nashel thought about what to tell him for the umpteenth time. It was clear he would keep insisting until he got an answer. She wanted to keep him by her side, but she knew he would freak out if he discovered the truth. She decided to give it a try, she could undo it easily and make a new plan.

"I want to give them the war they are so fond of," she told him when the camp was ready, and she was calmer.

Alistair's eyes bulged out and his jaw dropped almost comically. He opened and closed his mouth multiple times before he was able to speak. "What? How?"

"I want to destroy the Void."

If possible, his previous reaction was even more exaggerated after that last sentence.

"B-but..." he gaped.

"There had never been a war," she explained. "It's all a lie. The Void is a Container. They used it to trap the Triggennan's power after they took it from them."

"You found confirmation, then," Alistair concluded.

"Yes, the stories in *The Second Sunset* are true. I think a mix of all versions."

"And you want to destroy the Void?" Nashel nodded in response. "But what will happen to all that power?"

"I found out something else," she added somewhat tentatively.

Alistair cocked his head, but didn't press.

"The Triggennan," she continued. "It wasn't triplets, it was quadruplets."

"What?"

"There was a fourth member. She was their fail safe; she's the one who wrote the book in the first place."

"Oh, wow." Alistair was speechless once again. "They *were* too good to fall into that trap."

"Yes, they were."

"There's something else, isn't there?" he asked.

"She had a child, who had a child, who had a child," she replied vaguely.

"Okay..."

"She lost her powers when the others were killed."

"Did you find out how they were killed? The book was very vague about it."

Nashel nodded, but before Alistair could ask his next question, she added, "I'm their heir. The child of the child of the child a few times removed."

Alistair froze. It took him a few moments to process, but he was a smart guy and soon made the connection. "You don't want to just destroy the Void. You want to absorb the power."

"Reclaim it," she corrected. "It is mine."

"And taking it down will give them a chance to fight for real..." he continued.

"Yes."

"But why here? Why do you need a community of flairs?"

"You've read the same book I did. You know it took many people to create the Void and contain the power. It will take many people to destroy it."

She didn't have to say she required the powers of those people, not the people themselves.

Alistair looked at her, confused. "How do you know they're going to help?"

"I know," she replied with a shrug.

"What if they don't?"

"They will," she said with finality. "But if they don't, we'll find another way."

Not that she doubted herself.

Alistair still seemed unsettled, but after a moment, he laid down, turning away from her. "I'm going to sleep."

She rolled her eyes but didn't say anything. If he made such a fuss for a vague plan to make those flair help, what would he do when he found out she wanted to Drain them?

She settled down for the night as well, burying the little exposed skin around her eyes under her sleeping bag, shivering at the freezing temperature. She would deal with him in the morning.

It wasn't the sun rising or the heat that woke her up; it was movement, a prodding against her outer ward. Her training kicked in an instinct and she threw a camouflaging Expression in a low dome over herself and Alistair, while she rolled over to him, pressing a hand on his mouth and a finger on her own lips. He started awake and trashed under her for a second until his eyes focussed on her and he nodded. She let go and answered the pressing question that was making his eyes bulge. She mimicked something (her finger) hitting a wall (her hand). He nodded again, understanding, before his glance expressed the next question, "What do we do?"

She pointed towards their camp to pack everything and get ready to go. But go where? She stopped, taking a moment to think. The word prodding was coming at seemingly regular intervals from one point only on the ward. Her lessons taught her it could be a trap to make them go another direction where the enemy would be waiting, so before making a decision, she concentrated on seeing the Trace. She knew it was rare enough that they wouldn't know she could, so she used it to her advantage.

She saw the prodding was actually a feeler, which meant they knew the extent of her outer ward, but not that she had an inner one and a camouflage done too.

She followed the feeler path back to its origin, finding a flair not too far out, with other two next to them. She checked the rest of her surroundings, but nobody else was there. So not a trap, she should've expected that, Sunrise were not that cunning. Alistair passed her her bag, and she shouldered it before whispering to him. "Three flairs about 500 metres that way," she pointed.

He nodded. "What do you want to do?"

She took a minute to think. "Can you take over the inner ward?"

"Yeah," he replied, a glint of excitement in his eyes.

"Do it. Let me know when you're done," she said, even though she would see it for herself.

A couple of minutes later, she saw a strong new ward shimmering just a foot away from hers, and Alistair gave the nod. She let go of her own inner ward, which would give her some more power to work with – cursed that stupid, weak place.

"We're going to breach the wards that way," she pointed a quarter of the way to the flairs' right. "And circle them from the flank."

Alistair couldn't help but grin at her military terminology, which earned him a glare.

"We're going in between their feelers so they won't notice."

"Are we..." he paused, his eyes darting away, "killing them?" He finished in a small voice.

"No, chances are they can lead us where we want to go. We'll kill them only if we have no other choice."

He sighed with relief, took a deep breath and nodded.

They moved as she kept the camouflage dome on them, giving them another advantage. Thankfully, the moon was out, giving them enough light to see each other and where they were walking, but not too bright to give their position away.

They passed the first ward, and Nashel raised a fist to stop them. She studied the incoming feelers, timing their gap to find the right time to breach. They were not precisely regular, but left enough time to cross in between. Nashel waited until the last one dissipated, then dashed through the outer ward, Alistair in tow.

"You can let the ward down," she breathed so low that she wasn't sure he heard her.

They walked in a wide arc to flank the flairs that were still sending feelers. They had no protections up and became easy targets for Nashel as soon as she could lay her eyes on them.

She let go of the outer ward, but didn't give them time to realise it she commanded the sand under their feet to swallow them. It was amazing using her elemental powers, but she also felt her head spinning for the effort. The three flairs gasped and screamed in terror, trying to fight the sand in vain and after only a few heartbeats, they were buried in it up to their necks, only their heads out so they could keep breathing and, more importantly, answer her questions.

"You have two choices," she told them without preamble. "You either take us to your community or you die here. Which will it be?"

They looked at her with fear that changed into arrogance when they realised she was young.

"You better run. As soon as we're out of here, you're dead."

Nashel grunted in mockery. "I could've buried you alive, and you didn't even realise I was that close. What makes you think you can get out, let alone kill us?"

She saw them try to get free, but the sand kept its clutches. She smirked and waited, but they didn't budge. She rolled her eyes and made the sand shift so that one of them sank deeper. Sand got in his mouth as he tried to scream, tried to keep his head up, but she was relentless.

“He has about a minute before he suffocates, and about two before panic gives him a heart attack. So I’ll ask you again. What is your decision?”

“Alright, alright,” the one who seemed in charge said.

“I’m waiting...” she sing-songed.

“About a twenty-minute walk north-west,” the third one replied.

“Thank you,” she replied sarcastically, Alistair inhaled sharply. She saw him take a step towards her, as if he wanted to stop her. She ignored him and focussed on the men in front of her. The process was simple, but she had used quite a lot of power already, and she had the impression Alistair was going to stop her if she didn’t hurry. Nashel focussed on their core, so much brighter than the animals and the apos, and once she felt it inside her, she sighed of relief, and it was so blissful she didn’t hear the shrieking of her victim or the other flair. She was well aware the one she buried was about to die, so she swiftly turned to him. She took just a moment to enjoy the feeling before she turned to the last one.

Cadets at the Academy, and even students at the Sunrise one, experimented with drugs. Some went far over the edge and became addicted to the point that they couldn’t function. She never understood the appeal, she never tried drugs herself, but now, oh now, she got it. She wanted more, she didn’t want to stop, ever. She wondered what it’d feel like to have that power back home.

“We’re awake. No reason not to get closer now,” she told Alistair. “Let’s go.”

Nashel didn’t even have to form a fully conscious thought that what remained of the flairs, not much admittedly, was buried under the sand. She started to walk north-west but after a few steps she realised Alistair was not following. She turned, eyebrow raised before remembering he could not see her. “What?”

“That was awful,” his voice broke mid-sentence. “Is that

what you plan on doing to these people?" His disgust was palpable.

"Yes," she answered truthfully.

"No!" he exclaimed. "You can't do that. It's monstrous."

She sighed. "If you want to leave, feel free to do so."

"No, I just don't want you to do this!"

"I will do whatever it takes to complete this mission," she told him coldly. "You can go if you don't agree, but I'm not stopping."

"There is no mission!" He exclaimed, Nashel just looked at him.

"Fine, I will do whatever it takes to avenge my ancestors and reclaim what's mine."

"So what? You're just using me and throwing me away when you don't need me anymore?" his voice rose throughout.

She took a deep breath, keeping her anger in check. "You are a good person, Alistair, but this is my legacy. This is what I'm meant to do."

"No," he insisted. "Your legacy is the Void. I get you want to get back the power that was stolen from the Triggennan. But Draining? That is what they did to them, and it is awful."

"So what? They can't get a taste of their own medicine?" she challenged.

"They are all dead!"

"I need the power."

"There are other ways!" he was shouting by then, but they were still away from the community and there was nobody around to hear them or spot them.

"No, there really aren't," she shrugged.

"You can ask for help. The people who created the Void did, you said it yourself."

"Help from whom? The weaklings that pass for flairs in this Sunforsaken country? My people, who lied to me and sent me away because I'm too good?"

He gaped, but couldn't reply to that.

"I am doing this whether you want it or not," she said with

finality.

He shook his head.

"Go home. You don't have to be here."

"And you think that makes it okay?" He laughed humourlessly.

"I don't know what makes it okay for you." He was more hysterical, and she kept calm. "Do whatever it is that does it."

"What if I try to stop you?" he raised his chin in challenge, and she rolled her eyes.

"Don't. You are smart, you are powerful, but you don't stand a chance against me," her tone changed to cold and menacing.

"Maybe not, but I have to try."

She shook her head, saddened. She liked Alistair, perhaps even loved him, but she wouldn't stop because of him. "I don't want to hurt you, Al."

"That's what gives me a chance!"

He attacked her. It was a sloppy, predicable burst of power she deflected languidly.

"Alistair," she warned him. "Don't. It won't end well for you."

He didn't listen and tried to attack her again, but he was not trained, and she had just Drained three people, her power was almost as strong as it had been at home.

With a lazy flick of her hand, she had the sand form into a sort of ropes, tying his wrists and ankles, immobilising him. He struggled against his binds, but it was in vain.

She saw the challenge die in his eyes, and he hung his head in defeat.

"We're setting camp. We lost too much of the night to approach now, and I prefer to do it with the help of darkness, so we'll wait until tomorrow."

"That's it?"

"I told you," she sighed, annoyance seeping out. "You are welcome to stay or go. Either way, I'm doing this."

Nashel heard Alistair's breathing slowing and deepen as he fell asleep, but she stayed awake, looking at the night sky without really seeing it. She was scheming, planning her next move. Alistair could become a problem if he insisted on stopping her. She knew there were no other options, even if he couldn't see it. She needed the power, and she would get the power. If she had to add him to the list of people she'd Drain, so be it; this was bigger than him and their relationship.

She shook her head, clearing her thoughts, knowing she had to focus on her goal. She would use the day to gauge the layout and size of the community. They wouldn't attract much attention if they were careful. The flairs wouldn't suspect they were looking for them. They would underestimate them. Then they'd wait till night, and she'd take them one by one. She knew she wasn't good enough to take them all at once. She tried with the three she had just took, but it didn't work. She noticed, though, that the sense of wrongness she felt with the apos and the animals wasn't there. She closed her eyes and focussed on the feeling she had when she first Drained the rabbit, and the ones after that, then the apos. The feeling had always been there for the few moments it took to settle in. Then she recalled the fresher memory of the flairs and realised it was never there. The only difference was the presence of power. She wondered why it made a difference. Everyone and everything had a spark of power, a life force. That's what she'd taken from them all. It was just in a larger amount in flairs that allowed them to manifest it in various forms. Maybe the amount made the difference, maybe the fact that they had power and she had power made Draining more seamless. Maybe, now that she thought of it, it was possible to Drain without killing the victim, not that she cared. Draining completely was definitely quicker and easier, but it was interesting to consider the possibility, even just theoretically.

CHAPTER THIRTY-FOUR

A question of Love

When morning came, they followed her plan, went around the community, pretending to be on one of those extreme adventures they saw advertised. Alistair mostly gave her the silent treatment, but at least he stopped insisting. That changed when night fell and she readied herself.

"I can't let you do it." He stood in front of her, back straight, chin raised, fists clenched to white knuckles.

"And what do you plan to do?" she asked dismissively.

"I'll raise the alarm," he replied.

"I'll just kill them," she shrugged. "There will be a small window to Drain them after that. I might not be able to Drain them all, but I should get enough power either way."

"I'll fight you!" he added desperately.

"You tried that, and you lost," she replied, trying to convey the threat he would face if he did.

"Nashel, please," he changed tactics. "If you love me, if I mean anything to you, please don't do this."

She shook her head and took a deep breath. "I'm sorry," she told him as she looked him in the eyes and spoke in the tone that would make her control his mind. "You were right on one thing. I need help. You will help me."

"I will help you," he repeated slowly, his eyes glassy.

"You will follow my orders and will fight by my side."

"I will... orders... side."

She was tempted to add 'even if it meant killing them', but she knew that would destroy their relationship, and if she needed to absorb the Void, she needed someone to help her keep away unwanted eyes. She let go of her control. Alistair blinked a few times and waited for her move.

They had camped approximately ten minutes from the community, so it didn't take them long to reach it. For the first time since she left, she thought about her squad. It would've been useful to have them there. They were a well-oiled machine, complementing each other. The mission would've been a piece of cake if they were there. She manipulated the Trace to create an entrance undetected, leaving just a sliver opened behind her in case they needed a quick escape and it would take too long to re-do the process.

The village was eerily quiet. There were no lights, no people on the streets. Nashel grinned. They were overconfident, putting too much faith in their wards. Well, they would pay the price soon. She approached the closest house, Alistair following meekly behind. There was nobody on the ground floor, so she led the way up the stairs, where a simple bedroom occupied most of the space, only leaving enough for a small landing and a bathroom. The door wasn't even closed, so she entered the bedroom easily. Two flairs slept side by side, unaware their end was near.

"Make the room soundproof," she instructed Alistair in a whisper.

He didn't reply, but he obeyed as her control compelled him to.

"If she wakes, keep her busy." She pointed towards the woman as she concentrated on the man.

It turned out to be unnecessary. The man stirred and gasped, his expression twisting in pain as she Drained him of his power and life, but he didn't scream. She made quick work of the woman, and only after she gave herself a moment to feel the flow of power in her veins. It felt like her blood was singing.

They moved to the next house and proceeded in the same way. Here too there was a couple, and they didn't writhe or scream either. Nashel had to struggle to keep focus as the new power in her desired her attention.

The third house was different. It had two bedrooms, the master housing a sleeping couple, and the smaller one belonging to their child. Nashel stopped on the landing, considering whether Draining the child was required. She didn't care that they were children, but the younger ones would not have the same amount of power the adults would. Draining still required her full attention, and using it to something almost useless was not ideal and could cause problems. She also imagined that Alistair's mind would process the sight and struggle against her control, while she needed him to stay as he was for the moment. She decided to focus on the adults first, the process becoming easier with each victim.

Alistair soundproofed the room, just as he did the previous times, but neither of them thought the child could wake and seek the parents. When they realised it, it was too late. Nashel was in the middle of Draining the father, the corpse of the mother already Drained, lying next to him, when she caught a flash of movement. Alistair saw it too, as they turned at the same time towards the door. It took her a moment to realise the child had seen them and ran.

"Go!" she ordered Alistair, who jolted after the child as she finished with the father.

It was too late. It wasn't Alistair's fault. The child was fast and knew the terrain better. By the time Alistair and Nashel exited the house, the child had already raised the alarm. Flairs appeared from every direction so quickly Nashel would've been impressed if she weren't the one surrounded.

She didn't wait for them to coordinate; she attacked them, releasing the power she had just taken. It was wonderful, to feel so powerful again. The air and sand around her answered her summon immediately. Projectiles flew in every direction, attacking the gathered flairs. Alistair turned her back to her and attacked the ones behind, protecting her. Screams and shouts filled the air, but these people were not ordinary Sunrise magicians. They didn't live hiding their abilities.

Nashel hoped she had been right when she told Alistair there was a short window after death when she could still Drain, because it would be a shame if they were in so much trouble for nothing. Still, she relished every second of the fight.

The flairs didn't counter her attack in a manner she knew. They took their wands and pressed them on their forearms, lighting up intricate runes that glowed in light pink, then put their wands away. In unison, they raised their arms and created a shield. Nashel stood transfixed for a moment. She had never seen such a practice, and she was fascinated despite the situation.

She tested the strength of the shield by sending another volley of air and sand, Alistair still standing alert blind her, ready to deflect any attack. The shield absorbed her strikes.

"Wow," she found herself murmuring. It had been a long time since she was challenged in such a way. If Eira knew about it, he would die of envy. The thought made her laugh out loud, giving the impression of being crazy. Not that she cared.

The flairs didn't give any indication of wanting to attack. They didn't strike, or closed in on her, which made her pause. What did they think they could achieve? Yes, she was trapped within their shield, but if they didn't attack and she couldn't break through, they would be at an impasse forever. Were they waiting for something or someone? Did they hope she would exhaust herself with useless attacks?

She took a moment to scan the crowd more thoroughly. The first line of flairs, the one with the glowing pink rune, was the one sustaining the shield, but the others behind it stood inactive. Why? She cocked her head, trying to figure out their strategy, wishing Siora was there to do it quickly, when she caught a movement towards the back of the group. Her grin widened.

She sent another attack, pretending to try to breach the shield, but it was a decoy. She really aimed at the movement she saw: a child, maybe even the same as before, who was being led away to safety. The earth erupted from underneath the child's feet, swallowing them. The flair leading them away shouted in distress, and several of the last row turned in horror. They hadn't extended the shield under- or above ground, and that was a mistake.

Still, she hadn't killed the child like she did the man in the desert, but merely commanded the sand to take them and bring them to her. They were spit out at her feet, disoriented, and Nashel finally saw him. A boy of ten, still in his pyjamas. He took a moment to understand what had happened, and when he turned to Nashel, his expression was of pure fear.

"Let us go or he dies," she used a sliver of power to amplify her voice so that everyone heard her. In the meantime, levitated the kid by the throat, and he struggled, gasping for breath, against the vincible grip of air.

Instead of answering, the second row started to chant, another form of power she didn't know. She wished she could study these people instead of Draining her, but her mission came first.

"No, no. No funny business," she hissed. She knew they wouldn't listen, but she was enjoying herself.

The chant surged, and with it a wave of power. Before they would launch it against her, though, she started to Drain the child.

"NO!"

The voice didn't come from the flairs. It came from Alistair. Nashel's head snapped towards him. Shock coursed through her: his eyes were clear. Not a trace of control left.

"I can't let you kill him!"

She laughed softly, the sound maniacal and unhinged. "You're not strong enough to stop me."

"I was strong enough to break yo—"

The shield imploded with a deafening sound of broken glass, the shards carried by a tidal wave of power that crushed into her and threw her to the ground, making her lose her grip on the child. Black dots swam in her vision for several moments as she tried to inhale through locked ribs. She knew she was in a vulnerable position and, without thinking, she enveloped herself in a cocoon of power that would give her the time to assess her body.

She pushed through the pain to take a deep breath, revealing broken ribs. The back of her head felt wet, and when she touched it, her hand came out dark in the soft glow her protection offered. Despite the bleeding, she didn't feel dizzy or confused, so it was probably just the impact against the hard ground or a rock, but not a concussion or worse. She could move her arms and legs, but a sharp pang alerted her that she had an injury in her left leg. She wasn't sure if it was a broken bone or an open wound.

She could heal herself easily with all the power she Drained, but she didn't want to spend too much time in the cocoon, unable to know what was happening outside. So, she only healed her ribs to allow herself to breathe normally, then stood up. The child she Drained wasn't too far from her, dead. She wasn't sure if it was because of her or them, but she didn't care. Alistair was groaning a few feet behind her. She didn't spend much time assessing him, more concerned with the enemy and their next move. They seemed to have erected another shield and were waiting for her to react.

"You saw what we can do," one of the flairs said. She couldn't see who it was, but it didn't matter. "Surrender yourself, and we'll let you live."

She laughed again. She was a Sunset. Surrender was not in her nature.

She noticed the runes on the first row now glowed blueish, not pink, telling her there was something different in the shield. Part of her mind wondered briefly about their execution of powers and how it would be a weakness, the change in colour, if only she was privy to their tactics. She tested it again to see if they had learnt their lesson. She commanded the earth again to swallow a random person. It worked.

"How stup—" she was about to mutter, when she felt herself suffocate, as if her mouth was full of sand.

Understanding flashed into her mind, and she freed the flair, throwing them against the wall of one of the houses. The impact took Nashel's breath away, as if she, too, was thrown, but she also realised the flair died and she didn't.

Her enemies exchanged a glance, an understanding running like a current through all of them, and they all started to chant again. This time, though, it didn't last long and didn't end in an explosion. A ripple ran through the shield, making her weary.

If the shield had the power to make her experience what her victims experienced, there was only one way she could beat them. The only way that would make it impossible for her to Drain them after. Fire.

"You have one last chance," another voice called. "Surrender."

A murmur rose from everyone around. "Surrender. Surrender. Surrender," they repeated as if it could convince her. Perhaps they were attempting mind control, but she didn't seem affected.

"I surr—" Alistair's voice muttered from behind her.

She turned towards him in anger. "You will do no such thing," she snapped, and somehow it worked. He looked at her confused, as if he wasn't aware what had just happened, confirming her suspicion.

She considered what she knew. The shield made it so that whatever attack she launched would reflect on her. They also did something else, if the short chant was any indication, and she wasn't sure she wanted to know what it was. Fire seemed her only option; at least she was immune to that. She didn't like that she wouldn't be able to Drain them, though, so she hesitated, studying her enemies and the terrain.

What if she didn't attack, but created a diversion? If she managed to distract them enough for them to drop the shield, she could attack unopposed and make quick work of them. Fire was the answer, after all.

She looked at the houses surrounding them and concentrated on one right behind the enemy line. She had control over all the elements, but fire had always been her favourite, and houses were notorious hazards.

"What are we doing?" Alistair whispered approaching her. She heard fear in his voice, but she didn't have time to decipher if it was fear of her or their enemies. She didn't have time to coddle him either.

"Just you wait," she replied, knowing he would pester her if she didn't.

The fire started small, as all fires do, but it didn't take long to envelop the entire house, flames licking the outside walls, tending to the sky. She smiled. She had always liked to watch the flames dance. The last line of flairs shouted, panic and warning mixing together, as they moved away. Nashel had one of the tendrils reach across and set the opposite house on fire too. The group pushed towards the front, trying to get away from the quickly growing inferno. Spark by spark, house by house, a circle of fire surrounded the enemies. Still, the shield held.

She pushed the flames closer to the people, making them push forward, elbowing each other as panic settled even more. Finally, they crashed into the first row, and the shield wavered. Nashel didn't wait any longer. She attacked through the gap, not aiming at anyone in particular, but hoping to sow more chaos.

She heard voices over the roar of the flames trying to cajole the people to keep their heads, but it didn't work. She closed the circle even more, the heat forming blisters on the skin of those closer to it.

Alistair screamed.

She risked a glance towards him, and he was looking in shock at his arms, red and covered in sores.

"The shield," she muttered, understanding.

The flairs realised she was stronger and wouldn't let the reflection distracting her, but they realised Alistair was weaker and tried to use him as bargaining chip. She was so close! She couldn't let them win. Not even for Alistair. They expected her to stop; they counted on it. She wouldn't give it to them. If she could break the shield, she could annihilate them all. If she timed it well, she could even save Alistair, healing him with all the power gained. It was risky. She wasn't entirely sure how the wavering shield would affect Alistair, and it would be close. Close, but worth it.

"Be strong," she ordered him, despite not having control over his mind anymore. "I will get you out of this."

Dead or alive, she didn't add.

She let the flames surge, not closer, but higher, hungrier. A few were burnt, Alistair immediately shouting in pain as well.

"Be strong," she repeated, but didn't stop.

More people pressed against the shield, and more cracks appeared. She gathered her strength. If she was to pull it off, she would have only one chance. She took a deep breath, tuning out the sounds around her, focussing only on inhaling and exhaling. Once. Twice. The third time, it wasn't only air she let go of. She let her power free. Unshaped, unfettered. A blast that shattered the shield and knocked the flairs back with such force that some flew into the jaws of the fire, immediately turning to ash. She was aware of Alistair's screams turning to whimpers and soft cries, and saw him fall to the ground in the corner of her eye, but she didn't stop.

She Drained the first flair before they even touched the ground, and she was on the second as they did. Some had died on impact, and she discovered there was no window after death for her to Drain them. She methodically Drained those closer to her, as the few uninjured were busy trying to save the others. Then, she heard it. A single breath. It shouldn't have been so loud, but it reached her like a gust of wind. The last breath of a person. It almost seemed to whisper her name, and she immediately turned towards the only person who knew it.

Alistair laid motionless.

Nashel hesitated for only a blink. An impossible choice in front of her. She could keep Draining the flairs or she could revive Alistair and heal him. She needed the power to attempt to destroy the Void, but she also needed Alistair.

She chose him. She rushed to his side, grabbed him and teleported both to safety.

CHAPTER THIRTY-FIVE

I Choose You

Safety was a relative term. She took them away from the community, but still in the desert. It wasn't easy to teleport someone else, pass through a small breach on a very well constructed wall and get too far off destination, while injured. Not even with all the power she Drained.

She checked Alistair's chest for movement, but saw none. She tried his pulse, but couldn't find it. Still, it had only been a short time, and she was confident she could heal him. She forgo setting up wards to keep anyone away. She doubted any of the flairs would be able to find them and counted on them being busy with the fires and injuries.

For the second time that day, she wished Eira were there. He was a much better healer.

"Damn it, Alistair," she muttered, her fingers hovering over his absent pulse. "Don't do this now. I told you to be strong."

She didn't waste time checking for other injuries. She would do that once his heart was beating again. *If* his heart was going to beat again.

She rubbed her fingers together, summoning a spark of power. She knew she had to be careful, that a jolt too strong would do more harm and that she would have one chance due to Alistair's state. She pressed her charged hand flat against his chest, right on top of his heart, and let lightning fly.

Alistair's body jerked violently, his torso arching off the ground, his head snapping back. His eyes opened, but they weren't seeing.

She pressed her finger on the side of his neck, and there was nothing.

"Damn it!" she shouted, punching Alistair's chest in frustration.

He gasped, air rushing into his lungs like a drowning man, startling her. He coughed, choked, but he was alive.

Nashel sat back, satisfied. "Told you I'd get you out."

He wasn't listening, though. Nashel wasn't sure he could. Now that he was alive, he would feel pain again. He cried out once, then his head fell back, lolling to the side. Nashel made sure he was still breathing before she focussed on his body. Every inch of exposed skin was covered in blisters and burns. His clothes were in tatters, and she imagined the wave of power she released had injured him internally too.

She had her own injuries to consider as well. Her leg and head throbbed in unison, hammering her brain as she tried to focus. She finally looked at her left leg and saw a gash there, trickling blood. She gingerly pressed a hand on the back of her head, feeling the bump that formed, but she found it had stopped bleeding. She had been right: it wasn't a concussion.

She decided to focus on Alistair first. She had sustained worse injuries and could bear it for a while longer. She rummaged through her bag (she wasn't sure how she still had it) and found a t-shirt. She pressed it and tied it around her leg, hoping it would stop the bleeding completely while she healed him.

She concentrated on the burns. Healing wasn't her best skill, but every cadet was trained on the basics, and she was very familiar with fire and its behaviour. She poured her power out, hands hovering over one limb at a time, as she reduced the redness and burst the blisters. He whined but didn't regain consciousness. She rolled her eyes at his weak behaviour, but he couldn't see her. She wasn't good enough to heal him completely, or prevent any scar, so when she was confident the burns were no more than a mild scald, like the result of a hot summer day spent in the sun, she moved to the invisible injuries.

"Don't worry, you'll still have a pretty face," she muttered.

Her blast reflected by the shield in its last moments left him with cracked ribs, bruises and internal bleeding. She couldn't figure out which organ was affected, maybe his liver or his spleen. She didn't have the skills to heal it properly; she could only stop the bleeding and repair his ribs. It would have to do until they could reach a city and have him assessed. Hopefully, even in that Sunforsaken country, there were flair healers and not just apo doctors.

When she was sure Alistair was out of danger, she turned her concentration on herself. She undid the makeshift bandage and looked at her leg. It was a deep wound, but nothing too concerning. She healed it, using as little as possible, not worried about adding another scar to her already littered body. The bump on the back of her head was just that, so she ignored it. It had stopped bleeding and would only give her a headache she could deal with.

She rolled both sleeping bags, using a trickle of power to slide Alistair's beneath him, and she laid down too. Her body was sore, but her mind was running a hundred miles a minute. It wasn't the first time she had botched a mission, but it hadn't happened in a while and not on one so important. She forced herself to relive each moment, analysing it to find her mistake.

She had underestimated the flairs. She thought they were useless Sunrise, just like everyone else she had met that far. She should've considered they could've been different since they had decided to alienate themselves from the rest of their society. Nothing could've prepared her, though, for the

Expressions they were using. She had never encountered anything like it. They used runes and chants, techniques she thought not even the Sunset was aware of.

She should've left Alistair, sent him back home or temporarily trap him somehow, because having him there, albeit under her control, cost her greatly. She should've taken the child first, without thinking how he would've reacted if he were in his right mind. She should've warded the child's room if she wanted to take the parents first. She should've instructed Alistair to be the lookout and deal with disruptions by any means necessary.

She was proud of the fight itself. She was facing an unknown opponent, and she held her ground. Again, though, she shouldn't have hesitated and finished them off, even if the price was Alistair's life. She still needed him for the next phase, but she could've found another way. If she had Drained the entire community, she would've had enough power to erect her own shield, securing her back while she was busy with dismantling the Container and absorbing the Void.

She glanced at Alistair's now peaceful slumber. He would wake up in pain, but only in a few hours. A few hours would be enough to go back and finish the job. A tactical retreat didn't mean failure. It didn't mean never going back.

Before she could even finish processing the thought, she was already on her feet. She quickly worked a ward that would keep anyone out (and Alistair in), left him with water, food, and a small fire, and a message informing him she would be back soon, just in case he woke before she returned.

She could almost taste the anticipation of more power. It was a wonderful feeling as she teleported back to the community. She entered through the hole she had created, nobody yet repaired it, and she shrouded herself in darkness.

Smoke was rising everywhere, the sound of the inferno she created still loud, as were the shouts of those coordinating the people. She approached them stealthily as a precaution, but she immediately saw they were too busy to notice her even if she were wearing a neon light dress.

The smell of burnt flesh was strong closer to the battlefield, and she could distinguish more noises as she approached it. Whines of the injured. Cries of grief. She smirked, knowing that it would not last long; they would all be reunited in death soon.

She started with the stragglers, those farther from the centre, those who weren't injured too badly, but weren't helping too much. Nobody noticed her as she Drained the first, then the second, then the third. She paused, licking her lips as if she had just eaten something delicious, and appreciated the power coursing through her veins for a few moments.

She Drained the injured next. Waited until the healers were focussed on others and silently claimed victim after victim. Another idea struck her. They had healers. If she took one prisoner, she could take them back to Alistair, make them heal him properly then Drain them after. She knew she didn't have much time before they realised something was happening and would understand that she had returned. She had to act fast. She interrupted the Draining and observed those healing the injured to find the strongest. They were all just patching up the worst, making sure to save lives, and presumably would return to finish the job after the emergency was over. Nobody stood particularly out, so she chose a random person.

Darkness still covered her, so she approached the closest one, knocked her out, and dragged her away to a safe spot where she could return after she finished with the others. The sand answered her command easier than ever as she ordered it to bind the woman.

She went back to the battlefield and knew her time was up. She noticed the flairs were more alert and had noticed both the dead and the absence of one of them. She made the fires still burning rise in a circle again, surrounding every survivor and pushing them closer to each other.

They tried to chant and form another shield, but she made the flames interrupt them, singeing them whenever they tried to speak, burning their flesh whenever they tried to activate their runes.

"I don't fail," she told them.

She picked them one by one, making the others watch as her victims screamed in pain only to fall on the ground an empty casket. First, she took the children from under their parents' arms. They didn't have that much power, but at that point it was a matter of principle, of victory, and not just need. She took the injured from the loved ones caring for them. She took spouses and lovers, targeting those that huddled together in useless hugs. She took the stoic ones, those standing straight, accepting death with a challenge, last in a show of respect she didn't think they appreciated.

Her mind solely focussed on completing the mission, she took the healer and teleported back to Alistair. He was still unconscious. Nashel woke the healer with a violent shake. It took her a moment to realise what had happened, and that she wasn't home anymore.

"Heal him, and I'll spare you," she lied.

The woman's eyes widened. "Where am I?"

"It doesn't matter. What matters is that your life is in your hands. Heal him, and you'll live. Refuse or trick me, and you die."

"My fam—"

Nashel place a gentle finger on her lips and smiled a creepy smile. The woman started to shake. "Shh. No questions."

The healer nodded, finally convinced. She turned towards Alistair and hovered her hands over his body. A soft glow enveloped them as she scanned him.

"You did a good job," she told Nashel in a whisper that sounded like a whimper. "His spleen ruptured. It would be better to take it out. Is-is that okay?"

Nashel knew enough to be sure one could live without a spleen and the woman wasn't tricking her. "Yes."

The healer resumed her job with a nod before taking out her wand and placing the tip by the affected organ. Nashel rolled her eyes at the ridiculous piece of wood, but didn't say anything. The healer started to chant under her breath, and a soft glow lit the wand. Nashel wasn't sure how the woman was removing the spleen, but Alistair didn't move or expressed any pain. It took the healer a few minutes, sweat forming on her forehead with the effort.

"I stopped the bleeding and removed the organ," she explained when the wand stopped glowing.

"Do the rest," Nashel ordered.

"I don't think I can do everything," the woman trembled, tensing as if expecting an attack.

"Excuse me?"

"It's not that I don't wan to!" She rushed to explain. "I don't have enough magic."

"After the display I saw back there, I highly doubt it," Nashel replied coldly.

The healer shook her head. "That's only because we share," She admitted.

Nashel masked her surprise well. It explained the runes and why the flairs were so powerful.

"Not a problem," she shrugged.

Nashel forced a sliver of her power on the woman. The healer gasped, eyes widening in shock, but she knew better than to ask questions, and turned back to her patient. With precise flicks of her want she moved through Alistair's body methodically. Nashel studied him, noticing the small winces of pain followed by a more relaxed expression, and she knew the healer was being true to her word.

"Can you heal his burns so they won't scar?"

"Yes," the healer replied. She was visibly tired but didn't complain.

When she finished, she sat back down, sighing heavily. Relief was all over her. Fool.

"He will be okay," she smiled.

"Thank you," Nashel replied.

The woman opened her mouth, undoubtedly to ask to be returned home, but Nashel didn't let her.

"You have my power now," she told her as she started to Drain her. "I need it back."

It was a lie. She never intended for the woman to live, but she liked to toy with her prey. The healer screamed and writhed in pain until every ounce of her power transfused to Nashel. With a dismissive wave of her hand, she set the body to ash and dispersed it to the air.

Only then, with her mission accomplished, did she let herself feel the rush of power. It was almost overwhelming; it felt like it wanted to burst out of her, as if she couldn't keep it in. She was stronger than she'd ever been, even in the Sunset. She knew she would be successful and destroy the Void once and for all. She just couldn't wait.

She was tempted to leave Alistair behind and go immediately, but something kept her there. She wanted to know if he hated her. If he remembered much of what had happened, if he blamed her for gambling with his life.

The wait for Alistair to wake up seemed eternal. Nashel has so much energy that it made her even more impatient and made it seem as if time slowed down. She went for a run, hoping she would tire herself. When it didn't work, she exercised more with push ups, pull ups and all the repertoire of cardio. She cooked a small meal, saving a portion for Alistair. She tried to nap, but couldn't stop feeling the power, couldn't stop thinking about how close she was to her final goal.

When dawn broke, Alistair finally roused, as if he were tied to the sun. His eyes fluttered open, but then he startled awake, sitting up in a rush, alert and ready to defend himself. Nashel tensed for a moment, but when he recognised her and realised they were alone, he relaxed, and so did she. Still, she didn't speak, but let him take the lead.

Alistair looked around, taking in the desert and the absence of a town. He saw their sleeping bags rolled out, the food waiting for him and seemed confused.

"How?"

"I took you here when you passed out." When you died, she wanted to say, but better to ease him in.

He looked down at himself, noticing the absence of any injury or wounds. He patted his chest as if to test his insides were still there.

"I thought..."

"You were healed," Nashel explained.

He cocked his head, even more confused.

She was waiting for him to remember the mind control, the Drained child, the shield that reflected their attacks before she explained in more detail. Alistair's eyes moved left and right as he remembered the events that took them there, and Nashel saw the moment he realised.

"You!" Anger had replaced confusion.

"I had no other choice," she told him.

"You could've let me leave!"

"I did give you that option several times," she reminded him. "You refused."

"You could've—" he stopped, shaking his head. "My mum was right. She told me you were dangerous. She told me if you found out your mission was fake, you'd be stopping at nothing."

She interrupted him before he could continue. "Answer me one question. Are you more upset about me controlling your mind or about what you witnessed?"

He opened and closed his mouth a few times, unable to answer. His shoulders sagged dejectedly when he couldn't find the right one.

"Both," he said weakly.

Nashel shrugged.

"I broke free," he murmured unsure.

"You did," she confirmed. "My concentration was spread too thin, and what you saw was too shocking for you."

He nodded, agreeing. "Can I trust you to tell me what happened?" he asked after a pause.

"I can show you," Nashel answered, extending a hand for

him to hold. "You won't like it."

"I don't like this fuzz I feel right now," he countered, steel in his tone.

"Very well."

He grabbed her hand, and she recalled the memories from the moment they breached the community's wards until the moment he died and she took him away.

"You chose me," Alistair commented, eyes wide in surprise when she finished.

She considered what to say next. She didn't really need him anymore, she had enough power to protect herself when she would attempt to dismantle the Void, but she wanted him there. If she told him the truth, that she didn't have to make a choice, that she saved him and went back to complete her mission, he would not be pleased.

She nodded. "I kidnapped a healer," she said, because he would soon be questioning the absence of scars. "I'm not that good at that."

"You Drained them after?"

She nodded. "I need the power."

Alistair took a deep breath and stayed silent for a while.

"I'm heading back to Amasyr," she told him. "And from that to the Void. I don't expect you to come with me. I understand if you don't ever want to see me again. But if you do, you are welcome to come."

"Can I think about it?" he asked shyly.

"Yes," Nashel answered. "I promise I will not control you anymore."

He nodded, but didn't look convinced. "Thank you for showing me the truth."

CHAPTER THIRTY-SIX

The Void

The journey back to Amasyr was awkward. Alistair was brooding and didn't speak a word to Nashel. Several times she noticed him taking a breath as if he were about to say something, but then he would change his mind and shake his head. Nashel forced herself not to roll her eyes.

"Do you even love me?" he muttered under his breath.

Nashel waited, unsure if it was meant for her.

"Do you love me?" he repeated louder, anger seeping through.

"I do," she replied simply.

"You have a funny way of showing it," he whispered.

"Perhaps," she shrugged. "Perhaps I just have different priorities."

He shook his head again. "Was any of it real?"

"The memories I showed you? You know they were."

"No, us. Was it real?"

Nashel turned to look at him, confused. "Yes. I just told you I love you. Of course it was real."

He sighed. "My mum was right," he told himself.

Nashel's anger flared. "You think she's such a saint?"

Alistair was startled. "No. She told me that when she

understood, she was angry too. She wanted to destroy them too."

Nashel tsk-ed. "But she's no heir to the Triggennan."

"Exactly, so she had to give up and make a life for herself."

Nashel didn't like his tone. It seemed to suggest she had to give up too. She was tempted to tell him about his father, just to spite him, and make him realised Raven wasn't such a good person after all. But then she realise it would be a waste of breath. She didn't reply.

"I get you want to reclaim what's yours, but there are ways that don't involve killing people."

She groaned. "Not this again. I needed the power."

His eyes were glistening, and Nashel hoped he would not start to cry because she had not time nor will to console him. He hang his head in defeat and stopped talking to her.

When they arrived back to Amasyr, it was a relief for Nashel. They stopped at the first cafe to enjoy the cool air conditioning and a cold drink. The silence was deafening, even for her.

"I believe those extreme adventure people organise tours to the Void," she told him just to fill the quiet. "It'll be faster to travel with them."

It'd be faster to teleport, but she didn't want to use her powers; she wasn't sure she's consume it and be dry by the time she reached her destination.

Alistair didn't look up. "Do you really want me to come?"

"You are welcome to," she shrugged.

"I don't want to kill anyone," he said through gritted teeth.

"I'm not asking you to," she replied softly.

"Then why do you need me?"

She bit her tongue to avoid rejecting the notion. "Because once I start, I will not be able to see or hear anything that's going on."

"And?"

"It will attract people, even if just apos living nearby."

He nodded. "You want me to stop them."

"I want you to have my back," she rephrased it.

Alistair was torn, but in the end decided to follow Nashel. He was still not happy with her, but he stopped arguing. They replenished their supplies and made their way to the organisers.

The journey was uneventful and quicker than walking. The people with them were a mix of apos and some flairs who were trying their best (and failing) at hiding their useless wands. Some of the apos looked at them sideways and muttered insults under their breath, but nothing happened.

When they arrived at the Void, their reactions were hilarious. Some screamed in utter fear, some refused to get off their vehicles, one fainted and one wet their pants. Nashel took great pleasure in imagining their faces when they'd discover the Void was no more in a couple of days.

They were left to their own device, given a time to return to the meeting, paint and warned they would be left behind if they were late. Of course, the organisers stressed how important it was to stay at a safe distance, but looking at the people around her, there was no danger of that.

"I studied the map of the area," Nashel told Alistair once they were out of earshot. "We'll walk about a day south. It should take us to a relatively safe space."

"Okay," he shrugged and followed. Monosyllables were the most he had spoken to her since the desert, but she wasn't concerned.

They walked for the rest of the day and half the next. The South was light years away from the fast-paced luxury of Soloed, or even the modesty of Amasyr. It was a dry, poor land where "farmers" (if they could be called that at the edge of a desert) had to fight for the most meagre crop, and the few animals were thin and sad. The people weren't much different, malnourished, grumpy and hostile. They looked at them as if they wanted to kill them with their stares, or a sickle, whichever worked best.

They stopped at what Nashel thought was a reasonable distance from the last one they encountered. The people seemed even more dejected and disillusioned that close to the Void; they were mostly apos (she checked), so she was positive they wouldn't run to it if they realised something was happening to it, but the opposite way. At least she hoped they had enough common sense to do that. She decided to start at night to further minimise the chances someone would stumble upon them, but also she wanted to revise her plan once more. They shared a meal of canned food and decided against a fire. The temperature dropped, but it wasn't as freezing as the open desert.

"What do I have to do?" Alistair asked as she was scanning the book about Containers. His tone had changed from detached and angry to apprehensive.

"I told you. Have my back," she replied simply.

"I don't think those villagers will bother," he pointed towards the direction of the last village.

"No, but once I start, they'll notice."

"And they'll come or call for help," he concluded.

She nodded.

"What do you need to do?"

"The Container needs to be breached for me to be able to absorb the power," she explained. "But if ever a tiny drop of it escapes, it will be disastrous."

"So how can you breach but not breach?" he asked, confused.

"I'll block it with my body."

"I thought touching the Void would kill you instantly if you're not a Drifter."

"It normally does, but not to me. It's my power, it recognises that."

"So, what could happen to you?"

"The Void could overpower me and absorb me instead of the other way around."

"You could die?" his eyes widened, and his voice rose. He wasn't completely done caring for her after all.

"That would be the lesser consequence."

"But it knows it's yours!"

"It does, but it also wants to be free," she agreed. "I'll be the weakest link in the Container, and it'll do anything to push past me."

"But you're sure you can do it..." It wasn't a question, but he wasn't convinced either.

"Yes," she said with finality.

He took a deep breath and sighed. "Okay, I'll do what I can."

"And Al," she added. "No matter what's going on, what I do or what I say. Do. Not. Touch. Me."

His eyes widened, but he nodded.

The Void was calling to her as she stood and faced it, as if it knew what was coming. She took a step towards it, then another, focussing her full attention on it. The hum intensified, reverberating in her veins, raising the hair on her arms, giving her goosebumps.

Her hand reached out, her fingertips crackling with static, but nothing happened to them, just like the first time she touched it.

She thrust her arms in up to the elbows, stepping closer and closer, feeling the pressure of the Container trying to push her out and the Void trying to pull her in.

She carefully positioned herself so that the front half of her body was inside and the back half outside, the Container pressing on her silhouette. She focussed on that feeling, she had to make a breach that was a precise cut-out of her shape, making sure that even the tiniest gap was sealed and that she didn't move too much or it would be catastrophic.

She followed the instructions she had read and hoped they were accurate. She felt the Container give way ever so slightly and rushed to "grab" it with her power, moulding it around her. The effort took her breath away, black spots dancing at the edge of her vision, her head spinning. The Void took advantage of it and pulled harder. She almost stumbled, but planted her feet firmly on the ground. The ground. That gave her an idea. She called up the earth, willing it to wrap and harden around her calf, effectively grounding her in place.

Keeping the hold on the Container, she shifted her focus to

the Triggennan's power, trying to claim her. She let it crawl up her arm, feeling her out, but stopped it from harming her.

"Yes, it's me," she thought at it, knowing it would hear her. "You want out?"

She felt as if the buzzing intensified in response. "I'll let you," she told it, feeling sure and a bit silly at the same time. "You just need to get in." Talking to it wasn't part of the Expression, but it felt right.

She focussed on a point in front of her, it wasn't any different from the others, just convenient. She prepared to fight the pull of the Void when it shimmered, forming a shape that slowly revealed itself to be human. "You came back," the shape told her, and Nashel recognised the voice immediately.

She blinked, and the shape consolidated in front of her: Nightshade.

"I told you I would," she smiled at him.

"I'm glad you did." He looked at her with affection. "And that you can touch it without dying. You were right."

"It's mine," she told him. "All this power is my legacy. I need to take it back."

He nodded. "You should."

"You're not mad? Afraid?"

"No, I lived my life," he replied seraphically. "Out there, it was a miserable, hateful one. In here, time doesn't exist, and I've lived an eternity of happiness."

She nodded.

"But remember, a Drifter cannot live without the Void."

"Are you sure you're okay with what I'm about to do?" She asked again. "Are you here to deter me?"

Nightshade laughed. "No, go ahead. I told you, I'm more than fine."

She looked at him for a moment, trying to understand his words, but couldn't. She mentally shook her head and refocused on her task.

"Thank you for freeing me," Nightshade told her before he disappeared without waiting for an answer.

The power thrummed around her, and she latched on to it, feeling it pull, overwhelming her. She called to it as it called to her, and they started fighting for control.

The Void felt she was the weak link in the container and tried not only to absorb her but also to push her out and escape. Most of all, it wanted to break out. She tried to convey to it that the only way out was through her, in her. She wouldn't beg for it; it wasn't in her nature, and she was sure the Triggennan's power wouldn't appreciate it.

She felt it struggle, but she was strong, strong enough to counter it, and soon it knew it. She felt the moment it gave in, letting her absorb it. She felt all the lives it took through the centuries flow through her. She felt the Triggennan themselves let go of centuries of struggle and pain and welcome the freedom their heir would give them.

She felt Nightshade brush against her. "Remember," his voice was distant and soft. "Drifters..." he couldn't finish the sentence.

Power rushed to her, sneaking up her legs, her arms, her torso, wrapping around her neck and starting to squeeze, thrusting into her rib cage, trying to crush her heart and rip it from her body. Pain flared in every part of her as the power kept grasping for her, getting inside her Ears, eyes, nose and mouth. She wanted to shout, but she couldn't. Something was wrong, very, very wrong.

She tried to think, but the pain was too intense, and all that came to her was the last of Nightshade's words. "Drifters—"

Drifters cannot live without the void. He had told her that, and it's what he meant in the end too, she was sure of it.

Drifters cannot live without the Void.

Drifters cannot live without the Void. She wasn't a Drifter, though, was she? He confirmed she wasn't. Drifters cannot live without the Void. They could not live without it! He said "without", not "outside".

Drifters could not live without the Void. That's what was wrong, what was tearing at her. Not all of the Triggennan's power was around her. The tiniest part was with the Drifters.

She called out to them, down in the recesses of the base's dungeon, in their dark, sad cells and wherever they were kept in the Sunrise because she knew they had some as well. She called to each and every one, promising freedom and peace.

She felt them answer, one by one, as the power around her lost its grip with each that came through. She started to feel more confident, the adrenaline of victory slowly replacing the receding pain.

Something touched her, making her shiver with its weirdness. It wasn't coming from the Void; somebody was touching her back outside!

"El?" a tentative voice reached her. "Everything okay?" Only one person called her that. The one person she instructed not to touch her.

"Why are you calling for me? What can I do?" Alistair asked.

Call for him? She didn't.

Drifters cannot live without the Void. Nightshade's words resonated in her mind once more, and something clicked that time. Alistair was a Drifter. He had never crossed the Void, but he was born on the wrong side, and that's what made Drifters. She had called to him. She had called to all of them, whether in captivity or not 'initiated'. Nightshade had tried to tell her, but she didn't understand until then: Alistair could not live once she destroyed the Void.

"Step in," she sent the message back to him. "It's safe, I promise."

She felt his hesitation as he slid his hand from her back up along her arm, holding her hand tight as if she were his anchor. She led him in front of her and smiled.

"See? It's okay."

He looked around apprehensively, but nodded.

"I know what you're thinking," she continued. "It goes against everything you've ever known. But I promise, it's alright. I can't do this without you."

"For real?" he asked, surprised.

She nodded. "For real. Drifters cannot live without the Void."

His eyes widened in shock and fear.

"It's okay," she reassured him, her hand resting on his cheek. "You're going to be okay."

She didn't wait for more questions; she kissed him like never before, and he relaxed into it, letting go of his reluctance, believing he was safe with her.

In a way, he was. Nothing could ever happen to him anymore.

She felt it, the last of his power left him and got into her, and his body dissolved into the Triggennan's power. And with his last breath on her lips, she had completed her task.

The shattering, deafening sound of the Container breaking into millions of invisible pieces echoed what the part of her who loved him felt. She wiped the single tear that rolled down her cheek, the single moment of grief she allowed herself, then she took in the scene around her. The desert was still arid and barren, but she could see the Sunset now, and she could feel the sigh of relief that pervaded everything around her now that the flow of power was restored to its natural state.

She had done it. She had completed the mission. Found her legacy. She felt the Triggennan inside her, all four of them, proud of her achievement, finally free. Only one last thing was left: revenge. She had promised the two nations a war, and she was going to deliver.

As she foresaw, the villagers had called for help. A group of magicians appeared, teleported nonetheless. She smirked as they took in the wasteland and her. She knew something had changed in her, she could see the soft glow she emanated, even in the scorching sun, and knew they were afraid.

Before they could muster themselves and attack, another group arrived. Their uniforms dark blue, their formation perfect. Field Marshall Stormbreaker at the head of them. Her people. They, on the other hand, didn't hesitate. Their coordinated attack hit her, but didn't touch her. One of the flairs also attacked the magicians, imprisoning them in a cage.

Nashel turned towards the general. "Remember me?"

The general's eyes widened in shock as he recognised her. "Cadet Under Officer Nashel," he muttered.

"Volatile nature," she quoted. "Expendable assignment."

He schooled his expression fast, but she saw his emotions, his surprised.

"I guess in a way you were right," she conceded.

"What have you done, foolish child?!"

"You wanted a war, general," she replied icily. "Now fight."

She waved a hand, and the cage imprisoning the magicians disappeared. The two groups looked at each other, then at her. She shook her head as they both attacked her again, but nothing could touch her anymore.

"Gather your armies. Fight each other. It's what you asked for." She laced the order with control that affected both the general and whoever was in charge of the Sunrise, wherever that person might be.

Stormbreaker reacted immediately, ordering a regroup. The Sunset flairs disappeared as quickly as they had arrived. The Sunrise group looked confused and uncertain. They realised by then that they would not win a fight against her, but at the same time they didn't want to go. Nashel made the decision for them. She teleported them back where they came from.

They could have their war. They could fight for a while. She would watch them like she watched the children on the playground playing with their tin soldiers. Soon the Sunset and Sunrise would be no more.

Only a united land would exist, under one rule: hers. A new Golden Age had just been born.

Acknowledgements

The Two Suns' journey has been a long one. I had the initial "vibe" over fifteen years ago! I wanted to write a book where the protagonist was a villain, but I didn't want it to be a redemption arc or an apology for her behaviour.

At the time, the only details I knew were the world divided in two and two magical schools, a good one and an evil one.

A lot has changed since then. I have changed since then!

This latest iteration of *The Two Suns* started in 2020, when I decided to make it more than just vibes and vague ideas. I can't believe it actually took me five years and another book in between to finish it.

While *The Two Suns* is not my debut novel (Time Wave is, check it out!), it is my baby. It's the idea that resided in the back of my mind whenever I thought about writing.

It wouldn't be here if it weren't for a few people: The Bookdun and BoB communities; Natalia for letting me vent and helping to develop Nashel as a character; my ARC readers, for taking the time to read and review it; my followers for liking my attempts at marketing videos.

And you, the reader. Thank you for stepping into this world. I hope you enjoyed your journey just as much as I did.

Also by K.S. Sanral:

- Time Wave

✷ ✷ ✷

About the Author

K.S. Sanral's journey into writing began at the tender age of seven, when she ambitiously set out to pen her autobiography, only to pause when she realized her story had just begun. Since that moment, writing has woven itself into the fabric of her life, an ever-present companion guiding her through the realms of imagination and creation.

Stay connected:

Website: kssanral.com

Mailing list: http://eepurl.com/iRrOzk

Social media: @kssanral

☀ ☀ ☀

Thank You for Reading *The Two Suns*!

If you enjoyed this story, please consider leaving a review on Amazon or Goodreads. It helps more than you know.

👉 Stay connected for the next book:

• Join my mailing list: http://eepurl.com/iRrOzk

• Follow me on: @kssanral

Your support means the world, and I can't wait to share more stories with you!

~ K.S. Sanral

☀ ☀ ☀

www.ingramcontent.com/pod-product-compliance
Ingram Content Group UK Ltd.
Pitfield, Milton Keynes, MK11 3LW, UK
UKHW010245080126
466772UK00001B/41

9 781068 704260